SO-ANR-661

Play It Again, Samantha

NOTE: "Universe," as used in this text, is synonymous with God, the Creator and Creative Forces.

Carolyn Douglas

Inkwell Productions

Copyright © August 2002
by Carolyn Douglas
Scottsdale, Arizona

First Printing, February 2003.
All rights reserved.
Printed in the United States of America.
No part of this book may be reproduced in any for or by any means
whatsoever without written permission from the publisher.

ISBN#: 0-9728118-3-4

Library of Congress Control #: 2003104264

Published by
Inkwell Productions
3370 N. Hayden Rd., #123-276
Scottsdale, AZ 85251
Phone (480) 315-9636
Fax (480) 315-9641
Toll Free 888-324-2665
Email: info@inkwellproductions.com
Website: www.inkwellproductions.com

Dedication

The author is deeply indebted to the 'angels' who assisted her in so many ways:

Carole Sheely ... proofreader and special friend for her eagle eye and suggestions for the perfect words which improved the text.

Virl M. Swan ... my brother, a jazz musician, educator in the field of music, and symphony conductor, who was always available to provide the appropriate musical selections.

Patricia Turpin ... for her highly skilled and professional editing and guidance.

And so many special friends who assisted when transportation, research and encouragement were needed.

Most of all, my love and extra special gratitude goes to my son, Robert D. Harmon, for his talent, special skills, thoughtful assistance, dedication, and patience that provided the drive and sparkling energy that enabled the text to come to life.

Table of Contents

Prologue

It is early December. A young man in his early 20s, well dressed, with a solemn expression, reaches out to ring the doorbell of a beautiful home in Central California. The door is opened by another young man, about the same age, casually dressed.

"Good afternoon. I am here to see Casey and Connor Malcolm."

The young man answers, "I'm Casey, and if you wait a moment, I'll get my brother." The two boys quickly return and look expectantly at the visitor.

"Gentlemen, my name is Manny Wong and I have something of importance to discuss with you. May I come in?"

The boys stand aside and show him into the living room. Once seated, Manny Wong speaks. "My ancestors came to America from China five generations ago. As the youngest member of my family, it is my honor to fulfill a pledge made over a century ago." He looks at each boy solemnly and says flatly, "It concerns the two of you."

Manny Wong stands and with a slight bow and both hands extended, presents an envelope to the boys. "I'm sure you will find this letter most interesting. As you can see by its condition, it has made a long journey through my family for many years. Now I honor that pledge made by my ancestor and deliver it to you now. It is our hope that its contents will bring you understanding and peace."

Casey, frowning, reaches out to take the letter. Before he can ask any questions, the young caller presents a business card saying,

"Perhaps you will have questions. You may reach me at this number." He then smiles, bows his head, and leaves the house.

Once the door is closed, the two brothers examine the envelope which is yellowed with age but still well preserved.

"What is it?" asks Connor.

Casey shakes his head. "I don't know. What do you think? Should we wait for Dad to get home?"

"Well, it's addressed to us. We can at least look at it."

Taking a sharp knife, Casey carefully cuts open the envelope. Inside is a faded letter and another envelope. He unfolds the letter with Connor looking over his shoulder. As they read, they both gasp in wonder and look at each other. The opening words are clear and inviting, and as they read, their excitement and surprise grows with every word.

Chapter One

I ran away from home.

I, Samantha Malcolm, with very little thought and a modicum of common sense, threw a variety of belongings into a backpack and walked away from Rocky Crest, a lovely second home in the Sierra Nevada Mountains in California. The primary reason was to distance myself from Harland, my complacent husband, and his strong willed, domineering mother, Delilah. But there were other reasons.

This was no sudden decision. The major elements had been there, bubbling away in the back of my mind for at least five years. It took a series of disappointments and a dedicated program of self-realization to bring me to this point.

But most of all, it took a heartfelt, desperate prayer to the Universe.

That one act opened my life to unbelievable experiences, exceptional people, and the development of my life as I wanted it to be, not what others expected of me.

Oh yes, the Universe responded, but not the way I had hoped. I can attest that the Universe works in mysterious ways.

Here is what happened.

I guess it began when Harland and I discovered the place that we named Rocky Crest, high in the Sierra Nevadas, sitting in the center of what used to be the mining and prospecting areas of the 1849 Gold Rush. Miles away from small towns and ranches, it consisted of five acres in the midst of those high mountains with numerous outcroppings of rocks and boulders, ranging from pebbles to giants, pushed up through the soil. The landscape was stark, but the view of the surrounding mountains was breathtaking.

In the middle of this, Harland installed a three-bedroom, three-bath mobile home. I was allowed to fill each room with colorful and pleasant furnishings. In shades of turquoise, tan and maroon, the final effect was low key and comfortable. Also scattered about were a series of paintings and water colors by local artists that added to the visual pleasure of our second home.

For many years my boys Casey and Connor, my husband Harland, and I enjoyed this patch of serenity and history. The boys joined their father on some of his rock-hunting expeditions, or they explored on their own. As they grew, we brought up mountain bikes so they could follow the old trails still remaining from the early days of the Gold Rush. My role was to tend to the home fires or shop for supplies at the small towns miles down from the mountains. It was a pleasant, satisfying environment, though I found it lonely at times.

When Harland suggested that we spend a month at Rocky Crest to ease the empty nest status that had just come upon us, it was not my idea of Paradise. Just days before, I had helped the boys pack for college – Casey for his third year and Connor for his first. Both had chosen colleges on the other side of the continent, so with a lump in my throat I assisted in the preparation. It would be an exciting new world for them, but a quiet one for me.

As usual Harland was terribly busy. His hardware stores were flourishing with number four just recently launched. Therefore,

I helped with the boys' preparations, drove them to the airport, and bravely sent them on their way.

As they were leaving, the boys were loving and concerned, and did their best to cheer me. They promised to phone and write often, but their eyes and attention were clearly focused on the boarding gate and the plane waiting just beyond. After quick kisses on my cheeks, they were on their way, and I returned to the empty house waiting for me.

I sat on the sofa in the living room to meditate and find the center of my feelings about the recent changes. However, images of my life kept intruding. How did I get here? My mind wandered, searching, and it filled with an image of the first time Harland and I met.

It was at a lawn party given by my parents for a local politician. Then I was Samantha Jane Logan, only daughter of Sarah and Frank Logan, living in Fresno – one of the larger cities in central California. I do admit that my parents spoiled me with dance lessons, piano lessons, and pink dresses lovingly made by Mom. They took great pride in any and all of my accomplishments, especially the piano recitals where I played my little heart out starting at age 5. By the time I was in high school, I accompanied various choral groups, as well as rehearsals of musicals presented by the music department.

Then I was a tall, slender girl with light brown hair in a ponytail and I never lacked for dates. Even in college there was a never-ending line of eager, panting young men. Sailing through with a minimum of effort, I majored in liberal arts and piano studies.

At the age of 21 I looked at the rather challenging world and wondered what was next. Then I met Harland Malcolm. His angular body towered over my 5 feet 8 inches. His fine brown hair had lovely waves that curled a little on the neck and behind the ears. His smile was sweet and his deep blue eyes sparkled. And though he did not present a strong or bold character, he was well mannered and eager to please. Ten years my senior, he was then owner of two hardware stores. He generated an air of success and luxurious well-being, a man well-known about town. Radio and television ads for Malcolm's Hardware aired daily. How could I help being flattered when Harland was clearly smitten from the first at that party in my parent's backyard. That summer, when he wined and dined me in the best restaurants in town, showered me with flowers and little surprise gifts, my immature and inexperienced heart was his.

His proposal was irresistible. "My life would be so full and rich if you would only be mine, dear Samantha. Please say yes so we can marry and start a wonderful life together."

This was the last time he was so lyrical, at least in my presence.

Very much in love, I never wondered why he had not married before this. I assumed he was so involved in the growth of his business that he had no time to be romantically involved, which was partly true. Then I met Mother Malcolm whose presence overwhelmed me like a battleship in heat, and her first words were far from welcoming. Eyebrows raised, she looked me over and announced, "I suppose it's time for my Harland to marry, and you'll do as well as any other young lady in this town. He's convinced that you, and you alone, can make him happy. We shall see." This did not help to strengthen my relationship with Delilah, and it planted the seed that our marriage might not be made in heaven.

Delilah Malcolm was one of the social queen bees in our city. She cut an imposing figure with her ample bosom and a trim figure set on two shapely legs. She was always smartly dressed. When we met, her bright blond tresses were skillfully piled on top of her head, which added another two inches to her dignified stature. That plus her piercing blue eyes let me know right away that she was the top bulldog in the Malcolm yard.

Harland, of course, was the center of her world, which she directed as artfully as a DeMille epic. He was Moses, Ben Hur and Superman combined, while I was one of the extras in the background. In time, I am proud to say, I became a feisty terrier nipping at her heels.

Caught in the first blush of young love and courted during a lovely summer, I stepped over a rose-covered cliff in August and Harland and I were married while my bewildered parents looked on in dismay.

"Samantha, dear, are you sure you want to rush into marriage so soon after college? Shouldn't you get out and see a little more of the world?" Their words did not touch the glow of first love.

College does provide an all-around education, but marriage gives a novice sober and unending training on many levels. My maturation began almost immediately with a honeymoon about as exciting as a fallen soufflé.

Oh, we did have two weeks at a beautiful lodge in Carmel. Our activities were walks on the beach, checking out the lovely little shops, early dinner and bed. That part was not what you think. Harland was proud of his golf game and cherished an early tee-off time at Pebble Beach. His efforts to teach me golf did not go well, even when using his gift of the finest and most expensive clubs. My fingers knew well what to do on a piano keyboard, but the proper grip on a golf club did not come easily. After two days of instruction, he left me on my own.

"My dear Samantha, why don't you book the pro for lessons. Or, if you prefer, take my credit card and buy whatever you want in those little shops."

The pro was booked solid, none of the ladies at the club seemed approachable for friendly conversation, so I shopped for useful, useless items to enhance my new household. When we got home, my days were busy finding space and/or a good use for my purchases, and adapting to the Harland I was still getting to know.

After a while, some of his habits caused doubts and questions to dance about my brain. For instance, he introduced me to friends and associates as "my little lady" or "the new Mrs. Malcolm, my wife." He seldom mentioned my name. I pointed this out to him, but he failed to grasp the problem. "I'm proud of my little wife," was his reply.

Life with Harland went smoothly once I adapted to his routine – getting him off to work in the morning, making sure dinner was ready when he returned, entertaining his business and political associates, attending dances at the country club, and arranging meetings and conferences at the house. However, I was not privy to the details of his professional activities.

To Harland, his work was a noble crusade. He had affection for every hammer, screwdriver, lawn mower and plumbing fixture in his stores, and when one of his own went through the door, it was like sending his children out into the world.

Next was golf, and then his great passion for collecting rocks, stones and fossils. Many of his weekends and vacations were devoted to this hobby, and one room in our house was dedicated to specimens, rock and gemstone displays, polishing and buffing machines, tools and other items sacred to the hobby. I never quite reconciled his passion for the highly useful tools of his business to the sit-there-and-do-nothing world of rocks.

The interior of our house displayed a vast array of his discoveries. He sliced an outstanding piece of rose quartz, as big as a breadbox, into five pieces, then arranged them like dominoes on our enormous coffee table. The entry-hall table displayed a geode stone the size of a football. Cut in half, it revealed an interior bursting with sparkling purple and blue quartz crystals. These treasures multiplied from year to year, thanks to his determined exploration of the earth.

At first I was rather proud of a man so dedicated to his work and hobbies, until I realized that I came fourth. Was I dismayed? No. As a dutiful wife, I settled into my role as Mrs. Harland Ridgemont Malcolm, wife of that enterprising young man in the hardware business.

While the marriage was young, Harland was loving and attentive, and sex was new and interesting. Aside from some necking and heavy petting as part of my high school and college curriculum, I was very new at the game. Harland was gentle and caring, and at times he could give a sensitive touch when it was needed. But it had none of the Burt Lancaster/Deborah Kerr passion in the surf, or the breathless anticipation of Rhett carrying a weak but willing Scarlett up the stairs. However, it worked, and in short order we had two wonderful sons.

In two rare instances of defying his mother, Harland left the naming of our sons to me, which ruffled Mother Malcolm's feathers to such a degree that they did not settle for several years.

"And what is wrong with Harland Ridgemont Malcolm, Junior? It's a traditional family name, my maiden name, and should remain in the family. 'Casey Logan,' indeed!" She raised and squared her shoulders in outrage. I heard the same remark when Connor Joshua was christened two years later.

Becoming a mother gave me more grit and somehow I stood my ground and came through victorious. She never quite forgave me for this defiance.

Harland and I communicated while the boys were small, but it soon became rather mundane. A bit formal at this point, we had no endearing names or nicknames for each other. But the love and affection were still there though not outwardly shown.

Ten years later my lovely sons, bright of mind and strong of limb, filled the house with their shouting and constant movement, not to mention their friends who came for swimming and tennis. They were involved in anything that required them to move – football, basketball, soccer, animals.

Both had light brown hair, which bleached out in the summer sun. Their father, meanwhile, had lost his crown of lovely curls except for a few locks carefully combed over the top. His face had matured, but I decided it made him look much more interesting. His body was still angular, and his custom-made suits fit a man who had challenged the world and succeeded.

By then, I was custodian and caretaker of an impressive two-story house containing four bedrooms, numerous bathrooms, a library, the rock room, a good-sized swimming pool, and a double tennis court. As for me, I dove into all that the city could offer in volunteer work and companionship. With the boys in school and busy with their outside activities, and Harland increasingly and lovingly attending to his stores, there was oodles of time for me to perfect my imitation of June Cleaver, which rated a faint nod from Mother Malcolm on rare occasions.

The Westside Tennis Club steered me into their board of directors (a position not coveted by many of the members). I became the one active member of the entertainment committee at the Westside Golf and Country Club, reluctantly involved in the P.T.A., and a spare for the Ladies Bridge Club. (I did not play that well.)

In my one statement of self, I changed my name from Samantha to just plain Sam. It was informal and friendly, and it fit me nicely. But to the boys I was "Mom," to Harland I was still "Samantha, dear," to Mom and Dad I was "our baby Samantha," and to Mother Malcolm I was still "your wife" or "that girl, Samantha."

During this time, dialogue between Harland and me was rather hit-and-miss, like tennis serves that were never quite returned.

"Where are the boys?" He usually asked this question as he went through the mail on the hall table.

"At soccer practice. They're having hamburgers with the team."

He would say absently, "That's nice. Did you pick up my gray suit from the cleaners? And did you get a chance to pick up some new underwear for me and the boys? You know, the new style jockey shorts in different colors?"

"Yes, Harland," and seeing that he was still involved with the mail and messages, I added, "and the earrings to match."

He stopped at the bottom of the stairs, turned to me with raised eyebrows and shook his head sadly. "Yes … ah …yes, my dear. And what is this phone message? I can't read the numbers. I've asked you this before – please tell Thelma (our part-time maid) to make an effort to take messages carefully so I can read them."

"Yes, Harland."

"And Samantha, there's something I wanted to tell you."

"Yes, Harland." An unanticipated bright spot in my day.

"Please remember that Mother will spend all Sunday with us. I'll pick her up after my foursome. Be sure not to serve anything with sour cream or green peppers. She said an upset stomach kept her awake the whole night after she dined here the last time, and she wanted me to be sure to tell you."

"Thank you so much, Harland." I had not forgotten, but I had now learned to present my comments with care, while my mind privately shouted answers that were not very proper.

"And I have a dinner meeting tonight so I won't be home until late," he would say on his way upstairs to change.

"Have a fun time, Harland, and good night."

My thoughts fast-forwarded another five years. At this time my inner voice (which began talking to me a lot) was saying, *There's more to life than this, kiddo. You're giving out a lot more than you receive. Let's take a look around and see what kind of changes could bring more sparkle into your life.* I found my inner voice, on occasion, had some very neat things to say, so I often tuned in to that frequency.

So, farewell, Board of Directors; I'm not available, Country Club Entertainment Committee; I've done my bit for the P.T.A. Let's see what's out there for nice ladies like me whose lives have less fizz than day-old ginger ale. Let's find me some challenges and excitement.

I turned to Mom and tried to describe what I was feeling. In return she sounded rather vague and bewildered. "Well, Samantha, dear, that's just the way life is. We all have to work through times like this until things get better."

Bless her heart, I could not put much faith in her advice since she was speaking over her portable phone from a Disneyland-type retirement community in Florida. She had no grasp of my situation, and now, instead of being the cherished only child with their full attention, I was now a grown woman whose parents were having playtime.

One day while brushing my teeth, the inner voice spoke to me once more. *All right, Sam. What are you going to do for yourself? With the men in your life out of the house more than they are in, you should look around for something to fill your days with more significant endeavors.*

Step Number One: I found a meditation class, so I spent hours cross-legged on the floor, eyes closed, looking for the inner me. Nothing dramatic presented itself except an opportunity to sample marijuana (it made me dizzy). Meditation didn't expand my inner vision, but it did bring the old life to a standstill and allowed me to contemplate my navel, the world, the Universe and, above all, life with Harland.

Step Number Two: I joined an exercise class to put my body,

which bordered on great 15 years ago, back into Olympic shape. After two children, this was more difficult since the cargo had shifted somewhat. But in time the contour slowly returned to its former glory.

What my lovely home had been lacking was a piano, and I had not realized how much I missed playing, especially during the holidays. After many discussions, Harland agreed to install a baby grand in our huge living room. Soon I was deep into arrangements, and all sorts of wonderful sounds.

Step Number Three: I took night courses at the local college on piano and jazz and filled my repertoire with music from the 1930s to the 1990s – jazz, swing, rock 'n' roll.

From the boys: "Mom, we like your music, but do you have to play so loud? We can't concentrate when you play that thing. Try to keep it down." I argued that it was no louder than their rock 'n' roll, but they persisted. We negotiated a truce. They turned down the rock 'n' roll, and I played softer or while they were in school.

From Harland: "Samantha Jane, do you have to spend so much time at that piano?" I was "Dear Samantha" when called upon for mini concerts for special gatherings of friends and associates. "Aren't there more useful things you could be doing, like helping Mother with her shopping or going for groceries?"

"She had my services yesterday. Today is my time to practice the piano, Harland."

"Oh well, try to do it when I'm not in the house."

"All right, dear, and thanks for your support."

During these five years, in addition to the piano, my life consisted of daily meditation and yoga exercises. I took a front row seat at seminars on "How to Discover Your Goal in Life" or "Spiritual Growth for Women." My mind reeled after lectures on reincarnation and life after death. The thought that I might have known Harland in a past life and could possibly meet with him in the next led to more than a few sleepless nights. Then it occurred to me that in my next life I could possibly be his father or mother, sister or brother, or not even see him at all. I slept deeply and soundly after that.

Without a thought for my feelings, Harland registered his disapproval. We never again discussed my extracurricular activities. My duty and devotion to him was continuing and constant and he seemed contented. However, my life became a patchwork of those projects which, in the end, provided a brighter view of my world, a loving understanding of my sons and husband and, above all, what bright and unique souls we all were. It also made me a detached, rather bemused observer of my own life and provided insights that helped me deal with it all without hitting myself on the head with one of Harland's very useful tools.

Of course, just when I attained this high level of under-standing, the next level threw me a major curve.

Chapter Two

My growth and maturity was a gradual opening, like a flower reaching out petal by petal to the warmth and understanding of a benevolent sun. Little by little I gathered information through classes, seminars and workshops.

Harland, already set in life's pattern and routine, had no interest in my inner transformation. Whenever I tried to share my discoveries, his eyes wandered or he cleared his throat, looking for escape. By this time he was 45; I was 36 and a spiritual late bloomer.

I awoke each day with enthusiasm and a broader appreciation of life. The meek, submissive, eager-to-please Samantha was changing into a together, self-confident Sam, and I was delighted with her. Harland only noticed that I was not as pliant as usual and there were a few waves developing upon the waters of his serene lake.

Little by little my routine changed. With Harland off to work and the boys rushing to classes and sports events, the quiet house was mine. Rather than dashing to meetings and not-too-interesting gatherings, I put my house in order and then turned to my inner temple to meditate, read and reflect. The more I perceived, the more I found ahead of me to be discovered.

There were times I would look at Harland reading the paper or sitting at the dinner table and wonder who he was, what were his lessons to learn in this lifetime, and why were we together? What did we have to learn from each other in the process? I would smile as I explored this idea, and if Harland caught me he would smile back, probably interpreting my demeanor as contentment, and in a sense it was.

As I mentioned, this inner process brought expansion. My love for Harland, Casey and Connor grew as I realized that we were four souls sharing this lifetime, separate but connected. However, I could not demonstrate this growing spiritual awareness forthrightly or I might alienate them. Therefore, I gladly gave them my love and care, which they willingly accepted, but I did not attempt to make them a part of my personal growth.

At one point I was drawn to crystals and began wearing them, nicely mounted on long silver chains, or as bright earrings. Before my studies began, I assumed that only dramatically gowned mystics wore crystals, together with colorful scarves, multiple rings and bracelets. But this was not so. As my studies continued, I found that stones and crystals have been meaningful to many civilizations, and in this century were important in the development of electronic equipment, condensers, capacitors and transducers. Many New Agers held crystals during meditation to help develop intuition and healing. They even slipped them under their pillows to heighten the interpretation of dreams.

All of this was lofty information for a simple California housewife, but I brought it down to a more pragmatic level. To me, crystals were like nourishment from the earth, like the food of life — carrots, potatoes and other things from the soil. Unlike diamonds, which are hard and cold, I found some crystals had a warmth that seemed to reflect the energy I shared with them.

At one Sunday dinner, Mother Malcolm made a point of remarking to Harland, "Why does your wife insist on wearing jewelry made of glass? Now you're so successful, haven't you given her any diamonds or other precious stones to wear in public?"

Though ready and willing to stand my ground and set the lady straight, Harland raised a finger to stop me and came to my defense, a rare event. "Mother, Samantha is wearing crystals which are very dear to her. Many of them I found on my digs in the mountains. In fact, there are several large pieces and clusters in my workshop that are rather attractive. I'll take you there after dinner so you can see for yourself."

The lady shook her hands in a negative manner and said, "No, that's not necessary, my dear. I'll take your word that such stones are acceptable and stylish."

A small victory, but it was a delight.

And so my education continued and I became a stronger, more confident Samantha equal to almost anything. Not quite! Being enlightened was wonderful, but I found it doesn't give you much of a bat to swing when life throws you a few curves, and one came at me shortly after the boys left for college.

After returning from the airport, I sat quietly at home, reflecting for over an hour, feeling like a deflated tire and confused about what to do next. I finally gave in to my mood and moved to the piano to play every sad melody I could think of while I had a good cry. I was still huddled over the keyboard when Harland arrived, and for once he seemed sensitive to my frame of mind.

Sitting beside me on the piano bench, his arm circled my shoulders in comfort. "I know what you're going through. I'll miss them too. I came home early to bring news that will make you feel much better and help us so we won't miss the boys so much."

Needless to say, he had my full attention.

"The new store is doing well. I'm satisfied the manager and the sales personnel are performing on a high level, so I've decided to take time off, about a month. We can spend it together." He looked quite pleased with himself.

My mind raced with bright possibilities. "Oh, Harland, I've really wanted to travel — to London, Paris, or maybe a romantic cruise! There's no one to keep us home now."

Harland's voice brought me back from the far reaches of my

imagined journeys. "No, nothing like that. I thought we could have a good, long stay at Rocky Crest. That should be great fun. There are areas up there I've been wanting to explore." He smiled in anticipation of my reaction.

For a moment I tried to bring up the enthusiasm he wanted. "Yes, Harland, it would be wonderful to spend so much time together." Then my deepest urges rose to the surface not to be denied. "But dear, we really haven't traveled anywhere else for so many years. Can't we take some of this time and go somewhere, even if it's within the United States or Canada?" I substantially reduced my goals to come closer to his.

He frowned and stood up. "Why on earth would we want to do that when we have everything we need at Rocky Crest? Now, don't worry about it. Once up there, you'll have a wonderful time with lots to do. We might even drive over to Nevada and spend a few days at Lake Tahoe or Reno. That would be a good trip, don't you think?"

He had used this tone for appeasing the boys when they were younger. He seemed pleased he could be so reasonable when I was not as responsive as he had hoped.

Then he added the topper. "When I mentioned it to Mother, she said she would join us for a week or two, and perhaps bring a friend along. That should be fun, and they would be company for you."

"Let me think about it, Harland," I replied. "Perhaps I can come up with something you would enjoy for part of the time." I turned away sadly and headed for the stairs. The future was not promising, and I had to decide between running away from home, joining a convent, or beating a drum for the Salvation Army.

Harland called after me, "There won't be time. I want to leave Sunday, that's only five days. Let's organize the gear and food, plus all of my equipment, and whatever things you want to bring along." Any or all of those three options danced in my mind and began to look more and more appealing.

Five days later, in a bright new van he had gifted to himself, Harland drove us through the Central Valley of California, through the foothills, and on up into the higher elevations of the Sierra Nevadas to Rocky Crest. As usual it looked to me as stark as a lunar landscape. The surrounding mountains, though, were green and lovely in the fading sunlight.

On the long drive up, Harland was full of plans and ideas — what he would be doing, what I could be doing. As far as I could determine, my role was cook, housekeeper and companion. Like the pioneer women who came before me, as long as I kept a fire in the hearth and a pot on the stove, I would be treasured.

However, my thoughts went in another direction. Perhaps this would be a good time to rebuild the love and affection we had shared in the early days of our marriage. I had high hopes for some uninterrupted time together before Mother Malcolm descended upon us.

After settling in, Harland established his routine. Up early for a hearty breakfast, he would pick up his tool kit, sandwiches, bottled water, a Thermos of coffee, and head out to vigorously seek the treasures of the earth. I was left to my own devices — cleaning and straightening the mobile home, planning the evening meal, reading, walking, and trying desperately to maintain the comfortable perspective I had created during the last five years. Meditating outside, breathing deeply of that wonderful air, reviewing my past, present and future was the routine of my days.

The soft mornings of warm togetherness I had anticipated were punctuated by long phone conversations concerning one, some, or all of Harland's stores. His managers faxed inventory sheets and sales figures, which he would digest after dinner. My attempts to rekindle our once loving bond were inhibited by the movement of nuts, bolts and pliers.

"It's a beautiful night, Harland. Let's go outside and look at the stars. We could bundle up and be nice and cozy keeping each other warm." I wasn't too good at seduction, but I was giving it my best shot.

"Sounds good, Samantha, but I have a little studying to do. It's been a tiring day, and I want to hit the computer first thing tomorrow for the next batch of reports. I really want to turn in early."

On another cold evening, I suggested in a low voice that we go to bed early and snuggle like we used to.

"Sounds great, Samantha, but do you know what occurred to me today? We haven't played Gin Rummy in so long, and I think I'm ready for a real challenge tonight."

After that last statement, we made and held eye contact for about 30 seconds. During that look it finally occurred to me that Harland was seeing the old Samantha that he had created, not the new, improved model.

During dinner one night Harland announced, "I received a letter from Mother today. She and her friend Mavis will be joining us next Sunday for a week or two. That should be fun, and the four of us can spend the evenings playing bridge. We'll all help you improve your game."

I was stunned and speechless and could not think of a proper, civilized response. I think he interpreted my silence as joyful assent. The thought of spending my days in the company of Mother Malcolm and Mavis sent a shock through my body and all I could think was: *HELP! What do I do now?* I could not find the words to respond to him.

We spent the next few days shopping for food and other items that would please our guests. All too soon it was Sunday and Mother Malcolm sailed up the road in her Cadillac and unloaded

Mavis and five suitcases.

Mavis was a lady to be taken in small doses. Weighing about 100 pounds soaking wet, her small, seemingly frail body hid a strong and determined character. Her gray, tightly curled hair framed an elongated face that featured bright, searching brown eyes. Standing equally as high on the social ladder as Mother Malcolm, they were no threat to one another. When talking together they chirped like two robins in a tree using a kind of social shorthand.

When in a group discussion, Mavis tended to pounce on the subject like a bird discovering a worm, and in a flash it would be hers to capture and eventually gobble up. She was not one to let a conversation go by unchallenged.

I ushered the ladies to their separate, rooms which I had taken great pains to prepare. Entering her bedroom, Mother Malcolm looked about and sighed, "This is even more rustic than I remem-bered."

Showing Mavis to what I thought was the better of the two bedrooms, I said, "I do hope you will be comfortable here during your stay."

Mavis put her suitcase on the foot of the bed, pulled back the bedspread and checked the sheets. "There isn't much you can do with these funny little mobile homes, is there?" Then she launched into an extended report about a cousin and his wife who once owned a mobile home and somehow had managed to turn it into a cozy and comfortable domicile. I stood there politely for over 10 minutes before she finally paused to take a breath. Then I smiled and excused myself.

As I walked into the kitchen to fix dinner, I was over-whelmed by an urgent need to don my armor and shield and prepare for battle.

The next morning Harland left early to put in a few hours of rock hunting, and the first shots were fired.

From Mother Malcolm: "My dear, this house isn't as tidy as it should be. You must have seen the dust around the doors and windows. Haven't you noticed, Mavis?"

The silver curls on Mavis' head danced up and down as she nodded her head in eager agreement.

From me: "It's hard to keep up with it in this dusty area, Mother. And besides, our stay up here is also my vacation time."

Mavis chimed in. "One should always be watchful and not allow one's environment to become shabby or ill-kept. One must always keep one's surroundings bright and sparkling. My cousin's mobile home was always in pristine condition."

Of course, the "one" meant me, and I was the "one" who did the cooking, cleaning, made the beds — all under the watchful and critical eyes of Mother Malcolm and Mavis. Dressed in her bright silk casual pants suits and comfortably settled on the sofa, Mother Malcolm was dedicated to the proposition that all present were to be properly cared for.

The first major battle took place at dinner four days into their stay. It came out like sulfuric acid with enough destructive bite to corrode the soul of a saint.

"Beef stew, my dear, is a rather common dish, don't you think? It's all right for the pioneers or people who camp out, but with your lovely kitchen, why can't you attempt a more varied menu, more interesting meals? Don't you agree, Mavis? Harland?" I glared at Harland, daring him to join the attack, but he ignored me and replied, "Well, yes, Mother." Then glancing at me he added, "Samantha is so capable, I'm sure she could create something new and tasty if she really tried."

I returned fire by sweetly suggesting, "Mother Malcolm, with all of your experience, why don't you prepare dinner for the next few nights and then I could learn from you." It took a great deal of effort to keep my tone reasonable without sarcasm.

"My dear, my days of cooking are over; and besides, you could use the practice." She raised a manicured finger as if scoring a point, which she had. Game, set and match.

Mavis joined the attack by describing, in great detail, how a kitchen properly organized, with food carefully purchased and available, could deliver banquets with the greatest of ease if the cook had only the right training and attitude.

I looked at Harland, but his expression seemed to reflect embarrassment and disappointment in me rather than irritation at his mother. No help there.

Silently I reviewed the future entrées — fried rattlesnake, French fried possum, filet of coyote. But retreat seemed the best move, so I quickly excused myself from the table and walked out into the starry night where I sat upon one of the larger rocks and asked for answers and options.

For a few moments I reviewed my life. Realistically, there had been no tragedies or major crises in my life. Compared to many others, my own existence had been an easy one. I played the roles that were offered to me—dutiful wife to a hardware store tycoon; acceptable daughter-in-law to his mother; doting and attentive mother to our sons; loving daughter to my distant parents. When it came to the quality of life, mine clearly seemed a bit dented.

Looking out at the brilliant stars, I began to pray. "All right, you wonderful Universe. I seem to be backed into a painfully dark corner tonight. I can no longer tolerate this life gracefully. Please, please help me find some purpose and meaning in my life, find an existence that will bring some measure of satisfaction, acceptance and appreciation for all I have tried to do. Please help me to find more positives and fewer negatives, more successes and fewer failures. I must have done some good in this life, my dear Universe, and surely I deserve better than this!"

Focusing on the bright stars, I repeated this prayer over and over until my voice became hoarse and my body was weary. Hours later I entered the darkened mobile home and joined Harland in our bed. As I crept closer to him for comfort, he roused slightly, patted my shoulder, then turned over to resume his soft snoring.

I touched his shoulder. "Harland? Can we talk a minute? I really could use some tender, loving care."

He looked over at me and yawned as he said, "Samantha, I'm very tired and sleepy. We'll talk in the morning."

At breakfast Mother Malcolm was very cool. She and Mavis, and Harland as well, found it hard to make eye contact with me. She stated firmly that while Harland was out searching for the perfect rock, she and Mavis would drive to the nearest city, 40 miles away, to check out shops worthy of their attention. While there, they would assist me by purchasing their carefully selected list of groceries that even I could transform into a presentable evening meal. I smiled weakly, too weary to come up with an appropriate zinger to suit the occasion. Then after a peck on my cheek, Harland hurried off, forgetting his promise of the night before. Mother Malcolm, with a brief nod in my direction, sailed off in her Cadillac with Mavis.

After the dust had cleared, I finished the chores — kitchen clean, beds made, everything in order — and then paused for a moment to review what should come next. Without making a conscious decision, I went to the closet, pulled out a backpack and began to stuff it with underwear, a pair of athletic shoes, a change of clothes, cosmetics, and a variety of other items that came under my hand. Since it was cool in the mountains, I put on worn blue jeans, a T-shirt, a flannel shirt, and my tan, down jacket. As an afterthought, I threw in a knit cap and the satin case holding my jewelry — gold chains, earrings, crystal pendants on chains, assorted rings. I included the pieces Harland had given me on the birth of each of our sons. Gifts from his treasures — a ring made from a beautifully cut aquamarine mounted in handsome gold, a long necklace made from brightly faceted pieces of obsidian, and a huge ring made from a gold nugget.

Packing finished, I pulled on my boots, filled a pint canteen with water, picked up the backpack, surveyed the house, walked out the door and carefully shut it behind me.

Harland had taken his van, and the Cadillac was transporting Mother Malcolm and Mavis down the mountain. What do I do now? Where do I go? An inspired thought brought me to the storage shed where I found the boys' sturdy mountain bikes. Strapping the backpack on the rack of one, I carefully pointed the bike down the one-lane road leading away from Rocky Crest and bravely headed …where?

I seemed to be in the process of running away from home.

Searching for roads where the bicycle could travel easily, or taking shortcuts where it seemed provident, I soon became quite lost, even though I had traveled through this area many times. Also, I became terribly thirsty and often drank from the canteen. I did not think to bring food on this expedition, and as the day wore on, the need for a snack of any kind was badly felt. But I charged forward with good intentions, my resolve still strong, though it was beginning to get a bit ragged around the edges.

Stopping more than a few times to get my bearings, rest, and take in some water, I did not notice the many hours go by. I hurried, searching for civilization, any kind of a house or structure. I was sure there would be a farm or ranch somewhere, and my eyes scanned the horizon as I pedaled the bike more rapidly than before.

As the sun continued its journey into the west, food and shelter became uppermost in my mind. Coming to the top of a dirt path, I saw a small valley, and in the center, a cluster of buildings. As I approached I could see houses and shacks on the mountain slopes facing the center of town. This encouraged me to rush downhill toward the promise of assistance and a hot meal. Just then the bicycle struck a rock, skidded over to the side, and came to a dead stop as I tumbled over the handlebars. Stunned, I sat for a moment before checking my body and bike for damage. I came through fairly well, but one wheel was badly bent. After collecting my wits and backpack, I began walking toward the buildings. Twenty minutes later I entered the outskirts of the small town.

There was no sign of life on the street — no people, cars, activity of any kind. A faded, weather-beaten sign said "Welcome to Boone Valley," but that was all that greeted me. I slowly walked up the dirt street to find drab, dried-out buildings on each side. No lights, no convenience stores, no cafés, no gas stations. On one side, the remnants of a stone building stood with blank spaces where the doors and windows had once been. Farther on to the left, a one-story brick building seemed intact with iron plates covering the entrance and windows on each side. It clearly showed the aging of many years.

Walking along the dusty street, I found all of the buildings in similar condition. Four wide steps led up to a wooden walkway fronting faded and crumbled structures, and I began going from one to another, looking through dirty windows or bare window frames. All the buildings were clear of furniture, with nothing but dirt and debris on the floors.

Swearing was not part of my upbringing, but I could not help saying aloud, "Oh shit! *Super* shit! A ghost town! How can I be so lucky?" Then I screamed, "Where did everybody go?" In the stillness I waited, but there was no answer.

The sun rushed on its western path and shadows darkened the streets and buildings. Moving away from the buildings to the middle of the street, I continued my desperate exploration, but the silence was deafening and the approaching darkness daunting. I kicked at the rubble in the street in frustration, and cold anger came with it. As it bounced away from my feet, the fading rays of the sun glinted off one of the rocks, so I reached down to pick it up. It was not a rock but a crystal formation. It was a good size, almost filling my palm. Two spears were joined together at almost a "V." Their lower areas were milky, but the five sides and points were bright and clear. Early prospecting in the red earth covering these mountains must have brought many of these quartz formations to the surface. Harland certainly had more than a few in his collection. I slipped it into my jacket as I returned to the warped wooden stairs and sat down. I examined more closely the deserted streets and rundown and dilapidated buildings. Nothing moved.

In an effort to rest comfortably, I shifted the backpack to my knees, rested my head on my arms and, after carefully reviewing the situation, began to cry. My sobbing was unrestrained, like a child's. After awhile, like a child, I mercifully fell into a deep, deep sleep.

Chapter Three

Someone tugged on the sleeve of my jacket. Someone patted my right shoulder insistently. I was reluctant to back out of a very comfortable sleep, but the pats and tugs continued without pause.

"Lady! Lady? Are you all right? Are you dead, Lady? Wake up! Come on, wake up, Lady."

Slowly I raised my head, opened my reluctant eyes, and attempted to clear my mind. Two children stood before me — a small girl with red curly hair that obviously hadn't seen a comb in days, and an abundance of freckles over her little pug nose; the other, a boy several years older. He looked a bit shabby and very serious for his age with straight brown hair spilling over his anxious eyes.

"Lady! Are you all right? Why are you sittin' here? You've been sittin' here for a long time."

I was at a loss how to reply as I searched my mind for logical answers. I was groggy and disoriented. My eyes wandered to the street and the buildings in the morning sun. I turned back to the children, then came to a dead stop, eyes and mouth open in amazement. Shoving my backpack aside, I jumped up and put my full attention on the streets of Boone Valley. The buildings had been repaired. The black paint of "Assay Office" was now readable. The Boone Hotel was upright, looking important and ready for business. Down the street was a bright yellow building with "Majestic Saloon" clearly lettered in bright green. Added to this were the many people on the street as well as horses and wagons. And there were the odors — dust, horse droppings and food. `I turned to the children in shock.

"How long have I been here? When did all this happen?" I gazed around in amazement and felt a little scared. "How could I have slept through all of this?"

Then the answer came to me and I smiled. "I get it! They're making a movie here, aren't they? They brought in a big crew overnight to get ready to shoot a movie! Are you in it?"

The girl moved closer to the boy, and they continued to stare at me. Upon inspecting their clothing, I decided they were part of the cast. Her brown plaid dress was far from clean, a bit ragged, and over her shoulder was a gray knitted shawl for warmth. Her long cotton stockings were wrinkled, and the brown shoes quite worn. The boy's shabby brown pants came just below his knees, his shirt looked homespun, and his wool tweed jacket was about a year too small and a button short. Well, the costumes were authentic for a Western, that was for sure.

The little girl turned to the boy and asked, "What's she sayin', Warren?"

He looked at me warily and answered. "I dunno. What're you talkin' 'bout, Lady?"

Trying not to frighten them, I changed the subject. "Well, who are you two? Where do you come from?"

The boy straightened, looked me in the eye and replied, "We live here, Lady! What d'ya think?"

To calm him, I said, "Well, my name's Sam. I got lost and I'm just passing through. What's your name?"

He relaxed a bit and shot back, "My name's Warren. This here's my sister, Sumpin. She's 6 and I'm 9 years old."

I turned to the girl. "Sumpin? Where did you get a name like that?"

She still had a finger in her mouth, so her brother answered. "Momma Bertha told us that when she was a new baby with all that red curly hair, she said, 'Now, she's really Sumpin,' and we called her that ever since." The little girl nodded vigorously in agreement. I couldn't imagine a mother who would burden her child with such an unattractive name.

"Children, I need to find an adult who can help me. Is your mother nearby?"

Not only did I want to find out where I was, I needed a cup of coffee as badly as a cactus needs rain. Secondly, it was imperative to find the nearest restroom. It had been a long night and a lot of water from the canteen. Warren surprised me with his answer.

"We live over at the saloon, and Mamma Bertha's sleepin' now. We can't never bother her before she wakes up." Sumpin nodded in agreement.

Urgently I told them, "Kids, I'm desperate. I need a cup of coffee, but first I need to find a bathroom."

Warren looked at me curiously. "You wanna take a bath?"

"No, dear. I need a rest room, a toilet ... you know, answer Nature's call?" When he did not answer, I tried again. "An outhouse?"

"Oh. There's one over behind the saloon. We'll show you where 'tis."

Going before me, the children walked down the middle of the crowded street toward the saloon. This gave me an opportunity to examine the buildings more closely. They had all been fixed up and were busy with people coming in and out of the doorways. A horse brushed by as we walked, and the rider stared down at me. Then I noticed that most of the people on the streets were gawking at me. They were dressed as extras and, I assumed, ready for the filming of the movie to begin. I thought someone might yell at me to get off the set, but no one said a word.

As we passed the bright yellow saloon, the children turned onto a path between two buildings and led me to an outhouse. Wonderful! Handing my backpack and jacket to Warren, I walked in.

Gritting my teeth against the waves of unbelievable stench, I quickly chose one of the six wooden holes. I emerged in record time and found the children patiently waiting.

I knew I should go find someone in charge, but I really needed a cup of coffee to clear the cobwebs. I asked the children, "Where can I find a decent cup of coffee? I'm really desperate for one."

They looked at each other, then led me to a doorway in back of the saloon. We entered a long dark hallway. Warren opened a door and I saw a large kitchen. I felt the heat radiating from a huge, black, cast-iron stove. On each side were shelves and cupboards filled with cans, small bags and boxes of food. An assortment of pots and pans hung from the walls. To the left were four tables, each with four chairs. Behind them on the walls were shelves and cabinets holding a variety of crockery and enamelware.

In the center of the kitchen was a long wooden table to which were attached knives and cleavers of all sizes and shapes. Working at the table was a man of Chinese ancestry wearing what looked like black pajamas and a small black hat. A black pigtail hung halfway down his back. Upon seeing us, he rushed to the children.

"What you do here? Go 'way! You come here only to eat! Mistah Smitha's be very mad!" His hands motioned, trying to shoo us out the door.

Warren stood his ground and pleaded my case. "Wong Kee! This lady here is new, she's hungry. Can she have some coffee?"

"We no give food! Mistah Smitha's no want. Go 'way!"

I took it from there. "Wong Kee! I'm a very weary traveler, I seem to be lost, and I badly need some coffee just to get myself together and find my bearings. Could you please spare a cup?" I tried my best to look terribly sad.

After looking me over, the cook turned to the stove, picked

up a huge pot and poured hot liquid into a large tin cup. Handing it to me, he said, "Drink now, then you go!"

I took the cup gratefully. "Thank you, thank you so much Wong Kee. You've saved my life!" Then I took a sip. Well, it was like nothing I had tasted before. But it was hot, dark, very strong, and wonderful, and I could feel my red corpuscles coming to life. The shutters of my brain opened, and I became more aware of my surroundings.

As I sipped the coffee, Warren explained that Wong Kee was the cook for the saloon, and that he fed everyone who worked there — the bartenders, gamblers, piano player, his mom and five other Waiter Girls, and the owner, Orrin Smithers. I got the impression that Smithers fed the children only because they belonged to one of his Waiter Girls.

My thoughts were interrupted by Wong Kee who had been eyeing me from head to toe. "You dress funny. You have no woman clothes?"

After another sip of coffee I replied, "You mean a dress? I've been wandering around these mountains, and a dress wouldn't do. Lots of women now wear pants anyway. Haven't you noticed that?"

He shook his head, then walked over and felt the material and stuffing in my jacket. I explained, "That's a special material, and it's stuffed with goose down so it keeps me very warm when it's cold."

He nodded his head then turned away and walked to the worktable. Pulling out a loaf of bread, he cut three thick slices and brought them over to the children and me. "You go, take this other room so Mistah Smitha's no see." He then waved us out of his kitchen and closed the door.

Warren opened a door directly across the hall from the kitchen to a room holding six round tables with five chairs around

The room had an odor of its own — old cigars and stale whiskey. Over to the side was a large object covered with burlap.

The two windows overlooking the outhouse brought in the sunshine, and the children and I sat at a table and smiled at each other while we ate the bread. Soon I felt ready to take on a tiger, or at least a few cubs.

First, I needed to find a telephone, or a bus to take me down the mountain to Jackson. And a store for food and bottled water—I was not about to be caught without those staples again. As my head cleared I made the decision to head for home, not to Rocky Crest, and consider my options from there.

Warren walked to the object in the corner, pulled back the dusty cover and proudly pointed to a small part of it. "Lookee here! Ain't this purty?"

Beneath the covering was a piano. I helped him remove the burlap, and there stood a beautifully crafted ebony spinet, though very dusty and neglected.

"This is a beautiful piano, Warren, but it's a shame it's not being used. Do you play?" Two heads shook in a positive no. On an impulse I said, "Would you like me to play something for you?" Two heads nodded in agreement.

Taking a bandanna from my backpack, I wiped off the dust, lifted the lid to uncover the keyboard, then brought over one of the chairs to sit on.

"Do you have a favorite song?" Two heads wagged back and forth in another "no." My fingers played a series of chords while I searched my memory for an appropriate song. The piano was badly out of tune, but remnants of its beautiful tone were there. It took a moment, then I knew what to play.

The song was about a candy man and the luscious confections he could make. The melody was light and happy and the children were entranced. My Cub Scout troop sang this at one of their annual shows. We practiced the words over and over, so I was able to sing every verse. When I finished, the children were smiling, displaying teeth that probably hadn't been brushed in days, and clapping their hands. Sumpin was jumping up and down shouting, "More ... more!"

With such a great audience, I went immediately into an encore about the wonderful things that could be found beyond a rainbow. Once more the children listened silently, intent on every word. Just as I played the last chord, the door flew open and a man burst into the room. His eyes were cold and he spoke in a deliberate tone. "Who told you kids you could play with this piano?" Then he turned to me. "And who the hell are you?"

Dressed in a black suit with an off-white shirt and black string tie, he glared at me from under heavy black eyebrows. His curly black hair came to his collar and was badly in need of a decent haircut. Under a scraggly black mustache his mouth was curled and ready to shout when I began to laugh.

"You must be the owner of the saloon, the one who gives the hero a bad time."

"Whaaat?" The heavy eyebrows raised high on his forehead.

"Aren't you one of the actors working on the movie? You look perfect for the part. And the town looks so real. Was it built just for the movie?"

He became even angrier. "What the damn hell are you talkin' about? I ain't no actor, and I can't make no sense outta what you're sayin'. Now get outta here. I don't need no strange woman around upsettin' things."

This brought me to a dead stop. Now wait a minute! I needed to ask some questions, but I wasn't sure I would like the answers. I tried to placate the man.

"Mr. Smithers? My name is Samantha Malcolm, and some-how I lost my way in these mountains and ended up here in Boone

Valley. Are they shooting …" I tried another tack. "Why are there so many people on the streets so early in the day? Is there a celebration?"

He looked at me like I just stepped out of a UFO, then spoke again in that cold, frightening tone of voice. "How in hell can you be in these mountains and not know what's goin' on? Why else would all these folks be here? They're all lookin' for gold!" He shouted the last sentence.

It took me a moment to digest that bit of information. All those people, dressed like a scene from "Gunsmoke," searching for gold? No, it couldn't be. Another question occurred to me.

"When did they get here?"

"Lady, they been a-comin' here ever since they found gold back in '48. Hell, this town ain't more than 5 years old. Folks keep comin' here to make a fortune, one way or another."

My heart began to beat in double time. I had to ask. "One more question, Mr. Smithers. What is the date?"

He frowned, scratched his nose, then answered, "It's somewhere 'bout the 20th of August."

My body turned cold and my next question exploded from me. "I've been lost in these mountains for quite awhile. Tell me, what … year is it?"

"You must have been livin' in a cave somewhere, woman. This here's the year 1852. Now, no more of your damned questions. I got a saloon to run and the men will be comin' in here to play cards. You take these kids outta here and leave the piano alone!" He strode angrily from the room.

My mind was like a Ferris wheel spinning out of control as I reviewed the startling facts I had been given. I stood and began to pace the room, trying to reconcile the present I was living in … yesterday, with the present I seemed to be in today. The obvious conclusion could not be possible. Where could I go for answers?

What could I do next?

As I paced the floor, my eye caught a piece of paper nailed to the wall near the door. Moving closer I could see it was a handbill bearing an interesting announcement.

PUBLIC NOTICE.
All citizens of Boone Valley are
respectfully invited to attend the
HANGING of MERCER OATES,
CLAIM JUMPER. Meeting will be
at the Lucky Shamrock Saloon,
MINER'S COURT, August 24th, 1852,
7 o'clock, NIGHT.

Clyde Parkins, Sheriff

The paper was fresh, and the black ink seemed to be heavy, dark and new. My eyes fixed on the date, and I reached out and rested a finger just below the year. I can't remember how long I stared, but after awhile I began to giggle quietly, and then laugh, and then I could not stop myself. My laughter grew in volume and my eyes filled with tears. Stumbling to the nearest table, I sat and buried my face in my arms. Never before in my life had I given in to tears, but not only had I cried myself to sleep last night, but now I surrendered to a regular Niagara Falls of weeping.

What I was feeling was a combination of fear, dismay, helplessness, despair, bewilderment and dread. Could this be true? *If it is, stop the world. I think I'd like to get off now, thank you.* I slowly came back to myself as I realized little hands were patting me on the shoulder, stroking my hair.

"Mis' Samantha, you all right? Don't cry, don't cry."

I had forgotten that four young eyes were witnessing my

storm of tears. As I raised my head I could see they were frightened and concerned, bless their little hearts. For their sakes, I sat up, wiped my eyes, and managed a crooked smile. Sumpin was shaking, but Warren seemed intent on helping me become a sane person once more.

"Warren … Sumpin, I'm so sorry you saw me carry on this way. Don't worry, I'm all right now. But I surely had a good cry, didn't I?"

Warren managed a smile and said quite seriously, "You sure did that, all right." Leaning forward, I grasped a hand from each of them and tried to explain.

"My little friends, it seems I'm in deeper trouble than I ever imagined. What I need now is to find a few answers. I need a quiet place where I can think things through and make some decisions."

Warren nodded. "So, what're you goin' to do?"

I struggled to quiet the storm within me.

"Warren, you seem to know your way around town. Is there a good hotel where I can get a room?"

Both children smiled, and Warren answered, "Hotels are full all the time and people are sleepin' in the lobby, and even in the streets just like you."

"What about here? Could Mr. Smithers rent me a room?"

Warren shook his head. "They're all full, too. They have people in 'em day and night."

I was getting desperate. "Now think, children. Is there any-place in this town where there might be some space? How about a nice house where I could rent a room?"

They exchanged a few whispered comments, then Warren suggested, "The nicest house in town belongs to Mrs. McKee. She owns the Mercantile Store. She's kinda mean and don't like us kids around her store, but she lives in a big house all by herself."

A small ray of hope. "Could you take me there so I can at

least talk to Mrs. McKee?"

The children nodded to each other, then Warren took my hand and led me out the back door, around to the busy street, and once more through the crowds of people. As I walked, my eyes swept across the crowds moving about me. Some looked me over as they walked, but many others did not. Except one.

One tall figure stood on the wooden walkway in front of a store, not moving, his eyes fixed on me. He wasn't wearing odd pieces of well-worn garments. His outfit was more put together, the shirt, jacket and pants well coordinated. A narrow-brimmed, tan Stetson placed just above his eyebrows topped the outfit. He stood out in that greatly diverse crowd and, as I glanced at him, our eyes connected, but just for a second. Warren pulled at my hand, urging me to keep up as we hurried down the street.

A few moments later, as we were passing one of the narrow side streets, our attention shifted to an argument taking place. Loud voices were accusing, swearing, then we heard scuffling, an exchange of blows.

"Damn your hide! Stay away from my claim and my food, and don't let me see you 'round there no more!"

Warren looked up and smiled. "Happens all the time. No need to be scared."

The dirt road leading through town left some of the shops and crowd behind and I began to see more of the mountains surrounding Boone Valley. The odd shacks and structures I had noticed before were more clear. They dotted the lower elevations, and I could see men and women going about their business around them. Small vegetable patches were growing by many of the shacks, and lines of rope held the day's washing to dry. Trees were absent on the lower slopes, which were devoid of green growth of any kind. It occurred to me that wood on those slopes had long ago become the fires for cooking and warmth.

Later I realized my inner computer was taking in all of these details as an interested observer, but I had not yet accepted the unquestionable proof that I was indeed in this time and place. The various buildings of town were now behind us as we continued our walk down the dirt road. We passed what seemed to be a church, and then a series of houses more sturdy and larger than those upon the mountains. Fifteen minutes later we reached a house much nicer than the others. It was a white, two-story, Victorian style with a broad porch about the entrance, and a widow's walk on the roof. The trim on the porch railings and shutters was blue, and the effect was charming.

As we came up the long walk, the front door opened and a woman in her 50s rushed out and yelled, "I told you kids not to hang around here or my store. Now git!"

She was dressed in black with the long sleeves covering her wrists and the high neck almost to her jaw. Her faded brown hair showed streaks of gray, and her face reflected a lady who was far from contented.

Quickly I removed the S.F. Giant's cap, ran my fingers through my hair, and walked closer to the porch.

"Mrs. McKee," I began in my most pleasant manner, "my name is Samantha Malcolm and I'm new in town. I desperately need a place to stay for a few days and was wondering if you would rent one of your bedrooms."

"Never! With all the riffraff coming to town, I'd sooner open my home to a pack of monkeys. I don't know you or where you come from." Her eyes examined every detail of the blue jeans, the flannel shirt, my uncombed hair, and a face that showed the effects of a crying jag. She was not impressed. She added, "We may be in the wilderness, but decent ladies don't dress like you. It just isn't done."

"I do apologize, Mrs. McKee. I wore these clothes to be

comfortable and had no inkling I would end up so far from home."
I was determined not to let go of this chance, slim though it seemed.
"I'll gladly tell you about my background and anything else you
would like to know. Here's the situation. Somehow I became separated from my husband and two sons, and I really need a quiet place
to think through what I should do next."

The lady frowned and shook her head. "Young lady, I do not
make it a practice to bring strangers into my home. I've heard lots
of hard-luck stories, so don't think you can tell me anything new."

"I promise you," I urged, "you haven't heard this one. Please
think about it,"

She hesitated while she continued to look me over. "Well,
we can talk. But the youngsters can't come in. They'll have to wait
out here on the porch."

I turned to the children. "Will you wait for me?"

They both nodded and settled themselves on the top step of
the porch.

Mrs. McKee opened the front door and impatiently
motioned for me to enter into a dark entry hall. The house smelled
of new wood, paint and kerosene.

As I walked through the dark rooms, I felt disassociated
from sanity, like I was in an audience waiting for the actors, dialogue
and story to begin.

Chapter Four

Mrs. McKee led me to a small parlor and indicated a wooden, straight-back chair. It was a pleasant room with a flowered rug, red velvet settee, and arm chairs scattered about. The room was cool and quiet, as if very little activity intruded on the silence.

As she settled into a comfortable chair, Mrs. McKee shook her head in disgust and asked, "Well, what is it you have to say? What can you tell me that I haven't heard before?"

"For one thing," I answered, "I'm lost and have no idea how to get back to my family."

She snorted. "This happens, I know that for sure. My husband, daughter and I came all this way from Missouri, and it wasn't easy. People can be separated and lose each other. I'll grant you that."

"Exactly. Right now I'm at a loss as to what to do and what steps to take to find my family. I need rest and time to review my options. I promise, Mrs. McKee, I'd be a good tenant and cause you no trouble."

She shook her head. "With a stranger in my house? My mind wouldn't be easy!"

Just then there were thumps on the porch where the children were waiting. Mrs. McKee hurried to the front door and called out, "You be quiet out there." The thumps stopped. There were other admonishments I couldn't hear.

During her absence I studied the parlor and the room on the other side of the entrance. In a far corner I could see another beautiful piano. This one was rosewood, exquisite in detail with a matching bench. Walking closer, I ran my fingers over the wood, then couldn't resist touching the keys. The tone was lovely and perfectly in tune, and I played a few chords.

"What do you think you're doing, young lady?" Mrs. McKee was furious. "No one plays that piano anymore!"

"But where did you get such a beautiful instrument? I've never seen one quite so lovely."

She showed her disapproval. "Martin, my husband, took it in trade from a German man looking for gold like all the others. He gave the man much too much in supplies, but he wouldn't listen to me! He wanted it for our daughter, Rosalie, but before I knew it Martin died of consumption and Rosalie ran off with a gambler. As far as I'm concerned, it can rot here."

With my hands on the keyboard, I searched for some way to reach this lady. After hitting a chord, I began singing a song from "Oklahoma." Out of the corner of my eye I could see her standing there, hands folded, not moving. She wasn't objecting, so I continued.

She moved to sit in the chair nearest the piano and listened while I sang the lyrics. When I played the last chord, I looked over to see how the lady was reacting. She was looking down at her hands, so I waited until she raised her eyes and said softly, "We had this piano a very short time. Rosalie could play it a little and sing the songs we liked. Martin and I loved hearing her sing in the evenings. After he died she wouldn't touch the piano again, and then in a few weeks she was gone without a word. It's been very hard for me to forgive her, but I do miss the sound of her sweet voice in the evenings."

I found it hard to find the right words. "Mrs. McKee, I am so very sorry to learn about Martin's death, followed by Rosalie's departure. How terribly sad it must have been for you."

We sat silently for a few moments. What else could I say that would comfort this lady?

"Mrs. McKee, if it would help you at this time, I know many songs and lovely melodies that I could share with you. If you let me stay here, I will play and sing for you every evening. Would you like that?" From the expression on her face I could see I had given her some comfort.

She looked at me quietly, then said hesitantly, "I think I'd like that. That was a pretty song. Reminded me of Missouri when I was a girl. I saw many a morning like that."

Once more she inspected me from my rumpled hair to the heavy boots, then commented. "Well, from the way you talk and play that piano, it's clear you've had a good bit of music and book learning."

Adding another talent, I said, "Also, I'm a pretty good cook, and I'd love to help out in the kitchen and maybe cook something you may not have tasted before. May I please stay here with you?"

She seemed to be considering the pros and cons of taking in the rumpled and dirty stranger before her. Finally she said firmly, "All right, Missy. You can stay and see how we get along. I'm not the easiest person to live with, as Martin often told me. But if you'll play that pretty music for me, it'll give me something to look forward to every night besides checking inventories and doing the books." That decided, she stood and asked, "Do you have a suitcase or a trunk?"

I indicated the backpack. "This is all I have for now, but I intend to find suitable clothes as soon as I can. I'll have to work that out later."

Her mind made up, she started for the stairs. "Let me show you the room you can use."

I hesitated. "I'd better tell the children to go home, and I'll visit with them later."

Looking out the front door, I could see Warren and Sumpin waiting patiently.

"Hey, kids, you've been a big help to me today. This kind lady has a room, so I'll be staying here. But I'll be looking for you in town. I don't want to lose my new special friends."

They smiled, waved goodbye, and began their walk back to town.

As I closed the door, I remarked to Mrs. McKee that they were sweet children to help me in my distress, and especially to lead me here to such a lovely home.

She shook her head. "They're a handful, running around town, nobody minding them or taking them to school. It's a scandal that they live in that saloon with their mother."

"Well, they seem to love her and appear pretty well cared for, though they could use some decent clothes."

As she led me up the stairs, I noticed the details of her clothes. Floor length black cotton, obviously handmade, no zipper, tight bodice, full skirt, and looking a little worn. Here again were additional clues that I was indeed coping with 1852.

She opened a door to a bedroom bright with sunlight from two windows overlooking a garden. There was a four-poster bed and a matching wardrobe, dresser and vanity off to the side. On top of a small table was a large china bowl decorated with blue flowers, a matching pitcher sitting inside: one more reminder that time was playing a trick on me, and there was some serious sorting out to be done.

I commented on the lovely room but noticed that the lady's face was full of pain.

"This was my daughter's room," she said. "I don't come in here no more, so you might as well use it."

"I do appreciate your letting me stay, and I'll take good care of everything. And Mrs. McKee, I need more of your help, if you don't mind."

I motioned her to sit on the chair in front of the vanity and I sat on the bed. "You see, I'll need to buy clothes since this is all I have with me. When I walk down the street, everyone stares, so I should get some proper dresses right away. I brought some jewelry with me, so I could sell that to get started. Maybe you can advise me about what I could do to earn money to live on."

She walked to the wardrobe, opened the double doors and pointed to the contents. "Rosalie left these behind. She packed a bag and ran off one night while I was sleeping. As you can see, she left most of her things behind."

Her voice choked, but she caught her breath and continued. "Look through here and the dresser and take whatever you want for now. Whatever else you need will be at my store, and I'll give you credit 'til you get a few dollars together."

I was overwhelmed by her kindness. "Mrs. McKee, an hour ago we didn't even know each other, and now it seems we could be friends. I'm very grateful."

Waving a finger in my direction, she said, "Mrs. Malcolm, you seem to have an honest face, even though you're dressed so funny. And you can call me Hattie." Looking at me sharply, she continued, "I think we'll get along. And if we don't, you'll hear from me!"

Her face reflected pain and caution as she left the room. My tension eased a bit and the first of my major problems was solved. However, as the door closed behind her, I allowed myself to slump on the bed and give in to the dismay and panic I had been suppressing. It was almost like a dream. My mind and body seemed disconnected. It took an effort to move, and the riot in my head had to be stilled and brought under control.

My God, what do I do now? Here I am in an alien world filled with manners, customs, situations and people new to me. I can't share with anyone who I really am, where I have come from. Will I ever be able to return to Harland and the boys?

I tried to picture what Harland and his mother were going through. By now it had probably occurred to him that I had disappeared. Was he panicked and searching frantically for me? Or having coffee with Mother Malcolm and Mavis and discussing how badly Samantha was acting? Was he certain that I would show up at the doorstep, contrite and asking for forgiveness? Had he called the authorities? The search parties, if any, would look in vain.

I allowed myself to smile at the thought of Mother Malcolm and Mavis doing the kitchen chores. The smile faded when Casey and Connor came to mind. I missed my dear boys. What anguish will they go through?

How can I get back? When can I go back? What did I do to get here? How could I reverse the process? My head ached with questions for which there were no answers. There was a knock on the door. Hattie came in carrying a pitcher of water and a towel. "You might want to clean up a bit before you come downstairs. Take your time and I'll throw together some vittles for lunch."

I accepted with gratitude, and as the door closed I filled the basin with water. Stripping to panties, I sponged away the dirt and tears of the day and the night before. The water felt cool and refreshing, and I began to feel more centered and perhaps capable of facing my new situation.

I explored the contents of the wardrobe. It was like looking through a rack of an antique store. The dresses were polished cotton and bombazine, long, of soft colors, and trimmed with ribbons and lace. Hattie and Martin evidently doted on their daughter, providing an abundance of fine clothes.

Checking through the dresser, I found bloomers, camisoles, half-slips trimmed with satin ribbons, nightgowns, and two pair of long cotton stockings. Well, if I'm going to participate in this masquerade, I may as well dress the part. One by one I tried on the clothes. My days at the gym paid off. The underclothes fit very well.

After the slip and camisole, I pulled on a blue gingham dress with a narrow white lace trim, long full skirt with a ruffle, and a wide collar that covered the shoulders. The sleeves were long and full with lace trim at the wrists. The dress was a bit loose and hit above my ankle. Rosalie must have been a big girl, but inches shorter than me. Looking into the mirror, it seemed I might fit into Boone Valley without calling attention to myself.

Getting a few things from the backpack, I brushed my hair for the first time in 24 hours. It fell just to my shoulders, which would fit into this time period. There was a blue ribbon among the contents of the dresser, so I used it to tie back the sides of my hair, which I hoped was the style.

A pair of shoes in the wardrobe proved to be woefully small. Of the shoes in my backpack, the athletic shoes were out, so the boots would have to do. With a last glance in the mirror, I noticed my gold wristwatch. That, together with my diamond engagement ring, went in my backpack. The platinum wedding ring with its intricate design I left on.

As I walked down the stairs, wonderful smells met me, so I searched through the lower floor until I found Hattie in the kitchen. She looked up as I entered.

"My, you sure look a sight different than when you first came in. You do look pretty, though that dress is a bit short and the boots just won't do. I'll take you to the store after lunch and see what we have in your size. How about some fried eggs and boiled potatoes?"

I was so hungry I could eat a grizzly bear, so the meal, though a bit heavy in carbohydrates, was most welcome. She served the eggs and potatoes with bread, hot coffee and cream, and I ate every bite washed down with two cups of coffee. Now I was ready to tackle Boone Valley. First, I borrowed a cape from Rosalie's wardrobe, then checked into the jewelry case to see what I could convert into 19th Century cash. The gold nugget ring plus a small but heavy gold chain should do the trick. Then I hurried to join

Hattie for my first shopping trip in Boone Valley.

It was a brisk, cool day and the 20-minute walk to the center of town was an eye-opener. Many houses were built around Hattie's, but none as large, and most were only one story. All were wooden frame construction and typical of the time.

Once more I looked up at the slopes of the surrounding mountains and the shacks and lean-tos scattered about them. Plumes of smoke curled upward from many of them, and here and there a man or woman carried wood and walked on the dirt paths.

I listened with interest as Hattie spoke of the early years when she and Martin traveled by wagon train from Missouri. After selling their small store in Missouri, they loaded the inventory onto two strong wagons.

"Samantha, I can't tell you how hard it was, walking for so many miles or bouncing around on a wagon. And the worst part was those dear people who fell by the wayside — some dying of fever. Or when their mules or oxen gave out, they stood by their wagons helplessly. It made you heartsick. But somehow Martin and me made it. But I don't like to think on that part of the trip."

Upon reaching Sutter's Mill in California, they filled two more wagons with goods and supplies, hired drivers from the many men eager to travel to the Mother Lode, and headed where gold was attracting people from all over the world. They were among the first settlers in Boone Valley. Their wares were much in demand, and at first they were sold from the backs of the wagons. Once the store was built, Martin and Hattie had a thriving business outfitting customers with the tools they would need at the gold fields, as well as providing food and other materials for the more permanent citizens of Boone Valley. Within three years the store had grown into a large enterprise.

"Someone told me a week or so ago that there's about 20,000 people living and working here, though I don't know how they figure it. I see mostly those passing through, and that amounts to hundreds. They head up to the diggings pretty quick, so they don't stay around to be counted. However, they do leave wives and children behind to wait for them."

Hattie reported the town now had a thriving sawmill, brick-yard, flour mill, two churches, one schoolhouse, three banks, two blacksmiths, a livery stable, post office, boot maker, telegraph office, newspaper, a brewery, and 13 saloons — the largest was the Majestic run by Orrin Smithers. In the early months Martin and a few others invested in the sawmill and lumber yard, and that helped in the early construction and growth.

Hattie's home was closer to town than many others since it was one of the first to be built by Titus Boone, a carpenter. She remembered the house sitting in the field by itself upon completion. Soon the entire valley was filled with tents, shacks, and structures of every kind.

"Samantha, Martin and I spent many days and nights starting our business, I just can't tell you. But it grew to what it is now, and I have wagons coming in every other day from San Francisco, Stockton or Sutter's Mill. Our shelves seem to get empty awful quick these days. Now I have three clerks to take care of things. Wish we had 'em earlier 'cause those long hours and cold nights working on the account books took their toll on Martin, and he died a little over a year ago."

She choked a bit when she spoke of her loss. I already admired this lady for what she had endured.

The road was now crowded with men, horses, carts, teams of oxen, mules, and off to the side, small groups of women and children. A stagecoach and its team of four horses rushed by, causing the dust on the road to swirl around us.

We came to the Assay Office and Hattie directed me through the door. There were several people in line, but it moved quickly and soon Hattie introduced me to Aaron Ross who examined my gold nugget ring.

"Where did this come from?" he asked.

"My husband found it when he was … exploring."

"The setting I have not seen before. What is it?"

"I understand the nugget is pure 22 carat, while the ring and setting are 18 carat. It was made … back East," I answered.

Hattie interrupted. "Aaron, this here's a friend of mine, and I hope you'll do right by her. And be sure you use the real weight!" She smiled with this last remark.

Aaron smiled back. "Right, Miss Hattie. You know I always do the best I can."

He turned to carefully examine the ring. Finally he sat up and commented, "Altogether this ring has about two-and-a-half troy ounces of pure gold. I can give you $50 for it. If I can sell it for more to someone, I'll give you the extra money. How's that?"

Fifty dollars didn't sound like much to me, but Hattie nodded in agreement. I then handed over the beautiful gold rope chain, which I'd bought for $375. This, too, was carefully examined until he asked, "Where did this come from? It's well made."

I hesitated. "It was made in … Europe, where many talented craftsmen make beautiful jewelry. I believe it cost about … $400.

He shook his head. "A great amount which I cannot pay. I can pay only for the troy weight of the gold."

Hattie interrupted. "Why don't you display it here and see if anyone has enough gold to buy it?"

I agreed that would be best. Tucking the $50 into the pocket of the dress, I followed Hattie to her store to look for shoes.

We walked on down the street to a building with a sign across the front entrance: "McKee's Mercantile." The double doors of the entrance were wide open to admit the crowd of people entering and leaving. Inside Hattie introduced me to each of the busy clerks —

Ambrose Baxter, Frank Newhall, and Jim Bidwell. To the latter she directed, "Help this lady get whatever she needs, and start an account for her."

Jim Bidwell nodded respectfully and returned to the waiting customers, while Hattie proudly showed me around. The store was divided into two sections.

"Over here on the right are the heavy items — shovels, pick-axes, metal pans for panning the gold, metal cooking and eating utensils, lanterns, candles, blankets, nails, hammers, knives, tents, chisels, guns, rifles and rope. Over here we have shoes and boots, and hats."

She guided me to the other side of the building, which was overflowing with barrels and bags of flour, sugar, beans, hardtack and salt. There were also huge containers of coffee, dried fruit, salt pork and canned goods. The store was bursting with odors coming from the merchandise, the smoke from the kerosene lamps placed about, as well as the sweat from those anxious to buy the items so necessary to their lives. No wonder Hattie's business was doing so well.

After my tour, Jim Bidwell showed me the shoes in my size. The shoes were sturdy and practical and not built for style or appearance. A few were made for dancing or wearing in town, but most had heavy soles for winter wear. I settled on a pair that were comfortable but not too heavy. To my delight, they cost only $3.50, so I brought out some money from the sale of the ring. Hattie pushed my hand aside. "You hold on to that until you know what you're going to do. We can settle the bill later." I decided that Hattie was my kind of lady.

Hattie took time to go over the receipts with the clerks, check on inventory and orders, and then indicated she was ready to return home. She gathered supplies for her kitchen, which I helped carry back to the house. I offered to contribute something for the food, but she would have none of it. "We'll work all that out later. Don't you fret about these things for now."

That night we had a meal of stewed chicken, dumplings, and cabbage from her garden. She had never heard of creamed cabbage, so I got busy at her large, wood-burning stove and whipped up my part of the dinner. Hattie was pleased with the result. "Well, this is very tasty, and something I can certainly do myself!"

It was late in the day, and we lit two kerosene lamps to see our food and find our way for the washing up. Hattie filled a bucket from a sturdy pump next to the sink, then placed it on the stove. This was the hot water we would use to wash the dishes. No hot water heater in this day and age. I was gradually adapting to this life, though at times I felt I was playing a part in a play.

With everything cleaned up, Hattie moved to the room next to the kitchen. It was clear she was anxious to talk, and learn more of my history. We carried the lamps and settled in comfortable chairs. By this time I was truly tired after an incredibly emotional and wearing day, but I remembered what I had promised this fine lady and moved to sit before the piano to play for her.

Chapter Five

That first night at Hattie's the house rang with music. Taking more than a page from "Oklahoma," I played many of those lovely melodies, and it proved to be a special experience for both of us. To me, it was like a visit home, reminding me of who I was and what I had left behind. The colorful scenes from the movie flashed through my head as I played. Once more Hattie seemed to be transported back to her childhood in Missouri, her face shining as she listened.

Just as the concert began, Hattie left the room and returned with a bottle and two glasses. "Martin always had a bottle of whiskey on hand when his men friends visited, and I managed to put away a few bottles of sherry for medicinal or monthly ... discomforts. Let's have some now."

"Hattie, what a wonderful thought. I can't think of a better time to celebrate."

"But what can we possibly celebrate?"

"Anything, everything. My coming here. You taking on a new boarder."

As the evening progressed, we found many things to toast — sentimental songs from her past, Martin's favorite song. By the time the visit to Oklahoma was over, the bottle was half empty and Hattie was slumped in her chair deep in thought. Holding a sherry glass in one hand, she uncurled and pointed a finger at me. "Samantha, it's time to tell me. Who are you? You, my girl, clearly come from a place different from anything I know about. You're ... different."

"Just how am I different?"

She narrowed her eyes and looked at me closely. "The way you talk. The way you walk. The way you handle things. You're so sure of yourself. No woman I know acts the way you do. You look people right in the eye and say just what you mean. No beating about the bush. Do all the ladies act like that where you come from?"

"I think most of them do."

Drinking the last of the sherry in my glass, I set it carefully on the table next to the piano. "Hattie, all I can tell you is that I have come here over a very long distance, and somehow in the process I became separated from my family. I don't know if, how or whether I'll find them again. I wasn't prepared to find myself in the middle of the Gold Rush, all alone, having to take care of myself."

Hattie nodded sympathetically. "Tell me about your husband."

Answering presented a problem. How to be truthful without disclosing the facts of my incredible journey? "My husband, like yours, is a merchant specializing in tools and hardware. Like Martin, he put a great deal of time, effort and thought into his work." I didn't know what else to say. Hattie refilled our glasses and we silently drank, each in our own thoughts.

Hattie sniffed, leaned forward and said, "It just isn't right! We both lost our husbands and we're separated from our children. It's bad enough living in this God forsaken country, but without friends or family, it's downright hard."

Sitting back a little unsteadily in her chair, she continued. "There aren't many women in this town I have really gotten to know. And most of them are scattered all around the place. So I have no real women friends like I had in Missouri. They come in the store and buy their supplies. I see them in church and we nod at each other, but they're scared of me because I own the store and work for a living. After Martin died and Rosalie ran off, they didn't bother to invite me to their tea parties or socials."

She sat quietly for a moment, then burst out, "Damn that Martin, dying on me! I told him not to work so hard, to get more help, but he wouldn't listen. That store was everything to him and he'd come home only to eat or sleep a little. I hardly saw him at all during his last years, and we barely looked or talked to each other. And now he's gone and I'm alone in this house and that store to run." The sherry had opened the dam and the tears were ready to fall.

I hastened to reassure her. "Hattie, you are a remarkable woman, and you should be proud. Coming out here by wagon train — what a hard and wrenching experience that was. And then helping to set up the store, and now running it on your own. Few women could accomplish as much. Yes, it hasn't been easy, but you've tackled everything that was thrown at you and succeeded, and I really admire what you've done."

She looked at me with eyes slightly out of focus. "Really? You really like what I've done?"

"Of course! Why, you're a pioneer in more ways than you realize."

"Am I, Samantha?" She paused for a moment to think it over, then said proudly, "Yep, I suppose I am."

"Hattie," I continued, "we have so much in common. We really could become friends. In fact, I've never had a real close friend to share things with, confide in. Do you think you could stand it?"

Slowly her face began to crumple, the tears began to fall and she sobbed — not silently, but loudly, leaving her gulping for breath. I moved closer, put my arms around her and held tight for several minutes. Finally she paused and, using a napkin, loudly blew her nose. Embarrassed, she sat up straight and looked away from me. "Land o' Goshen, I never cried like that in my life, and I'm sorry you had to see it."

Consoling her, I said, "You're certainly entitled after what you've been through — losing Martin and Rosalie, and dealing with problems at the store. I'd say that was a good, first-class, thunderstorm of a cry, and I bet it made you feel better."

She drew back and looked at me. "Young lady, you sure do have a different way of looking at things, and I must say it's real nice. Maybe we really can be friends."

I nodded. "Well, it could be an interesting and bumpy ride, but it will be fun." And she smiled happily while wiping the last of the tears from her face.

I turned to the piano and impulsively began to play and sing;
"Show me the way to go home,
I'm tired and I wanna go to bed.
I had a little drink about an hour ago
And it went right to my head.
Wherever I may roam,
On land or sea or foam,
You will always hear me singin' this song
Show me the way to go home."

Hattie began to laugh and laugh, and then stopped to say, "Well, that's sure true of us, Samantha. Luckily we're already home and nobody will have to show us the way."

The lady was having a lovely time, so I asked, "Hattie, how would you like to hear a really naughty song?"

"Would it be proper?"

"I think it's very funny, but I'll leave it to you. I'll only sing a verse at a time. Are you ready?"

She nodded uncertainly, and I turned to the piano and sang the first verse of "Lydia, the Tattooed Lady."

"Lydia, oh Lydia, say have you met Lydia,
Lydia the tattooed lady.

She has eyes that folks adore so,
And a torso even more so.
Lydia, oh Lydia, that encyclopedia,
Oh Lydia, the Queen of tattoo.
On her back is the Battle of Waterloo,
Beside it the wreck of the Hesperus, too.
And proudly above waves the Red, White and Blue.
You can learn a lot from Lydia."

I looked over for Hattie's reaction. She looked as stunned as a maiden lady who stumbled into the Dallas Cowboys' locker room.

"It's up to you, Hattie. Are you ready for more?"

Her eyes never left mine as she reached for the sherry bottle, poured more into her glass, then took a healthy sip. When that was done, she nodded her head very slowly.

"When her robe is unfurled
She will show you the world,
If you step up and just tell her where,
For a dime you can see Kankakee or Paree,
Or Washington crossing the Delaware."

At the end of the second verse I turned to find the lady wearing a lopsided smile. "That sure was a scandal, Samantha. I don't know all them folks you're singing about, but was there really such a lady?" Her words slurred a bit, but her eyes had a devilish gleam.

"I don't think so, but it's fun to think about how she might have looked, don't you think?"

She hunched her shoulders, giggled softly and said one word. "More."

"Lydia, oh Lydia, say have you met Lydia.
Lydia, the tattooed lady.
When her muscles start relaxin',
Up the hill comes Andrew Jackson.
Lydia, oh, Lydia, that encyclopedia,

Oh Lydia, the queen of them all!
For two bits she will do a mazurka in jazz,
And a view of Niagara that nobody has.
And on a clear day you can see Alcatraz.
You can learn a lot from Lydia!"

Then I turned to Hattie. "Are you ready for one last verse?"

"I wouldn't miss it for all the gold in these mountains," she slurred.

"Oh, Lydia, oh Lydia, that encyclopedia,
Lydia, the tattooed lady.
She once swept an Admiral clear off of his feet.
The ships on her hips made his heart skip a beat.
And now the old boy's in command of the fleet,
For he went and married Lydia!"

At the end of the song we had a good laugh while draining the last drops from our glasses.

"Samantha, you're a caution, and I do believe you'll be a very bad influence in this house." She reached out a hand and I helped her to stand, a bit unsteadily. "In the meantime, m'dear, you can help me to my room."

With a kerosene lamp in one hand and Hattie in the other, I struggled up the stairs where we said a fuzzy good night, and entered our bedrooms.

Slowly and with difficulty, I removed the layers of clothing, slipped into one of Rosalie's nightgowns, climbed into bed and turned out the lamp. I was more than ready for a night's rest.

I tried to pray and meditate, and to ask the Universe what else it had in store for me. Though I struggled to bring my scattered thoughts together, it was no use. My mind was like a litter of kittens, stumbling in many directions. I gave up and snuggled under the warm comforter.

As I slid into sleep, it occurred to me that it would be highly interesting to see where I would wake up in the morning. The last time I closed my eyes …

Chapter Six

As I woke the next morning, I kept my eyes closed for a few moments, testing the environment, listening for clues. Would I be like Dorothy freshly returned to Kansas from Oz, staring into the kind face of Auntie Em? Or would Mother Malcolm, the Wicked Witch of the West, be bending over me and voicing disapproval? The sound of a rooster announcing the new day left no doubt, and I opened my eyes to see the four-poster bed and other furniture about the room. All right, Sam, you lucky lady, back to your version of the Yellow Brick Road.

Pouring water from the pitcher into the basin, I managed a thorough wash-up job, but dearly missed my morning shower. Next I brushed my teeth with the last drops from the pitcher.

A quick inventory of the contents of my backpack showed: toothbrush, hand cream, moisturizer, foundation, eyebrow pencil, mascara, eye shadow, lipstick. I gathered the cosmetics and returned them to the pack. It would not be fitting to use any of them during my stay. Then I realized even the other items — toothbrush, shampoo and conditioners, things that I thought of as necessary — must be hidden away, even the little packet of tissues, the breath mints, the ballpoint pen and the notebook. My heart sank as I scanned the contents of my wallet — driver's license, photos of Harland and the boys, a variety of 5, 10, and 20 dollar bills from another time, and lastly three useless credit cards. Everything was returned to the backpack, then stored well back in the wardrobe. Once more I resisted the panic inside me and tried not to think of what I might be facing.

I finished quickly, pulling on the cotton stockings and new

shoes, and one of Rosalie's dresses. After checking the mirror to verify an image suitable for 1852, I paused to say a little prayer that I would be equal to the challenges ahead of me. My wristwatch indicated 7:30 am before I hid it away and rushed down the stairs to join Hattie.

She was grinding coffee in a hand-operated mill and greeted me with a smile. "Good morning! What would you be wanting for breakfast?" Her face was softer and seemed to glow in the aftermath of the confidences we had shared the night before.

"First of all, Hattie, how's your head? Is it as fuzzy as mine after all that sherry?"

"Hardly a twinge, and I slept like a baby. So, how much breakfast d'you want? I have oatmeal all ready."

She dished out a large helping into a bowl, then placed it in front of me. It smelled good and I was hungry.

Hattie added a jar of molasses, a small pitcher of milk, poured the coffee, and breakfast was ready.

We were finishing the last of the coffee when I expressed my nagging concern about finding employment to earn the money I would need for food, housing and clothing.

Hattie was sympathetic. "I understand why you're worried. I'll ask around town. Wish I could use you at the store, but my clerks don't want a woman in what they think is a man's place. Even when I go check on things, I know they're glad to see me go out the door so they can get on with the real work. When Martin was alive, there was no question about me helping out all day, but now I let them outfit the miners and fill the orders. I'm busy enough ordering supplies, checking inventory, and doing the books."

"Could I possibly find work at the newspaper office or at one of the hotels?"

She shook her head. "With the town so chock full of men and women living hand-to-mouth, there's always someone willing to work for very little."

Further discussion brought few possibilities, and I was quite concerned. Then I had a thought. "There's something I can do very well, and that is play the piano. But where?"

Hattie thought for a moment. "We have a town hall. You could play your nice music there and give recitals."

"Perhaps. But I need something steady to depend on. It's either go out and find my own gold mine, or use the skills my years of study have given me."

Hattie shook her head. "You're a pretty lady and smart. We'll think of something. I do have some influence, you know. But today I must check the supplies coming in from San Francisco. Would you like to come along with me?"

It would be a good time to look around town and get familiar with the layout. I nodded in agreement.

As we reached McKee's Mercantile, I decided to look for the children. Hattie frowned. "That saloon is no place for a proper woman to be. You just be careful with all the drinking and what all goes on there."

Reassuring her, I headed for the Majestic Saloon just down the street. As I walked along, I was struck by the undercurrent of activity, the urgency. The boardwalks were filled with people, mostly men dressed in remnants of suits, and a great assortment of hats — stained, dirty, misshapen, wide brimmed, knit caps, early versions of the Stetson. Everyone was moving quickly, I assumed on errands that would enable them to head to the gold fields. Dressed as I was, I did not stand out, and in a short time I reached the saloon, its yellow paint shining brightly in the morning sun.

The children were not in sight so I hesitated to enter through the front door. I turned to the path between the buildings and used the back door leading to the kitchen. Wong Kee was working at a table filled with vegetables. He paused to looked me over, then nodded. "Pretty dress. Much betta."

I smiled. "Good morning, and thank you, Wong Kee. I'm looking for the children."

"They eat in other room. You want coffee?"

I shook my head. "No thanks, I've had breakfast. I'll just go in and say hello."

Crossing the hall, I found Warren and Sumpin sitting at one of the tables and eating what looked like oatmeal. They smiled as I sat beside them.

"Well, good morning to you. How are you today?"

Warren answered. "We're good 'nuff, I guess. You look purty now you ain't wearin' funny clothes." He turned back to the bowl and continued to eat. Sumpin looked at me shyly as she spooned the cereal from her bowl.

I sat on one of the chairs. How subdued and quiet they were. Then I noticed Warren had a bruise over one eye and a red mark on his cheek. Sumpin had bruises on one arm as if a strong hand had grabbed and held her.

I touched her arm, then turned to Warren. "What on earth happened? Who did this?"

"You shouldn't be here," he replied nervously. "Mr. Smithers don't like us bringin' nobody in the saloon." Sumpin nodded sadly.

"You mean that terrible man did this just because you brought me here for a cup of coffee?" It was hard to believe they would be punished for such a minor kindness. "Where is that man? I want to talk to him!"

The children became terrified when the man in question came through the door. Grabbing the remainder of their breakfast, they scampered out of sight.

"You're here again," Orrin Smithers growled as he glared at me.

"You bet I am, Mr. Smithers, and I want to talk to you!" I was furious, and had no idea where the accumulation of anger came from, but I rose and stood toe-to-toe with this man. "How dare you hit those children just because they were kind to me."

"They know better'n bring in strays from the street or botherin' Wong Kee in the kitchen. This is my place and I set the rules." His eyes were icy under the black eyebrows.

"But two helpless children less than half your size? That was very brave of you. I'm the one who asked for help, so maybe you should hit me too, or do you want me to pay for the coffee? It's unbelievable that you beat them like that."

"Woman, who the hell do you think you are tellin' me what I should or shouldn't do?" His expression became more fierce and his hand raised and became a fist.

I hesitated, then lowered my voice. "Mr. Smithers, I know this is none of my business. But it's in my nature to be shocked when it comes to the mistreatment of children."

His answer was abrupt. "They know the rules. I feed 'em, give 'em a place to sleep, and after that they gotta keep out of sight and not bother the girls, the bartenders or Wong Kee. And the same goes for you. You don't belong here gettin' in the way."

"I agree, Mr. Smithers, but these children are important to me. You see, I recently lost my husband and two sons, and just talking to Warren and Sumpin eases my sense of loss. And maybe I could share some of my music with them, just as I did with my family. When I saw this lovely piano yesterday and played for them, it made me feel a little less sad. It's really a beautiful instrument, though badly out of tune. What a shame it's just tucked away and not being used."

He shrugged and said impatiently, "I took it from a guy who gambled everything he had. Damn fool lugged it all the way from San Francisco hopin' it would bring 'nuff money to stake a claim. It was all the sucker had, but it sure ain't worth the money he owed me."

I pressed my case. "Why don't you let me play something and you might feel it's good investment after all?"

He shrugged again and nodded. "Go on, play."

I hurried to the piano, uncovered it, and sat down.

A song popped into my head and my fingers began playing the introduction to "September Song."

Glancing over, I could see he sat down, crossed his legs, put an arm over the back of the chair, and listened as I began to sing the lyrics. Now, my voice isn't the greatest, but it does a pretty fair job on a song. At least I could give some meaning to the lyrics, and somehow I knew they would appeal to Mr. Smithers' ego.

After the last chord faded away, I turned to him and waited. I could see the words of the song might have touched a soft spot, if there was any such thing under that rough and stubborn personality.

Gruffly he said, "You play purty good. Not as good as my regular piano player, but purty good."

"Thank you, Mr. Smithers. Now, when this room is not being used, may I come and play for the children?"

He shook his head impatiently. "I'll think about it."

Curiosity got the better of me at this point. "Mr. Smithers, may I ask one more favor? Since it's still morning and things must be quiet, may I take a quick look at your saloon? I've never seen one before."

"Woman, you're a bother. Outside of my Waiter Girls and dancin' girls, none of the women in town have been inside my place."

He snorted in disgust, then rose from the chair. "Well, come on, and take a quick look around." He gestured impatiently and led the way into the hallway, then into a large area the size of two large tennis courts.

The morning sun shone through four large frosted windows at the front of the building, and kerosene lamps lit the dark corners. The front door was open with a separated frosted glass panel covering the entrance so no one could look in. At the far end of the room was a small stage with a battered upright piano on the floor to the right. To the left was a door, then the beginning of a massive bar, at least 30 feet long, the dark wood shiny and well cared for.

Smithers rubbed his hand proudly along the rich surface of the bar. "Brought this up in pieces all the way from San Francisco. Them mirrors come by ship and then by wagon, all wrapped in straw, and not one cracked. I told the freight company I'd skin 'em alive if they broke just one."

Four large, matched mirrors hung on the wall behind the bar, and on the counter underneath were rows and rows of bottles and glasses shining brightly, waiting for the day's business. Wooden beer kegs stood every 10 feet or so on the bar itself. I almost laughed aloud when I saw the brass spittoons on the floor below — right out of an old Western movie.

In front of the stage and extending back about halfway into the room was an open area, the floor well polished but showing the scuff marks of many boots. Not exactly the Paradise Ballroom, but it must have an interesting collection of couples dancing the nights away.

All about the sides of this area were numerous round and square tables with chairs. Beyond the dance floor and continuing to the front entrance, the tables filled all available space except for a walkway from the front door to the stage. The floors seemed clean and well kept.

Stairs on one side of the room led to a balcony that ran along two sides. Around the balcony were doorways to at least eight or 10 rooms.

Looking at Smithers, I nodded. "This is quite an operation,

and I'm impressed, Mr. Smithers. Is this room filled with people every night?"

He allowed himself a small smile, puffed out his chest and answered, "The men like comin' here to drink, dance with the Hurdy-gurdy Girls, play cards. I do all right."

Just then a man walked out of one of the upper rooms, yawning and scratching his head and stomach as he came down the stairs. He had sandy hair parted in the middle, a bony face, thin lips clamped on a lit cigarette. As he reached us, he deliberately looked me over then muttered, "Mornin', Orrin. Who's the dame?"

I quickly answered, "My name is Samantha Malcolm, and Mr. Smithers has been kind enough to show me his saloon."

The narrow jaw dropped as he looked at Smithers in surprise. "He what?"

"Shut up, Willis. This here lady is new in town and I'm thinkin' about letting her and the kids visit in the back room." He gestured, "This here's Willis Weatherby. He plays piano for me nights when things start gettin' busy."

I smiled. "How do you do, Mr. Weatherby. I'd love to hear you play sometime. I also play the piano."

Weatherby turned away and headed for the kitchen. "Ya don't say!" he drawled as he walked through the door and slammed it behind him.

Turning to Smithers, I offered my hand. "I won't take any more of your time. Thanks for the tour. And if you don't mind, I'd like to spend a little time with the children before I meet Mrs. McKee."

He said gruffly, "So you know Mrs. McKee. You a school teacher? You sure talk like one."

"Not really. I've just had the benefits of a good education."

Warren and Sumpin were standing in the hallway as we entered, and turned to run away. I hurried to stop them. "It's all right, kids. Mr. Smithers says he'll think about letting us meet in the back room when it's not being used. Isn't that right, Mr. Smithers?" I turned to him.

"Yeah, we'll see," and he hurried back to the floor of the saloon.

I herded the children into the side room, closed the door, then asked, "Are you all right? You're not badly hurt?"

Warren answered, "Nah. He hits us sometimes when we're in the way, but we're all right."

"Well, you didn't deserve it, and if I have anything to say about it, that will never happen again. And while we're here and no one else is around, what can we do for fun? Shall we talk, play games?"

Sumpin jumped up and down and clapped her hands. "Rainbow! Play the rainbow song!"

With such an appreciative audience, I sat down at the piano and once more sang about candy and rainbows. I followed these with songs about raindrops, the doggie in the window, smiles, silver linings, anything that would please them.

Our impromptu concert was a bit spoiled by the jarring notes of the out-of-tune piano. Lifting the lid and peeking inside, I could see the strings were very much like an upright. Perhaps there was a tool at Hattie's store that I could use to tune this piano. Perhaps Willis Weatherby had one.

Suddenly the door opened and two people entered, their eyes intent on the children and me. One was Willis Weatherby, the other a girl in her 20s, her face heavy from sleep, her auburn hair long and straggly. Her garish red satin robe was lightly tied, barely covering a white camisole and bloomers. She wore black cotton stockings and black high-button shoes.

Willis spoke first, pointing in our direction. "I tol' ya, Bertha, them kids was in here with this here woman. Orrin told 'em they could be in here. No tellin' who she is or what she wants with your kids."

"Well, no one asked me; that's for dang sure," she said, pushing the tangled hair back from her face. There was no doubt that this was Bertha, loving mother to Warren and Sumpin. "What do you want with my kids?"

"Your children were very kind to me when I first came to town, and I think they're very sweet. They remind me of the two children I recently lost. I mean no harm. I'm only chatting with them and playing songs they seem to enjoy."

Bertha, a hand resting on one hip, looked me over with a cold and critical eye. "Jes' so you know that these are my kids, they do what I say!"

"No question about it. May I call you Bertha? Would you like to join us and hear some of the songs they like?"

"Naw. I ain't had my breakfast yet, and I want 'em sittin' with me in the kitchen while I eat." Bertha was not happy.

Warren interrupted. "Momma, it's all right. We ain't doin' nothin' we shouldn't. You'll see."

"All right. But don't you go away." And she flounced out of the room.

Willis stood there with a sly smile on his face, rather pleased with what he had engineered. Turning away, he said, "You go ahead, play your little tunes and see where they get ya." Then he left the room. Warren led me and Sumpin into the kitchen where we sat at one of the tables.

Bertha carried her breakfast to the table and sat down, still looking me over with suspicion. As she tackled the food, she attacked. "What you want with my kids? Ain't you got none of your own?"

I told my story once more about the recent loss of my husband and two sons, and how I found myself in Boone Valley lost and confused. "Your children, Bertha, were kind to me, brought me in here for a cup of coffee, then led me to a house where the owner agreed to rent a bedroom until I could get my bearings and make some decisions. The owner, Mrs. McKee, has kindly given me shelter, which I never could have found without the help of your children."

Bertha turned to the children and said sharply, "You took this woman to Hattie McKee's house? She's a mean lady and hardly talks to anyone. She's always yellin' at the kids to keep away."

Warren assured her, "She was kinda nice to us and this lady, so it was all right."

Bertha shook her head in disapproval, and the children and I waited. She said no more until she finished eating, then ushered the children out of the room, saying, "Lady, I'm goin' to keep an eye on you, so watch it!"

I looked at Wong Kee who was shaking his head sadly. "She not nice. She not want others be nice to kids."

Oh, great! Just two days in town and I'd made three new friends, and now three enemies. My score would have to improve very soon or they'll be lynching me outside the Lucky Shamrock Saloon!

Chapter Seven

Job hunting was discouraging. In each shop the man in charge was busy, short-tempered, or had no time for a mere woman. I tried to appear meek and vulnerable, but that didn't help. One "gentleman" told me firmly that he found me forward and aggressive, while another looked me over and said, "I don't have time for you right now, but come back later so we can *talk* about it." It was clear the job market in Boone Valley was flooded. There was no place for me.

At one shop, Miss Ida Penny, seamstress, greeted me with one of the few smiles I received that morning. Small but trim, she stood with her back straight, head up, and her hands out in welcome. Her light brown hair was in a neat bun on the top of her head, where she had added a perky blue bow. Her soft blue eyes winked at me behind gold wire spectacles. Her smile was one of surprise and pleasure.

"My, my. You must be new in town! How nice of you to come into my little shop. What can I do for you?"

After introductions, I explained that I had no dresses to my name, and perhaps she could provide the items necessary for my continuing life in Boone Valley.

"Oh, it would be my great pleasure, Mrs. Malcolm. As you can see from some of the materials and items hanging here, I can make any and all of the clothes you need. How much do you want to spend?"

I hesitated. "Right now I have only $50 to my name, but I hope to find work to earn what I'll need to live on. Why don't you tell me what just the basic items, a dress, underclothes, will cost?"

To my surprise she answered, "Well, the prices here are probably higher than you were paying at home, but it's because of the demand and availability of material, thread, buttons and ribbons. For a cotton or calico dress, the price is $3. A serviceable skirt with appropriate trim and decorations, $2. A white or matching shirt, 1 dollar 50. For undergarments — panties and camisoles, and under-skirts, anywhere from 50 cents to $2. Does that sound like too much?"

I gasped. At these prices, the $50 seemed like a fortune, so I gave my first order to this gentle lady.

"I'll be needing one dress, one skirt, two blouses, and the necessary undergarments."

Ida suggested, "You'll be needing a corset, won't you?"

I declined and silently hoped it would not cause a scandal. By the time all measurements had been taken and material selected, Ida and I were on a first-name basis and busily chatting about Boone Valley: who was who and who was scandalous, who was upright and who was a rogue.

After conversations with Hattie and Ida, the tone and temper of Boone Valley was taking shape in my mind. I began to feel I could belong. Here I was, a fascinated spectator who knew that the energy, highlights and growth would within 100 years be nothing but rotted lumber and dust. All at once I was enthralled with the gift I had been given and eagerly anticipated the experiences that were before me.

Whatever forces had brought me here, for whatever reason, I silently thanked them. The inexperienced girl I was as a bride, and the far-from-worldly woman/wife I had become over twenty years, might not have the intelligence or awareness to make the most of this journey, but by golly, I was going to hang in there until the end, whatever it might be.

It was past noon when I returned to Hattie's house tired and

very hungry. She was at the stove frying chicken and boiling potatoes. She waved me away when I offered to help, so I stood nearby
and told her of my morning. She frowned when I described my tour
of the Majestic Saloon.

Hattie was concerned. "Orrin Smithers and I have done
business for more than a few years, and I will say he pays his bills
on time. But I don't like the man. I've heard stories about the way
he treats his girls. And those unfortunate children. Hanging around
that saloon to visit with them doesn't seem very smart to me. Orrin
and Bertha sound like two people you'd best steer clear of."

"I can handle it, Hattie. But I feel sorry for Sumpin and
Warren."

Hattie nodded. "Well, while you're helping them, be careful.
And I'm so glad you got to meet Ida Penny, one of the good ladies
in town. I've been meaning to take you over to see about some new
clothes. You have made another new friend in Ida Penny."

I walked to the back door, which was open to allow the
warm sunshine to come into the kitchen. Looking out I could see a
well-kept vegetable garden, and a border of colorful flowers around
the outer edge of the property.

"Hattie, that's quite a garden you have out there. How do
you find the time to take care of it?"

"Heavens, I'd never be able to take care of a garden. My
neighbor, Hector Cortez, tends to it. I pay him a little and he takes
the rest in vegetables for his family."

"This morning I thought I heard a rooster when I woke up.
Do you also raise chickens?"

"Yes, 'way in the back you can see a shed where I keep
about 50 chickens. Hector feeds and cares for them as well. The
eggs his family and I don't use, along with the extra vegetables, I
sell to Rev. Norton for his restaurant."

"What great planning. Was that your idea or Martin's?"

"Oh, Martin came up with it, and it's certainly paid off. That plus our farm about 10 miles down the mountain. A man there and his family raise cows, sheep and geese, and twice a week he brings in milk and butter. We really need a few more men to help with the cattle, but as soon as we find one that works out, he gets gold fever and skedaddles."

"I wondered where that delicious cream and butter came from."

As we talked, I watched as she removed wood from a pile next to the stove to feed the flames.

"What about the wood, Hattie? You certainly don't go out and chop it up yourself."

"Land sakes, no! There's a Chinee man who drives his wagon load of firewood through town twice a week. He knows to stop here and add to my woodpile if it gets low. Hong Shen I think is his name. He also chops up the kindling when that gets low. He's very quiet, but very reliable."

I was impressed. "It sounds like you've got everything covered — the store, meat, vegetables, milk, butter and wood. And you have this lovely house which is as fine as anything you can see in San Francisco."

"That's because Martin owned half of the lumber yard, so we had all the wood and paint we needed. It was started by Titus Boone, a fine carpenter and one of the first people to settle here. He earned money for his claim by building most of the stores you see on the main street, and the town was named for him. Martin helped him start the lumber mill, then Titus took off the minute he got enough money to buy a large claim. We see him when he comes to town to put some of the profits in his pocket. He comes by the store for supplies, then back he goes to his prospecting. He hasn't had as much luck digging as he has with the lumber mill, but he's convinced there's a big strike waiting for him. What a fool!"

I nodded. "Yes, I've read … heard that gold fever can be very compelling. That German gentleman must have found it hard to give up the beautiful piano you have, just so he could dig some of that yellow metal for himself."

Hattie snorted. "He treated it like a baby. Before he finally took off, he was over here almost every day under foot, playing it, polishing and tuning it until it sounded just right. He got to be a pest."

That statement got my attention. "Hattie! He tuned his piano? Tell me, how did he do it?"

"Oh, he had a funny looking metal thing he used. I didn't really watch him because he was fussing over it so much. But I think the tool is inside the piano somewhere."

I rushed to the piano, lifted the lid and there, hanging on a hook to one side, was the key and tuning fork. It didn't look so complicated, so I decided to tune the piano in Orrin Smither's back room.

"Lunch is ready," Hattie called, and I rushed back to the kitchen, ravenous and full of plans.

Early that afternoon, tuning tools in hand, I entered the saloon card room, and happily it was empty, but the smell of spilled whiskey and stale cigar smoke remained from the night before. Lifting the back lid of the piano, I surveyed the strings and rods. I used the tool on the nearest rod and found it was a perfect fit. After a tone from the tuning fork, I found middle C and began the tedious procedure to correct the strings of this beautiful instrument. I touched each key as lightly as possible as I brought it to the level of true pitch. I did not want my project to attract Orrin or anyone else who would find it annoying. Fortunately, I was undisturbed for over an hour until at last, to my ear, the full tonal beauty had been achieved.

Putting down the tuning fork, I struck a few chords, then

found myself playing a beautiful melody from a 1930's collection I enjoyed. Its title, "What'll I Do," was most appropriate. It was a sad reminder of what I had left behind and my bewildering prospects.

After the last note, I sat deep in the memories that had bubbled to the surface until I heard a sound behind me. Grouped around the open door were four young ladies looking at me with surprise and curiosity. They were dressed in brightly colored but shabby dresses, and their young faces were covered with heavy makeup. I motioned for them to come in and close the door.

"I didn't want anyone to hear me, especially Mr. Smithers. But I just had to tune this beautiful piano. How did it sound to you?" One slightly chubby girl with a happy face stepped forward. "That was real purty. Don't know when I ever heard a tune as nice as that. We heard you out by the bar and just had to come and see who was playin'."

"I'm glad you liked it. It's one of my favorites." I smiled. "My name is Samantha Malcolm, and Warren and Sumpin are my special friends. Mr. Smithers is allowing me to visit with them when this room is not being used."

"My name's Abigail, and this here's Flower and Maggie. And Naomi. We're Waiter Girls for Mister Smithers." She came closer to the piano. "We sure hear about you from Bertha. She thinks you're going to teach her kids bad things."

"I don't know how talking with them or playing songs could be bad. They were my first new friends since I arrived, and I've become very fond of them."

"You sure don't sound like you would harm those two nice kids. Could you play somethin' else before we go back to work?"

"Sure, I'd love to. I'll sing the words to the song you liked." I couldn't resist a responsive audience and turned to the piano to play and sing the words as meaningfully as I could for my enjoyment as well as theirs. As I finished, I turned to my audience and found almost everyone in tears.

Abigail wiped at the moisture in her eyes, smearing some of the black makeup. "That sure was beautiful … simply beautiful," she sniffed. The other girls nodded. "We have to go back now, but when can we hear some more?"

"Whenever I visit the children, you're welcome to join us."

They turned to leave, but Orrin Smithers blocked the door, one arm raised in anger. "What the hell are you broads doing here? I've been lookin' all over for you. You're supposed to be servin' drinks, not wasting your time in here! Get back in there and get busy!" The girls hastened from the room as he came forward and closed the door very deliberately.

"Here you are again! Woman, I'm gettin' sick and tired of findin' you here where you don't belong, taking my girls away from their work. Now, get out!" His fists were clenched by his sides.

I stood to face him, put out an arm with the palm of my hand extended. "Now, wait just a darn minute, Mr. Smithers. There's a reason I'm here, and if you will just simmer down I'll tell you what it is."

He stopped, but his anger was at the boiling stage.

"I've just done you a favor, believe it or not."

"Like what?" he bellowed.

"Tuned your piano, my dear sir, and now you have a second usable piano in your establishment. Now, just cool down and listen."

He hesitated, stared at me for a moment, then sat on a nearby chair. Slowly he leaned forward with his arm on one leg, still sailing on the wave of his anger.

Turning to the piano, I began the song that I played for him before, "September Song," which had appealed to him. I played it beautifully, if I say so myself, covering nearly all of the keyboard in the process. He may not have enjoyed it, but I had a great time showing him what glorious sounds that piano could make.

When I played the last note, I swung around to face him. He had settled back in the chair, and some of the wind seemed out of his sails.

"Well," I asked, "what do you think? Doesn't it sound much better? You don't have to thank me, but I do hope tuning this piano will pay you back for that damn cup of coffee I took from your kitchen."

His tone was quieter, but still harsh. "Woman, what do you expect from me? So you tuned the piano and, yes, it sounds better. Now what good does it do sittin' in this back room? This room is for playin' cards, not playin' tunes."

Like a light bulb shining brightly over my head, a solution to my employment was there before me. I had only to convince this difficult and obtuse gentleman. Leaning forward, I said, "Mr. Smithers, I've got a proposition for you."

At this, his eyes lit up and he began to look me over rather crudely.

"No, nothing like that! Now listen. How would you like to move this piano out into your saloon, clear to the other side of the room from the other one, by the front door? I could play for your customers earlier in the day, during the cocktail hour, and maybe my music would bring in more people."

"What in hell is the cocktail hour?"

"Oh, that's what they call it back East in the big hotels." I was picking up speed now. "It's the time of day from early afternoon until early evening when people are coming in from work, or going to dinner. I could play, say, from one in the afternoon, until sundown when Mr. Weatherby takes over. What do you think?"

He stood up. "Woman, you're out of your mind! I don't need another piano player."

I stood up beside him. "Think about it. If it works, it would bring in some of the men who usually go to the other saloons, and you might have a full house earlier in the day. When do you usually have your largest crowd?"

He hesitated, then answered, "About 8 at night when the Hurdy-gurdy Girls come in. But that don't mean I'm considering this crazy idea of yours."

"What do you have to lose? Why don't you try it for a few days and see if it works? I'll only play the piano. I wouldn't interfere with the bar activities, or card games, or anything your girls are doing. But I'll give your customers entertainment that none of the other saloons have. How about it?" At this point I sounded more confident than I really felt, but I was trying to be persuasive.

"Woman, you've done nothing but pull on my chain ever since you stepped foot in here. Why should I let you start this nonsense?"

"If I bring in more customers, wouldn't that be worth trying?"

"Well, if you know Hattie McKee, she would not approve of a lady friend of hers playing in a saloon." And he almost smiled as if he had found an easy way out.

Pressing my case, I offered, "If Hattie comes over here and tells you that she approves, will you give it a try?"

He nodded. "She won't. But ask her anyways. And I still ain't sure I want you or your music in here."

"Even if I promise to play your special song whenever you ask for it? You seem to like it very much."

He motioned to the door. "Get yourself out of here. Maybe we'll talk about it another time. But don't count on it!"

"Certainly not!" Hattie was adamant. "Have you working there every day with those smelly, drunken men? And work for that Smithers man? He may be a very good customer of mine, but as your friend I'll never tell him I approve of you working in that place!"

We were sitting at the kitchen table, the remnants of dinner before us. This conversation had been going on for some time.

"But, I would only work in the afternoons until sundown. I'd be home for dinner. And this is a perfect way to earn money, plus any tips I may get if they like me." The more I argued, the more it seemed the perfect solution.

"But your reputation!" she exploded.

"Hattie, I don't know anybody in this town except you, Ida and the children, so who cares about my reputation?"

She looked at me shrewdly. "You got everything figured, I will say. I don't know of a decent woman in this town, or anywhere else, who would be willing to earn money this way. But as I said, you're different than any woman I met before. You're so dang sure of yourself! But I don't know you well enough to tell you what to do. As you said when you first came to this house, you have to decide for yourself what to do now that your husband and children are missing."

"Does that mean you'll tell Orrin Smithers that you approve?"

She looked at me thoughtfully, then suddenly slapped the table with her hand.

"Samantha, I'll not only tell Orrin that I approve, but I'll insist that he hire you for at least a week to see if your fool idea will work. And it will pleasure me to do it."

"Hattie, you're a dear." Leaving my chair, I brought her up to her feet and administered a bear hug. She seemed to find it too intimate and quickly turned away.

"Haven't you ever been hugged before?"

"Now and then by Martin and Rosalie, but not very often. It just isn't done, Samantha." She was visibly flustered.

"Well, my friend, you'd better get used to it. I always hug

the people I love, or just anybody who wants to be hugged, with the great exception of my mother-in-law. But that's another story. My dear Hattie, hang on to your bustle 'cause you're going to get hugged again!"

This time she did not resist, and I think she even hugged back, just a little.

Chapter Eight

Orrin Smithers was fit to be tied when Hattie and I confronted him the next morning. Bringing Hattie through the back door of the saloon, we entered the kitchen to find him drinking coffee and talking with Wong Kee. At the sight of us, he put down his cup and raised his hands to the sky.

"I can see this ain't my lucky day," he exploded. "What in hell do you women want?"

"Orrin Smithers, watch your language," Hattie protested. "We just want to have a little talk. Samantha told me all about her idea. I not only think it's a mighty fine one, but I know you'd be real smart to give it a try. I definitely approve."

He put his hands to his hips in exasperation. "Hattie, the men who come in here just want to drink, play cards, and dance with the Hurdy-gurdy Girls. This here ain't no place for a tea party. No ma'am!"

"Now you just listen to me." Hattie stepped forward and brought one pointed finger close to his chest. "It won't hurt to give this lady a chance. The afternoon is your slow time, isn't it? Your dancing girls come in later. Maybe what you need is another kind of entertainment. Let her try it for a week, and if your business doesn't get better, then that's it."

We could see by the look in his eyes that the possibility of more afternoon business was attractive. On the other hand, he didn't like to give in to a woman. Finally the thought of increasing business in the afternoon won.

"Hattie, you're a hard woman. And your friend here is no better. All right, she has one week startin' tomorrow afternoon. I'll move the piano out. Now, good day, ladies."

Hattie did not budge. "What about pay? What are you going to pay her?"

Orrin scratched his head. "Oh, Lord, you are persistent. All right. If she lasts a week, I'll pay her what I pay my Waiter Girls – $34 a week, less expenses."

Without hesitating, Hattie came back with, "First of all, she won't be serving drinks or dancing with your customers. She's a lady! Next, she'll have her meals with me. No telling what sort of food she'd get here!"

That last comment was punctuated with a loud bang and commentary in Chinese. Wong Kee had imbedded a large knife in the wooden worktable.

At this point I had to interrupt. "Wong Kee, I'm sure your cooking is just fine. I know your coffee is great. But it would be easier if I had my meals with Hattie."

The flood of Chinese subsided and Wong Kee turned away. Hattie continued. "I know firsthand how beautifully Samantha plays the piano, and if she's hired after the first week, she should be paid $45 a week."

"For only five hours of playin'? And seven days a week?"

Once more I interrupted. "Six days a week from one until sundown, and I get to keep the tips."

Orrin was still objecting. "Why, $45 is what I pay my regular piano player."

Hattie was persistent. "Then, pay her $40, and that's fair!" She nodded her head firmly for emphasis.

Orrin glared at the two of us, and then a sly smile came over his face. "Sure, I'll let her try for one week. We'll see how she likes the noise and the boozin', and the drunks hangin' all over her. If she stays through the first week, I'll hire her full time, Hattie, at $40. But I don't think she'll last more than a day or two. And I don't think Willis will take too kindly to her doin' his job. We'll just see what happens." He turned to me. "You be here tomorrow about one and I'll have the piano moved out. Then we'll see if this fool idea of yours will work."

Hattie looked over at me, eyebrows raised, but I nodded with much more assurance than I felt. "All right! Hang on to your hat, Hattie, because tomorrow this rocket takes off for the moon!" Hattie and Orrin looked at each other in confusion.

That evening and the following morning I was busy at Hattie's piano, developing and listing the music I would play. Then I chose one of the prettiest dresses from Rosalie's wardrobe to wear for my first experience as a working lady. The dress was a soft-polished cotton with a pattern of pale pink roses and green leaves. The low-cut neckline was trimmed with a ruffle and a small green velvet bow. The puffed sleeves were full to the elbow where they were decorated with larger bows of the same material. Hattie called in Ida Penny to lower the hem. As an added bonus Hattie found some leftover material, so Ida made a rosette for my hair.

When it was time, Hattie helped me get ready. She brushed my hair, then brought it forward in a large curl to hang over one shoulder. I added the rosette, then we checked the final effect in the mirror.

"If you ask me," Hattie commented dryly, "you look much too good for that place. How are you feeling?"

"A little nervous," I confessed. "I've never played for this many people before, and I'm not sure they'll like me."

Hattie was positive. "No worry there. If they've got any sense at all, they'll know that you're something special, and you'll play the best piano they will ever hear. Just be sure none of them gets too friendly with you."

"I think I can handle it. We'll know by tonight if my kind of music appeals to them."

When Hattie went to her room for a coat, I sneaked some of the cosmetics from my backpack and applied a hint of eye shadow, eyeliner, mascara, also a touch of pink on my cheeks. I lightly touched the lipstick to my lips, then checked the result in the mirror. The warm colors of the dress combined with the makeup came together in a lovely blend of rose and pink. I felt like a 19th Century knockout. However, the real test was how Hattie and the rest of Boone Valley would respond.

Putting my watch and list of selections for the afternoon in the pocket of the full skirt, I grabbed the wool cape from the wardrobe and headed downstairs. Hattie was in the parlor, and as I entered she looked me over.

"My word, what have you done with yourself, Samantha? Is that color on your cheeks and lips?"

"Oh, Hattie, is it too much? I just wanted to add a little bit of color to go with the gown."

"Well, you do look very pretty. Rosalie only wore that party dress once, but you do it proud. I'm not used to seein' that much color on a woman's face, but you do look elegant. Just be sure those men don't think you're one of Orrin's painted girls."

Hattie insisted on walking to town with me. Working our way through the crowded streets, we stopped short of the saloon and looked it over. All seemed quiet. With a few words of encouragement and a pat on the shoulder, she sent me on my way.

Just as I was turning to take the path to the side door of the saloon, I noted a man who had just opened a door to a shop across the way, but he was frozen, not moving, staring at me.

I found myself also frozen, unable to move. I recalled seeing this man my first day in Boone Valley. He was the well-dressed man, different from others on the street, who had watched me. Now our eyes locked for a moment until, slowly, he lifted his hat, nodded, then entered the shop, closing the door behind him.

Well! Stunned, unable to process what had happened or why it happened, I shook my head then forced myself to focus on where I was going and the possible employment waiting for me.

It was 12:30 when I opened the door to the kitchen. As usual, Wong Kee was busy at the wooden worktable, and across the room Warren and Sumpin were eating their midday meal. Wong Kee paused and looked me over.

"You too pretty for saloon woman. You sure you want work here?"

"I need the money, Wong Kee. You heard Mr. Smithers say I've got one week to prove I can bring in more customers. Do you think I'm crazy?"

He shrugged his shoulders and looked directly into my eyes. "You nice. Good to young ones. You do good, pretty music, smile. Good fortune be with you."

I was touched, and studied the face of this kind man for the first time. It was golden tan, smooth. The brown eyes were topped by soft black eyebrows. The only wrinkles on that serene face were three horizontal lines crossing his forehead, as if he continually examined the Caucasian world where he must live. I decided I liked this gentleman, at least what I had seen so far.

"Your good wishes are very much appreciated. Thank you."

I gave the children a quick hug and sat with them for a moment. Warren spoke up. "Wong Kee says you're playin' the piano t'day. We can't come in the saloon, but we'll be outside the front door listening."

I touched their sweet faces. "It makes me feel better to know you'll be there and I'll include some of our songs with the others. Wish me luck?"

From Warren, "Sure do!" Sumpin nodded and smiled.

And with such support from three special people, I was on my way.

I hung my cape on a peg near the door, then opened it, saying, "Well, here I go, ready or not!"

I quickly entered the main room of the saloon. The afternoon sun shone through the front windows and a few kerosene lamps lit the dark corners. An assortment of men, some in suits, and some in grubby work clothes, sat around many of the tables, bottles and glasses before them. Behind the long bar were two men in long white aprons and white shirts with the sleeves held in place by black garters. They were busily washing and wiping glasses and beer mugs and setting them on the shelves behind them. Many eyes followed me as I approached the nearest man behind the bar.

"Hello, I'm Samantha Malcolm and I'm supposed to play here this afternoon. Has the piano been moved in here?"

The bartender, the towel in his hand suddenly still, looked me over carefully. "It's over in the corner by the front door. Orrin told us you'd be coming. I'm Corbett, but most folks call me Corby."

Corby had a friendly and welcoming smile. He looked like a figure out of the Gay Nineties — dark brown hair, parted in the middle and slicked back with some kind of grease, and a dark handlebar mustache. His eyes were kind and I appreciated the warmth they reflected.

Corby motioned to the other man behind the bar. "That's Elmo."

Elmo nodded his mostly bald head in greeting and continued polishing the glasses. "Pleased to meetcha!" He spoke out of the side of his mouth, and the smile was the most lopsided I had ever seen, but he, too, seemed pleasant and friendly.

Corby came closer. "You look like too nice a lady to be working in a saloon. Elmo and I was just saying we've never seen such a thing like you're going to be doing. You just be careful and don't let the guys with a snoot full get too friendly."

This concerned me. "What shall I do if they get rough? Give you a high sign?"

Corby grinned. "We have ways to make 'em behave if they bother you." He reached under the bar and pulled out a wooden club about the size of a baseball bat. "If this don't work, Elmo has something to back it up." Elmo walked to the far end of the bar, reached underneath and pulled out a large, black revolver. "They sure behave when they see this here Peacemaker. A feller walked in here one night carryin' this and makin' quite a nuisance of hisself. After a while he left feet first, and the gun stayed behind."

Even in his large hand, the firearm looked enormous.

"That's a wicked looking gun," I commented.

"This feller was really braggin' about what a special gun it was, but he sure didn't know how to use it proper. Played with it like a toy. It's what he called a Colt Walker .44, made just for the Texas Rangers to use when fightin' with them Mexicans south of here. Wanna hold it?"

He handed me the gun, and my hand crashed against the bar with the full weight of it. Elmo and Corby exploded with laughter. The barrel must have been at least 8 or 9 inches long, and I laughed as I tried to manage it. I said, "This weighs a ton," as I handed it back to Elmo.

"We guess about 4 pounds. It's a handful, all right, but it's one of the ways we keep the peace around here real good!"

"I'll certainly call on you if I have any trouble."

"You can count on us, Mis' Samantha." Corby was most reassuring.

Just then a shadowy, dark form filled the front entrance. It turned out to be a husky but non-threatening man wearing well-worn clothes, boots caked with dirt, and a shapeless cap. When he saw me, he removed the cap and held it nervously in his huge hands. His face, round and rosy from many days in the sun, had a kind quality to it, and his light-brown eyes darted from me to the floor. Corby greeted him. "Well, if it ain't old Barnaby, and so early in the day. Did that dry and useless claim of yours give you any gold today?"

Barnaby lowered his head, and fumbled with the hat in his hands. "Ah, Corby. My claim is a good one. I just' ain't found the right place to dig. But look what I dug up today!"

Reaching into a pocket of his shapeless pants, he pulled out a nugget the size of a small walnut. Corby whistled, brought out a scale and placed the nugget on one side. When the scale balanced, he whistled again.

"Well, Barnaby, you sure did good today. This looks like it's high grade, and you got about two ounces here. That's the best you done in a long time, so you'll be buyin' more than a couple of beers tonight! And as is the custom around here, the first one's on us."

Barnaby beamed with happiness at the mug set before him.

Pointing a thumb in my direction, Corby announced, "This here's Mis' Samantha, Barnaby. She'll be playin' the piano for us this afternoon."

I reached one hand out. "I'm very pleased to meet you, Barnaby."

He stepped back in confusion, looking at me, then at Corby who gave a hearty laugh and patted him on the shoulder. "Don't mind him, Mis' Samantha. Barnaby's very shy."

Turning to the confused man, he said, "Barnaby, she just wants to shake hands. It ain't exactly the custom 'round here, but she just wants to say 'How d'ya do'!"

Barnaby raised one large hand, wiped it on pants already well covered with red dust, then tentatively brought it forward. I grasped his warm but very calloused hand and shook it firmly.

"I'm very pleased to meet you, Barnaby." Wanting to be friendly, I asked, "What's your last name, Barnaby, and where are you from?"

Corby tapped my arm that was resting on the bar. "I guess bein' new here you don't know better, but 'round this part of the country we never ask a man's name or his history. It just ain't done. First names is about all you're ever gonna get."

I was nicely put in my place. "Oh. Thanks for telling me, Corby. I'll never make that mistake again."

Corby leaned across the bar. "Barnaby, today is the first time Mis' Samantha's goin' to play the piano for us. Why don't you take your beer over by the piano and see that the fellows don't bother her?"

The muscles in his face relaxed, he smiled and nodded. "I'd sure be glad to do that, Corby. I'll look after her real good."

"Good man, Barnaby. You just do that."

I nodded to Barnaby. "Wonderful. And it's time, so here I go, fellows. Wish me luck!"

"You betcha, lady!" said Corby.

Barnaby picked up the beer and followed as I walked over to the piano. It sat in a far corner under the second floor balcony, almost hidden by the tables around it. Motioning to Barnaby, I asked him to move it out from the wall, near to the front window, but a few feet more toward the center of the room. It was still dark in that area, so I asked for a kerosene lamp to set on top of the piano. This done, I brought up a chair, sat down, and faced the keyboard.

I removed the list of selections from my pocket and set it on the music rack. The songs were a bit tongue-in-cheek, but only for me. I began with "Nice Work If You Can Get It," followed by "Getting To Know You." When the key was right and the lyrics came to mind, I sang with the music.

While deciding what to play next, I glanced up and was pleased to see that many of the men had moved from the tables at the far end of the room to those nearer to the piano. Some were standing at the bar adjacent to me. I could see Orrin leaning against the bar watching closely. Also, Corby and Elmo were serving drinks to the tables closer to the piano. I wasn't even aware so many people had congregated into such an attentive group, but now I had a real audience and was not sure how to proceed.

Looking at the men sitting at a nearby table, I asked, "Is there anything special I could play for you?"

No one spoke. They sat, looked at their drinks, shuffled their feet uneasily.

"What would you like? A love song? A sad song? A happy song? No requests? All right, you just listen and tell me what you like."

Turning to the piano, I reviewed the list and decided "Let Me Entertain You" from Gypsy sounded appropriate. I played the melody once through, then sang the chorus. This was fun! Then I went into "Everything's Coming Up Roses," working through the melody and the lyrics. Remembering the young audience outside the front door, I played two choruses of "Over the Rainbow," then sat back in my chair and took a short break.

The men sitting at the nearby tables had grown to twice the number and I heard, "Purty music" and "That was sure good on the ears." Their applause, with a few cheers thrown in, was most encouraging.

I could see Orrin glaring at me, and could not help giving him a big victorious smile in return. My smile faded, however, when I saw the angry face of Willis Weatherby beside him.

Facing my audience, I announced I would take a five-minute break and then continue the program. Then I went to handle the matter of the resident musician before it grew to titanic proportions. "Mr. Smithers, did you tell Mr. Weatherby about our arrangement, that I would be playing here in the afternoons?"

Orrin smirked. "Why, no, Mrs. Malcolm. I thought you'd

want to work that out with Willis yourself."

Facing my rival squarely, I said, "Well, Mr. Weatherby, you probably know that Mr. Smithers has agreed that I would have a one-week trial playing from one until sundown. We're hoping it will bring in more customers at that time. What do you think?"

Willis clearly was not happy. "Lady, what makes you think you can come in here and take over. I give 'em the music they want for drinkin' and dancin' and they don't need nothin' else!"

I pointed to the crowd assembled near the piano. "It doesn't look that way to me. They seem to enjoy what I've been playing so far."

Willis took a step toward me, mouthing off a string of epithets that I had never heard before. Holding up my hand, I stepped closer and lowered my voice.

"I don't think it would be wise to make a scene, Mr. Weatherby. Those people over there are watching us and waiting for me to come back. If you give me a hard time, some of them may not take it kindly and think you're not a very nice fellow. Now, if you've a mind to, why don't you step over there and ask them if they would like me to go away?"

Willis saw that most of the eyes were on us. Clenching his fists in frustration, he growled in a low voice, "Lady, you ain't gonna be 'round here for long, I'll see to that!" And he stalked off like a furious wet hen.

Looking at Orrin, I said, "Well, it looks as if I've won the first round, don't you think?"

Orrin answered casually, "Looks like, but Willis can be real mean when he's a mind to."

"You're his boss. Aren't you going to set him straight? I thought you ran this saloon the way you wanted, with no trouble or problems."

"We'll see. I'll just let this little set-to run itself out to the end."

"Thanks a lot," I growled, and returned to the piano.

The next few hours went quite well, and more men came through the front entrance until almost all the tables around the piano were full. Corby and Elmo were busy serving drinks and mugs filled with beer to the customers. The men at the far end of the room were still busy playing poker, but they too seemed to be listening. On the whole, the audience was quiet and applauded with enthusiasm after every group of songs. And through it all, Barnaby sat close by, watching anyone who approached the piano.

When I noted that the light coming through the window was beginning to dim, I secretly checked my watch. It was almost 6 o'clock. I closed with another two choruses of "Let Me Entertain You," then stood up. Smiling, I thanked everyone for listening and announced that was the end of the concert, but that I would be back tomorrow at the same time.

As I stood, some of the men gathered about, smiling and telling me how much they liked the "purty music." One man rested his hand on top of the piano, and when he removed it a small gold nugget was there. With a "Thank ya, ma'am," he drifted back into the crowd. This happened again and again, and soon there was a small pile of gold.

As the crowd cleared, Barnaby walked over and pointed to the gold. "They sure did like you, ma'am. I ain't never heard such good music before. If you're goin' to be here again tomorrow, I'm sure goin' to be here too."

"I'm glad, Barnaby. Tell me, what am I supposed to do with this gold? I can't put it in my pocket as it is."

Reaching into his pocket, Barnaby brought out a small leather pouch. "Take this here, ma'am. Here's where I put my gold, when I find it."

"But I can't take this. You may need it!"

"I got plenty more, ma'am. Never had 'em all full, but I 'spect to some day. I'd be pleased if you take it."

With his help I transferred my own personal bonanza into the leather pouch, then to the safety of my skirt pocket.

Several of the Waiter Girls walked by, trays filled with glasses. Noting that Orrin was still leaning on the bar, back turned, they whispered, "Business was really booming when we came to work. Good on you, Mis' Samantha."

I headed back to the kitchen and cheerfully reported to Wong Kee, "Everything went very well!"

Giving a slight bow, he answered, "Is good. Maybe good fortune be yours. You make many friends, you stay even if everything new."

I stepped closer to look into his eyes and saw understanding there. I couldn't stop myself from saying, "I think you know that I come from another place very far away."

He nodded and said, "I know," and turned back to his work.

For several seconds I was frozen by the impact of those two words. I knew Wong Kee and I would have more to say to each other at another time. I put on my cape and went out the back entrance, Barnaby still beside me.

"Mis' Samantha? Can I walk you home? It's almost dark."

"Why, that's very nice. I'd like that."

As we reached the street, Warren and Sumpin came up and took my hand. "We sure liked listenin' to you, Miss Samantha," said Warren. "When will you come and play for us again?"

"Little friends, it's hard to say since things have changed and now the piano's out in the saloon. I'll talk to Mr. Smithers and see what I can do, okay?"

And so, tired but happy, I completed my third day in Boone Valley and had much to think about — doing well at my first job, a new friend walking beside me, and a dedicated enemy to deal with.

I took a deep breath of the early evening air. The streets were still filled with a noisy assortment of wagons and carts and people. They didn't seem so strange to me now — in fact, I was beginning to deal with this time, this place, and somehow it seemed right.

As Barnaby and I reached the edge of town, I could see Hattie hurrying toward us. She was eyeing Barnaby and said breathlessly, "Samantha, I got worried about you walking back by yourself and thought I'd better fetch you home."

"I'm perfectly fine, Hattie. This nice gentleman not only sat near the piano while I played, but he offered to walk me home." Barnaby, hat in hand, lowered his head and shuffled his feet in embarrassment.

"Hattie, this is Barnaby. And Barnaby, this is Mrs. McKee, my new friend."

Hattie looked him over and just nodded, while Barnaby mumbled, "Evenin', ma'am."

Hattie spoke, not very kindly. "Well, that's nice, but I'll walk Samantha home from here. You can go back now." Her hand moved in a dismissive gesture.

Head still down, Barnaby turned away and started back to the saloon. I called after him, "Thanks for everything Barnaby, and good night!" He gave a small wave in return.

I turned to Hattie. "Why were you so rude to that nice man? He was very kind to me, and I was hoping we could ask him in for some coffee."

Hattie snorted. "Why he's just another of those dirty miners. I bet he ain't had a bath in weeks and weeks. I don't want a man like that in my house!"

I was astonished. "Dirty or not, he was good to me and I intend to be kind to him, no matter what you say."

Hattie shrugged and altered her tone of voice. "Well, you do what you like. Maybe under those filthy clothes is a good man. If he cleans up, maybe you can ask him in the next time. We'll see."

I took her arm, and we slowly walked back home in the dusk while I reported on my first day as an entertainer.

Later, in the privacy of my room, I giggled as I imagined the expression on Harland's face, or better yet Mother Malcolm's, if they could have seen the events of my day. Me, Samantha, playing the piano for a room full of 49ers! I went to sleep smiling at the thought.

Chapter Nine

For the next three days my programs grew in popularity and so did the number of men crowded around my piano. Barnaby still watched over the behavior of the audience, which really wasn't necessary, and I settled nicely into the routine of my job.

Orrin and Willis were there as well, standing at the bar, heads together. The growing number of men who came through the door and settled down to enjoy the music must have pleased Orrin, but as yet he had said nothing to me. My routine was to finish the concert with a rousing tune, then chat briefly with some of the attendees. Barnaby collected the gold that appeared on the top of the piano, I said good night to Corby, Elmo and Wong Kee, then walked back to Hattie's with Barnaby at my side. I congratulated myself that I had become an accepted part of Boone Valley. I was able to drift off and sleep more easily that night.

My self-congratulatory mood was short-lived. A few days after my concerts began, Hattie and I were finishing breakfast when there was a hesitant knock on the front door. Hattie left to answer it, and soon returned with a disapproving look. Following closely behind her was Barnaby, hat in hand, looking very uncomfortable.

"This man says he has to talk to you. He says it's important."

"Hattie, is it all right if Barnaby sits with us while we talk? Do you have any coffee left from breakfast?" I directed Barnaby to a chair at the kitchen table.

Hattie snorted her disapproval, but reached for the pot on the stove, poured a cup of the hot brew into a white mug and set it firmly in front of Barnaby.

"Barnaby, has something happened?"

"You're not goin' to like it, Mis' Samantha," he began. He was visibly shaken and could not meet my eyes. The words came out slowly and reluctantly.

"Last night Corby and Elmo told me I should come over first thing this mornin' so you'd know about it right away."

Now Hattie was sitting and waiting as expectantly as I was.

"Yes, yes, Barnaby. What is it?"

"It's Willis. He ain't very nice and all last night he was tellin' everybody stories 'bout you."

"What kind of stories?"

There was a pause before Barnaby went on. "Willis says you come from San Francisco, but you ain't no widow, in fact he says you was a whore afore you came here. Beg pardon, Mis' Samantha, but that's what he says. Everyone was listenin' and sayin' things that weren't very nice."

Hattie exploded. "I knew it! I knew nothing good would come from you working at that place. Well, you're not going back, and that Orrin is going to hear from me the next time I see him."

"Let's get the whole story, Hattie." I turned to Barnaby. "What else did he have to say? Tell me everything."

Barnaby's gaze shifted from me to Hattie and back as he continued. "Well, Ma'am, he says you was a high priced … what I said … for a couple of years, and then there was this big scandal about some important man and that you had to leave town. That you weren't doin' any playin' or singin' there, but just … what I said. He says you ain't no lady like you pretend to be."

He looked stricken. "I just know that ain't true, Mis' Samantha, but Willis wouldn't stop talkin' about you all night. The men were all snickerin' and laughin'. It made me mad, and Corby and Elmo, too."

I leaned forward. "What did Orrin Smithers have to say about it?"

"Oh, he jus' smiled and snickered with the rest of 'em."

The three of us sat silently at the table, digesting the information. Barnaby finished his coffee, then looked at me. "What will you be doin', Mis' Samantha? Will you be playin' the piano there any more?"

"Not if I have anything to say about it," Hattie said firmly. "In a town like this, folks just love to gossip, true or not. You know yourself the talk in that saloon is just lying and bragging. How can you tell anyone it just isn't true? They won't listen 'cause the lie is more entertaining than the truth."

"But if I don't go back, they'll assume it's true and I'm too ashamed to show my face. There's no way I'll let Willis get away with this."

Standing up suddenly, I said, "Let me think about this a moment, Barnaby. I'll be right back."

As I left the kitchen I could hear Hattie saying, "Have more coffee, Mr. ... Barnaby?"

Upstairs I said to my troubled expression in the mirror, "Well, Sam, as Oliver Hardy often said, 'This is another fine mess you've gotten me into!'"

What resources or experiences could I use in a case like this? What would John Wayne or Clint Eastwood do? They'd strap on their guns and go out to face the bad guys, that's for sure. Of course, someone like Willis would never dare to say a discouraging word to either of those men. Weren't there any strong females in those Westerns? Let's see, there was Miss Kitty at the Long Branch Saloon, and she didn't let anybody get away with anything.

As I sat there, I spotted the crystal I'd found in the dusty road of the Boone Valley ghost town. It was there, next to the china basin. Taking it into my left hand, I closed my eyes, took three deep breaths, and began to feel more centered. For a few moments I sat quietly, calming my mind and body, and soon the outrage and anger dropped away. I was fully aware that women living at this time were not allowed to be assertive. In some cases they were treated with great respect, but in others they were badly used. But that was before Samantha came to town! It would be up to me to control or change the situation; it was not necessary to take this insult passively. Returning to the kitchen, I addressed Barnaby.

"Please go back to the saloon and ask Elmo, Corby and anyone else who doesn't believe these lies to meet with me as soon as possible. Now, where could we meet secretly and talk about this?"

Hattie offered a small room in the back of her store, and we told Barnaby we would meet him and the others there in fifteen minutes. That should do. And people could come in through the back door, away from the street.

After a hasty breakfast, dishes done, hair combed, cloaks and gloves in place, Hattie and I hurried through the cool morning to her store and into the storage room. A quick look at my watch told me it was still early, eight in the morning.

Soon Corby slipped through the door of the back room, then Elmo, followed by Maggie, Naomi, Abigail and Flower. The girls were dressed in soft cotton dresses in various shades of blue and gray, covered by warm wool coats. Without the harsh makeup they wore when working, they looked fresh and friendly. Barnaby stood hesitantly outside until I motioned him through the door, then I turned to face my troops.

Corby spoke first. "We asked the girls to come, all 'cept Bertha and Zola who make it plain that they don't like you much. All of us here don't like what Willis is sayin'."

I was touched. "Thank you so much. Please believe me when I say that there's absolutely no truth at all in the lies Willis is spreading. For your information, I've never, ever sold my ... favors to anyone. I've been to San Francisco twice, and that was with my husband for a few days at a time. You all know that playing the piano at the Majestic is the only way I have to earn money, and I rather enjoy it, but Willis is making it very difficult."

They were all silent until Maggie spoke. "I think it's just terrible what Willis is doin'. He's just jealous, that's all. He don't like you gettin' the attention and playin' as good as him."

Abigail broke in. "He's always makin' trouble so he'll look good. He's had things to say about all us girls that ain't true. So why can't we all tell a few lies about Willis to pay him back?"

Corby shook his head. "That'd only make things worse. What we all can do is tell everybody that those stories just ain't so. If anyone badmouths Mis' Samantha, we can just say that it ain't the truth and there ain't no proof. We can talk to the fellows who drink at the bar, and you girls can put in a good word whenever you hear someone talk bad about Mis' Samantha."

Elmo spoke up. "Mind you, we can't be mean about it or start any fights. Anythin' like that and Orrin will be on our backs, or worse."

Everyone around agreed. I spoke up. "That sounds like a great idea. Remember, don't bring up the subject, but if someone starts talking, just say that you know for sure the stories aren't true. And if they are in doubt, they can just ask me."

Corby stood at this point. "We're for you, Mis' Samantha, and we'll do the best we can. Now, Elmo and me have to get back to the bar and finish cleanin' up or Orrin will be on our tails if everythin' ain't ready for today's business. Them night bartenders don't do a very good job. Will we be seein' you later?"

"I'll definitely be there, gentlemen, wearing a suit of armor if I can find one."

Frowning and shaking their heads, Elmo, Corby and Barnaby waved goodbye. That left just the ladies, and we certainly had a lot to say to each other. Abigail settled her full, round body in a chair and patted her frizzy, strawberry blonde hair.

"We sure do admire the way you're standin' up to Orrin. He ain't the easiest man to get along with. We see the way he treats them youngsters and sometimes he hits on us when he gets real mad. But we're gonna help you all we can."

I said, "Now, see if I remember, isn't your name Abigail?"

She was pleased. "Sure is, and this here's Naomi, Maggie, and our little Flower who's younger than any of us."

She pointed to the slight figure sitting to her right. Flower's hair was light blonde, almost white. She had a sweet expression on her pretty face, and her soft blue eyes balanced her pale skin. She ducked her head in embarrassment, but raised it when she saw that we were all smiling at her, and she gave us a smile in return.

Pointing to Hattie, I said, "I'd like you all to meet my new friend who has given me shelter in her lovely home. This is Hattie McKee, who let us meet here in her store."

Hattie nodded her head to the murmurs of "how-d'ya-do" and she smiled and returned a "nice to meet you all."

Once more I told the story of being separated from my family, and finished by saying, "So here I was without friends, family or money. If it hadn't been for this kind lady," I pointed to Hattie, "I don't know what would have become of me. But like all of you, I'm just trying to earn a living and keep body and soul together."

To Flower I said, "It's so nice to know you. You look too young to be serving drinks in a saloon. How old are you?"

She looked over at Maggie for approval, and then replied softly, "I reckon I'm about 14."

I was touched. "It must be hard on you, carrying those heavy drinks around. Are you very tired by the end of the evening?"

Her fragile shoulders shrugged. "Oh, it's all right. What I don't like is when the men get too … friendly. I get tired when I have to pull away or make 'em let go."

"But isn't that what you're supposed to do? Just serve

drinks? Isn't that why you're called Waiter Girls?"

Maggie explained. "That's all we're hired for, but Orrin keeps tellin' us that we're supposed to serve drinks and still be 'friendly' with everyone. Some of the men think we should take 'em upstairs to pleasure them — but we don't do that, unless we want to. Anyway, Orrin don't like any of that goin' on. He says it causes too much trouble. But that don't stop Zola and Bertha from sneakin' upstairs and makin' extra money on their own."

Hattie frowned and shook her head in disapproval.

Abigail continued. "That's why Orrin has the Hurdy-gurdy Girls come in every night. That's how he makes lotsa money."

I looked at Hattie who just shrugged. "What on earth are the Hurdy-gurdy Girls? I've never heard of them."

Abigail explained. "Orrin has about 15 of 'em he brought in from San Francisco. They come in about 8 o'clock, after you go home, and they dance with the customers all night. They don't live in the saloon like we do, but out in town. Some are even married, or have men friends to support 'cause they make such good money. But most of 'em are stuck-up, thinkin' they're better'n us regular girls."

Hattie nodded. "I've seem them around town, walking on the streets toward the saloon. Do they wear white muslin dresses that come just to their shoe tops, and ribbons and tassels in their hair?"

"That's right. They wear their dresses shorter so the miners won't stomp on 'em while they're dancin'. And they put their hair up in nets and ribbons so it don't fall down with all the jumpin' around they do."

Maggie shook her head. "I sure wouldn't want to be one of them girls."

Naomi reached down and rubbed one of her ankles. "I would if my sore feet would take bein' stepped on by them heavy boots.

Why, them girls make up to $25 a night, or more!"

"How on earth do they do that — just by dancing?" Hattie was intrigued.

Naomi explained, "Them girls get paid for the dancin' and the drinks they sell. After each dance, the fellas gotta buy the girls a drink. It's supposed to be expensive wine at a dollar a glass, but it's really just tea. So the girls get a cut, 25 cents, plus part of all the drinks they can get the miners to buy. By the time the dancin' is over at two or three in the mornin', they take home a goodly amount."

Abigail commented dryly, "That depends on whether or not they get to keep it. Everyone of 'em got a husband or lover waitin' at the door to take it away and put it in their own pockets. Ain't but a few of them get to keep some for themselves."

I was curious. "If you don't mind my asking, how are you girls paid? Do you get back something for all the drinks you serve during the night?"

Naomi answered. "Orrin pays us girls $35 a week plus 1 cent for every beer we serve, 3 cents for whiskey, brandy and other drinks."

"Does he pay you every night like the Hurdy-gurdy Girls?"

"No, ma'am. He settles up with us every Saturday. So, we can make almost $60 or more a week, before Orrin takes out 'expenses'."

"What's that for?"

"Oh, $10 for our rooms and meals, another $5 for our beddin', towels, laundry. Of course, we pay for our dresses, and they get worn out pretty fast."

"I can see Orrin does just fine with all the money you and the Hurdy-gurdy Girls bring in. Do you manage to save or put away any of it for yourselves?"

The girls were silent. Abigail answered hesitantly. "It's hard. There's a bank quite a walk from here, but the owner don't like to see us girls in there. We don't see how us depositin' our money can hurt his reputation. We try to hide money in our rooms, but sometimes someone sneaks in and steals it while we're workin'." The other girls agreed sadly.

I protested. "Well, how are you going to save for your future? You surely aren't going to serve drinks the rest of your lives, are you?"

Abigail shook her head. "We sure don't want to, Mis' Samantha, but can't do nothin' about it."

Hattie exploded at this. "Well, I can do somethin' about it! I got a nice strong lockbox in my house, and if you girls'll trust me, I'll keep your savings nice and safe for as long as you want. You work hard for your money, and you sure deserve to have it put away safe."

Maggie was all smiles. "We would be so beholden to you, Mis' McKee."

"Shucks, it's a pleasure to put something over on the menfolk from time to time. You just give Samantha your deposits, and I'll keep records just like a bank!"

As we were saying our goodbyes, Flower asked shyly, "You be comin' in to play today, Mis' Samantha?"

With a little more bravado than I felt, I assured her, "You can bet I will!"

Once they were gone, Hattie frowned. "Are you sure you want to go in and take on Willis and Orrin, as well as those dirty-minded men?"

"I'll have to tough it out sometime, Hattie. I'll see how it goes, and then come up with Plan B if necessary. I have something in mind that might work to get Willis or Orrin to change their tune. And you, Hattie, I'm proud of you."

"What on earth for?"

"For offering to help the girls and keep their money safe.

That was a lovely thing to do."

"Well, land sakes, I couldn't help but feel sorry for them. I don't approve of what they do, but they are nice little things once you get to know them. Let's just keep it to ourselves what I'm doin' to help out."

A few hours later Hattie and I stood across the crowded road from the saloon. Hattie held onto my arm. "Are you absolutely sure you want to go in there today?"

"Yes, I simply must deal with this now. I'm going to face Orrin and Willis and then take it from there. If nothing else, I can appeal to the customers in the bar. Wish me luck!"

With a brave smile that I did not feel, I worked my way through the traffic, then hesitated just an instant before I opened the door to the kitchen.

As usual, Wong Kee was working and something was bubbling in a large pot on the huge iron stove from which a welcome warmth radiated. He looked up as I entered, set aside the huge knife in his hand, then looked me over quietly.

"Why you here? They say bad things 'bout you."

"Wong Kee, I must face my enemies. I cannot run away."

"Not easy, you must be strong." He stepped closer and looked deeply into my eyes. "I see strong, not big strong. You have fountain of fire inside. Remember, think strong and keep temper. May gods watch over you." He nodded as if satisfied.

"Your words are helping, and I thank you," I replied. He looked at me for a moment, then returned to his work just as Orrin Smithers entered the kitchen.

"Well, look who's here today, that fine lady from San Francisco!" The grin on his face was like a cat ready to play with a mouse.

Focusing on his eyes, I pulled myself up straight and said, "Mr. Smithers, do you believe all the nonsense that Willis is spreading?"

"Woman, how do I know what he says ain't true?"

"You know it, because I say it's as far from the truth as you can get. It's something that Willis has created in his mean little mind."

Orrin was unconcerned. "That's what you say. But, you just go on out there and play your music and don't pay no mind to what the customers will be sayin'. They got their own ideas and maybe you can change 'em, but I think you'll be runnin' for home real soon."

The all-knowing grin was still on his face, and I could feel my anger rise. But remembering Wong Kee's wise counsel, I stepped back, looked at him without flinching, and managed a smile.

"All right, Orrin. Here I go. But I'm giving notice that before I'm through, Willis is going to look very silly." And with my head held high, I made what I hoped was a grand exit.

On entering the saloon, I approached Corby and Elmo behind the long bar and whispered, "How does it look now? Are the bandits getting ready to attack?"

Corby laughed when he said, "No sign of them yet, Mis' Samantha, but there's been a lot of whisperin' and laughin'. We've only been able to talk to a few, but most of 'em still are set on believin' the worst. You take it easy, and if you have any trouble today, you give us a high sign."

I thanked them, then looked around for Barnaby, my protector. He was already in place next to the piano. Many of the tables were already crowded and I could hear the whispers and snickers. All eyes were on me as I neared the piano. Barnaby stood, then glared at the assembled congregation as I stood, faced my audience and smiled. "Good afternoon, gentlemen." (I stressed that last word.) "I have some very special music to play for you today, and I hope you listen carefully to the words because there is a message there for all of us."

A rumble of voices rose, then quieted as I sat down and began playing, and singing, "You'll Never Walk Alone."

I played the melody through again as sweetly as I could, then once more sang the lyrics, providing a big dramatic finish.

There was a scattering of applause, but many eyes were downcast and did not meet mine as I turned to look around. One rough voice said, loudly, "What else d'ya play at besides the piana? Fun and games, we hear!"

Many of the audience responded with shushing noises and demands for quiet. Barnaby jumped to his feet and eyed the speaker with his huge fists clenched at his side. When all was quiet, he sat down and said, "You go on and play some more, Mis' Samantha."

The incident unnerved me for just a moment, then I went on with the program. Next on the list was "Oh, What a Beautiful Morning," followed by "Look For the Silver Lining," and then "Blue Skies." I was actually beginning to enjoy myself. Next came "Over the Rainbow."

The applause was stronger after each selection, and soon the muttered remarks and laughter had faded. Every now and then I glanced over at the bar, and sure enough Orrin and Willis were watching like two vultures in a tree. In one quiet moment between songs, I caught their eyes and gave them a bright smile of victory. They responded by turning their backs and facing the bar, heads together.

Time went quickly as I played a series of waltzes, and before I knew it, Barnaby was beside me saying, "Time t'go home, Mis' Samantha."

I stood and faced the crowded tables to say goodbye. There were more than a few smiles in response, and nods of approval. As before, a number of them approached the piano and mumbled "thank you" as they placed small pieces of gold on the top. Some could not make eye contact, but many nodded and tipped their dusty and well-worn hats.

Barnaby gathered the gold from the top of the piano to put into another of his leather pouches as I walked over to the bar. Orrin and Willis were nowhere to be seen, but Corby and Elmo came over. "You done good, Mis' Samantha," Corby said. "We never thought everyone would behave, but things just might turn out all right."

Elmo whispered, "Don't be too sure. Lookee over there!" He motioned over to the tables around the piano that were still filled with customers. We could see Orrin and Willis standing at one of the tables, leaning over in conversation with the occupants. Every now and then there would be a loud roar of laughter, then they would move on to other groups.

My heart sank with the thought that today's battle was not only far from won, but still fully engaged. With a brief goodbye to the bartenders, I headed for the kitchen, Barnaby close beside me. As I picked up my cloak, I looked over at Wong Kee and sadly shook my head.

"I thought it went well, but now I'm not so sure."

Wong Kee bowed and said, "Brave man must face dragon more than once. Remember, stand strong, face dragon."

"Thank you for your good advice. Good night, Wong Kee."

As we left the building, Barnaby looked at me anxiously. "What are you goin' to do now, Mis' Samantha? You gonna do what the Chinee man says? You comin' back tomorrow?"

"Of course, Barnaby. There's much more to be done, though I'm not quite sure what at this point. I'll think about it tonight. And thank you so much for bringing the word to me. If I had walked in there without warning, it would have been disastrous."

Farther down the street we met Hattie walking our way. "I just couldn't wait another minute. What happened, Samantha?"

"I thought it went well, but now I'm not so sure. I'll have to come up with Plan B, whatever that may be. Let's talk it over tonight, and I'll do some cogitating as well." Turning to Barnaby, I said, "You do a wonderful job as my protector, and I thank you so much for being there. Can I depend on you tomorrow? I feel it may be a little rough for a few days."

"You can count on me, Mis' Samantha. G'nite to you." Turning to Hattie, hat in hand, he bowed awkwardly and said, "G'nite to you, Mrs. McKee." And turned back to town.

Hattie and I walked back to the house, had a quiet dinner, and retired early. I wasn't up to the usual evening concert, but promised I would play again very soon. She, bless her heart, understood.

Sleep came very slowly that night. A series of scenes from many westerns went through my mind. Confrontations in bar rooms, the hero winning over the villain, the good guys vanquishing the bad guys. But the only good guy was me, and I wasn't about to pull out my trusty six-shooter and blaze away. As I slipped into sleep, the image of me standing off Orrin and Willis with a gun in my hand took hold and my last thought before falling asleep was, "Atta girl, Samantha. Stand your ground!"

Chapter Ten

The next morning I opened my eyes slowly. The shock of my surroundings was declining and acceptance was taking over. But the impermanence of the situation was like a constant buzz in the back of my mind. Could it be that one of these mornings I'd awaken in my own bed at Rocky Crest with all of the nagging dissatisfactions still with me?

Sliding through time to Boone Valley surely brought my former life's journey to a crashing halt. What day was this? Friday, Saturday? No, Saturday. I'd been here just eight days and had to deal with survival and confrontation — two issues that were never problems in my other life. Here I'd made friends, worked for my livelihood, and stood up to the obstacles in my path. The old Samantha never had such challenges, but this might be just what I needed to shake and force me to open up to changes and new experiences. Was this what the Universe had in store for me?

Harland certainly could have used such challenges, but on reflection I knew that he found every emotional need fulfilled in the daily activities of his hardware stores. I thought of my boys and how I missed them. Memories of their strong faces filled my mind, and the pain of this separation brought tears to my eyes. I longed to be there to see their transition from college to emerge as young men ready to go out into the world. Shaking my head, I could not deal with that question right now. Heaving a sigh, I rose from the bed and prepared for the day ahead of me.

At breakfast, Hattie and I reviewed the trouble at the saloon and possibilities before me. Nothing concrete came to us, and soon, in silence, we finished our coffee. Then I heard a horse and wagon coming to the back of the house. I raised my eyebrows at Hattie.

"Oh, that's just the Chinee man who brings wood once a week. He fills the wood box on the side, whatever I need. Today I owe him some money."

She left the table, then returned with her drawstring purse. Through the kitchen door I saw a wagon loaded with chunks of wood with two horses waiting patiently. A small man wearing black pajamas and a black hat with a narrow brim, moved bundles of wood from the wagon to a box just outside the kitchen.

He bowed as Hattie approached, then held out his hand as she counted out coins one at a time. When he nodded, she closed her purse and returned to the kitchen.

"A nice man," she commented, "but we don't talk much. He just brings the wood, I pay what I owe, and he goes on his way. I know he's as honest as the day is long, so we get along just fine." We could hear the sounds of the wagon moving away from the house.

I decided it would be best to appear at the saloon earlier than usual in case there were issues to deal with. I put on the blue dress from Rosalie's wardrobe. If work at the Majestic somehow lasts longer, I'd better order a few dresses from Ida Penny. However, there are problems to sort out before I become a regular at the saloon.

I enjoyed the morning walk through the cool air, then greeted Wong Kee as I entered the kitchen.

"I've come early to fight a few dragons, Wong Kee. Have you seen any around?"

He did not smile, but I could see his dark-brown eyes sparkle in response. "They no come out yet."

"Do you think I need a sword and shield today?"

"Remember, stand strong. Keep temper."

I pulled myself erect, then left the kitchen with a pounding heart. Six or seven men were standing along the bar, drinking and talking. Seven or eight tables near the stage were filled with men drinking or playing cards. At one table a group was in deep conversation with Willis.

As I walked to the bar, Corby joined me, frowning. "You're here early, Mis' Samantha. Orrin's doin' some business way on the other side of town, but you can see Willis over there. He's been busy all mornin' telling all kindsa stories about you. They been laughin' and carryin' on for quite a while."

A big burst of laughter came from the men at the table. Willis grinned and pointed at me. "There she be, boys. The whore from San Francisco."

Turning to Corby, I said, "I've had enough of this, and I'm going to do something about it NOW!"

He put a restraining hand on my arm, but I pulled away and sailed toward Willis like a battleship ready to fire. Ignoring the onlookers, I stood almost toe to toe with him, and he looked me over with a smirk on his face. All conversation stopped and the room suddenly became very still.

"Willis," I said as loudly as I could, "You've been telling lies about me, things your little mind has created that are far from the truth."

Willis took a casual stance, looked around at the crowd, and drawled, "Well, lady, how do we know they ain't true? Can you prove to the contrary?"

"My word should be good enough for anyone. And I demand that you stop telling these terrible stories."

Willis loved playing to the onlookers, and he said casually, "Now, just how can you stop me?"

My mind was racing, but in a burst of inspiration the image that put me to sleep last night came to me. There I was facing Orrin and Willis with a gun in my hand.

"I'll tell you how, Willis." I came closer and pointed a finger at his nose. "You've been damaging my good name, and I'm not going to stand for it. I demand satisfaction."

Willis sneered, "Yeah, I understand you're quite good at that!" He grinned around at the crowd, proud he had returned a witty reply.

I snapped my fingers at him. "Wake up and pay attention, Willis! We're living in new times with new rules. You've smeared my reputation, and by God I'm going to prove what a liar you are."

"And just how are you expectin' to do that?" Willis sneered.

"I'm challenging you to put your own reputation on the line. I challenge you to a duel!"

Willis' smile changed to great surprise as he backed away. "Nah, no woman ever fights a duel!"

I went on. "So, let me be the first. What do you want, Willis? Guns? Swords? Sabers? Knives? Rocks? Slingshots? Which do you choose?"

Willis was uncomfortable as he anxiously eyed the gathering crowd, then looked back at me.

"I don't know nothin' about them things, never have. And you don't neither, I'll bet. Nah, you're crazy, woman." And he looked to the crowd for support.

"You're right, Willis. I don't know much about those weapons. But I do know something that we're both good at, and I challenge you, right here in front of everyone, to a duel ... a piano duel."

There was a great outburst from the crowd as Willis stepped back, then smirked in reply, "Well, just how you gonna do that? I can outplay you with one hand behind my back!"

Laughter rose here and there, but it quieted waiting for me to respond.

"I'll tell you what it's going to be, Willis. A piano duel — on my piano since it's just been tuned"

My mind was racing now. What have I created, and how can such a thing be structured? Verbally shooting from the hip, I improvised.

"We'll select five pieces each, music that we play especially well. We'll each play one, the crowd will decide which of the two they like the best. After we have played all five of our selections, whoever has the most points wins. If you win, I'll give up the afternoon programs and leave. If I win, you will apologize and take back the stories you've been telling about me. Do you agree?"

Willis looked at the men grouped around him for backing, but he found only eager smiles.

"Well ..." he stalled. The men around him cheered before he could finish and a few slapped him on the back.

Then a thought occurred to me and I raised my hand for silence. "All right, the duel will not take place until Willis says he is absolutely ready. But I have one condition that I insist on."

The assembled men waited expectantly while Willis scowled and his narrow chest seemed to sink into itself.

"From this day until the duel is over, I want his promise that there will be no further stories, lies, or wild tales of any kind about me. Is that understood, Willis?"

He did not answer but stood like a child who had been caught with his hand in the cookie jar. "Well ..." he began again, but the remainder of his words were lost in the cheer that rose from the men.

Playing to the crowd, I said, "Will everyone help to make sure that Willis meets this condition?"

From the crowd came loudly, "Sure will," "You bet," and "Yes, ma'am!"

I was mighty proud of myself as I walked back to the bar where Elmo and Corby waited, king-sized grins lighting their faces.

"You sure done it, Mis' Samantha! You sure faced that Willis and fixed his wagon good," Corby said. "You just wait 'n' see. Everyone's goin' to be talking about your duel and waitin' for the day when Willis says he's ready."

Elmo clapped his hands in agreement. I suddenly felt a little weak in the knees and leaned against the bar.

"Elmo, what have you got to drink that won't knock me off my feet?"

"We got sarsaparilla, ma'am. I'll getcha some."

The drink, while not cold, was refreshing and I began to feel stronger. Just then Orrin walked in, looked over the crowd and saw Willis off to the side, standing alone, shoulders slumped. He also took in our group at the bar — Elmo, Corby and I, all wearing bright smiles. "What the hell's been goin' on?"

Willis rushed to his side, then pulled him through the door leading to the card room.

Corby laughed. "I sure wish I could hear what they're sayin' to each other!"

After finishing the drink, I went to the card room and knocked. I wasn't about to let Willis backslide or waffle out of the challenge. There were about 12 men in the room who, I assumed, were quietly playing cards until Orrin and Willis burst in. All conversation stopped when they saw me. I smiled as sweetly as I could and pointed to Willis.

"Willis, in the next day or so, let's make a list of the five pieces we'll each be playing. They could be posted where everyone can see, and it might make the playoff more interesting."

I closed the door quietly, and laughed when I heard the outburst of voices that followed my exit.

I couldn't resist opening the door to the kitchen and waving at Wong Kee who looked up from a huge pot on the stove.

"I have met the dragon, Wong Kee, and got a good whack at

his tail. The first battle is mine! What do you think about that?"

Wong Kee brought his hands together and bowed, and I think he came very close to a smile.

"You do good. You have good mind I not see before. This dragon not see foe such as you. May you soon stand over his body in victory."

Grinning, I held my hands together and bowed to him in return.

Back in the saloon, I found all six Waiter Girls gathered about the bar. They surrounded me as I approached. Maggie spoke. "We was all sound asleep when we heard this commotion and had to see what was happenin'. Elmo and Corby told us all what you done. Good on you for standin' up to Willis."

Most nodded in agreement, but a tall, rather skinny girl I had not seen before spoke up. "You sure think you're sumpin', coming in here and talkin' your big talk, makin' a fool outta yourself."

I found later that this was Zola, the self-appointed queen bee of this little group. She had curly black hair, black eyes, and a rather haughty, I-am-in-charge attitude.

I said firmly, "All I did was stand up for myself and deny the lies that Willis has been spreading. Don't you agree that any woman is entitled to fair treatment and dignity?"

"Who are you kiddin'? All we do here is serve drinks and get paid, and don't give Orrin no trouble."

Bertha, not my candidate for Mother of the Year, stood beside her and moved her head in agreement. "Yeah, that's right!"

To break the tension, I suggested, "Since you're all down here and not working, why don't you come over to the piano and I'll play something special for you." I walked over and sat before the piano as the girls gathered around — Zola and Bertha rather reluctantly.

I don't know why this song came to mind, but the words and

music were especially appealing, about a maiden praying for some-one to watch over her. Four of the girls drew up chairs and sat, ready to listen. Only Zola and Bertha remained standing, Zola with crossed arms, looking up at the ceiling.

I played that lovely song to the end, relishing the melody that was so beautiful. When I finished, I turned to see my four new friends were enchanted. Shaking her head, Zola walked away and Bertha hesitantly followed behind.

Maggie clapped her hands and smiled. "That sure was one of the sweetest songs I ever heard. Made me want to cry."

Flower nodded in agreement, as did Maggie and Naomi. Just then Willis walked up. All was quiet.

Willis growled, "I'll have the list of my music by tomorrow afternoon. No trouble at all." He turned his back and stalked away. The girls used the silence that followed to wave to me then quickly scamper up to their rooms.

During lunch Hattie clapped her hands when she heard the details of my exchange with Willis. "Lady, you are a caution. I can't get over how you walked right up to the man and challenged him to a duel, of all things. Wherever did you get such an idea?"

"Last night I was thinking I should demand a retraction or an apology at least, but felt Willis wouldn't consider it. I knew I had to challenge him in some way. Then I pictured myself facing Willis with a gun in my hand, and it all just fell into place before I knew what I was doing or saying!"

"Well, I'm sure proud of you. And you're going to show up Willis very nicely."

Dressed once more in the rose-patterned dress, I entered the saloon kitchen that afternoon just before one. Turning, I found Sumpin and Warren finishing lunch at a small table by the window. "Well, hello there you two. I haven't seen you for a few days and I've missed you. Where have you been?"

They seemed glad to see me, but smiled rather hesitantly.

"We been around," Warren replied. "Mama Bertha don't like us to be seein' you, and Mister Smithers makes us stay outside during the day. We try to listen through the front door, but it's hard sometimes."

They both looked tired, and I noticed again their worn and tattered clothes. I turned to Wong Kee. "Are these children being properly cared for?"

"Mother not happy," he replied. "She not want them near you. Not treat them nice. I try feed and keep in warm kitchen. Mistah Smithas makes them go."

I was outraged. Turning to them, I asked, "What do you do all day, where do you stay?"

Warren shrugged. "We go into stores 'til they run us out. When it's cold, we go to old shacks or stables 'til we can come back here."

I hugged each child. "I'm on your side, and remember that you can come to me if you have any trouble. Will you do that?"

With downcast eyes they nodded. My mind was troubled for the children and I resolved to find a way to help them. But right now I had to go to work.

I entered the saloon and saw a large crowd already assembled. A great buzz of conversation filled the air. As I connected with Corby, I raised my eyebrows. He came to meet me at the end of the bar.

"What we got here, Mis' Samantha, is all these men want to look you over and hear how you play. Word's spread all over town about your duel, and they're real anxious to see what kind of a lady you are. They've been flockin' in for the past hour."

Barnaby joined us. "That's right, Mis' Samantha. They're all a-waitin' for you. I told 'em they all gotta behave if they want to hear you play. I think they're gonna be fine. I'll be close by if you need me."

He was looking quite nice with a new green wool shirt and tan trousers. The usual stubble on his face had been shaved, and his hair was nicely combed. The shapeless hat was gone. In its place he wore a brown felt hat with a narrow brim. It seemed that his new assignment as my protector had given him a sense of purpose and he fitted the part of my guardian angel just fine.

Naomi hurried by with a tray full of drinks. "We're sure busier than usual today. They're all thirsty and ready to hear you play!"

As I sat before the piano, a familiar figure caught my eye. A man sitting in a chair just inside the front door wearing a tan Stetson set low over his eyebrows, and a well-fitted jacket. Because of the crush of people, I couldn't make out any further details. But the repeated appearance of this individual began to intrigue me.

It was a landmark afternoon. No matter what I played, there was thunderous applause and vocal appreciation. Within a few hours, there was standing room only around the entrance and along the walls. Barnaby stood guard by the piano, but his services were not required. He smiled and nodded with pride as I played. Willis and Orrin were nowhere in sight, which pleased me. This was my day, and I didn't need a dark cloud to spoil it.

Barnaby reminded me when it was time to go, so I stood and said goodbye to those in the audience, and they smiled back. A line formed and many of them passed by the piano — some tipping their shapeless and worn hats, and some smiling and nodding. More than a few commented on the duel, that it was something they were looking forward to.

When the crowd thinned out, I found Barnaby carefully bagging the gold dust that had been left on the top of the piano. I had no idea how much had accumulated over these last few days, but it looked like I had earned my way rather well.

After saying good night to Corby and Elmo and waving to the Waiter Girls, I retrieved my cape, gave a quick report to Wong Kee, then headed out the back door with Barnaby at my side. When we left the building, a cold, moist wind hit us. It had been cool during the day, but the unexpected briskness made me pull the folds of the cloak closely around me.

Hattie was waiting across the road and motioning frantically for us to join her. Her expression was grim.

"Why so gloomy, Hattie? We had a wonderful day."

"That can wait, Samantha. I have something to show you."

She led us down the street to the wooden stairs of a walkway, then turned and pointed underneath. There, in the growing darkness, I could see Sumpin and Warren huddled together in the cold. They looked quite lost and very miserable.

"My God, Hattie! What can we do for them? They're freezing!"

"Let's take them down to the store. The potbellied stove there was nice and warm when I left to meet you."

Barnaby lifted Warren into his strong arms, and I could easily carry Sumpin's small body. She made a soft, mournful sound as she snuggled against my shoulder. Soon we settled the children in chairs before the warm stove, and Hattie bundled them into wool blankets from her stock. When I removed their worn and soaked shoes. I could feel their poor feet were ice cold. I rubbed Sumpin's small feet between my hands and motioned Barnaby to do the same for Warren. The children were silent as we ministered to them.

"Hattie," I asked, "do you carry children's clothing that will fit these two? Let's get them into the warmest that you have, everything from the skin out. Barnaby, give her the bag of gold we earned today."

Hattie waved her hand in dismissal and said, "We can settle that later. Right now the children need something hot in their stomachs. Let's get them to my house right away. I've got a big pot of soup on the stove that'll be just the thing. I'll be right back with the clothes."

Barnaby stood up suddenly. "Lemme see if I can find someone with a cart or wagon to carry us all to Miss Hattie's house. I'll be right back."

Hattie returned with an armful of clothes just as Barnaby entered. "I gotta man with a cart. He'll take us all to Miss Hattie's for a small nugget."

We carried the children, blankets and clothes, into the wagon, and in no time were unloading in front of Hattie's. The wonderful smell of soup met us as she opened the door and led the way into the kitchen. She efficiently ladled the hot soup into bowls while Barnaby and I settled the children at the table.

Seeing their dirty hands and faces, I suggested. "Let's put on some water to heat. These two could use a bath before they put on their new clothes. Heaven knows when they were washed last."

The children sipped the hot soup, and began to unfold from the blankets like young flowers opening to the sun. Hattie brought out a big washtub and filled it with warm water. Once deposited into the tub, the children began to smile as they played with the soap and wash cloths. Once they were well washed and scrubbed, they emerged squeaky clean, ready to be dried and wrapped in enormous flannel towels. The sight of their shaggy, mussed hair gave me a thought.

"Hattie, could you get me a comb, scissors and a mirror? I think these two could stand a first-class haircut."

Hattie was skeptical. "Do you think you could do a proper job?"

"Oh, easily," I laughed. "I was barber-in-residence for my two boys for many years until they insisted they were big enough to go to a regular barber. I think I'm rather good."

As he fidgeted on the chair, I proceeded to give Warren a

first-class, 20th Century haircut, and trimmed the bangs out of his eyes. When I handed him the mirror, he surveyed the completed job before he turned to me and grinned.

Sumpin was next. Her curly red hair was long and tangled, but by the time I finished, it framed her pretty face. She contemplated her reflection in the mirror for a moment before she finally smiled back at it.

I turned to Barnaby. "How about you, Barnaby? You look a little shaggy, and I'd like to pay you back in some way for your services as my guardian angel. How about a trim?"

He ducked his head and looked at Hattie and me in dismay. "I ain't never had a real haircut. I just cut it off when it gets too long."

"Come on, Barnaby. I think you'll like it!"

With encouragement from Hattie and Warren, Barnaby lowered himself into the chair. When the layers of his sun-streaked brown hair were snipped from his forehead and neck, there emerged a rather nice looking man with a finely shaped head. Sumpin even said, "You look real good, Barnaby."

Even Hattie concurred shyly. "You do look very nice, Mr. .... What is your name anyway?"

Quietly he replied, "Barnaby Tinker, ma'am."

Lowering her eyes, she said, "Well, you look very nice, Mr. Barnaby Tinker."

A bit flustered, Barnaby looked long and hard in the mirror, and then nodded with pleasure.

Hattie broke the silence by saying, "Well, let's get these youngsters into their new clothes and see how they look."

Warren donned warm tweed pants, a blue shirt and sweater, with a heavy wool jacket on top. He slipped his feet into knit socks and heavy brogans, and I retrieved the brown knit cap from my backpack to complete the outfit. He was far from the wet, miserable child we found under the stairs.

Sumpin's dress was dark blue flannel with long sleeves and a dark red trim around the collar and cuffs. The skirt reached almost to her ankles which we covered with long, black wool stockings and heavy black shoes. The wool coat was long for her, but it had a hood and would last for several years. They were both beaming as we praised how grand they looked, and they whirled 'round and 'round to show off their new clothes.

Barnaby volunteered to deliver them back to the saloon and Mother Bertha before it got much later, but I felt I should also talk to her, so the four of us headed back to town. I expected Bertha would not be happy with us for "interfering" with her children. I was right.

Chapter Eleven

When we reached the saloon, we found Wong Kee in the kitchen. Upon seeing Sumpin and Warren in their new finery he raised his hands in the air, then squatted down to eye level with Sumpin.

"How pretty you! And Warren, so handsome! What happen?"

I explained how we had found them. "Has anyone been asking about them? Has Bertha been worried?"

"She not ask. She thinks I feed then send to bed. Mama Bertha not miss."

I hesitated. "Better tell her the clothes came from Mrs. McKee, not from me. That's true for now."

Wong Kee nodded as Elmo came through the kitchen door carrying two containers. "Hey, Wong Kee, we need more hot water and hot coffee out at the bar. Lotsa people ordering hot toddies 'n' coffee with brandy to warm up." Seeing the children, he looked surprised. "Well, now. Who are these two handsome young people? Do I know them?"

Sumpin ran to him and opened her arms. "It's me, Elmo! Me and Warren! We got all wet 'n' got some soup, and a bath, and a haircut, 'n' everything!"

Elmo picked her up as he smiled his crooked smile. "Well, so it is. You look so fine and dandy, I didn't recognize you!"

Warren ran to him as well. "Me, too! Mis' Samantha even gave me this nice cap!"

Just as Wong Kee handed Elmo the refilled containers, I heard a terrible pounding and the building seemed to shake. There was no reaction from the people standing in the kitchen, so I had to ask, "What on earth is all that noise? Is there a storm?"

Elmo chuckled as he headed for the door. "Them's the Hurdy-gurdy Girls just startin' their dancin' for tonight. The men are always ready to dance as soon as the girls get here."

Before he went out the door, I called to him. "I'd love to watch them. Can I peek through the door?"

Elmo took a second to consider the question. "Best come in the front way and stand in the back so Willis and Orrin won't see." Barnaby and I stepped out into the hallway. The door of the card room across from the kitchen was slightly open. Putting a finger to my lips, I peeked inside.

Since the piano had been removed, Orrin had added another table and five more chairs, making seven tables in all. The tables were full, and the men occupying the chairs were focused on the cards, bags of gold dust, coins and nuggets in front of them. The room was hazy with clouds of smoke filling the air.

At each table a well-dressed man was deftly going about the business of dealing cards. The Dealers stood out in their black suits, white frilly shirts, and colorful brocaded vests. They were quite a contrast from the dusty, ill-dressed men occupying the other chairs. I softly closed the door, then motioned Barnaby to follow me.

Once outside, I asked, "Who are those men dealing the cards? Do they play cards all night?"

Quietly he answered. "Them in the fancy suits are gamblers from San Francisco who rent the tables from Orrin. They play all comers 'til sunup or later, any game you want to play — poker, faro, three-card monte, blackjack. They're slick as can be, and I betcha they make a lotta money. I know better than to play with 'em! Don't have enough gold, nohow."

We walked around the building, through the front entrance, then stood against the wall to watch the action. The dance floor was filled with couples. About 15 women in white dresses were dancing with assorted men — men from the mines still in their work clothes, men in suits or parts of suits, and all wearing hats that had obviously seen many days of inclement weather. The men danced vigorously with the women in their arms — not gliding across the floor, but stomping with great enthusiasm. No wonder the building was shaking.

I couldn't see the women very clearly, but some of them looked like farm girls—sturdy and plain. Leaning over, I commented to Barnaby, "Those Hurdy-gurdy Girls don't seem to be very pretty, at least from what I can see."

"Don't matter, ma'am. They're women we can dance with, talk to, and it's real nice when they smile back at us."

It was difficult to see Willis through the mass of people, but I could hear his piano, together with the sound of a violin. They were playing "Sweet Betsy From Pike," and I must say Willis' skill on his well-used upright was impressive; he used the full range of the keyboard to accompany the dancers. He played three or four selections, and then everything stopped. In the silence Orrin called out, "Gents, take your ladies to the bar."

At that, everyone rushed for the bar or the tables where Waiter Girls busily served from trays filled with drinks. In less than 10 minutes, Orrin yelled, "Now, gents, take your ladies for a dance." The music began once again, and the floor quickly filled with couples. This time Willis and the violinist were playing a very spirited melody I hadn't heard before.

Barnaby and I moved outside to the cold and misty wind of the night. The streets were damp and a new layer of mud made the walk home more difficult. Hattie was looking anxiously out the door as we arrived and seemed greatly relieved as we approached.

"I was beginning to worry; this weather's getting so bad. But you're just in time for supper." She looked shyly at Barnaby and added, "You're welcome to stay to supper if you like, Mr. Tinker."

Barnaby sheepishly bowed his head, then lifted it to reply, "I'd be pleased to join you, Mrs. McKee. Thankee, ma'am."

The meal was delicious — some of her hot soup, then roast beef, boiled potatoes, carrots and apple sauce. After the gangbusters of a day, I was ravenous and ate like a lumberjack. Hattie had found time to bake a small cake, even after a solid afternoon of work at the store.

Thoroughly content, we enjoyed the last of the coffee at the kitchen table.

I turned to Barnaby, "What's happening at your claim these days? What with all the time you've spent watching over me, have you been able to work on your mine? How's it going?"

He seemed embarrassed and looked about the kitchen before answering. "Well, it ain't goin' too good since you ask, ma'am. Ain't dug up much gold for a while 'cept for a nugget or two, and I gotta get back. When I'm away so much, fellas start sniffin' around my claim. And if I'm away for three days or more, I could lose it. That's the rule."

I was shattered. "Barnaby, you've been spending too much time protecting me. I'll never forgive myself if things go bad for you after you've taken such good care of me."

Hattie was shaking her head in sympathy.

He hastened to say, "I'm real glad to do it, ma'am, just as long as you need me. I don't mean to make you feel bad."

"Dear Barnaby, you've helped me through a difficult time, and now it's time for us to take care of you. Tell me, where is your claim?"

"Oh, 'bout four miles east of here."

"You mean you walk four miles to town every day just to look after me? Well, I don't know how I can ever repay you, but I'm going to try. "

In a flash of inspiration, I pushed back my chair and raced

upstairs to my bedroom. Returning to the kitchen, I placed before Barnaby two of the largest pouches containing my tips.

"Here. I have no idea how much is there, but it's all yours."

Barnaby shook his head. "Ma'am, I just can't do it. You earned this, you keep it."

"No, Barnaby, I want you to use this so you'll have plenty of food and supplies while you work your claim. How about this? Call it an investment. I'll be a partner and back you as long as you need it. When you strike it rich, you can pay me back. What do you think, partner?"

His face brightened considerably. "It sure would be nice to have someone interested in my claim and how it goes. Then I wouldn't feel so alone workin' up there."

We all leaned back in our chairs, quite pleased. Then Hattie added, "Mr. Tinker, I want you to come by my store and get whatever you need. You probably could use a warm coat, some extra blankets, extra boots and socks when your feet get wet. Where do you sleep? Do you have a tent?"

Shaking his head, he replied, "No, ma'am. I fixed me a lean-to outta scraps of wood and canvas, but I should close it up before it gets real cold. Last winter I lived in the mine, back in the tunnel, but that wasn't so nice and it was hard to have a fire goin' and keep warm."

"All right, then," Hattie said firmly. "You get all the tools, nails and canvas you need at the store and pick up what you need at the lumber yard. You just fix yourself a proper place." Then she added, "And while you're at it, take some of that gold and get yourself a mule to help carry everything up to your claim. If you run out of gold, I'll extend you credit and you can consider me a partner, too."

Barnaby was at a loss for words.

I asked, "What kind of a claim do you have? How large is

it?"

"Well, ma'am, it's a good one. It's right on the river; it's part of the mountain that comes right down to the water, and it's about 25 feet across. I built me a nice tunnel going into the mountain, but so far I only got a bit of gold dust or a nugget here and there. But I ain't givin' up. I jus' know there's a good bunch of it in there waitin' for me."

Then he ducked his head in embarrassment. "Sorry, ladies. I ain't talked this much in a long time. I sure do appreciate your kindness."

Hattie went to make more coffee, and though rather tired, I picked up one of the kerosene lamps, excused myself and went to the piano in the parlor to work on music for the duel. I began with a list of 12 possibilities and worked through them, trying different arrangements, judging how a crowd of rough and tough men would enjoy them. Two hours later, I came up with a fair approach to each piece, but could not decide which five to select. I returned to the kitchen to find the dishes done, everything neat and tidy, and Hattie and Barnaby sitting at the table deep in conversation.

Hattie looked up, "Through already? Mr. Tinker and I have just been talking a blue streak. Did you know he's from Missouri, too? Why, it's just like a visit with home folks."

"How wonderful for you," I answered.

"And we've been listening to you play, and I've made up my mind to sneak in the back door of the saloon and listen to the duel. I'm determined to be there and hear everything. The men at the store have been talking about it, and they say the saloon will be packed with people."

Then I yawned and announced, "It's been quite a day and I'm rather tired. I'm heading for bed."

Barnaby quickly rose to his feet. "Sorry to stay so long. Thanks for a fine dinner, Mrs. McKee. G'nite, Mis' Samantha."

It occurred to me to ask, "Barnaby, are you going to walk all the way back to your claim at this time of night in this bad weather? You'll be soaked."

"I'll be just fine, ma'am. Jasper at the livery stable lets me sleep there sometimes when it's late or the weather's bad. Besides, he's got a mule out back he's been wantin' to sell. I'll talk to him first thing in the mornin', then stop at your store, Mrs. McKee, then get myself right back up to my claim."

"I'll get to the store early to tell the boys to give you any credit you need," Hattie added. "Your new partners agree that you'd better get back to work as quick as you can."

Barnaby bade us good night, then Hattie and I each took a lamp and mounted the stairs to our bedrooms. Before we parted, Hattie remarked, "Y'know, that Barnaby isn't half bad once you get to know him." Then she yawned and entered her bedroom.

The next morning over breakfast Hattie began talking. "Samantha, I been thinking about those children and how splendid they looked once they were cleaned up and you cut their hair so nice. It's a real shame there's no one to really take care of them. And those Waiter Girls, why they are just girls, young girls trying to get along in the world."

She took a minute, then continued. "What do you think about inviting them here for lunch? The girls can bring their money to put in my safe, then we can just visit. They can get away from that awful saloon for a change. And they could bring Sumpin and Warren with them." Then she hastily added, "Of course, I wouldn't want it to get around town what we're doing here, but I think it might be enjoyable. What do you think?" She raised her eyebrows and waited for my reply.

"I'm sure they would love to come. The children and I haven't been able to get together. And the Waiter Girls, with the probable exception of Bertha and Zola, would be so pleased to be in a lovely home like this after living in that saloon."

Hattie suggested, "What about tomorrow for Sunday lunch? Do they work? Can they get away?"

"I'll find that out. They shouldn't be working seven days a week, but knowing Orrin I wouldn't be surprised."

We cleaned up the dishes and straightened the kitchen, then I headed for the saloon. Hattie stayed home to work on the store accounts, so I walked alone that day. The skies were clear and the cold and mist from the night before had moved on. Taking a deep breath of the fresh mountain air, I reviewed the panorama about me: the houses, tents and shacks scattered about the surrounding hills and mountain slopes, smoke coming from the chimneys.

As I hung my cloak in the saloon kitchen, I noticed four men sitting at a table on one side of the room. Their clothing indicated they were gamblers. While deep in conversation, they were finishing breakfast and the last of the coffee before them. They paid no attention to me as I walked to the other side of the long room to greet Wong Kee.

"And a good day to you, Wong Kee. How are you today?

With a slight bow he said, "I do plenty work. You want coffee?"

"Would *love* some, if you don't think it would cause another fuss."

"Not today," he said firmly as he handed me a cup filled with the hot brew.

As I sipped the coffee, I asked, "How big is the town or the village where you live. Are there many people there?"

He looked down at his work, but answered, "Many Chinese come here, run from bad times in China. Some work in mines, work where they make beer, chop wood, wash clothes, some cook. Work very, very hard."

Suddenly I was aware of voices from the tables across the

room. I could hear, "Who does she think she is, talking to the Chink that way?"

I turned to see several angry faces and at first was unable to grasp the situation.

Another voice said harshly, "She must be that whore from San Francisco everybody's talkin' about."

They waited for my reaction, and I wasn't about to let it pass. Oh, how I wanted the shadow of John Wayne to help me stand my ground. Mentally I hitched up my gun belt, walked over to the table, looked into the eyes of every man there and said as kindly as possible, "Well, 'everyone' also says that all gamblers are crooked, double-dealing rascals. Is that true?"

The men glared at me in silence, so I plunged ahead.

"I don't believe it's true of all gamblers, even if that's what 'everyone' says. You all look too intelligent to believe vicious gossip."

I paused to glance around the table, trying to read every face staring at me. "I believe that all women are entitled to respect and courtesy until their behavior indicates otherwise. And since you're dressed like gentlemen, I will assume that you know the meaning of those words."

"As for Wong Kee, he was kind to me when I first came to Boone Valley, without friends, funds or family. I feel I should treat him in the same way. In this life, one cannot have too many friends or helpful strangers, and if you gentlemen have ever read the Bible, I think you will find more than a few passages supporting my stance on this."

The men did not respond. Glaring at me, one by one they stood up and headed for the door. One turned and said abruptly, "I don't care what you say, my money's on Willis to win that damn duel of yours. We're giving three to one odds that Willis will whip you good. We intend to collect on those bets!" He was the last to leave the room, and slammed the door behind him.

I turned back to Wong Kee and found him bowing to me. "You most worthy opponent. Take care of tiny dragons good."

"Wong Kee, they had no right to say those things. Prejudice is such a terrible thing. Not only against people of different colors and races, but against women as well."

He turned from his work and looked intently into my eyes. "You good woman. Act different, think different, talk different. Have great knowing about many things."

I asked, "What do you think of me challenging Willis to a duel?"

His reply was thoughtful. "Any fight won without blood is honorable one."

Before I could answer, the door opened and in came the six Waiter Girls, all dressed in a variety of underclothing covered by colorful flannel robes. As they sat at the tables, Wong Kee served them bowls of hot stew and thick slices of bread. Bertha broke away from the group.

"There you are," she spit angrily, "the whore who's tryin' to steal away my kids. Who do you think you are takin' 'em off somewhere, dressin' 'em up, and who knows what else without askin' me? You're tryin' to steal 'em, admit it!"

Once more I found myself involved in a confrontation I certainly didn't want. "Listen to me, Bertha. Mrs. McKee found the children outside in the cold, wet and hungry. You were working and something had to be done. No harm was done or ever will be done to them. We know that you're their mother and always will be; there is no question about that. You should appreciate the fact that three people were willing to help your children when they were in distress."

Bertha began screaming. "You're just a lying whore from San Francisco, and everybody knows it. Stay away from my kids!"

Zola was beside her and joined the chorus. "You whore. Who do you think you are?"

Suddenly there was a huge crash as Wong Kee slammed his largest cleaver on the heavy worktable. The screaming women quieted as he pointed the cleaver at them. "No harm done. Tiny ones are flowers — need sunshine. No fight when there is no harm."

The seated Waiter Girls murmured agreement with Wong Kee. Bertha frowned and turned away, saying, "This ain't none of your business, Chink!" She walked to the other girls to say, "Y'all know I can't take care of my kids when I'm workin' and sleepin'."

Maggie patted her hand as she sat down. "Then why not let Mis' Samantha help you when she can? She didn't do nothin' wicked, and they sure looked extra nice when they brought 'em back."

Bertha just shrugged. I jumped in and told her of Hattie's invitation to have the children for lunch on Sunday. "While they're there, I can play for them, teach them songs, then bring them safely back here in time for dinner. Wouldn't that give you time to rest up after working so hard?"

Looking down at the table, Bertha nodded. "Yeah, I sure could use some extra sleep on Sunday mornin'. But I ain't sayin' yes. I gotta think on it first." She looked over to Zola, and the two conspirators quickly ate their food then left the kitchen.

I turned to the remaining Waiter Girls at the tables — Naomi, Maggie, Flower and Abigail. "If you don't mind giving up some of your day of rest, that lunch invitation includes you four. You can bring the special packages you would like Mrs. McKee to hold for you, then we can have music or just talk. Do you work on Sundays, or do you have a day off?"

Maggie answered bitterly, "Day off? What's that? All Orrin allows us is a few extra hours on Sunday. Most days we start servin' at 3 o'clock, and we're done about three in the mornin' when the

Hurdy-gurdy Girls go home. On Sundays we start work at 6 o'clock."

I was appalled. "That's not work, ladies, that's slave labor. Can't you do anything about it?"

"We tried, but Orrin jus' won't listen."

All my knowledge of the 20th Century fight for fair treatment for women bubbled to the surface of my mind.

"When you come to Hattie's on Sunday, we'll talk about this some more."

They were excited and interested as well as pleased to be invited to one of the nicest homes in Boone Valley.

Just then Willis came through the door and all talking stopped. He looked at me angrily. "Well, where's your list of five things you're gonna play? I already gave mine to Orrin. I've got the five pieces down good and I'm ready for your damn duel. Are you?" I shook my head, and Willis made a disgusted sound and turned his back. It was then that I noticed the crowd was already gathered for my afternoon music. Many were already settled at the tables surrounding the piano with drinks before them. Then I realized that I had not planned the program for the day so I was not sure where to start. But smiling to myself, I sat before the piano and began with a few Beatles songs — "Michelle," "Eleanor Rigby," and then "Yesterday." Then, for my own amusement, I played "You Ain't Nothin' But a Hound Dog" in waltz time, and followed with "Love Me Tender" and "Are You Lonesome Tonight?"

I had made a point not to play any song more than once or twice, since I did not want the music or lyrics to be remembered and carried into the future.

The concert went well. No jeers or lewd remarks. Just a warm response to what I was playing. Never in my other life had there been such appreciation and acceptance, and I loved it! When the program was over, the usual line of men passed by the piano.

More than a few mentioned the duel, that they would "sure be here when it happens."

Someone, probably Corby, had put a large beer stein on top of the piano, and when I turned to go, it was almost half-full of bits of yellow gold. I picked it up and carried it to the bar.

Orrin was there, leaning against the bar and surveying the crowd. I paused to remind him, "Don't forget, tomorrow is my day off. I think it has all been going very well so far. Don't you agree?"

He frowned, looking around at the men in conversational groups at the tables. "We'll see if they still like you next week. They may just get tired of that silly music. Or Willis will show he can play just as good, if not a whole lot better!"

With a broad smile, I answered, "We'll just see about that!" and walked triumphantly from the room.

Chapter Twelve

As I walked back to Hattie's, I reflected on the past week of unexpected circumstances. It had proved challenging, frightening and, at the same time, fulfilling. In my other life, I could not have risen to such challenges and faced them – not without Harland beside me taking charge. Would he live out his life believing that his bride of 20 years had suddenly deserted him? With Connor, Casey, and the strong unforgiving presence of Mother Malcolm beside him, I'm sure he will survive as a wronged and martyred figure.

As I entered Hattie's house, she came from the kitchen wiping her hands. "You must tell me about your day while we eat, but first I have something to show you. Ida Penny came by the store and left the things you ordered." She pointed to several neatly wrapped packages on the small settee in the parlor.

Opening the largest package, I found a dress made of a luscious, multi-printed soft blue material. The three-quarter sleeves had 2-inch cuffs of the same material and was trimmed around the neckline with velvet bows of a deeper blue. The full skirt was also trimmed with the same velvet, three rows running from waist to hem. It was beautifully crafted with its tiny stitches and splendidly executed trim.

"How lovely!" I cried. "Look, Hattie, this is perfect to wear when I play the piano."

"Indeed! Let's see what else she sent."

The next package contained a long skirt in a dark-blue brocade. It was not as full as the dress, but straight and slim looking. As an afterthought, dear Ida had crafted a matching cape that came to the waist. Included was a white cotton shirt with long billowing sleeves, and a neat collar with just a touch of the blue on the two points. The second shirt was fancier, with rows of white lace at the collar and around the cuffs.

Another package contained long panties, full under slips and camisoles, all beautifully sewn. What a joy to have some clothes of my very own.

During dinner, I reported my confrontation with the gamblers. Hattie was amazed. "Heavens, Samantha. I surely don't know how you found the grit to face those men. They're not used to a woman talking back. Of course, you do it in a nice way, but nonetheless, they're not used to a woman setting them straight, no matter how bad they need it."

I didn't dare reveal to her that my mentors were a variety of personable cowboy actors who reflected the straight-as-an-arrow code of the Old West. I only hoped they would have been proud of me, as Hattie seemed to be.

"You know, Hattie. I've just discovered something about myself."

"What's that?"

"I'm not the same Samantha who came to Boone Valley a week ago. The old Samantha could never have challenged Willis to a duel, let alone talk back to those gamblers."

"Now that I think on it, Samantha, you sure have a lot more spunk than when I first brought you into my house. What would your husband say if he could see you now?"

"I think he would frown, scold me severely, and send me to my room!"

We both giggled and Hattie said, "If my Martin could see us in the evenings with the music and the sherry bottle, and the laughing and carrying on, he would have a proper fit, that's for sure." Looking up at the ceiling, she put a hand over her heart and said, "And I only hope that he's having as good a time up there in Heaven as we're having down here!"

Sunday morning dawned beautiful and clear, with just a little cool air remaining from the misty rain of the previous days. Hattie invited me to accompany her to the nine o'clock service at the First Methodist Church. "It'll be good for you to meet some of the other folks in town, and besides I haven't gone myself for several weeks. Reverend Norton won't scold me too much if you're with me."

It seemed like a fine idea — connecting with God. I wasn't sure whether to thank Him or ask for His blessing, but I felt a conversation of some sort was in order.

I wore the new skirt and matching cape, and one of the lovely blouses. In Rosalie's wardrobe I found a black straw hat that completed my outfit.

Hattie was wearing a dark brown brocaded dress with a small brown felt hat and a black knit shawl. She pinned a cameo at the collar and was pulling on brown kid gloves. She looked quite elegant and in control.

I chuckled, "Let's go to church and give the congregation a treat!" And we went out the door arm in arm.

After a short walk through the morning sunshine, we approached a plain, square building of natural wood. Groups of people were coming together and entering the welcoming double doors. Hattie introduced me to Reverend Norton, a tall, lean, dark-haired man with a black mustache over a warm smile. He bowed in greeting.

"You're most welcome, Mrs. Malcolm. Since you're a friend of Mrs. McKee, we're proud to have you join us today."

The interior was pleasant with six rows of benches on each side, and a raised platform where the service took place. There were hymnals available but no organ. It was so fine to hear "Rock of Ages" sung a cappella by this gathering of 30 people.

Reverend Norton ministered to his flock in a smiling, loving way, stressing that sin was not to be a part of their lives, and that they should be mindful of the commandment to love thy neighbors at all times.

Afterward a small gathering mingled outside the church, and Hattie introduced me as Mrs. Samantha Malcolm, a visiting friend. I could not help but take note of these female pioneers and what their journey here and day-to-day life had done to them. Some of their faces were marked with worry and hardship. The wrinkles and creases on their foreheads made them appear old before their time. Their uncovered hands were calloused and misshapen by the horrendous efforts necessary to maintain comfortable homes for husbands and children. I silently blessed them all.

Everyone I met was cordial and obviously in awe of Hattie. Our conversations went well until a woman's husband joined us and blurted, "Well, now, you're the lady who plays the piano at the Majestic Saloon. I heard you play once."

His wife bristled a bit at this information until he assured her, "Don't you fret, Nancy. This lady plays in the afternoons with a chaperone, and she's a crackerjack performer. Plays the loveliest music you ever did hear."

A few more couples joined us and the reaction was the same. The wives were taken aback with the news, but the husbands were reassuring. I was quickly surrounded by several women and Mrs. Norton who wanted to ask about my "concertizing." Hattie stood to one side like a mother hen. Though the women were shocked that I worked in the saloon, they were also curious and sympathetic when I told them that I'd lost my family.

On the way home I asked about Rev. Norton.

"He brought his wife and daughter here three years ago and started his church. Poor soul, he didn't have much of a congregation in the beginning and almost starved until his wife talked him into starting a café where all the miners and merchants could get a decent meal. Della's a fine cook, and with their daughter Mercy helping, they've been doing just fine. I helped them bring up a fine cookstove from Sacramento, and now they're famous for their beef stew and pies."

"Is business good?"

"Norton's Café is chock full every day, and that's how he got his church built. He plans to have a steeple and even a bell very soon."

"He must feed a great many people. Where does he get his supplies?"

"Well, I gave him some of my chickens and a rooster to start, and now he's got quite a flock. Luke brings butter, milk and meat from my farm down the mountain, and I sell him the extra eggs and vegetables I can't use."

I was intrigued. "Could we go there for dinner someday? I'd like to see his café and sample the food."

"I guess we can do it some evening after we're done at the store and the saloon."

Once home, we began fixing lunch for our guests, the young ladies from the saloon. Hattie prepared and roasted chickens, and I gathered ingredients for a potato salad. Soon the potatoes and eggs were boiling on the stove. Since there was no mayonnaise, I used her stock of bacon grease whipped together with vinegar, and the result, I must say, was rather tasty. I garnished the potato mixture with carrot and celery sticks, and my contribution was ready.

I put the large bowl of potato salad and the huge platter of succulent, brown, roasted chicken on the table. Then there was timid knock on the door.

Hattie and I greeted Sumpin and Warren who greeted us with shy smiles. They were followed by Abigail, Flower, Naomi and Maggie. The girls entered shyly, hesitating as they looked about, and Flower seemed a little sad and withdrawn. All were dressed in their Sunday best—dresses neatly pressed, shawls of wool or knitted material, and a variety of hats. Sumpin and Warren were wearing their new clothes.

"Sure is a lovely home, Mrs. McKee. Thanks a bunch for askin' us over," said Abigail coming forward.

"You're most welcome," Hattie answered. "Lunch is all ready and you can come into the kitchen and get your plates. You'll have to bring them back into the parlor to eat since the table won't hold everybody. Come on."

With full plates, we sat in the parlor. Hattie spread two large napkins on the floor for Warren and Sumpin.

After lunch Abigail turned to Hattie. "Mrs. McKee, since you were kind enough to offer to hold our savings for us, we brought 'em along today. Is that all right?"

"You bet it is, ladies. You just come upstairs to my bedroom and we'll put everything away safe and sound."

Hattie led the four girls up the stairs, while Sumpin, Warren and I played songs on the piano. We had a wonderful time until we heard Hattie and the girls coming down the stairs, chattering away like old friends.

Naomi was smiling as she entered the parlor. "Mrs. McKee has a regular safe, and all of our money is put away nice and snug, and everything's recorded in a book, just like a regular bank. It sure eases our minds to know we can put this money here and it'll be there waitin' for us."

Flower had moved nearer to the children, and as she reached out to smooth Sumpin's hair, the sleeve of her dress pulled back and revealed a large bruise just above her wrist. I gasped and moved to take her hand in mine, but she tried to pull the sleeve down even more. I could see the discoloration of the bruise extended another three inches up her arm. She pulled back in shame.

"Flower, my dear girl," I said, "what on earth happened?"

There was a heavy silence until Maggie moved over to stand by Flower, a protective arm about her shoulders. "Orrin was after her last night. He left her alone when she was so young, but last night ..."

Just then Hattie stood up and took Sumpin by the hand. "Come youngsters. I might have cake left over from last night. Let's go to the kitchen and see if we can find it," And with a backward glance at me, she led the children out of the room.

I turned to Maggie and said quietly, "All right, what happened?"

She began slowly, reluctantly. "We shouldn't be talkin' about such things with a lady like you, but it's just the way things are in a place like that."

I motioned for them to sit down and said quietly, "If there's a problem, let's talk about it."

"Well, us girls are supposed to be Waiter Girls, that's what we do, and we don't entertain the men upstairs, though sometimes that's what Orrin wants us to do for his special friends."

I interrupted. "Are there saloons in Boone Valley that provide that kind of ... service?"

"Oh, lots of em," Maggie answered. "There's Whiskey Joe's, Diamond Nelly's, and the Green Clover. But some of the men come in thinkin' that's what us girls are for. It's hard to tell 'em different. But that's not the main problem."

"Is it Orrin?" I asked.

Maggie lowered her eyes and brought her hands together tightly. After some time she looked around at the girls and they nodded for her to continue.

"We know that he goes to them places oftentimes. Other times he pesters one of us girls to ... pleasure him. He's mostly with Zola and Bertha 'cause they don't complain, but all us girls have been with him. Either that or be thrown out in the street, as he always tells us. You must know he's got a bad temper if he don't get things his way."

"Indeed I do."

"Well, this mornin' when we were through workin', he went after Flower. We all try to look after her, but last night he just insisted. He took her by the arm and was draggin' her up to his room and some of us tried to stop him. He was awful mad and hit us, but then I told him that Flower had been feelin' poorly and throwin' up and he stopped. Well, he kept sayin' he had to have one of us. Then Zola come by and said she was willin'. We all know he does her special favors and gives her extra money. She really works at stayin' on his good side. So off they went. Poor Flower's been upset ever since."

We all looked at Flower in sympathy. Embarrassed, she lowered her head and pulled the sleeve of her dress down to hide the bruise.

Naomi spoke up. "It's bad enough having the men pull at us while we're workin', touching us in places we don't want to be touched. The work is hard luggin' those trays and drinks every night, and sometimes we get so tired we can't get enough rest."

I asked, "Where did the dresses and makeup you wear come from? That might have something to do with the way the men treat you."

Abigail answered, "Oh, Orrin had all that stuff brought in from San Francisco, and we know the dresses are gettin' worn and shabby lookin' so we don't look so nice. ...But what's makeup?"

"Oh, sorry," I said. "That's the color you put on your cheeks and eyes. I guess it comes from making up the face with color, shortened to makeup."

"Orrin brought that in, too. He likes to see lots of red on the cheeks and black stuff around the eyes. He says that's the way the saloon girls look in San Francisco."

"Well, it's not very flattering. You are all so pretty without it. And Orrin insists that you wear it?"

"You bet he does. He sets the rules and we got to mind him or get out," Naomi said sadly.

"Y'know, Mis' Samantha," Flower said wistfully, "what you're wearin' today is so pretty. I sure wish I could wear somethin' like that."

The idea was good, and I took it a step further. "You know, ladies, if you all wore something like this — a dark skirt, white blouse, and maybe a pretty apron, no one would doubt that you were indeed Waiter Girls. The clothes would be easy to wash, and it would help your confidence to wear them. It would be like a uniform."

They looked at each other soberly while considering the idea.

"And while we're at it, I could teach you how to use just a little color on your cheeks and around the eyes so you could be as pretty as can be. And if you like, I could trim your hair, just a little, so you can pin it up with a lovely big bow made of the same material as the apron. Would you like something like that?"

Flower breathed, "Wouldn't that be wonderful?" and she smiled for the first time. "I'd sure be proud to wear somethin' like that."

But Abigail, the cautious one, said, "Yeah, but what about Mr. Smithers? He won't take too kindly with us telling *him* what we want to do."

"Ladies," I suggested, "you can certainly ask. In fact, you can write it up as a petition, everyone sign it, and tell him exactly what you want. You can even get some of the customers to sign it."

Then Maggie stated the obvious. "Mr. Smithers would never agree. We girls don't have a say about anything — our food, clothes, hours we work. He tells us what to do, and there's no questions asked or wanted."

Then I asked, "What about your family or friends? Do you all have somewhere to go if things get bad?"

Abigail sadly shook her head. "All us girls are on our own. If we have families, they don't want to see us when they know what we're doin' to earn money."

I felt it was time to educate these used and abused ladies. Going to the kitchen door, I called, "Hattie, you'd better come in. I think you would like to hear this."

Then turning to the girls, I began, "My dear friends, let's get comfortable because I have a lot to tell you. I'm going to fill you in on some wonderful new ideas, starting with something called the Constitution."

Chapter Thirteen

I had read about the vital role women played in the settling of America, starting with the Pilgrims. Those women were confronted by an overwhelming wilderness in which they created homes for their families. Many hard years of backbreaking work passed before cold, starvation and harsh living conditions were overcome to allow a modicum of comfort. As civilization slowly crept across the continent, cabins and shelters had to be wrenched from a resisting environment. They fought to plant the gardens and crops necessary to maintain life, but their bounty could be taken away by one rainstorm, blizzard or drought.

How those women must have fought, giving daily of their energy, while countless fell by the wayside, overcome by exhaustion, fever or childbirth in the most primitive conditions.

I was aware of all this, but now I was seeing firsthand what it was costing those women who arrived, with or without their men, to be part of the Gold Rush. Whatever parts they were playing, none of them were easy. Those who came by ship or land and survived often buried husbands or children along the trail. Women came from Mexico, Peru, China and other lands for the sole purpose of providing physical comfort to the hordes of prospectors, adventurers and gamblers. Few landed on their feet with their health or the means to sustain life. I could not share these thoughts with the four young girls, but only hold this understanding within me.

What I was hearing that day in Hattie's parlor was the cruel reality of life in the new settlements. Women were being used with no thought given to their comfort or well-being. There were a few, I'm sure, who were able to marry miners who struck it rich, and live out their lives in relative comfort. But those who gave of themselves in the saloons or brothels were subject to the whims of the men who dominated them.

The Waiter Girls before me needed hope and a sense of the future, but what could be possible for them in the years to come?

Upon questioning, I found that all four girls were only vaguely aware of the magnitude of the document that was signed in 1789, just 63 years earlier. Hattie had enough schooling to know of Ben Franklin, Thomas Jefferson, and the others who created and signed the Constitution, but she was not sure of the details.

"Think of it, ladies. This document said in very clear terms that all men were created equal. That they have the right to life, liberty, and the pursuit of happiness." I paused to be clear on the facts I could give them. "This, my dear friends, does not include women, not in this day and age."

All eyes were focused on me, hanging on every word. "However, it may cheer you to know that there are some people, a growing number in fact, who feel very strongly this kind of freedom should include women. This has not happened yet, but perhaps some time in the future women's rights will be recognized. So let us hope we will all live long enough to see this happen."

From the expressions on the faces before me, I could see these concepts gave them a tremendous plateful of food for thought. There was a long silence until Naomi said hesitantly, "D'ya know what I'd really like? For us to have rules about how we should be treated at the saloon. For instance, the men shouldn't touch us the way they do."

Maggie inserted, "Yeah, and they shouldn't expect us to sit on their laps, or take 'em upstairs, or go home with 'em for the night if we don't want to. Some just won't take 'no' for an answer."

Abigail announced, "I heard about a saloon owner in Colorado who has house rules that everyone has to follow. Not only for how the girls should be treated neither. If a guy gets so drunk he can't stand up, he ain't served no more liquor and they take him outside to sit on the road. Same for anyone who starts a fight. And the gamblin', he won't let married men, especially fathers, lose all their money."

Maggie stood up and announced, "Yeah, that's just what we need. House rules, not only for us, but for the Hurdy-gurdy Girls. They get pretty roughed up some nights. I seen the bruises they get." There were sounds of agreement all around.

"And you know what else?" Abigail continued. "This nice man in Colorado lets the poor children 'n' orphans come in mornin's and pick up all the coins and nuggets they find on the floor!"

"I'd sure like to work for him," Flower said wistfully.

"You know, young ladies," I said, "there's power in numbers. If you all come together with a set of rules you would like for the Majestic, Orrin would have to listen. Tell him you'd go elsewhere if he didn't agree."

Level-headed Maggie suggested, "Well, maybe Mr. Smithers wouldn't listen to the four of us, but if we could get the Hurdy-gurdy Girls to join us, he'd be in a spot if all us girls told him. What d'ya think, Mis' Samantha?"

"No doubt about it. If you all stood firm, he'd be in a difficult position if you threatened to walk out. Why don't we start by writing out some of the rules you would like?"

Hattie stood. "Why don't I put the children in another room with some picture books. Then I'll get a pencil and some paper and we can start right now."

There was a buzz of conversation, everyone talking at once. Hattie returned and began writing, and within thirty minutes there was a tentative list of demands to present to Orrin.

1. All Waiter Girls and Hurdy-gurdy Girls will be

well-mannered and agree to serve and dance with all customers with smiles and good grace. It will be understood that no other services will be asked of them.

2. All girls are to be treated with respect and not be touched below the neck or above the knees, except what is customary for dancing.

3. Drunks who cannot sit or walk straight will be asked to leave or be taken out.

4. Customers who argue loudly or fight will be asked to leave or be taken outside.

5. Uniforms will be worn by the Waiter Girls, and they will be kept neat and clean.

Although all agreed that this was a good start, they also recognized that this approach would take more thought and discussion. Hattie invited them all to come the following Sunday to share more ideas.

I suggested, "Why don't we invite Ida Penny to come as well and bring samples of materials for uniforms? That would help you make some solid decisions regarding the uniforms and the wording of your demands."

The resulting smiles and comments continued until our guests headed for the door at 4:00, ready to return to work, but with hope for better working conditions.

As Hattie closed the front door behind them, we shared quizzical expressions and raised eyebrows. "Samantha, my dear, what have you done to those girls? You've given them a grain of hope, but there's trouble ahead. Any changes at the Majestic won't come easy."

I sighed when I answered. "You're right, Hattie. But these girls deserve more than the heavy-handed treatment they've been getting. And what's the alternative? Let them go on the way things are, or open their minds to other possibilities, other choices?"

"You may be right," she agreed. "We shall see."

When we settled down to a quiet evening of rest and reflection, my thoughts turned to the week ahead and the problems that could be waiting. I expressed my concerns to Hattie.

Hattie interrupted. "My girl, I can't help thinking what you've done for me these past two weeks. This big house doesn't seem so lonely, and there's so many new things to think about or look forward to. You brought in sweet music and new friends after years of silence. I'm so beholden to you, I just can't say!" Her eyes misted over, and she dabbed at them with a small hankie.

"Now, Hattie, it works both ways. Look what you've done for me. Took me in when I had nowhere to go, gave me a place to sleep, fed and clothed me. Where would I be if it wasn't for your kindness? There have been major changes in my life as well. And do you know what? I'm enjoying all of them!"

Hattie smiled through her tears. "Me, too." Then she stood up suddenly and headed for the kitchen. "And I think it's time to bring out the sherry bottle and celebrate!"

We shared another evening of good talk, good music, good sherry, and a general acknowledgment of the changing structure of our lives. I was tempted to tell this lady who I really was and where I came from, but something held me back. It was not yet time. Someday she would hear and accept my story, and it would change her life even more.

The next morning I sprang from my bed, ready to face the day. I washed up in the china basin, combed my hair, dressed, then paused to look in the mirror. *Here you go, Samantha. I think you're about ready for anything that comes to you today. Onward and upward, kiddo!*

Hattie had hot coffee and oatmeal waiting, and together we

planned our day.

I announced, "I think I'll go into town early and stop by Ida Penny's shop and pay for my new clothes. Then I'll look over any material she can suggest for the Waiter Girls. And, if it's all right with you, I'll invite her to lunch Sunday."

As we walked to town together, Hattie entered her already busy store and I continued down the wooden walkway. Farther down and a little beyond the saloon I came to Ida's shop. She was busily working and greeted me with a happy smile. Her blue eyes shone brightly behind her gold-rimmed glasses.

"Good morning to you, Samantha! And how do you like your new clothes?"

"Ida, they are delightful and fit perfectly. I couldn't be more pleased with the beautiful work you do."

Bringing out the leather pouch that held my gold, I watched as she expertly measured the bright metal. From my point of view, it didn't seem like much, but she seemed satisfied with the settled amount.

Ida thought that uniforms for the Waiter Girls was a splendid idea. She had all sorts of ideas about styles and colors that would be easy to maintain, and she brought out bolts of colorful gingham and calico to consider.

"And I'll need another pretty dress to wear when I play. I wore Rosalie's dresses all last week, and this week I'll wear the lovely blue one you sent. Don't start anything just yet, though, because my trial week ends on Wednesday and I'm not sure Orrin will want to keep me."

Ida exploded at that. "Well, I hope Orrin Smithers is not so short-sighted that he'll let you go! From what I hear, that place is filled every afternoon. And the duel between you and Willis has everyone talking. What a wonderful scheme that was!"

"Ida, you never know what Orrin will do, and we don't get

along too well as it is. Even if I win the duel with Willis, I may lose my job."

Ida brought out samples of bright brocades, polished cottons, silks and satins. We selected two that would make suitable "working" dresses and she put them aside until my future was more secure.

From Ida's I stopped by the saloon to see Willis. I found him practicing at my piano. I suggested to him that if the playoff went well, we could do a duet for an encore. He scoffed at the idea with a few rude comments, but I gradually persuaded him to select something that he knew and already played well. He began "Sweet Betsy From Pike" on the upper keys, and after playing it through the first time, I joined him on the lower keys and together we developed a very interesting arrangement. By the time we finished, he could not hide his pleasure. But then he left the piano abruptly. However, I called him back before he went too far.

"Willis," I began, "when do you think you'll be ready for the playoff?"

He seemed to like being asked, and after some thought he gruffly suggested the following Saturday afternoon. That would give us another four days to rehearse and work on the music we had selected. We hadn't noticed Orrin standing behind us until he came forward and took over.

"This is my saloon and I decide on what goes on here. I say this ridiculous duel will be held next Saturday at 3 o'clock. That'll give me time to pass the word around town and order extra seating and supplies."

So it was settled and there was nothing more to say. Willis walked off, but as I rose to leave, Orrin pushed me back in the chair frowning. "Don't you leave, Missy. You and I have to have a little talk."

He grabbed a chair, brought it around and sat, positioning it so that I was blocked next to the piano.

"Woman, what's this Zola tells me about you having a secret meetin' with my girls yesterday?"

Without flinching (which took a great effort), I looked into his dark eyes and said as calmly as I could, "Why such a fuss? The girls came for lunch. They brought the two children so Bertha could get some sleep, so what's so menacing about that?"

Orrin raised his voice. "In case you ain't noticed, I control these girls and they do what I tell 'em, and I don't need no busy-body tellin' 'em otherwise. I won't have you comin' in here giving them crazy ideas, do you hear me?"

I couldn't help but hear since he was yelling, but I held my ground and made eye contact the best I could.

He went on. "And so help me, if I hear you tellin' 'em things they shouldn't hear, I'll kick your ass right out of here. I don't care if the men think you play so good. You'll be out on the street and have a few bruises to show for it!"

Just then Corby appeared by me and said as positively as he could, "Mis' Samantha, Mrs. McKee is at the back door waitin' for you."

I stood up, pushed back my chair, and reached for his hand. "Thank you so much, Corby. It's time for me to go."

Orrin stood as well and snarled, "We ain't through talkin' yet, woman!"

As Corby helped me out of the tight arrangement of chairs, I replied, "Oh, yes we are, Mr. Smithers. Goodbye for now." And I walked away, holding Corby's hand tightly for support. When we reached the bar, I managed to say, "Corby, you're an angel. Thank you!"

He nodded with great understanding.

Hattie was waiting outside. As we walked down the street, I reported the exchange I'd had with Orrin, word for word. Her reaction was the same as mine. "How did Zola find out about our talking with the girls?"

"None of them would have told her, so she must have been listening to them talk together."

This was an unexpected development and I was concerned. "If Orrin finds out before the girls are ready to present their demands, he will stop everything."

We decided to have lunch at Norton's Café and continued our discussion. We were served a generous portion of the most delectable chicken and dumplings I have ever eaten. The handwritten menus at Norton's Café were interesting. They featured scrapple, buckskin hash, Boston baked beans, johnnycakes, fried mush, suet pudding, cornhusker brisket, quail and grouse pie, beef stew, bacon and eggs, and rabbit and duck stew (when available). Not at all bad for a remote town high in the Sierra Nevadas.

The café was filled with a mix of men, from miners in their dirt-stained shirts and pants, to men in suits, white shirts and ties, all eating with gusto. The miners were undoubtedly tired of their usual meals of hardtack, salt pork, beans, bacon and pancakes which, I understood, was standard fare at the diggings. Mercy Norton was busily serving the crowded tables, and her mother Della could be seen hard at work at the enormous black stove in the kitchen.

Lunch ended with a cup of powerful coffee, then we walked home in thoughtful silence.

Once inside the house, Hattie turned to me. "My girl, be very careful when Orrin's around. We must be on our guard when we see the girls next Sunday. I'll give some thought on how and where we can get together with Ida Penny and keep on with the planning. Do you think you should play at the saloon today?"

"I don't know why not. Barnaby isn't around to see me home, but perhaps I can get Corby or Elmo to take me."

"Don't worry. I'll either come for you, or have one of my

men at the store pick you up. But now you get yourself ready to go back to that place, and I'll walk you there myself!"

I dressed carefully in the new blue gown. With a minimum of makeup, I looked rather smashing, though my heart wasn't into feeling glamorous. I was determined to carry on with the best grit and fortitude that I could pull together.

That afternoon the area around my piano was crowded as usual, and all selections were received with warm applause and shouted praise. However, once I was into the second set, Orrin made it a point to pompously interrupt my playing and silence the protesting crowd.

"I've a special announcement to make," he said grandly, relishing the attention. "I've decided that we've waited long enough for this so-called duel to take place. I've set the date and time to be next Saturday at 3 o'clock sharp."

This announcement was followed by cheers, and it was clear that the word would spread quickly. He smiled at me smugly as he turned away, and made a gesture with his hand that allowed me to resume playing with his permission. I was seething, but managed to finish out the afternoon. To my satisfaction, everything I played after that was greeted with even greater enthusiasm.

After the last note, I stood to leave but was surrounded by a crowd of men asking questions. Was I ready? Was Willis ready? Was I nervous? Did I think I would win? What could I say except to invite them all to come Saturday and see for themselves. I caught Orrin's eye during this time and managed a smug smile of my own.

Turning to leave, I noticed that well-dressed man sitting at one of the tables near the entrance. His face was familiar to me now. Compared to the shabby and worn suits and stained garb worn by the miners and shopkeepers, this man's clothes stood out — not like the gamblers, but with good taste in a well-made tan jacket, patterned vest, white shirt and black string tie. The soft brown, modified Stetson sat firmly on his head, just above his eyebrows. Rather than the beards or full sideburns worn by many of the men, he sported a nicely trimmed mustache — not too thick, but just right.

When I approached the long bar, I quietly asked Corby if he knew the man. Corby reported it was Grant Douglas, owner of the largest brewery in town. Corby didn't know much more except that the man seldom came into the saloon, and was impressed by his personality and behavior. In fact, his feeling for the man bordered on respect.

As I walked through the door leading to the kitchen, I looked back at Grant Douglas and found he was still watching me. Strangely, a rush of feeling swept through my body and my heart began beating rapidly. Being a married lady of some twenty years, I hadn't had such feelings in almost as many. It felt wonderful, but I wasn't sure what I was going to do about it.

The sun had set and the streets were dark when I stepped outside. As she had promised, Hattie was waiting accompanied by one of her clerks, Frank Newhall. We had a safe and rapid walk home.

Over dinner, I casually asked if she knew Grant Douglas.

"Know him! Martin and I got to know him when we first came to Boone Valley. He seemed kinda lost, walking around town wondering what to do with himself — look for gold or settle down right here."

"How did he get here, Hattie? Did he cross the plains as you did, or by ship to San Francisco?"

"Now that I think on it, he never did say. We were all busy settling in. But he was a help to me and Martin getting the store started, though it was only wood and canvas to begin with. Then he worked for Titus Boone for a time, helping to build up the town." She frowned as she began to recall the details of that time.

"One day he rushed over to Martin and me at the store, saying he knew what he wanted to do. Since so many saloons were popping up, he said he would build a brewery and make beer. I recall he said that was something he really knew about, though he didn't say how. Martin and Titus loaned him the money to get started. On one of his trips to Sacramento, Martin found farmers who were growing hops and barley in the valley, so Mr. Douglas hurried on down there and found dependable suppliers. He sure is a go-getter, that's the truth. He and Titus, and some of the gold seekers needing to earn money, built the brewery, and in no time it was putting out beer by the barrels."

She interrupted her report to refill our cups with hot coffee. "We didn't see much of him after that, but he paid Martin and Titus back and then some. Everyone in town knows him. A real nice gentleman, and nary a cross or bad word has been heard from or about him. Why do you ask?"

"He was in the saloon today while I was playing, and he seemed to kind of keep to himself. I just wondered who he is. Corby told me his name."

"Why Samantha, girl, what's happening here? You're a married lady!" She eyed me suspiciously but said no more.

For the next three afternoons as I was playing, I made a point of looking over the crowd, and there was Grant Douglas sitting with his back against the wall, listening and watching me. He seemed to come early to sit at the same table by the door.

When I saw him on the third day, I smiled, and he in return doffed the brown hat and nodded his head. My hands were shaking when I turned back to the piano, so that the first selection came out slow while I gained control of myself.

Early Friday, I hurried to the saloon to tune the piano. The saloon was very quiet with one night bartender on duty and two tables of men playing poker. I began to work on the piano, concentrating on the tone and placing every note correctly. I was so focused on the work that I didn't notice when Grant Douglas walked up and stood at the back of the piano facing me. When I looked up, he put both elbows on the lid, leaned over to look deeply into my eyes and said, very softly, "Play it again, Sam. Play 'As Time Goes By.'"

My world came to a sudden stop at that moment, and all I could do was put one hand on my chest and say very softly, "Oh, my!"

Chapter Fourteen

I sat there, mouth open, hand over my heart, and stared at this man. His eyes were intense, looking deeply into mine. His expression was searching, questioning. He began to speak quietly.

"Now, take it easy. I know it's a shock and I can hardly believe it myself. When I first heard your music, I couldn't believe my ears. You were playing my music, not the music of 1852. Then I watched and listened to what you were playing, and I was sure. Do you realize what I'm saying?"

All I could do was nod.

He went on. "We can't talk now, but we must get together to make sense of all this, sort it all out. Don't you agree?"

Once more, all I could do was move my head in agreement, but now I was able to see that under his dark brown eyebrows were soft brown eyes that were very kind. His lips were nicely shaped under his full brown mustache, and I watched them carefully and waited for him to go on.

"How much longer will you be here?"

My mouth was dry but I managed to say, "About another hour, maybe less."

He whispered, "I'll wait for you outside and walk you home, or to some place where we can talk. Is that all right?"

Once more I could only manage a nod.

"All right. Take it easy and try not to hit the panic button. What we have here is a mystery to unravel. I'll see you later. Okay?" He smiled, tipped his hat and walked to the door.

I could not watch him walk away because my body was still in shock. I grabbed my shoulders and sat numbly before the keyboard going over his words. Could it be that someone else had been caught in the past as I had been? How did it happen for him? And are there others?

As I struggled to bring my scattered thoughts together, Willis suddenly appeared and pulled a chair to the keyboard.

"You ain't gonna outplay me tomorrow if I can help it. You'll have to go some to do it."

Pulling my scattered forces together, I managed, "Willis, you are quite talented, and it will be a challenge to come out the winner. But who knows? It may turn out to be a victory for both of us. Let's go over the encore once more."

We played through our arrangement of "Sweet Betsy From Pike." Then Willis left the piano smirking, full of himself. My thoughts were still on the handsome man with the soft brown eyes who was waiting outside. Hands shaking, my mind racing, I hurried to finish tuning the remaining keys.

Cautiously checking the watch in my pocket, I could see it was just past 9:30, and I knew that the next few hours would be dazzling. My body was numb with anticipation and fear combined.

Walking toward the street, I found my legs were not functioning as they should, my knees were weak and the muscles seemed to have a mind of their own. But there he was, waiting just outside the front entrance of the saloon. He walked over quickly, took my arm and guided me down the street.

For the benefit of the scattered of people on the street and walkways, he tipped his hat and said, "Good morning, Mrs. Malcolm. You're just in time for our meeting. It's just down the street a little ways." Then in a lower voice he continued, "There's a Wells Fargo office not far from here. An attorney friend, Andrew Locke, rents an office there, and he's letting me use it so we can talk uninterrupted. Is that all right with you?"

Still without a firm grasp on the situation, I could only nod, hoping that I did not look like an idiot. As we walked, however, I did note that he looked down at me from a height of at least 6 feet 2. He cut a rather striking figure in the 1850's clothes.

After a short walk, we entered one of the few brick buildings on the street. Inside was a hustle and bustle of activity and people waiting patiently at a counter. My escort waved to the man behind the counter, then guided me through a door into a small office containing a narrow desk and two chairs. Closing the door behind him, he motioned me to one of the chairs and we both sat down.

A few moments of very pregnant silence passed while we carefully inspected each other. He finally leaned forward and spoke. "Well, Dorothy, I have a feeling we're not in Kansas anymore. What do you think?"

Upon hearing those familiar words, all tension left my body and I relaxed, laughing and clapping my hands.

"All right! All right! This is like meeting a friend in a foreign country. Where are you from? How long have you been here? How did you get here?"

He held up one strong hand to stop my chattering. "First of all, my full name is Sheridan Grant Douglas. As you might guess, my father was a serious Civil War buff. Once settled here, I simplified it to Grant Douglas. My family called me Sherry, my ex-wife called me Sheridan, but my friends, back where I come from, called me Grant. Take your pick. And I understand your name is Samantha. Would you mind if I call you Sam?"

"That will be just fine," I managed. "And I'll call you Grant. You look more like a Grant than a Sheridan or Sherry."

"Fine and dandy with me. Secondly, I have a feeling we'll know each other quite well by the time we figure out why the hell we're here and what cosmic forces brought us here in the first place. We have much to tell each other."

After a pause, he asked, "How long have you been here?"

Thinking a moment, I replied, "Twelve or 13 days. Actually, it seems like a lifetime."

"Too right. At times it seems like I've been here forever, and then I remember all too clearly what was left behind, and those days are hard to take. It's been rough not having anyone to share this gut-wrenching situation with."

I asked about his friend, Andrew Locke. "Have you told him about any of this?"

"There have been times when I've been sorely tempted. He's a good man and a good friend to me, but I've never reached a point where I could open up about any of this. But let's start with you. Tell me your story."

And so I began the story of my life — Harland, my boys, Mother Malcolm, what it was like being the wife of a hardware tycoon, and how my life began to change with the overnight trip to Boone Valley. I included Warren and Sumpin, Wong Kee, and how Hattie had become a true friend. I don't know why I gave him so many details, but I felt some of the facts might be relevant to what had happened to the two of us.

He listened intently, asked few questions, and nodded with understanding when I described the process of adapting to 1852, along with some of the details of my work at the Majestic, the adversarial relationship with Orrin, the Waiter Girls, the knowing and spiritual awareness of Wong Kee, and the pending piano duel.

When I finished, he shook his head and smiled. "Sam, I do admire how you've toughed your way through all of this. I don't believe that Boone Valley has ever seen a woman with your grit before. You're giving them all lessons on how to treat a lady. Good for you!"

His words were like a pat on the back. I was not used to being complimented and could not help but smile with delight.

He smiled back and continued. "I heard about a new girl

playing the piano at the Majestic, but I wasn't curious enough to come over. Then several days ago I heard about the duel. That's what brought me over to check you out. The duel is tomorrow, isn't it?"

I sighed. "Yes it is, and it will either be a major event, or a fiasco. I'm not sure which. Will you be there?"

"Now that I know you, I wouldn't miss it for the world. Would it make you nervous, my being there?"

"Quite the opposite. It would be like having a friend from home to cheer me on. Sit in the back like you usually do so I won't be distracted."

"Sure thing." He smiled. "It is so great to be able to talk openly like this with no restrictions. I feel we could talk all night; there's so much I want to know."

I cautioned, "Right now there isn't much time left. I must hurry to Hattie's and change, then get back to the saloon for the afternoon program." Pulling the watch from the pocket of my dress, I noted it was almost 12. "I really must be on my way."

Taking the watch from my hand, he looked at it fondly. "You can't imagine how great it is to see something like this. The battery in mine gave out two years ago, and I really miss it." Then handing it back, he stood. "Let me walk you home and we'll talk along the way. Just like two friends, and that shouldn't cause any gossip. "

I laughed. "And on the way we can think of a plausible story to tell Hattie so she won't be scandalized when she sees us together."

Out the door and down the busy, dusty streets we walked, engaged in an animated, highly involved conversation all the way. Grant told some of his story.

"Sam, I love to fish, and I've been to streams and lakes all through these mountains and caught some beauties. Usually I'm with friends, but this time I came alone. This was four years ago. So, I stumbled onto this ghost town, and my Jeep — which usually performs like a trouper — died on me. The transmission went out, and there I was without a phone to call the auto club, or anyone else." He smiled. "You didn't happen to see a rusty old Jeep when you came into town, did you?"

"Didn't see anything like that, sorry. But, didn't you have a car phone? That's all the rage now, that is, then."

He laughed. "Sure, and this was when they were becoming so popular. I was in the process of getting one, but things got so busy I put it off, planning to take care of it when I returned from this trip. So here I am."

I was impatient to hear all of his story. "Please start at the beginning and tell me everything. Where are you from?"

Sticking his thumbs into his belt, he began, "Well, ma'am, I was born and raised in Sacramento, just north of where you were living. Went to school there, then got my degree at the University of California in Berkeley. Since San Francisco was just across the bay and a lot more challenging than Berkeley or Sacramento, I began working there and, through a series of happenstances, ended up with the Golden Brew Corporation. You've heard of it?"

"Of course. It's 'The Beer with the Golden Personality,' according to the ads on TV. My favorite drink is, was, sparkling cider, which makes me rather square."

"Not at all. That's a good vintage, and after several glasses you can still drive home safely." We both chuckled at this.

"But get back to your story. Were you married? Did you have any children?"

"I was married 15 years to a very nice lady, and the first 10 years were happy, but during the next five the marriage sort of crumbled. Two great children, girls — Christie and Leslie. My wife and I were divorced six years ago. She was very ambitious socially, and has since married a highly successful stockbroker. From what I hear, he's not tall and handsome, but he's given her the lifestyle she wanted. The girls are both in college in the east and, when I last spoke with them, they were happily settled in their selected colleges and dating the local boys. They both have good sense and I think they'll be just fine. At least I hope they have been fine these last four years. God, I do hope they're all right!"

He stopped and looked off into space. "I can only imagine what they might have been thinking since I disappeared. They could be out of college by now, maybe working or married, and I'm not there to be with them, or won't be. Jeez, this time scramble gives me a headache. The bad days are when I can't get these thoughts out of my head." We continued walking.

I shook my head and agreed. "I'm going through my own sense of loss where my sons are concerned. There is no way to avoid it."

"But tell me," I moved to a lighter note. "How did you get into the business of making beer for the saloons?"

"That was easy enough once I got myself together and the idea started, and that was a few days after I landed here. Here I was, like you, with a wallet full of money and credit cards, all useless. Golden Brew wasn't the largest brewery in the country, but it put out a first-class product and had an excellent reputation. I began as an apprentice in the plant where primary mixing and fermentation was done, then learned about priming, bottling, and aging. During those first years, I continued my education at night, received an MBA, was promoted to supervisor, then to plant manager. In time I went on to the corporate level. That was about the time my wife found it embarrassing to be married to a man engaged in the production of beer. It didn't suit her image."

"But it sounds like you were on a strong career path, on your way to the top."

He stopped walking and hit the palm of his hand with his fist. "Doggone it! I'd just made first vice president, and that damned fishing trip seemed a great way to celebrate. That night I put my sleeping bag under a tree near my Jeep, and after a short prayer to the powers that be to make my Jeep usable, I slept well. But, I woke up in 1849!"

He stopped and pointed to the rows of rough housing cluttering the sides of the mountain surrounding us. "Boone Valley was only a few tents and shacks in those days, but it grew, man, did it grow! Like a baby elephant! Saloons began popping up, and it didn't take any brains to see that the demand for beer would be heavy and constant."

He continued. "I don't know what I would have done if it hadn't been for Titus Boone, and Martin and Hattie McKee. With their help I found sources for the main ingredients, and started producing beer. It took awhile since I didn't have the capability to test the batches and create a consistent product. But I found ways, and now what we produce is first class, if I say so myself!"

"And now you're the Beer Baron of Boone Valley. A big man around town!"

He laughed. "I guess I am. I'm doing just fine, well known, providing beer to eight saloons, and I've got a good crew I can depend on. I pay them all quite well, so they're less likely to run off and search for gold."

We came to Hattie's house and I ushered Grant through the front door. We found her in the kitchen and she looked surprised and then pleased when she realized Grant was with me.

"Hattie, Mr. Douglas was in the saloon this morning, and since he's an old friend of yours, I introduced myself. He was kind enough to walk me home."

"Well, he's sure enough welcome here any time. Have some coffee?"

"Just a bit," he responded. "I've got business to take care of pretty soon."

"Hattie," I started, "we found we both came from the same general area. It's like talking with someone from home."

That was not quite the right thing to say, I discovered, since Hattie took over quickly.

"You don't say." She turned to Grant as she poured the coffee. "Well, did you know her husband? Do you have any idea where he is so they can get together?"

Glancing at me, he spoke, "Unfortunately, no. I didn't know the man or his family, and we lived too far apart to know the same people. But I sympathize with her plight and will do all I can to help her."

"Well, that's a blessing right there."

He hurried to change the subject by saying, "Hattie, you should see how this lady charms everyone who comes to hear her play. She's the best that I've ever heard."

"Well, I'm not surprised. She plays for me here many a night, and that makes me quite a lucky lady, having these evening concerts all to myself."

I jumped in, "This lady is very special to me, Grant, and we've become the best of friends."

"Grant! You two on a first name basis already? That's mighty interesting."

"Now, Hattie, don't get excited. Mr. Douglas and I seemed to connect in a very nice way, and having you as a mutual friend, it's almost like family. He's been telling me that wherever he goes people are talking about the duel. The playoff could be a big event." Grant finished his coffee and stood ready to leave when Hattie stretched out an arm to stop him.

"While you were gone, Samantha, something occurred to me and it's good that Grant is here to help out. I believe you've overlooked something very important regarding the duel."

Grant resumed his seat, and our eyes were pinned on Hattie,

waiting for her to continue.

"Samantha, my girl, you and Willis are going to play your music to see who will be the best. True?"

Grant and I both agreed.

"Then tell me this, young lady. Just who will make that decision? Orrin?"

I was a bit abashed. "Well, I thought the crowd would decide."

Grant stepped in. "Hattie's right. That may not work. We all know Orrin, and he's capable of manipulating people, even the large crowd that will fill the Majestic tomorrow."

I panicked. "What can we do this late? Is there any one person who could judge the music fairly, and stand by his decision against Orrin?"

Grant was thoughtful. "You're right, one person couldn't handle it. But, three people could." He stood and began to pace the floor. "How does this sound, ladies. We get three men who are well known and respected in Boone Valley. Let them decide." He warmed to his solution. "Each time someone plays, they will be judged on a scale of one to ten, ten being the highest number for approval. Then at the end, add up the numbers and there will be no question that the duel was judged fairly."

A wave of relief washed over me. "Mr. Douglas, that is a perfect solution. Now, who do you suggest for the three judges?"

He raised a finger and said, "I know just the men. Number one, Lawyer Andrew Locke. Number two, Rev. Luke Norton. Number three, Aaron Ross. Everyone knows Aaron is the most fair and honest man in town. And many times when I go into his assay office, he's working away and humming a tune. He's a good man and I'm sure he'd be happy to judge for you."

Hattie was delighted. "A perfect solution, I must say. Don't you agree, Samantha?"

"I couldn't be more pleased and relieved. And Mr. Douglas, would you please notify those gentlemen and, most troublesome of all, Orrin Smithers? I have a feeling he will not be happy at all."

Grant stood. "I'm heading back to town now, and it will be my pleasure to notify these gentlemen. I think they will be most happy to be part of your big occasion, Mrs. Malcolm. Then I will stop by the saloon and inform Orrin that three outstanding citizens of Boone Valley will play an important part in this duel."

He stood and smiled, "Ladies, please excuse me. There are important errands I need to take care of."

And he went on his way.

Hattie stirred the large pot on the stove. "Do you have time for some beef stew before dressing for work?"

A bowl of beef stew and a glass of milk later, I rushed up the stairs to get ready. My watch showed I had only 30 minutes before my afternoon concert.

Entering the saloon just at 1:00, I found the chairs and tables around my piano filled and there was a buzz of conversation. As I passed the bar, Corby caught my eye and said, "They've been comin' in for the past hour. It seems almost everybody in town wants to look you over and listen to what you might play tomorrow. And you should see Willis struttin' 'round braggin' about how he's gonna show you up. Be careful, Mis' Samantha."

"I'm not worried," I assured him."

As I stepped up to the piano, the gathering quieted. I stood before the keyboard and smiled at the faces before me, sensing that a statement of some kind was expected.

"Gentlemen," I began. "Thank you for coming today. You may have heard that we are having a special concert tomorrow. Somehow I feel that you are already familiar with the circumstances and what it will accomplish."

There was a ripple of laughter through the crowd.

"I hope you all will be able to join us tomorrow and celebrate whatever victory there may be. As for the music I'll be playing today, I'll keep the theme happy and positive."

The rest of the afternoon went well, and after the last selection, I stood and turned to find that many of the men wanted to talk to me. There were compliments, questions, awkward comments, bits of conversation. But all were most kind and anxious to cheer me on for the duel tomorrow.

Grant worked his way through the crowd to say quietly, "See you outside and I'll walk you home." And he disappeared.

Moments later as I turned to leave, I found that the beer stein on the top of the piano was filled more than halfway with nuggets, coins and gold dust. I had almost forgotten that this was part of my income, and probably more than half of the salary that Orrin had committed to pay me. I would have to discuss my salary with Orrin very soon. I decided it would be best to wait until after the duel, and ask Hattie to be with me as a witness and for moral support.

It was comforting to find Grant waiting, all smiles. He commented as he took my arm, "You should have seen Willis busy at the other end of the room anxiously beating his own drum and boasting about what he'll do to you tomorrow. The crowd around him, however, was nothing like the one around you."

I laughed. "That's good to hear."

As we left the building, he said quietly, "There hasn't been time to call on Andy, Rev. Norton and Aaron Ross, but that's the first thing on my agenda. I'll have more to report later."

I told Grant about the salary arrangement with Orrin that was yet to be solidified, and I was not looking forward to it.

"Sam, from what you've told me and what I've seen, you seem to be holding your own fairly well."

I sighed. "It seems like I've had one crisis after another since arriving here. Wong Kee tells me there are dragons of many sizes that I must conquer."

Grant laughed. "Well, no matter what battles you have ahead of you, my very best wishes are with you."

All the way to Hattie's we had a great time describing the sizes and ferocity of dragons we both had to fight since becoming a part of Boone Valley, California 1852. It was the nicest, sweetest conversation I'd ever had with any man. It warmed me like a roaring fireplace in winter. I could even feel sparks rising up out of that fire, but at this place, in this time, I didn't mind one bit!

Chapter Fifteen

On reaching Hattie's, Grant said, "I won't come in this time. Let's sit here on the porch for just a minute and talk, if it's not too cold for you."

"No, I'm fine," and I seated myself on the steps.

"Sam," he began, "I can't tell you what a great pleasure it's been to find you and become friends. It's one thing to move to a new town or city by choice, but being dumped into a new way of living and thinking, as we have, does shake one up. Do you think the powers that be are trying to get our attention?"

"They certainly have mine," I said gravely. "You told me the night your Jeep broke down you said a prayer before you went to sleep asking for help. Let me tell you how I think this happened to me."

He moved closer and looked at me intently.

"The night before I ran away like an unhappy child from our home in these mountains, I sat outside under the stars and sent out some serious prayers to the Universe about bringing substance and meaning into my life. I asked for a life with grace and positive direction where I could be a participant and not a puppet acting out the roles that were given to me."

"That must have been a pretty powerful prayer," he observed.

"But there's more." I went on, "That day I stumbled into Boone Valley, I was angry, tired, hungry and thirsty. By the time the sun went down, I was furious with myself and the Universe. I literally cried myself to sleep, but not before I made it clear to the Universe that I was not pleased with what it had done for me thus far.

When I awoke the next morning, the changes were made. You must admit that in Boone Valley I have found change, direction and meaning. Of course, it's not clear where all this will end, but it's evident that the Universe has provided the music and I guess I'll have to dance to it for the time being."

Grant smiled. "I do admire the way you put things into perspective, Sam. You'll have to admit, though, it's startling to be a part of history, seeing the way things really were at this time, and knowing what is yet to come."

I shook my head. "It's like peeking at the last pages of a book to see how everything turns out. These people have no inkling what's ahead, and we have no right to tell them."

"Not to mention the Civil War — that's only a few years away. It will change the lives of many of the people who have become important to us. But the one blessing, Sam, is that you and I don't have to go through all this alone. We can keep each other sane and on track." He reached over, took my hand, squeezed it and smiled. Returning the pressure of his hand, I smiled back while we shared a meaningful silence.

I interrupted the moment and stood. "Well, I've got to get some rest tonight to prepare for the playoff, and also for the meeting with Orrin."

Grant stood and took my hand. "And remember, we are no longer singular, but together in this. Thank you, Sam for coming into my life."

He leaned over, kissed me lightly on the cheek, then turned and walked away. As I moved toward the door I watched, and was delighted to see him turn and wave before he went on.

Of course, I could reveal none of this to Hattie that night. She, on the other hand, was reporting at length what she had heard in town. "Samantha, everybody's talking about your piano duel. Some of the men are very definitely on your side, but others seriously want Willis to win. They would hate to see a woman get the best of any man. It's like a horse race, and I hear there's heavy betting going on!"

I had not heard any of this and began to worry that the expected crowd would find the piano duel anti-climactic or dull, and nothing would be served. It hadn't occurred to me to be nervous until that moment, and my stomach began flip-flopping at the thought of the calamity that could result. I placed my hands over the area that was churning.

Hattie became alarmed. "Now, girl, don't let this get to you. What you've planned is bound to be entertaining so try not to fret. You get yourself upstairs and have a good night's sleep. I'll clean up the kitchen and we'll talk more in the morning."

But sleep did not come easily that night. Mentally I went over and over the music and the imagined response of the crowd, but no clear resolution came. If I came out second best, Orrin would have just cause to send me out the door without settling the money I'd earned, and once more I'd be job-hunting. My mind spun like a top most of the night, but I managed to close my eyes and sleep for a short time just as the dark sky became a light blue.

Hattie let me sleep until 9 o'clock, then shook my shoulder to bring me to a groggy awakening.

"Time to get up, Samantha. Here's some coffee and oatmeal, so you just be comfortable right here and have a quiet breakfast. I was afraid you wouldn't sleep much, but now it's time to get up and face the new day!"

I sat up, my body and mind in first gear, but the charge from the hot, strong coffee helped to put me in second gear.

Two hours later I was fed, washed, powdered, dressed and ready for the big event. Ida's blue-on-blue creation looked grand and helped to raise my spirits. A smattering of makeup added color to my pale cheeks, and I brushed my hair to one side with a jaunty bow to hold it in place.

I cautioned Hattie to come into the saloon kitchen just before three and wait there until the playing began. Then she could open the door to the central area and listen. As we sat there quietly talking over one last cup of coffee, there was a knock on the kitchen door. Grant was there. He bowed to Hattie, who brought him coffee and got him settled in a chair. He frowned as he removed his hat and ran fingers through his hair.

"I came hoping you were up and ready to take on the duel today, but there are some things you should know."

After a swallow of coffee, he began. "Last night I met with Aaron Ross, Andy Locke and Luke Norton. They said they would be delighted to judge the segments of the duel and vowed their decisions would be fair and well considered. We discussed how the music would be presented, and to follow the pattern of judging we discussed yesterday."

This was good news, but Grant had more to say. "The four of us agreed that Orrin should be informed of these details as soon as possible. We went directly to the saloon about ten o'clock and finally got him to sit down and talk with us. We informed him that Aaron, Andy and Luke had agreed to judge the event."

"Let me guess," I said. "Orrin responded with an objection or two."

Grant shook his head. "It was like a thunderstorm. He was assuming that he and he alone would be the judge. When we pointed out that it would not be fair, that he might be a bit prejudiced, he exploded, saying it was his saloon and he would make all the decisions."

Grant sighed. "It was a prolonged battle, and it took some time and bargaining. Finally Orrin agreed, but only if Willis can play any five songs he chooses — rather than being limited to the five on his list. And he demanded that Willis would always be the first to play." He sighed. "I do hope that's all right with you. Can you work with it?"

It took me a moment to think it through. "It could work out. Whatever Willis plays first, my selection will be what best fits the mood of his music." Then I clapped my hands in satisfaction. "Yes, it will work. If he plays a march, I'll play a march. If he plays a waltz, I'll do the same. Make sure that Orrin announces at the beginning of each segment what Willis will play. When it's my turn, I'll tell you what I'm going to play, and you announce my selection."

Hattie smiled and sat back in her chair. "Leave it to you, Samantha, to find a way to keep up with Orrin."

Grant was smiling as well when he announced, "I didn't think it would be proper for this lady to walk to work today. There's a horse and buggy waiting outside, and I would be proud to take her to the battleground!"

I groaned, "Please don't say that! I'm nervous enough as it is. But thank you, that's a lovely thought."

Winking at Hattie, then taking my hand, Grant led me out the door saying, "Then come, my lady. Your chariot awaits. And by the way, you look simply m-a-r-r-velous!" He slurred the last word, which brought back a distant memory that made us both laugh.

While driving the buggy into town, he looked over with concern. "How are you doing this morning? Any butterflies?"

"A whole squadron, thank you."

He frowned and said, "Now you listen here. I've heard you play, and this whole situation you've created is right and logical." Then he said with emphasis, "Just you keep in mind that it's going to go well; the audience cannot help but be entertained, and I absolutely know you'll either be a gracious winner or a courageous loser."

I could only look at him and shrug my shoulders. "Look at

it this way," he grinned. "What would John Wayne do in a situation like this?"

I laughed. "Probably clean his rifle and look at the situation from all angles."

"All right then," he said. "That's just what you should do. John Wayne didn't play a mean piano like you do, but he managed to be equal to any predicaments he had to deal with. Remember, this isn't a life and death situation. There won't be any blood on the street when it's over. It's only a plan you created to clear your name. Go in there and have fun with it. Okay?"

My shoulder and neck muscles began to relax. "Okay, coach. I'll go in there and do my best!"

There were crowds milling about in front of the Majestic, trying to push their way through the door. When several of them saw me in the buggy, they began to cheer.

"Go get 'em, lady. Give Willis what for!"

Grant drove to the side of the building and moved to help me down. "Now, Sam, you're going to be just fine. Try not to be nervous, and just play as competently as you always do. I'll be close by when it's time to announce your music." He planted a lovely kiss on my cheek as I stepped from the buggy.

Wong Kee looked up as I entered the kitchen. Naomi and Abigail were also there, loading their trays with plates and glasses. Abigail rushed over and took my hand. "Mis' Samantha, you can't imagine what's been happenin'. People been crowdin' in since 10 this morning, and the place is full already. Orrin brought in extra chairs and they're takin' up every space there is. He even made us girls start workin' early."

The girls did look frazzled. "I'm so sorry. I had no idea it would turn out like this."

"Don't fret yourself," said Naomi. "This is the most excitement we've had in ages. We'll survive."

Wong Kee looked concerned. "You ready for dragon? Very big one today."

"As ready as I'll ever be. How's Willis holding up?"

Abigail groaned. "He's been practicin' since early this mornin'. Kept most of us awake, even though we tried to stop him."

The afternoon program went well, though the audience was a bit distracted, waiting for the main event to start. Finally it was 2:30 and there was a groan of disappointment when I stopped playing and headed to the kitchen for a drink of cool water.

My challenge had become a large event, much larger than I could have anticipated. I was unable to visualize where I would be at the end of the day.

In the kitchen Warren and Sumpin were eating at one of the tables, and several gamblers were sitting at the other tables looking grim.

One of them frowned and complained, "Not much for us to do with all that fuss going on out there. How much longer are you going to go on with this nonsense?"

"As long as people out there want me. Be patient, gentlemen. It may be over in a few minutes, then you'll have your tables full again."

"Sure hope so, lady." And they turned away and returned to their conversation.

I went to the gentle man working at the stove. "What do you think, Wong Kee? This has turned into quite a circus, hasn't it?"

He shook his head and continued working. "Much going on. Big day. Many know your name when this day over. Much more than that. You see."

"I'm not anxious that they *know* my name, only that it was slandered and I want it to be cleared. That's what this is all about."

Taking a cup of water, I sat with Warren and Sumpin.

"Hello there, youngsters. Haven't seen you for a while. Are

things going well with you?"

"We be fine, Mis' Samantha," Warren answered. "We sure hear people talkin' 'bout you, 'n' Willis sure has been practicin' and keepin' us awake all night. Sumpin and me surely want you to win. We'll try to get close so we can listen."

Sumpin came over to stand beside me. I put my arm around her small body as she leaned against me.

"We miss you," she said softly. "We saw you first, but don't get to see you much anymore."

I hugged her. "Don't you worry, kids. Once this is all over, there will be time for us. There are lots more songs to sing and stories to tell. Can you be patient a little longer?"

Their smiles assured me that they would. We sat and talked quietly together. One by one Naomi, then Flower, Abigail and Maggie opened the kitchen door, wished me luck, then hurried back to work.

Then Orrin charged through the door and said gruffly, "What're you doin, wastin' time in here? You started all this, so get yourself out there. And I mean right now!" He left abruptly without waiting for me.

Somehow that didn't bother me. Orrin was just being his usual cantankerous self, and I felt strangely calm and ready for what was waiting for me in the saloon. I kissed the children, waved at Wong Kee and moved toward the door. On impulse I stopped where the gamblers were sitting.

"Gentlemen, I'm off to fight the good fight. Do you wish me well?"

Only one turned to face me and said roughly, "Lady, you damn well know where our money is. We've been takin' bets that you're goin' to get whipped, and there's lots of takers!"

I was able to smile and ask, "Oh? What are the odds?"

Taken aback he replied, "Two to one."

Rather than dampen my spirits, I found this amusing. "Well, I do hope it's money that you can well afford to lose! I'll take 10 on the newcomer."

I'm not sure, but it seemed to me that they turned a little pale at the thought.

Opening the door leading to the saloon, I was shocked at the mass of assembled people. Even the stairs leading to the second floor were packed. The resulting noise was deafening.

I looked about the saloon, then noticed my piano had been moved. No longer near the front entrance under the overhang of the second floor, it was now installed at the far end of that large room, up on the small stage. It was actually the best possible location considering the size of the crowd. We would not only be more visible to everyone, but the acoustics, such as they were, would be better.

I paused by the long oak bar. Corby hurried over and said, "It's been like this for a couple of hours. We had to bring in the night bartenders to help out. Orrin's in his glory and Willis is as nervous as a mule with fleas. Gotta go. Good luck, Mis' Samantha!" He flashed a smile and was back dispensing drinks before I could thank him.

It was difficult to make my way to the stage until a few men saw me and cleared the way. I reached the stairs at the side of the stage and waited.

Orrin and Willis were already standing on the stage. Orrin was dressed in his usual black frock coat, white shirt and black string tie. And darned if he didn't have a haircut! He looked quite the man in charge.

Willis was slicked up in a new and terrible looking reddish-brown suit, the jacket covering his usual striped shirt with the high white collar. His thin blond hair was slicked back, making him look like a frightened seal.

Nearing the stage, I could see a table had been placed on the floor close by. Three chairs were placed facing the stage. Already seated and ready to go were Rev. Norton, Andrew Locke, and Aaron Ross, pencils in hand and sheets of paper before them. Each one gave me a smile and nod of encouragement.

On seeing me, Orrin raised his arms and quieted the crowd. Once this was accomplished, he brought Willis to the front of the stage and put one arm around his shoulder.

"Y'all know Willis who has played piano here for several years, and y'all know how good he is. He's a fine man and he's been challenged by this here woman. I'm sure y'all wish him the best."

There was a round of applause as Willis walked to the piano. One chair was positioned there, and a second chair was set to one side. Then Orrin pointed to me and went on.

"This here's the woman who started this tomfoolery, and we'll just see who is the better … ah … player. Now here's how we'll decide who comes out the winner." He cleared his throat, then continued. "Willis and this here lady will play one piece of music at a time. First Willis, then this (he indicated with his thumb) lady. I have arranged for three gentlemen to judge their playing on a scale of 1 to 10. These gentlemen are Rev. Luke Norton of the First Methodist Church of Boone Valley; Andrew Locke, Attorney at Law; and Aaron Ross, proprietor of the Assay Office." There was a round of applause until Orrin raised his hands for silence. He continued.

"When the playing is over with, these gentlemen will add up the scores, and then we will know for sure who is the winner of this so-called duel. I would like to announce that Willis Weatherby's first selection will be 'The Fluter's Ball.'"

There was a smattering of applause while Orrin abruptly walked down the stairs on the far side of the stage, while I made my way up on the other side. There was a nice round of applause, so I faced the audience and gave them a hundred watt smile until Willis snarled, "Sit yourself down, woman!" He was already seated before the piano.

Sitting on the chair that was to one side, I said to Willis, "Are you ready?"

"Of course I am," he answered sharply, and turned to place his hands on the keyboard.

Willis began with a lively rendition of that old Irish melody. Full of life and bright, it pleased the audience which erupted with applause and cheering. It took me back to the early days of my piano lessons. "Fluter's Ball" challenged my third year, but I managed to play all of the notes to the satisfaction of my demanding teacher.

Now it was my turn. Looking about, I found Grant climbing the stairs to the stage. I motioned to him, and when he leaned over I whispered, "About the best piece that will fit here is an old one I just remembered — 'Billy Boy.' I'll just have to wing it. Wish me luck."

He nodded and moved to the edge of the stage where he signaled for silence. In a strong, deep voice he announced, "It is my pleasure to announce that Mrs. Malcolm's first selection this afternoon will be 'Billy Boy.'"

I then replaced Willis at the piano. Never before had I played this particular song, but I knew it well, and I might say with all modesty that I did a super fine job bringing in humor and changes in tempo. The crowd seemed to agree since the applause and cheers were reassuring.

There was a short intermission while the judges reviewed their notes and graded the first selections.

Once more Orrin mounted the stairs, had a brief conference with Willis, then turned to the audience.

"Willis will now play a song well known to many of you. The title is 'Danny Boy'." There was an "aahhh" from the audience, indicating their pleasure.

Orrin slowly made his way down the stairs and Willis replaced me at the piano and began. To my surprise, he brought a softness to this sentimental Irish song that I had never heard from him. He played four different versions of the main theme, and I was impressed, as was the audience. There were even a few sniffs and blowing of noses.

As I listened, I knew exactly what would nicely follow this song. During the applause, Grant mounted the stairs, leaned over, and I whispered, "Greensleeves."

He smiled broadly and nodded in agreement. "Mrs. Malcolm will now play an old, and very beautiful, English melody. 'Greensleeves'."

I loved playing that beautiful song. It was as if there was no one listening. I played for my own enjoyment; the fingers on the keys had a life of their own. The melody wove in and out of the chords, and I could imagine ladies in lovely gowns, walking over green lawns, delicate umbrellas over their heads to shade them from the sun. When I finished, there were a few seconds of silence followed by a warm response. I didn't care what I scored; that was a beautiful musical journey that I went on.

The judges took a few moments to determine their scores, then there were nods to indicate we could move on to the third segment of music.

Again Willis surprised me with his next selection: "Last Rose of Summer." After so many nights of pounding out music for the Hurdy-gurdy Girls and their partners to dance to, I was impressed that he chose the lovely rendition of this old favorite.

When Willis played the last note, I felt I could match the quiet mood of that melody and whispered to Grant to announce "Believe Me If All Those Endearing Young Charms," which he did. The audience responded equally well to the music that Willis and I presented, and I relaxed knowing that all had gone well so far.

There was another short intermission, then Orrin announced that Willis would play "Rock of Ages." All was quiet while he played this lovely melody, and beautifully I must admit. I don't believe the piano in the saloon had ever played this ancient hymn, but it was a grand rendition, and I congratulated myself that my effort to tune the piano was well done. The applause was quiet and respectful.

When Willis finished the last note, there was no question what would come next, and when I whispered to Grant that I would play "Amazing Grace," he smiled and said, "Right on, Sam."

I played it slowly, reverently, starting the theme on two notes. Then slowly the melody began to build, until the fourth time around it was played grandly on the full keyboard. The response from the audience was heartwarming.

After another five minute rest, the judges agreed on their grades, and once more Orrin came to the front of the stage and announced, "Now we come to the last selection of this so-called duel, and Willis will play a lively song known to all of you. 'Red River Valley'." There were hoots and cheers of approval from the assembly and Willis once more sat before the piano.

All of the skills that Willis used to provide lively music for the Hurdy-gurdy Girls and their partners were clearly demonstrated. The music had rhythm and zip, and the listeners joined in by smiling and clapping in time. When Willis brought the music to a crashing climax, he stood and looked at me with a triumphant smile as if to say, "Gotcha, you poor woman."

When Grant kneeled by my chair, I said, "How can I possibly play to top that? All I can think of is 'Streets of Laredo' and to play the daylights out of it. Any other suggestions?"

He took my hand and said urgently, "Now don't you go soft on me. You can do it! Just pretend that it's a movie and you have the whole MGM orchestra behind you, providing a lush background to whatever you play. Now you play the socks off that song. Okay?"

I nodded, then stared at the keyboard as Grant made the announcement. The crowd became very quiet, not a sound could be heard except for the tinkle of glasses being washed at the bar. Grant left the stage, and all eyes were on me.

Taking a deep breath, I rested one finger on the keyboard and began the melody. Once the melody was established, I began a counter melody with another finger. Little by little I added to it. At one point the melody was played by the left hand on the lower keys, the counter melody on the upper keys. It was like weaving an afghan. Melodies went in and out, back and forth, building until both of my hands seemed full of intricate chords, going up and down the length of the keyboard. After three versions of the melody, I changed the key, repeated both the melody and counter melody, then finished with three crashing chords.

I sat back, exhausted. Gradually I became aware of the clamor coming from the floor of the saloon. Men were standing, shouting, clapping their hands, and Willis had a sour look on his face.

Then I looked down and saw the judges going over their notes, and sure enough Orrin joined the group to insert his wishes into their decisions. The judges sent Orrin to one side until they had determined the winner. Everyone became quiet and sipped their drinks until the judges finally stood and indicated they were ready. They sent Andrew Locke to the stage. There was not a sound as he mounted the stairs and faced the waiting crowd.

"The judges have made their decision. It is clear we have heard some outstanding music here today, and we have been challenged to reach a fair and reasonable decision. As you know, it was decided each player could gain up to 10 points for each selection. So, it would be possible to earn up to 50 points if it was so decided."

He paused to clear his throat while the throng waited patiently. He continued: "The judges have awarded Willis, for his five selections, a total of 47 points. Mrs. Malcolm, on the other hand, was awarded a total of 48 points, making her the winner of this contest."

There was a burst of noise. Applause, cheers and jeers, and a loud protest from Orrin. Willis joined him on the floor and it was clear they were objecting to the decision. While this was going on, I motioned to Andrew to join me. As he kneeled beside me, I said, "One point doesn't seem to be a clear cut victory. Your numbers are close to a tie, so why don't you suggest that a tie would be a fair decision?"

He frowned. "That's very generous of you. Are you sure this is what you want?"

"I think it would be best for all concerned. Why don't you check with Rev. Norton and Mr. Ross?"

He joined the other two judges at the bottom of the stairs, and I watched as their heads came together to consider my suggestion. When they all looked up at me, I nodded to confirm my agreement. Orrin and Willis joined them to complain, but they were cautioned to wait until Andrew made an announcement. He mounted the stage, stood with arms raised to quiet the crowd, and when all became quiet, he began to speak.

"It has been brought to our attention that there was not a wide range of difference in how we rated these two talented musicians. Only one point gave us the winner. Therefore, Mrs. Malcolm has suggested that this duel could be considered a tie, and the judges agree."

There was an uproar of cheers and agreement by the audience. Meanwhile, Orrin and Willis stood at the bottom of the stairs, mouths open in astonishment.

I searched for Grant in the crowd, and we shared wide

smiles of satisfaction. Then I caught Willis' attention and motioned him back to the piano for our duet.

He had a prolonged discussion with Orrin, then they joined me on the stage. Orrin said in a low voice to Willis, "Are you sure this is what you want?" A hasty "You bet!" burst from Willis. Delighted to bring the attention back to himself and Willis, Orrin raised his arms until the crowd was hushed.

"Well," he announced, "Willis tells me they have something special to play for you now." He couldn't bring himself to say "encore."

Willis brought the other chair to the piano and sat beside me. The crowd became quiet and we went into an extended rendition of "Yankee Doodle," which resulted in more applause and shouting. Everyone remained seated and it was obvious no one wanted to leave.

"Willis," I suggested, "Why don't we finish by playing "Home Sweet Home?" He nodded in agreement and began the melody on his side of the keyboard. It was fun, and I could see he was enjoying bringing different shades to this simple melody.

When it was over, everyone was standing, cheering. I took Willis's hand and pulled him to the front of the stage for a few bows. At first he tried to pull away, but I held on as we bowed together, again and again, to the enthusiastic crowd. After more than a few minutes, the clamor lessened and I pulled Willis to the back of the stage.

Making eye contact, I said, "All right, Willis. Have I made my point? Will there be any further lies about me ?"

He looked at the floor and didn't reply.

"Come on, Willis," I insisted. "Agreed? Or do we have to go through all this again?" And I smiled to soften the challenge.

He nodded slowly, and as an afterthought he added, "I'll do it on one condition."

"Which is?"

Shyly he said, "You teach me more music we can play together."

Laughing I said, "Sure thing, Willis. Tell you what. How would you like to join me at the piano just before I finish my afternoon concerts? We could play them at that time."

For the first time since I'd known him, Willis smiled at me. It was a crooked but genuine smile. That, I felt, was part of my victory, and I smiled back as I left the stage.

Orrin was at the bottom of the stairs, a fierce look on his face. As I approached he snarled, "Betcha think you're a smart ass. There's no way to keep Willis or anyone else from talkin' about you."

I raised my eyebrows. "Don't be too sure, Orrin. Willis and I have come to an understanding and I don't think there'll be any more trouble. And by the way, early Monday morning you and I need to have a quiet talk about my salary. You're three days overdue, and after today I think we may have to renegotiate the amount. Until then, Orrin, good day!"

My exit was well planned, because Orrin was clenching his fists and taking a deep breath that extended his chest and filled his cheeks. I didn't want to be near him when all of that rage and hot air was expelled.

As I made my way through the crowd, the men were bubbling over with compliments, shaking my hand and gently patting my back. Every face was smiling and laughing, and I heard encouraging words of praise and approval.

"Mis' Samantha, we won't stand for no more lies about you," one of them said as he eagerly shook my hand. "We just won't allow it. No, ma'am."

I moved on to find Grant standing before me. He was laughing as he took my hand. "We'll talk later, you can bet on it!"

It took awhile, but I finally worked my way back to the kitchen. Before entering, I passed three of the gamblers heading for the card room. I couldn't resist stopping to say, "Gentlemen, what do you think of the outcome of the duel? If you paid attention, originally I was the winner. You would be paying out a lot of money now if I hadn't suggested a tie would be a better judgment considering the close scores. Do I hear a thank-you from anybody?"

They had nothing to say, but the looks on their faces signaled another win!

Once in the kitchen, I leaned against the door to catch my breath. Hattie, Warren and Sumpin were jumping with joy and clapping their hands. Even Wong Kee, usually so calm and self-contained, was bowing, his face radiant with approval. But the wonderful surprise was Barnaby beaming and dancing from foot to foot. I rushed to give him a hug, forgetting how very shy he was. He didn't seem to mind.

"Barnaby, I'm so glad you're here. Now everything is perfect!"

Shyly, he said, "Heard all 'bout you up at the mines. Word got around and I just had to come see if everythin' turned out all right. You sure showed 'em!"

"Samantha, you surely did," Hattie exploded. "Your duel was a huge success. Nobody will be talking bad about you from now on."

Warren and Sumpin were holding my hands and saying, "You sure played pretty!"

The kitchen door opened to Elmo with his arms filled with bottles and glasses. "Me and Corby thought you'd want to celebrate, so here's a round of sarsaparilla from us."

As he was pouring, he added, "Me 'n' Corby are real pleased that everything turned out so good. Even old Willis is smilin' and walking around like he just found gold!"

When everyone had a full glass, I raised mine and said, "What shall we drink to?"

Hattie took over. "We'll drink, my girl, to you and your outlandish but wonderful ideas. We're real proud of you, what you did, and that we all can call you our friend. So, let's raise our glasses to the lady who showed them all — our Samantha!"

Before sleep came that night, my mind raced with a jumble of thoughts. If you had told the old Samantha a year ago that she would be experiencing such an exhilarating moment, it would have been beyond her comprehension. Look at me, I told myself. Look at where you are and what you're doing. To me, the now I was experiencing was by far the best of all times — the most challenging and rewarding of my life! Thank you, Universe, I said silently. No matter what happens from now on, my life has changed and opened up to unlimited possibilities. It was exactly what I prayed for that night on the mountain top under a star-filled sky.

Chapter Sixteen

When the celebration in the kitchen concluded, Hattie, Barnaby and I found Grant waiting outside with a horse and buggy. The four of us fit quite comfortably in the narrow seats, and in no time we were unloading in front of Hattie's.

"Time for dinner," she said with a sidelong look at Barnaby. "You're welcome to come in and share whatever vittles I can put together. C'mon in, gentlemen."

I excused myself and dashed upstairs to change into something more informal and comfortable. But really I wanted to look my best for the gentleman downstairs.

When I finally entered the kitchen, Hattie was bustling around the black stove. The kitchen was cozy and warm.

She was just removing a large skillet from the oven and said, "You can tell the menfolk they can come in now."

Going to the door of the parlor, I found Barnaby and Grant deep in conversation and chuckling. "What's so funny, gentlemen?" Grant responded, "Barnaby was describing the look on Orrin's face when you and Willis were playing the encore. It was obvious Orrin didn't expect you to do so well. He really wanted Willis to come out the clear and undisputed winner."

Barnaby agreed with a laugh. "Yeah, that Orrin sure looked surprised when it was all over."

We were laughing as we entered the kitchen and found Hattie ready to serve her culinary concoction.

Hattie began, "Before we start, let's take a minute and thank the Almighty for helping our Samantha do so well at the duel today, and bless this food before us in celebration."

After heartfelt "amens" we shared a most enjoyable dinner. During coffee we all relaxed, tummies full, and smiled at each other, contented with the triumphs of the day.

Barnaby cleared his throat, then said softly to Hattie, "I brung somethin' for you and Mis' Samantha."

He got to his feet and dug into a pocket of his brown trousers. When his hand emerged, he opened it to show two nuggets about the size of strawberries. He deposited one into the palm of my hand, and one into Hattie's.

"For you," he said shyly. "Found 'em yesterday and they're about the best I dug up yet."

Grant whistled. "Those aren't bad at all. Do you think there will be more like these where you're working?"

"Wouldn't be a bit surprised. I been a long time diggin', but I got a feelin' there are more of these in the mine."

I explained to Grant that Hattie and I had a special interest in the mine since we three were now partners.

"Good for you, Barnaby," Grant cheered. "Keep up the good work."

Hattie chimed in. "We want you to know that your partners are awful proud of you." Then she shyly covered her mouth with a hand and lowered her eyes in embarrassment.

Barnaby ducked his head to hide a happy grin, and Grant winked at me.

Something from my first day in Boone Valley bubbled to the surface of my mind. "Last week I saw a notice in Orrin's saloon that a claim jumper, I think his name was Mercer Oates, was on trial, and the fact that he would be hung was a foregone conclusion. Whatever happened?"

Without hesitation Barnaby stated, "He got hung, all right!"

Grant offered more information. "As you might guess, Mrs. Malcolm, justice here is swift when a man is caught in the act of taking over a claim, or working the claim when the owner has gone for supplies. Our law enforcement here is provided by just a few men, so when such a crime is witnessed, the penalty is expeditiously carried out. When a man is caught in the act, he has little time to show remorse or plead his case."

Barnaby added, "That Mr. Oates was not a nice man. We knew he killed and stole a fella's gold dust before, and he sneaked around a mine when no one was there."

"That's right," Grant agreed, "and this time there was no doubt about his guilt."

"That's brutal but very efficient," I commented.

"That's the way life was — or is during the Gold Rush of 1852." His slip was not noticed by Hattie or Barnaby.

Hattie stood and started clearing the table. "Sam, you take Mr. Douglas and go visit in the parlor. Mr. Barnaby and I will do what has to be done here. That is, if that's all right with you, Barnaby." And she smiled coyly and waited for his approval. He nodded his head in happy agreement as we left the kitchen.

"You know," I said quietly as we entered the parlor, "I'm beginning to think that our Hattie finds great pleasure in Barnaby's company."

Grant chuckled. "There's no doubt that he's sweet on her." Then after a slight pause he said, "Will you play something just for me? Something from our time?"

"Of course. Anything special?"

"Whatever comes to you. I'll just sit back and enjoy."

Thinking to please him, I began to play and quietly sing, "I left my heart in San Francisco."

When I finished, I turned to find Grant sitting forward, his arms resting on his knees, his head bent as he focused on his fingers. Though the light from the kerosene lamp was bright, the darkness of the room seemed to envelop and hold us. My eyes explored the contours of his face, the straight nose, the strong jaw line, the nicely shaped dark brown eyebrows, the few but strong lines on his forehead. I was quite drawn to this man, and the fact that we were sharing a monumental secret made our connection stronger.

He raised his head and looked into my eyes. I hastily apologized. "I'm sorry, Grant. I should have realized this song would push a button that must be very tender by now."

"Sam, it's all right," he said quietly. "In fact, as hard as it was to hear those words, it was rather comforting."

He reached over and picked up my hand and held it firmly. As he paused, I impulsively reached over with my other hand and covered his.

"Sam, as soon as it can possibly be arranged, we must find time to be alone and really talk."

Just then we could hear Hattie and Barnaby finishing the kitchen chores and approaching the parlor. To break the tension that I feared would be obvious, I turned to the piano and began playing "Do Nothin' Till You Hear From Me." Grant let out a sudden laugh. Hattie and Barnaby entered the parlor. "What's going on here?" she asked, eyeing me as they sat down.

"We were just trying to remember songs we knew back where we came from. But Hattie, we need to discuss tomorrow's meeting with the Waiter Girls."

She looked concerned. "You're right, we did promise to meet with them, but where?"

I was worried. "Orrin mustn't suspect we're coming together to talk about our concerns."

Hattie's face brightened. "I'll bet we can meet at Ida Penny's shop. She's a good distance from the saloon, and if anyone saw them going in there, they'd think she was making them dresses or something.

I asked, "How can we get word to her and the girls?"

Hattie looked at the man beside her. "Mr. Barnaby, when you go back in town tonight, could you have a beer at the saloon, and secretly ask one of the girls to pass the word to meet us at Ida Penny's at noon tomorrow?"

"Sure thing, Mrs. McKee. I'd be glad to."

Grant volunteered, "I know Miss Penny, and her shop isn't far from my house. It would be easy to stop by and give her the word. I don't think she'd mind a knock on her door at this hour if it's for a good cause."

It was close to 10 when Grant said, "Barnaby, I think we should let these ladies get some rest. Mrs. Malcolm must be tired after her very busy afternoon."

Barnaby stood to say his thanks. I shook his rough, calloused hand and said, "Good luck at the mine, Barnaby. Please send word when you can."

Hattie, her face beaming, said, "It's a pleasure to have you here, Mr. Barnaby. Do come again some time." Then she added quickly, "You, too, Mr. Douglas. It was surely an exciting day and happy evening."

Grant took her hand. "Hattie, it's always a pleasure to see you, and this was a special evening. Thanks for having me in your home." Turning to me he added, "And thank you for playing a song that brought back some fond memories."

I smiled in return as they headed for the door.

Once they were gone, I could not resist teasing Hattie. "It seems to me that you're finding that gentleman rather interesting."

She quickly shook her head. "Land sakes, Samantha, you come up with the oddest notions."

"Well, you have to admit that Barnaby has changed. He's able to speak up and not get so flustered, and he's showing us that he has a sweet and generous disposition. I do believe it's because of your influence, plus the fact that Grant treats him like a true friend.

Just bringing him into our circle of friends has boosted his confidence."

Hattie's response was thoughtful. "Now that you mention it, Samantha, he is changing from the man you first brought into my kitchen. But you had more to do with it than I did. He's a nice enough fellow, and so is Mr. Douglas. In fact, it's clear to me that you find him real nice. Does he come to the saloon to listen to you play?"

"Yes, almost every afternoon, but maybe not so much now that the playoff is over. We'll see."

She yawned. "Land sakes, we've got to make church in the morning, then decide what we can do for those poor girls. Looks like tomorrow is going to be another busy day."

The next morning was sunny with a brisk breeze which we enjoyed during the walk to church. After the service, a number of the men approached us to comment on the playoff and what a great event it was. Rev. Norton made it a point to shake my hand and add his congratulations. I, in turn, thanked him profusely for acting as one of the judges at my piano duel. Hattie stood to one side, bursting with pride.

We hurried home, then to Ida Penny's shop. We found her waiting by the door, motioning for us to come. Inside we found four Waiter Girls and three of the Hurdy-gurdy Girls — Clara, Jewel and Mary.

Once we were seated, Naomi began talking. "We hope you don't mind us asking these three to come along. We told them a little what you been sayin' about equal rights for women and all that, and they like the idea of tellin' Orrin that we want things to change."

I took the floor. "Young ladies, you live in a community where men outnumber the ladies by a great majority. There is such a thing known as supply and demand. Women are in high demand

and short supply. That gives you an advantage. If the working conditions and general situation are not to your liking, you don't have to stand for it. You have the right to speak up in order to improve your situation."

There were murmurs of agreement from everyone.

Mary, a sturdy looking girl with light brown hair, spoke up. "Mis' Samantha, we see how the Waiter Girls are treated and how awful hard they work. But so do we! We're dancin' with them rowdy miners seven hours straight, and we're plumb wore out. Not only is the dancin' hard on our feet, but them miners step on us. And you should see the bruises on our legs where we get kicked."

She stopped to catch her breath. "Our dresses get tore up, and we have to mend or make up new ones almost every week or so. Sure the pay is pretty good, but we earn it! We really do!"

I asked, "Have you ever asked Orrin to help pay for the dresses you have to replace?"

There was the sound of rueful laughter from everyone.

"And does Orrin ever give you time off to rest up, or if you're not feeling well?"

Once more the cynical laughter.

"Well, ladies, there is strength in numbers. If only one of you asked for better conditions, Orrin wouldn't even pay attention. But if all of you present your demands and threaten to walk out, he will have to listen and, in the end, make some concessions."

"He'll holler like a stuck pig, is what he'll do," said Abigail, and everyone laughed in agreement.

I directed, "We'll just sit here and talk about what you would like changed. Hattie and I will write everything down. Then you can present your ideas to Orrin. It won't be easy and he'll probably give everyone a very nasty time, but if you stand together there's a chance he'll have to agree to some, if not all, of your requests."

At first the conversation was hesitant, and then came a flood of ideas, then laughter, then hope.

These girls had been terribly exploited, but it was good to see them realize that the quality of their lives could be improved.

We spent some time discussing the proposed uniforms for the Waiter Girls — black skirts, white shirts, colorful aprons, ties and hair bows. The Hurdy-gurdy Girls decided to keep their white muslin dresses, but to cover them with a full, patterned overskirt that tied in the back, and a vest of the same material.

Hattie and I copied the final list, which Mary would share with the others who danced with the miners. All agreed that secrecy was most important. They would need to be cautious about showing the list or discussing it with others.

By late afternoon we began to leave Ida's one or two at a time. Ida was bubbling over with the results of the meeting, saying she was anxious to start on the uniforms. A tremendous project, but she was willing to work day and night.

On Monday, Hattie joined me when I confronted Orrin about my salary. After the rousing success of the playoff, a higher figure would be in order. Over breakfast we planned our strategy and resolved that the confrontation should be in the saloon so the presence of bartenders and customers would soften Orrin's reaction. Between us we decided that a fair weekly wage was not $40, but $45 plus tips. We would also suggest that Orrin consider raising Willis' salary since he was, in my estimation, a very capable musician. It would probably cause a reaction bordering on war, but we both felt we could be forceful if necessary.

At ten o'clock we entered the kitchen of the saloon where we found Wong Kee and, sitting at one of the tables, Corby and Elmo drinking coffee. Wong Kee motioned to us to join the two men, and brought two more mugs of the hot brew to the table.

"You should be durn proud of yourself after Saturday, Mis' Samantha," Corby declared, raising his mug in a salute. "All the rest of the night and Sunday everyone was talkin' 'bout your duel and what a dandy show it turned out to be. And Willis didn't lose, and he didn't win, and he was just as proud as he could be."

Elmo interrupted, "As a matter of fact, Mis' Samantha, one of the guys made a bad remark about you and Willis shut him up proper. He said he found out you were a real lady and that he wouldn't stand for any bad talk, nohow!"

"Well, that's news," I replied. "I do believe I've made a new friend. But I'm not too sure about Orrin. I understand he's not too pleased with the results. By the way, is he up and around yet?"

Corby nodded. "Yeah, he's had his breakfast, and we seen him go through here awhile ago."

I explained, "Hattie and I came early to talk with him about my salary, which he has managed to overlook so far."

Turning to Hattie, I said, "I'm ready when you are. Still game to fight this out with me?"

"Samantha, girl, it will be my pleasure to help Orrin Smithers see the light where you're concerned."

We walked into the saloon and nearly bumped right into Orrin.

"What are you two doing here?" he demanded.

Hattie spoke up, "Orrin, we have things to discuss, business that has been put aside long enough."

He glared at her. "You in on this, too?"

She looked at him calmly. "I surely am. I'm here to see that Samantha is treated fairly and squarely. It's time to start paying this lady a regular salary, and one that shows what she's really worth to you."

He stalled and turned to me. "I ain't had much time to think about it, let alone decide what your playin' is worth to me. I don't need you ladies pushin' at me right now." And he turned to walk away.

Grabbing my arm, Hattie was hot on his heels. And there, in front of the bartenders and the scattering of customers devoted to early morning gambling, she challenged him.

Speaking so everyone in the saloon could hear, she stated, "Mr. Smithers, this matter cannot wait and will not wait. If you want Samantha to play as usual this afternoon, we'd better sit ourselves down right now and talk about it!"

Noticing the onlookers who were moving closer to witness the confrontation, we waited patiently for Orrin to respond.

Chapter Seventeen

With all eyes upon him, Orrin Smithers examined his alternatives. He had several choices. He could exit the room without a word and let the rumors fly, but that would be backing down from the confrontation and he would lose face. He could use his limited but colorful vocabulary to throw a stream of rejection and censure at us and appear the villain. Or he could join us at a table and make it appear to others that he was in total control. With a look of disgust on his scowling face, he chose the latter.

Then I threw the first ball. "I'm sure it has not escaped your attention, Mr. Smithers, that I have been playing the afternoon concerts here for 10 days. However, I have yet to be paid for my work."

Orrin opened his mouth to speak, but I raised a hand to silence him.

"The agreement was, if you will recall, that if I lasted a week, I would be paid. Now Saturday, when you settle all accounts with your people — bartenders, Waiter Girls and Hurdy-gurdy Girls — has come and gone. Where is my salary?"

Looking around, Orrin took a minute to form a noncommittal response.

"As I told you ladies before, I ain't made up my mind, and I won't be rushed. We'll talk about this another time because I ain't ready to talk to you right now."

I interrupted. "Mr. Smithers, I assume you expect me to play this afternoon as usual, is that right?"

"You're damned right," he snarled.

Raising my voice a little, I said, "In that case, Mr. Smithers, it will be to your benefit to settle this here and now. You have had ten days to think it over, and I am not inclined to work here another day until we're clear as to what and when I will be paid."

He glared at me but said nothing.

I continued. "After Saturday's success, it seems fairly certain that the programs I present in the afternoons will be very well attended. So if I agree to continue, you will pay me $45 a week, plus any tips. And whenever the area where I play is filled to capacity at least three days of the week, I will be paid a $10 bonus for that week."

"Who the hell do you think you are? This is my saloon and I said I don't care to talk about this right now. And that's it, dammit!"

I turned to Hattie and raised my voice even more. "There must be other saloons in this town that would be happy to hire me. Tell me which saloons would be worthwhile, and we'll start calling on them today."

Hattie and I stood, ready to move on, but I wanted to leave Orrin with one last verbal shot. "You've had 10 days to think about paying me for the work I've done for you. Now you have 10 hours to make your decision. Pay me for my work or I quit."

I could see Corby and Elmo, glasses and towels in hand, standing still and taking in every word. The men at the far end of the room were now on their feet and drifting closer to witness the climax of this dispute.

Orrin rose to his feet and pointed one long finger at me. "You smart ass. You think you got me over a barrel, but you're dead wrong. That duel of yours wasn't that great, and things will go back the way they were. My saloon was doing just fine before you got here, and you can go to hell!"

Hattie and I looked back before exiting. The men who had been listening were now gathering about Orrin.

Once outside on the boardwalk, Hattie said, "Land sakes,

Samantha. What have you done? Orrin would've come around if we kept at him, but you'll get nowhere if you keep on pushing that way."

"Hattie, just give me the names of saloons in Boone Valley — those that are not totally dedicated to the personal ministrations of young ladies."

"Now, how would I know such a thing? The names of all those saloons, let alone what goes on inside."

That didn't deter me. Holding my head high and proud, I answered, "I'll ask Barnaby or Grant Douglas. And if those saloons are not interested in my music, I'll hire a hall and give concerts on my own."

As we walked along on the crowded boardwalks and dusty road, Hattie muttered to herself and shook her head.

I took a deep breath, "This is a nice day and it seems I won't be working, so the rest of the day is ahead of us. What can we do that would be fun? We can start at Norton's Café for coffee and pie and, as the song goes, 'review the situation'."

"Sounds fine to me, Samantha, and first I'll stop at the store and pick up last week's receipts."

On reaching McKee's Mercantile, I sat on a bench just outside the entrance and waited. It felt good to relax and watch the panorama unfold in front of me — animals, a few women walking rapidly, headed for specific destinations. Men strolling, hands in pockets, getting the lay of the land. There were shouted commands to animals, or one man greeting another. The assorted clothing was well worn, wrinkled, or downright stained and dirty. The hats were stovepipes, derbies, and felt hats from fair to shapeless condition.

A heavy odor was part of the scene — dust, animal droppings, smoke, food. The horses and mules waited patiently, tied to posts at the side of the street. Small groups of people gathered along the roadside — talking, observing, swapping stories of gold found and lost, claims useless and rich.

Hattie returned with several bundles. As she sat beside me, I could see she was upset.

"I got me a worry, Samantha. It seems I must visit the farm down the mountain to see about some things, then go to Sacramento to check on supplies. We just heard the people we've been counting on haven't been sending all of our orders. Either they need to be kicked in the rump, or I'll find a new sources. It's times like this I truly wish Martin was still around."

"I'm so sorry, Hattie. Can I help in any way?"

"No. It's just things only I can sort out. Frank will drive me down the mountain to the farm early tomorrow. Then on to Sacramento. All these things must be settled before winter sets in."

She looked concerned. "This means leaving you just when you're dealing with Orrin. You can take care of the house all right, but you won't have anyone to help with the Waiter Girls, and who knows what Orrin will do next."

"Please don't worry," I assured her. "I'll be fine, and I can call on Mr. Douglas or Barnaby if I really need help. You do what must be done, and I'll hold the fort until you return."

We walked back to the house where I made a pot of coffee while Hattie packed. I found some leftover roast beef and the last of her supply of bread, and had some pretty presentable sandwiches and hot coffee ready when she joined me.

"Now, Samantha," she began, "you go to my store and get whatever you need, and they'll put it on my bill. I already told them you would. There's plenty of vegetables and chickens, and I'll leave some money for you to pay the man who brings the wood."

A terrible confession burst out of me. "Hattie, I've never killed or plucked the feathers from a chicken in my life. What can I do?"

She stared at me, mouth open in surprise. "How on earth did

you get it ready for the pot? Were you rich enough to have a cook do it for you? What about turkeys, lamb, pork?"

That stopped me. "Where I lived we got all of that at a butcher shop. I really wouldn't know what to do!"

Hattie shook her head in disgust. "Well, that's a puzzle, and all I can figure is for you to go to Rev. Norton's café and either buy the things you need there, or get food already cooked and bring it here to eat. It wouldn't be proper for you to go there alone for your meals. Land sakes, I never heard of a woman who didn't know how to get a chicken ready for cooking!"

"Don't worry. I'll manage somehow. I can do everything else, so I'll be fine."

While I cleaned the kitchen, Hattie went through her receipts, and began a detailed list of supplies to be ordered for the winter. Meanwhile, I took the last of the roast beef, picked some vegetables from the garden, and put a pot of stew on the stove for our dinner.

About mid-afternoon there was a knock on the door. Grant stood there, eyebrows raised.

"There you are!" He looked worried. "I went to the saloon expecting to hear some wonderful music and found you wouldn't be playing today. Quite a crowd was there, but Orrin wasn't much help when it came to explaining your absence. He mumbled something about you not being able to make it, and he wasn't sure when or if you would ever be playing there. Some of the men stayed, but many of them were complaining and carrying on something awful before they went out the door. What's up?"

Once seated in the parlor, I reported the details of my confrontation with Orrin. Grant listened quietly. I ended by saying, "I know that you, of all people, would know what the other saloons are like and if there are any you could recommend. I could at least talk with a few to see if they would hire me."

He frowned as he spoke. "Sam, there is only one, maybe two, that would be of a proper atmosphere where you might want to work. The rest of them provide, shall we say, entertainment that wouldn't be to your liking."

"Everyone who came to hear me play today must have been at the playoff on Saturday, and they'll want to hear more. How did Orrin take it when they left after his announcement?"

"Orrin was far from happy, in fact he was offering free beer to everyone who would stay. I left about then, but didn't hear very many takers. There was quite a buzz of complaints, and Orrin didn't seem to have a handle on the situation."

"What do you think, Grant? Was I wrong to ask for more than he was willing to pay, then walk out when he refused to discuss it?"

"Of course not, Sam. Orrin will pay as little as he can get away with, and we know for sure he'll milk Saturday's success for whatever it's worth. He would be out of his mind not to bring you back at any price. But he's a proud and stubborn man and doesn't want to look like he's giving in to a woman, especially one who works for him!"

At this point I informed him that Hattie would be leaving in the morning, and I would have to continue this battle on my own. "Can I count on you to back me up if this fight goes into a second or third round?"

He laughed as he shook his head and commented, "We surely don't know where this is going, but don't you worry. Between us we can work it out."

There was someone knocking at the door, and I heard Hattie answer it. She then appeared at the parlor door, eyebrows raised. "You're sure going to be surprised to see who's here to talk to you."

She stepped aside, and Willis walked slowly into the room. The expression on his face and accompanying body language gave two diverse messages. The face reflected resolution and determination, but the stiffness of the body, shoulders hunched and hands deep in his pockets, clearly indicated he would much prefer being somewhere else. I directed him to a chair, then Grant, Hattie and I waited for him to speak.

"Ah … I'm here…" And he sat silently, trying to find the right words.

Grant took over. "Let me guess. Orrin sent you here to either convince Mrs. Malcolm to change her mind, or he's sending the message that he will agree to pay what she is proposing. Is that right?"

Willis changed positions in the chair and said, "Yeah, somethin' like that. He says to come back tomorrow and you all can settle everythin' then. He won't say so, but he wants you back real bad." He sat quietly as Hattie, Grant and I exchanged triumphant smiles. Willis kept his eyes fixed on his hands and looked angry.

"Something else on your mind, Willis?" I said. "What's wrong?"

Squaring his shoulders, the words burst out of him. "Ain't right, no, it ain't. You gettin' as much money as I been gettin', and I been with Orrin for several years. It'll make me look the fool."

Happily Grant stepped in with just the right words. "You're absolutely right, Willis. Mrs. Malcolm considers you a very talented musician, and feels that you should also be given a raise."

Willis' expression brightened and he sat even straighter in his chair.

I nodded when Grant looked over at me, then he went on. "We'd like to suggest an increase for you as part of the conditions for Mrs. Malcolm coming back. You should be getting, what, at least $55 or $60 dollars a week. Does that sound about right?"

Willis was now smiling and nodding with dignity.

"Also, Willis," Grant continued, "you're certainly entitled to a monthly bonus of $20 if the saloon is full at night. How about that?"

Willis was overcome. "Mr. Douglas, sir, no one ever spoke up for me before, and I'm right beholden to you for the advice. Would you please write all that down so I can give it to Orrin when I go back. That way he's gettin' it from you and maybe won't be yellin' at me."

"I'd be delighted, Willis, and we'll do it right now. Mrs. McKee, will you provide me with some paper, pen and ink? This is a document I'll enjoy writing."

As Grant and Hattie left the parlor, I advised Willis, "If Orrin gives you a bad time, tell him about our agreement to play more duets together. Impress on him that he'll have more to offer his customers than the other saloons."

His face was covered with a bright smile. "This is darn nice of you, Mrs. Malcolm, and it'll be interesting to see Orrin's face every time we play together. It'll be good for business, but he won't like it a bit, I can tell you!"

"While we're waiting, Willis, come over to the piano and let's work on something right now."

I played "Gather at the River." By the second time around Willis was taking over the melody and adding some chords on the upper keys.

"Now, doesn't that sound nice?" Hattie commented as she and Grant returned with the document. "You two will have that lovely duet to play when Orrin takes you back."

"Takes us back?" I protested. "You mean when we decide to continue our work at his saloon. Orrin won't know what hit him!"

A beaming Willis went out the door with the new agreement held firmly in his hand. Hattie turned to us as the door closed.

"Well, don't you two beat all? Willis comes in here scratching for a fight, and there he goes looking like he just found sunshine. By tomorrow Orrin won't be a happy man, but he'll have his place full of people, which should cheer him up a bit. If this turns out the way it's looking, it'll ease my mind that Samantha will be doing all right while I'm away."

Grant hastened to assure her. "Don't you worry a bit, Hattie. It will be my pleasure to watch over Mrs. Malcolm and help if she has problems of any kind."

Hattie looked at me slyly. "Can you help her kill and pluck a chicken? She tells me she's never done it before. Did you ever hear such a thing?"

There was a loud burst of laughter from Grant. "That's really hard to believe, but maybe I'll give her a lesson or two while you're gone."

I didn't care for the devilish look in his eyes, but I smiled and nodded. Hattie announced there was still work to be done on the details for her trip and she excused herself.

"Grant, no way will I learn to kill and pluck a chicken. I'd much rather become a vegetarian." And we both laughed at the thought. "But back to Orrin. It still isn't clear whether or not I'll return to work tomorrow."

"Well, tell you what I'll do, since I'm now involved in the negotiations, I'll stop by the Majestic and check on Orrin's reaction to the agreement. You plan to report to work tomorrow. If you don't hear from me, that means he's accepting the terms. If there's any problem, I'll bring the word myself."

I leaned back in my chair and stretched out both arms in relief. "I can relax now that you're on my team. Thank you so much, my time travel partner. And now I have a question I've been dying to ask."

"Go ahead, shoot."

"What is it you miss the most from that other life, since you've been here longer than I have?"

He thought for a moment, then answered seriously. "Hamburgers and French fries, cappuccino, that glorious fresh seafood at Fisherman's Wharf, San Francisco Bay and the bridges at sunset, dinners at those wonderful French restaurants, morning newspapers and, most of all, riding bicycles through Golden Gate Park on Sundays with my daughters."

He stopped suddenly and turned his face away. After a few moments, I turned to the piano and said, "Remember this?" and went into "Over the Rainbow," which made him smile.

"Do they still show that movie on television?"

"On the classic movie channel once or twice a year. My boys never missed it, even though they're almost young men."

He shook his head. "That's good to know. What were the words to that song?" We began singing as Grant tried to remember the lyrics. We laughed like fools in the process.

At one point I stopped. "Do you realize how significant those words are to us? Especially, 'one day I'll wish upon a star and wake up where the clouds are far behind me'?"

Once more I played that lovely refrain and we hummed along until Hattie called in from the other room, "Quiet in there! I can't hear myself think with all that noise!"

Grant stood, smiling. "With that ringing in my head, I'd better be off. There's business to be taken care of at the Majestic. With luck, I'll see you tomorrow noon and victory will be yours!"

When I saw him to the door, he took my hand and held it for a moment before he nodded and said goodbye. I must admit that it was a pleasure to watch him walk away in the twilight, the broad shoulders, the set of his head, the long stride.

I leaned against the door as I closed it and said to myself, "Wow!"

The next morning I rose early to share breakfast with Hattie, and to see her settled on the compact covered wagon that Frank

Newhall brought to the door. As I watched them drive off in the cool morning mist, I was jolted at the similarity to sending my boys off to school on misty mornings. Oh, damn! Where are they, and what must they think of their mother — or did they know that I'd disappeared? I allowed myself a few tears as the feelings of loss and hopelessness overcame me. Would I ever see them again? See them dating girls, graduating, married, parents!

And Harland! I had not thought of Harland in days, and there was no wrench of loss or longing when I did. What had he done with the days and weeks after I disappeared? Did he go through a mourning period, or lose himself in the details of his hardware stores and rock hunting? Would he feel remorse, loss, betrayal, or would he play the martyr with Mother Malcolm's happy encouragement? I couldn't help but smile as I wiped the tears away and allowed myself a few moments of fancy to visualize the range of operatic reactions those two would share. Well, so be it!

In my bedroom, I prepared for the day. With Hattie's absence I had privacy to review those items of the 20th Century that I'd brought with me. Spreading them on the quilt of my freshly made bed, I was suddenly keenly aware that they did not belong in this time: the wallet with the driver's license and all other plastic and paper identification; credit cards for food, clothing, gasoline; the satin pouch filled with cosmetics, skin care, deodorants — things that once seemed so necessary; a box of tampons that I needed a week ago. When they were gone, what would replace them? It was a question not easily asked. What would Hattie think if she knew that I did not know how that female condition was handled? The comb and brush and other items were made of plastic so I kept them in the dresser. The digital wristwatch, still faithfully keeping time, must be hidden. The blue jeans had zippers, so they must remain out of sight, as well as the bras with their lace and elastic.

Seeing and feeling these items helped me to keep the balance between then and now. I was still attached emotionally to the 20th Century, though I was dealing with 1852 on a day-to-day basis until the reality of one or the other kicked in.

I'd had no word from Grant, so I dressed for work in the rose print dress, grabbed the heavy wool cape, and firmly closed the front door behind me. It was still damp and misty, so I drew the cape and its hood about me.

On reaching the saloon, I entered the kitchen as usual. There was the constant presence of Wong Kee, and at one of the tables sat Grant and Willis. I was greeted by their smiles of victory.

"Well, you're all looking quite pleased with yourselves. I will assume everything went as planned. Right?"

Grant said, "Give me your hand, please." He placed a leather pouch in it, and I could feel the weight of the coins it contained.

I looked at Willis. "You, too?" There was pleasure in his nodded response.

"Why don't I hear any screams from Orrin?"

Grant stood and took the pouch from my hand and gently escorted me out the kitchen door and into the saloon. I was met by a room filled with people, standing, sitting, settling into chairs. When they saw me, a huge cheer went up accompanied by applause that continued until I worked my way through the crowd and reached the piano, which was still positioned on the stage at the far end of the room. There I turned and faced all the smiling and laughing faces. Some comment seemed to be expected, so I raised my hands and motioned for them to quiet down. It took awhile, but soon I was able to say the words that I hoped were appropriate.

"Thank you so much for being here today. It makes my heart glad to see you all, and I am more grateful than I can possibly say. Tell me, how many of you were here Saturday for the duel? Raise you hands."

A little more than half indicated they were there. The

remainder must have heard by word of mouth. It made me rather nervous to know that all were waiting expectantly for the same excitement as we'd generated on Saturday. Just then Flower went by with a tray filled with drinks and I caught her eye, leaned over and said, "Please ask Willis to join me as soon as possible, and to bring an extra chair." She nodded and soon was lost in the crowd.

I turned to the piano, mind racing, and began to play "Strike Up the Band." I had never played it before, but the chords and marching tempo were simple. By the time I repeated it for the third time, I had arranged the daylights out of it.

When the applause settled, I softly played a lovely waltz. Hardly any sound was heard — no clinking of glasses or shuffling of chairs. Following that I played, but did not sing, "Fly Me to the Moon," and went on with "Ghost Riders in the Sky."

During the applause between numbers, I scanned the faces pointed my way, and finally found Grant smiling broadly and signaling thumbs up. After two more selections, Willis stood beside me, and I motioned for him to position his chair and sit down. Once more I addressed the crowd.

"Gentlemen. I'm sure you're all aware that last Saturday afternoon Mr. Willis Weatherby and I were involved in a duel. We didn't throw rocks or knives at each other, but piano notes. I'm sure you've been in this saloon many times and heard Mr. Weatherby, who is a very accomplished pianist, play the night away. So, we had our duel, hurling music back and forth, and I'll tell you a secret. We had a wonderful time doing it. So much so, we've decided to continue playing duets for your entertainment. Is this a good idea?"

Applause and cheers erupted, and as soon as it subsided, I concluded by announcing we would start with the music that was the deciding factor in the duel, then sat down. The crowd waited quietly, expectantly while I whispered "Ready to go again, Willis?"

"Sure thing, Mrs. Malcolm," and he put his hands on the

keyboard. We played our duet, and then managed a 15-minute break to escape to the kitchen. I asked Willis if he wanted to stop since he would be playing that evening as well. He assured me he wanted to go on, so we planned the rest of the program, then returned to the stage to finish up as we had on Saturday — alternating our own versions of assorted melodies.

When it was time to quit, we knew without a doubt the crowd enjoyed what Willis and I gave them that afternoon. Very tired and highly satisfied, we worked through the enthusiastic crowd to the kitchen where we fell into the chairs to recover. It had been a strain, but we pulled it off.

I gasped to Willis, "For heaven's sake, what will we do for an encore tomorrow?"

Willis laughed weakly and shook his head. "I'm sure you'll think of somethin', Mrs. Malcolm."

I nodded to Willis and Wong Kee and said a tired, "See you tomorrow." Grant then escorted me outside to the horse and buggy. He helped me up into the buggy seat, wrapped the warm cape around me. He took the reins in his hands, then leaned over and said quietly, "Now this is our time. We have much to say to each other." He snapped the reins, and the horse pulled the buggy away from the saloon as my tired mind sent out neon messages: Whatever does he mean by that?

Chapter Eighteen

This lovely man must have read my mind. Rather than taking me to Hattie's to fix dinner in her antiquated (to me) kitchen, the horse and buggy took us to Norton's Café where we had dinner among a large gathering of patrons. Hard-working merchants, clerks, bankers, miners — those without wives waiting for them with a hot meal. Luke Norton greeted us with a cordial "Welcome! Seat yourself, folks. Just a few tables left since this is our busy time."

We made our way to the far side of the café amid greetings from Grant's acquaintances and curious looks from those who could take their eyes away from the loaded plates. Rev. Norton's daughter, Mercy, approached wearing a frilly apron over a green calico dress.

Smiling shyly, she said, "What would you like for dinner? Momma's had two delicious roasts on the stove all day, and now they're just right for servin'. They smell wonderful. How about some Swiss steak and rice, or roasted venison? The venison came in this mornin' and seemed rather old and tough, but Momma knows how to fix it so it's nice and tender."

I ordered the Swiss steak, Grant opted for the venison, then we settled down to talk until the food was served.

Grant looked serious when he cautioned me, "Sam, while we're talking, we mustn't look like conspirators or seem deeply involved in what we're discussing. Try to look prim, proper, and agreeably interested in what I may be saying. Any other attitude and it will be all over Boone Valley by morning. We'll just make it clear that I'm escorting you home after a pleasant dinner. Okay?"

I sat up straight and clasped my hands before me in a lady-like way. "I'm glad you warned me, and I'll try to keep the proper composure. But I'm dying to lean over and ask for the details of your meeting with Orrin. How did you ever get him to agree to our terms?" I tried to look mildly interested.

Grant smiled pleasantly and answered quietly, "I used the old reverse psychology. Told him I understood the spot he was in and that such a decision would be difficult. He roared, swore and waved his hands. I nodded knowingly and told him I didn't blame him a bit for feeling pushed. But I pointed out that the news of the playoff was racing through town, and it would be to his advantage to ride with the popularity it generated for you and Willis. He blustered a bit more, then grinned slyly as if he had thought of it himself. He agreed to the terms, but I'm sure he feels he can bounce you and Willis anytime it suits him."

I responded as if he were reporting a recent tea party. "Now, isn't that lovely? And Mr. Douglas, it looks like we'll have to keep our guards up and sentries on alert." I laughed pleasantly, one hand at my throat, and added, "We can plan a network of allies and spies — Corby, Elmo, the Waiter Girls. I'm sure together we can keep up with Orrin's devious mind."

We smiled and nodded just as the meal was served. The dishes were heaped with food that put forth a wonderful aroma. My Swiss steak was tender and full of flavor. Grant dug into the venison with gusto.

As we ate, I told Grant, "I'm anxious to fill you in on the meetings we've had with the Waiter Girls and where they want to go with changes in their lives. I'll go into detail when we get to Hattie's. But these ladies are now banding together for one common purpose."

Grant put down his fork and sat back in his chair, shaking his head. "Sam, my girl, you're advocating rebellion, giving these girls ideas that they may not be able to act on."

I tried not to look too intense as I said, "Yes, but at least I'm giving them hope, pointing out the possibilities. You know how women are terribly used during this period in history, but some of them grow stronger in the process and survive to provide cornerstones for the families that will come after them. We've read a lot about the Gold Rush from the point of view of the men who were part of it. But what did we learn about the women who came with them, creating homes out of canvas and bits of wood, bearing children, growing food, making clothes, tending the sick? Many died because of the hardships. On the other hand, scores were widowed in the process, and yet were strong enough to prevail and raise future generations."

He inclined his head to caution, "Sam, you're creating a crusade that these men are not ready for, and there may be casualties along the way. Please be careful, not only for yourself, but also for the girls at the saloon." He was silent until he finished his meal. Mine was only half finished and I was full.

Just then Mercy came by and saw the plate. I apologized, "This was just delicious, but I can't eat another bite. I do wish I could take all this home for my lunch tomorrow."

She nodded as she picked up the dish. "Don't you worry. I'll put this in one of Momma's pie plates, and you can bring it back when you're done with it."

As the horse pulled the carriage toward Hattie's, Grant answered my inquiry regarding the cost of the dinner. "Dinners cost $3 a plate, and 10 cents for each coffee."

"That's quite reasonable," I remarked.

"Very much so. But not for some of the miners who barely make that much a day at their claims. Luke Norton could make even more money to support his church if he would raise the prices a bit, but he deliberately charges just a little over the cost of the food in order to feed more people, and in turn they might be inclined to visit his church on Sundays."

We neared Hattie's house, and I asked, "Would it start a rumor if you came in for coffee?"

"Maybe not if I drive the carriage to the back of the house. You go in, and I'll come in through the kitchen door."

After lighting the lamps and a fire in the stove, I set the coffee pot on the fire. When Grant came in the kitchen door, I commented, "I do miss electric coffee grinders and automatic coffee makers. The coffee here is so strong. Boiled rather than brewed. Here we drink it out of tin cups or china, but I prefer a large mug of fresh coffee to get me going in the morning."

"How true," Grant responded as we sat at the kitchen table. Then he said quietly, "All right, Sam, let's talk."

My body felt a sudden jolt, but I was able to reply, "All right, Grant. Where do we start?"

"First of all, why do you think you and I, of all people, were brought here?"

It took me a moment to work through an answer. Then I faced him squarely. "Maybe we both were at critical points in our lives that opened us to the experience. I had reached a point where the life I was living had no purpose, direction or substance. Through the training, spiritual sessions and classes that enlarged my awareness of inner as well as outer growth, I brought into my life the feeling there was much more to existence than the everyday pattern where most of us land. There is such a thing as living life to its fullest, looking beyond the people in my life and accepting them as individuals who would help me find the lessons I was to learn. Maybe by bringing me here, the Universe is saying "Here is what you are seeking. Pay attention!"

When I finished, Grant was looking at me strangely. "Where on earth did you learn all of that? I've never heard anything like it before.

His head went from side to side in sympathy, then he commented, "This is all new to me."

I laughed. "You were probably very busy with a different kind of spirits — alcoholic rather than inner growth."

Grant said softly, "Sounds like we've been traveling down totally different roads." We both sat quietly, looking at each other more deeply, looking beneath the surface.

I continued. "And I must confess something. I've never before talked like this, sharing my thoughts with anyone else in the world. It's like opening a door I've kept closed for many years."

"Sam, I've felt from the start that we have a lot to share, not only why we came here, but who we were before and who we are becoming now."

Without realizing it, we were holding hands tightly across the table. Then the coffee boiling on the stove broke the moment. I rushed over to take it from the fire, then poured it into waiting mugs. I set one in front of Grant, then sat down to face him.

"Sam, let's face the fact that Hattie will be gone for the next few days, so our time together must be put to good use. We should decide if we're going to try, in every way we can, to get back to where we came from, our other lives."

I nodded slowly in agreement.

"Or, and this is a killer, would we rather stay in this time and live out our lives in the last years of the 19th Century?"

Thoughtfully, I added, "I've done a little thinking along those lines. The 20th Century and all that follows has so much that is not yet evident here. Air travel, automobiles, new medicines and cures, advances in science, new procedures and devices to make life easier. On the other hand, there is the dark side of that time — the elevating crime rate, pollution, waste, the homeless, hunger, the arrogance and corruption in politics and the corporate world, robber barons, another depression, growing unemployment, sending young men to fight wars in obscure and distant countries, and the escalating use of guns. And since you've been gone, Grant, Mother Nature has been flexing her muscles and showing her power — floods, fires, hurricanes and earthquakes on a greater scale than ever before. Mankind is finding it does not have control over the environment which was once thought possible."

Grant looked sadly into his coffee. "And yet, if we stay here, we'll live in a society that does not have decent laws. There is a Civil War and the assassination of President Lincoln yet to come, not to mention inadequate medicines and medical care. But we could witness the dawning of the West — new cities, railroads, inventions. We could take part in all of that if we decide to stay."

"That is, if we have a choice," I said.

We refilled our cups, then took them into the parlor and settled comfortably in the overstuffed furniture. That night we talked for hours about his childhood, his hopes and fears, how he was close to panic when he first realized where he was in time. We talked about the early days and growth of Boone Valley, and how he managed to create and launch a brewery from just a few dollars loaned to him by Martin and Hattie McKee. In turn, I told him about what I had left behind — the latest in movies, politics, heroes, villains, scandals, victories. Finally we both fell silent, deep in our own thoughts. ·

Grant broke the silence. "Even if I could go back, what do I have to go back to? I lived a solitary life after my divorce except for the time I was allowed to spend with my daughters. I dated now and then, but didn't find anyone I wanted to commit to. My career at the brewery was going higher and higher into management, and that was where I put all my thoughts and energy. At the time it seemed I had it made, but living here has given me time to rethink my priorities."

His face brightened. "It's amazing. I like having a business with competent people that runs pretty well on its own. I've taken the opportunity to pass the time of day with townspeople and miners coming or going; to ask their opinions about different things, how they think and feel. I've learned to care about these people. Knowing the future, I can help or guide them. Now and then I might advise them to look into other areas or investments, but I am careful, however, not to appear all-knowing or insightful."

Putting his coffee aside, he leaned forward eagerly. "Do you realize, Sam, that we would know exactly how to invest our money? The Comstock Lode, the silver mines, the Industrial Age, railroads. All this would be new and we would know how successful they would be!"

He stopped himself. "I'm talking as if you and I would be making these decisions together. I don't even know if you want to stay or try to return to your other life. Am I assuming too much?"

I was at a loss for words. I admit I was caught up with his ideas, and he painted an exciting future that would be hard to resist. I began slowly. "Grant, I admit that my marriage was not made in heaven. I played the roles that were given to me — cherished only child, the wife of a successful businessman, hostess, homemaker, and mother of two fine boys. What I'm feeling at this moment is that I would miss my sons terribly. But if I returned, I would fall back into those roles in order to be with them. Frankly, at this point I'm not sure I want to pay the price." I was close to tears and caught my breath to hold back a sob.

Grant moved from his chair to sit on the sofa beside me. Before I knew it, his two arms enveloped me in a very gentle and protective way. "My poor Sam. Here we are strangers, thrown together in this crazy time and place. We can either deal with the future together, or we can each take a different road and go our own way."

He held me away so he could look into my eyes. "I may as well tell you that going forward with you in this time and place appeals to me greatly. I've come to admire your charm, your spunk, your devilish mind, and you ain't bad lookin' either!" His soft brown eyes warmed with his smile. "If this is what the Fates had in store when they brought us here, I wouldn't complain a bit." He laughed softly, then continued.

"There now! Have I pitched a curve you weren't ready for?" Then his arms held me gently once more and there was silence.

After a few moments he released me and stood up. "It's getting late, Sam, and I've given you a lot to think about. And I won't be sleeping too well tonight, that's a positive. Walk me to the door and I'll be on my way."

Holding hands, we walked to the kitchen door and faced each other. "Do you mind staying here alone?" he asked.

"I'm fine, though these kerosene lamps are a bother. Often I find myself reaching to the wall for light switches."

That brought a laugh, then he said, "I'll say good night and sweet dreams." His arms reached out and held me, then he sweetly kissed me on the forehead and went through the door.

That night my mind was like a merry-go-round, switching from trying to return home to be with my boys, to staying here with Grant. Back and forth, no thought completed before another came to take its place. The boys or Grant. Harland and Mother Malcolm were not part of my considerations, though if I did decide to return, our relationships would undergo a drastic change, I was very sure of that.

My role here was that of a woman separated from her family. Morals and conventions were acknowledged strictly by some levels of the community, and in others they were kicked aside and ignored. And I could not escape the fact that I was strongly attracted to Grant. Since coming together, our communication had been on a deeply personal level, something I had not imagined could be possible.

I spent a good many of the dark hours in prayer, asking for guidance and comfort. As I meditated, I was tempted to hold the crystal I discovered on that first walk down the dusty street of Boone Valley, but hesitated for fear it might in some strange way change or alter my circumstances.

"Help me, dear Universe, to find my way, in whatever manner would best serve all concerned — Grant and his children, me and my boys. Help me to live out my days just as I asked you that starry night not too long ago — with meaning and direction."

I left my bed early, fixed a breakfast I could barely eat, and went through the routine of cleaning up and dressing only to find it was too early to report to work. At almost 10 o'clock, an impulse sent me in the direction of Ida Penny's shop. Since my work at the saloon seemed to be on course once more, it would be smart to order one or two more gowns to wear.

As I passed the saloon, two small figures ran across the busy road, dodging the animals, carts and pedestrians. Warren and Sumpin greeted me with great smiles. "Mis' Samantha, we sure miss you. We hear you a-playin' 'most every day, but we hardly get to see you any more," Warren said breathlessly.

"Tell you what, youngsters, why don't you walk with me to Ida Penny's and we can have a visit right now."

Taking each one by the hand, I walked happily with them down the boarded walkways, chattering away. As we reached Ida's shop, Warren was saying with a worried frown, "Sumpin's takin' a notion that she wants to change her name. She's sure stubborn about it, and Momma Bertha says it's nonsense, but she keeps talkin' about it."

Before entering the door, I said to Sumpin, "What's this all about, young lady?"

She stood her ground. "Sumpin's no name for a girl. I want a regular name like everyone else."

Ida opened the door and greeted us warmly, then showed us to the back of her shop where she sat the children next to a warm and welcoming potbellied stove.

"Ida," I began, "we got us a serious problem this morning. It seems that Sumpin doesn't like her name and wants to change it."

Ida turned to Sumpin, "What would you like to be called?"

Sumpin put a finger in her mouth — she wasn't used to being the center of attention. "Don't know yet," she said softly.

"We must do something about that," I said. "There are so many lovely names, let's see what we can do." Then I presented to her every name I could think of, from A to Z, past to present. At each one she shook her head. Finally, discouraged, I said, "We'll just have to put our minds to it and pretend we're going over the rainbow to find a special name for you."

Her face lifted and she said sweetly, "That's the one. You can call me Rainbow."

We looked at one another, then Ida went over to her and curtsied. "Then that's what it shall be. I'm very pleased to know you, Miss Rainbow. And to celebrate this great occasion, I'm going to make you a special jacket with all of the colors in the rainbow on it."

Rainbow/Sumpin responded with a beautiful smile and clapped her hands. Warren, however, frowned, saying, "Don't know what Momma Bertha's goin' to say about this. She may get mad at us, like she always does."

Ida said briskly, "We just won't tell her. This will be our special secret." And she brought out milk and cookies and we had what amounted to a celebration. I raised my glass high and said, "Here's to a new resident who has come to town — Miss Rainbow. Long may she grace us with her special charm."

And there were smiles all around, as well as milk mustaches and cookie crumbs.

Ida then announced, "Some of the Waiter Girls were here yesterday picking out material for their new uniforms and they're real serious about wearing them when they work. They said some of the Hurdy-gurdy Girls will come over today to do the same. Looks like things are going to change at that saloon if the girls have anything to say about it. So, I've got enough work to keep me up nights for weeks, but I'm hopin' things will change for the better once Orrin approves."

I answered wryly, "Ida, 'approve' is not a word we use when it comes to Orrin, but if he's smart he'll seriously consider the suggestions the girls present to him. If they show him they mean business, maybe he'll agree. But it won't be easy."

Ida showed me samples of materials just received from San Francisco, and I selected two that would make lovely gowns. Between us we sketched two garments using her sense of style and my memory of costumes worn by heroines in Westerns I had seen in movies. No bustles, though I knew they would be high style in a few more years, but full skirts and flattering lines would be fine for me.

Before walking back to the Majestic, I sat down with the children and cautioned, "Now remember, there are several things we will not mention in front of your mom or anyone except friends. One is Rainbow's new name. Two, the new dresses for the Waiter Girls. Three, the changes the girls will be asking of Orrin pretty soon. For now we will keep these special secrets. Agreed?"

I raised my hand as a pledge.

Bless their hearts, the children raised their hands and soberly nodded their heads in agreement. After a warm goodbye to Ida, we walked the short distance to the saloon. On entering the kitchen, we said a cheery hello to Wong Kee.

I approached him and said in a very solemn voice, "My friend, we've been busy making plans and have some lovely secrets to share. First of all, Sumpin has a special new name, and she will share it with you only if she feels you can be trusted." I winked at Rainbow and she grinned in return.

"Second, there are changes that more than a few people would like to see around here. They're all good and would make things better. But these will take time. It looks like there will be some improvements at the Majestic!"

Wong Kee stepped away from his work and looked us over. "You have funny smiles. Must be big secrets to be happy. Wise man say, 'walk careful if you not know way', so be sure of way before you act." He nodded approval as he returned to his work.

Just then a man entered the room and approached Wong Kee. He was in his 30s, I would guess, with a bony, angular face, not handsome but carrying an air of importance. He was dressed in black trousers with a matching frock coat, a dazzling brocaded vest of blue and gold, a white shirt, and a black string tie. There was a large gold ring on the little finger of his left hand. He ordered, "Give me some coffee right now, you heathen, and make sure it's hot."

Wong Kee did not speak but reached for a mug and wordlessly poured the hot brew. The man drew a silver flask from his pocket, poured something into the mug, returned it to his pocket, then picked up the cup and left without a word.

I asked Wong Kee, "Who on earth was that?"

Even with a cleaver in his hand and the vegetables before him, Wong Kee stood erect with dignity and answered, "New gambler. From San Francisco. Here two days. Not very nice."

"And what is the name of that very rude man?"

"Name hard to say," he answered.

Warren spoke up. "His name's Avery Singleton. He talks like that to everyone 'cept Mr. Smithers. Momma Bertha thinks he's handsome, but I sure don't. He yelled at me once and tried to kick me. Told me to keep out of his way, and that's what Sumpin and I try to do, that's for sure!"

I could not help but say, "Oh, great! Just what we need. Another villain to deal with. Looks like trouble has come to River City and not a sheriff in sight!"

Chapter Nineteen

The concert that day went well. Most of the chairs were filled and the response to the music, especially when Willis joined me at the keyboard, was most gratifying. It was cut short, however, when a miner by the name of Ol' George ran in, holding his worn hat high in the air and yelling over and over, "I found me some gold! I found me some gold! Them durn rocks in front of my claim finally paid off!"

As he reached the bar, Corby brought out a bottle and a glass and set them before Ol' George, who poured a healthy shot and drank it down.

Everyone in the saloon gravitated toward the bar to hear about the fulfillment of the dream of all miners.

"Them lousy rocks in front of my claim kept gettin' in the way, so I finally set my mind to clear 'em out and make more room. Worked my fool head off breakin' 'em down, then I started findin' ore rich with gold and nuggets in them little nooks and cracks. The river must have swept 'em down when it flooded, and there they were, sittin' there waiting for me to find 'em. So I began throwin' 'em in the canvas bags in my tent. Been doin' this for at least a whole month, until them rocks were all cleared out. Well, sir, when I finally looked at them bags I could barely lift 'em. Borrowed Barnaby's mule, I did, and brought two of them bags down here to Aaron Ross to check out. Next day I brought in three more bags, and by the time he looked 'em all over and tells me I've got about 60 pounds of gold. Sixty pounds! Fellas, the drinks are on me!"

As the crowd vacated my side of the room, I could see Willis taking it all in. I approached him to ask, "What do you think, Willis?

Are you happy for Ol' George?"

"Guess so," he said bitterly. "I heard this was the third claim he's worked. He started out at a strike in Georgia at a place called Dahlonega. Didn't have much luck at all, so he's been workin' his way over here. He's worked hard, no doubt about it. I only wish I had a gold nugget for every note I played on my piano!"

By this time Ol' George was sitting on the bar, holding his glass high, and yelling, "I'm goin' home to Nebrasky, yes siree. I'm goin' home!"

I touched Willis on the arm and said, "Let's work on our own gold mine, Willis. Our duets are going well, but we should develop new material. The best place to practice would be at Hattie's. Why don't you come over there tomorrow morning about nine. We'll invite Mr. Douglas and Ida Penny to come listen." Even though it would cut into his sleep time, Willis was agreeable.

During dinner that night at Norton's Café, I asked Grant if he could come to Hattie's in the morning.

He said, "Yes," and then with a gleam in his soft brown eyes, he continued. "You can work with Willis the next few mornings, but in the evenings, my dear lady, your time is mine!"

Cautiously looking about the café, I whispered, "Grant, I can't remember the last time a blush came to my ladylike cheeks, but if you continue in this vein, the spectators will have lots to talk about. Mind your manners, please, sir!"

He laughed softly, and finished his dinner without further comment.

Later at Hattie's when coffee was before us on the kitchen table, Grant came to the point. "Sam, have you come to any decision? Any thoughts?"

"No, just a dark night with my head filled with chop suey! What about you?"

He took my hand and said, "No matter how you look at it, it

seems we're going to be together in this. Whatever the future holds, it's up to the two of us to decide what it'll be."

"But should we even try to get back? Did you go back to where you first found yourself in Boone Valley?"

"Sam, at the spot where I awoke, I spent hours there, day and night, saying prayers. I didn't have any ruby slippers, but I kept closing my eyes and wishing myself home. I did it over and over until one thing stopped me."

"What was that?"

"Hunger. I couldn't last another day without food and, most important, finding shelter and a way to earn money. Then I ran into Titus Boone who was looking for workmen for his building projects. Most of the men he tried to recruit were dead set on staking claims and working on their fortunes. While in college I worked in construction so I had the skills and experience Titus could use. Luckily he staked me for my first meal, then put me right to work."

I reflected, "There hasn't been time for me to spend a night on the stairs where Sumpin and Warren first found me. And I'd look rather foolish just sitting there all night with people walking by." I shrugged. "I thought about it, really, but wasn't sure how to go about reversing the process."

"So, what do we do?" he asked. "We can just settle into 1852, or we can work it to our advantage and shape things the way we want them to be."

I smiled at him and quoted, "It's a puzzlement, as the King of Siam once said."

There were a few moments of silence. Grant stood and paced back and forth in the small kitchen, and then sat down.

"All right," he said decisively, "here's what we'll do. You tell me — no holds barred — what you want life to be like if you decide to stay in this time period. Tell me from your heart of hearts. I promise, scout's honor, to be just as truthful with you." His face was open, earnest.

I took a moment, then began. "Grant," I said hesitantly, "this kind of a choice is given to few people — to know the future and be able to change the present. The mind staggers when you think about it. The Samantha I was 10 years ago couldn't have understood or accepted such a concept. But here we are with a world of choices before us. And do you know what?"

Grant smiled. "What does the new Samantha have to say?"

"My old life, 'way back there in the future, looks rather pale by comparison to this one. Here life would be much broader, colorful, down-to-earth. Off the top of my head, here is what I think."

I stopped to take a deep breath and clear my head.

"I would dearly love to stay here and see the Gold Rush through to the end when Boone Valley starts to close. Then, go from here to settle in one of the fertile valleys in California and watch it develop, to enjoy the sun and the quiet and the bounty from the earth. And then, following the Civil War, move east somewhere. For my last years, I'd love to actually know and talk with the men and women who will be instrumental in rebuilding and shaping our country. I want to watch the process as it happens, to see history unfold."

Looking deeply into Grant's eyes, I finished. "This is what would be most satisfying to me. It's not clear where the money would come from in order to finance all of this, but you said no limits, no holds barred."

Grant stood up, walked over to take my hand and lifted me up into his arms. Before I knew it, he was kissing me, as sweetly and as thoroughly as I had ever been kissed. And I didn't want him to stop. But he did stop. He put his cheek to mine, held me close and whispered, "Samantha, you're a wonder, and what a lovely appreciation you have of life and its possibilities. What you just described sounds so — so right — and I could see clearly how it could be for us. And you do mean us, don't you? Because I couldn't imagine going on from here without you."

Once more he enveloped me in a kiss that tossed all of my inhibitions aside. I clung to him and kissed him back with the same joy and passion. We had come together and were bonded for the future, whatever it would bring.

As I clung to him, I began to feel an ache in the very center of my being, a rush of all those emotions that made me want to be closer to him, to blend with him on every level — body, mind and spirit. I had never experienced that rush of emotions with Harland, never imagined that such feelings could be shared with another being.

Well, I'd read enough romance novels to know what would happen next. I was a little shocked, but it all seemed so very right. The next thing I knew we were upstairs, sitting on my bed, side by side, still kissing. Grant broke from the kiss and said breathlessly, "Sam, what we have here is a connection we can't ignore. What I feel for you at this moment would be hard to describe. There are so many thoughts, emotions, visions of the future involved. But we're here, we're together, and something wonderful is happening. And it isn't just now, tonight, but it's the beginning of a lifetime. You feel it too, don't you? Please tell me you do."

As he spoke, I could feel the tears welling in my eyes and streaming down my cheeks. I nodded as he reached up and with a curved finger gently wiped them away.

Before I knew it, the clothing we wore while playing our roles as citizens of Boone Valley were put aside and we were joined, bare skin against bare skin, open and sharing ourselves on the highest level of emotion. Our coming together was a commitment, a bonding of our hearts and minds.

"My dearest darling," Grant breathed against my ear, "I've never felt like this before. It's like you've always been there, waiting to become part of me. And without knowing it, I've been aching to find you to fill the part of me that was missing.

I gently asked, "How can this happen so quickly? We've known each other for just a few days, and yet I feel deeply committed to you."

Things were moving too fast, even by 19th Century standards, yet everything seemed to be unfolding as it should. It just felt right. When the Universe responds to a prayer, it seems to be complete in every way. Our lives were in divine order.

He drew me closer, and beneath the cozy quilt of that lovely bed, we once again gave each other our gifts of awareness, appreciation and passion, acknowledging each other for who we were and would become in the future.

We slept a short while until I woke with a start and found the sun was beginning to rise and morning was almost fully in bloom. Grant was still quietly sleeping, so I leaned over to feast on the look of him, the lines and planes of his face, the strength of his mouth and chin, the dark lashes that feathered his cheeks. My finger reached out to trace his nose from his brow to the graceful lines of his lips. He frowned, moved his head slightly, then reluctantly let go of the dream that held him. "Time to get up, you lazy thing."

His fingers lightly rubbed the sleep from his eyes. "Why did you let me sleep? Have you been awake long?"

"Not long, and I took the time to look you over, sir, to check the merchandise."

One arm reached out to bring me close so he could kiss my eyes and temples. "And what did you decide, my dear? Will you throw me back on the pile, or am I a keeper?"

Playing the role of a particular customer, I answered, "Well, you seem to be well put together, and able to function for the next 10 to 20 years. You also look like one of the newer models with a very attractive finish. Is there a warranty?"

He laughed. "I come with a guarantee to serve, honor, protect and cherish you for as long as you want or need me. Also, all the moving parts are in good working order. Shall we try them out now and see if it's exactly what you have in mind?"

He moved even closer, but I shook my head.

"Grant, remember, Willis will be here at 9 o'clock to practice. It's getting late, my dear."

He jumped from the bed and dressed hurriedly. "Damn, I could sure use a hot shower right now. I'll get the horse and buggy back to the livery stable, change clothes, rent another, pick up Ida Penny and be back about 9 o'clock."

He sat on the bed and gently held me. "My dear, we have much more to discuss. Mainly the fact that to these people you're a married lady. If we are to really be together, that must be resolved in some way. We'll have to give your situation some very serious thought."

His goodbye kiss was wonderfully deep and lingering. "For now, my dear Sam, goodbye." Smiling his lovely smile he added, "My dear. It's wonderful to be able to say it and know what it means. You look beautiful, and I can't wait to see you again like this, with your hair all messed up and that sweet smile on your face."

He left the room quickly, and I could hear him racing down the stairs, and then guiding the horse and buggy away from the house.

Snuggling back into bed, I could feel my body still humming from the passion of the night. While contentedly reminding myself of the things we had said to each other, a startling, dark thought inserted itself into my reverie. Harland! My legal husband of 20 years. Considering the time/space distance now between us, would it be considered adultery? It couldn't be. Harland wouldn't be born for more than one 100 years.

My thoughts drifted back to the night before, and I smiled. With my mind at rest, I rose from the bed ready to start the new day. Standing before the china wash basin, I looked at my reflection in the oval mirror on the wall. My face was glowing with happiness, and there was a grin I could not alter no matter how hard I tried. This could be a problem, I reminded myself as I dressed — one look at my face and everyone, especially Hattie, would know that I was in love.

Looking into the mirror, I said, "Mirror, mirror on the wall, who's the luckiest lady of all?" The image in the mirror smiled back and said, "Sam, my girl, you asked the Universe for a change and you not only got your wish, but you hit the jackpot!" And looking upward, I said, "And to the powers that be, saints and angels, I send you my love and gratitude. Thank you all so very, very much!"

By 9 o'clock I was ready, coffee was on the stove, and the cups and saucers set out. There was a knock at the door, and I guessed rightly that it was Grant and Ida. I greeted them, avoiding Grant's sparkling eyes.

"Good morning, Ida, Mr. Douglas. So glad you could be here. Come, we'll have some coffee while we wait for Willis."

I returned Ida's gentle handshake, and then found my hand warmly and tightly grasped by Grant as he said, "And a happy good morning to you, Mrs. Malcolm."

Since Ida's back was turned, I winked and wrinkled my nose. "You are most welcome, Mr. Douglas."

Ida gushed, "I heard all about the piano duel and have been longing to hear you play. So this is a very special treat for me!"

There was another knock on the door, and Willis was standing there looking rather uneasy. After he had a cup of coffee, Willis and I worked at the piano, coming up with several new duets. When it was time to stop, Ida burst out, "Oh, so soon? It's been such fun and I'd love to hear just a little more."

Turning to Grant and trying not to smile, I said, "What would you suggest, Mr. Douglas? Any ideas?"

"Why yes, Mrs. Malcolm. I think Ida would really enjoy hearing "In the Good Old Summertime." And that's what I played and sang. Ida was enchanted.

They all left soon after that. Grant was the last one out the door. He turned to say goodbye and gave me a quick wink and blew me a kiss. That gave my body a happy charge that set me up for the day. He transported Willis and Ida back to town, which left me time for lunch and to dress for work.

I was hoping Grant would return with the buggy and escort me to the saloon, but he was not in sight when I closed the door and began walking. It was a little after noon and the afternoon air was cool and crisp, but rather pleasant. As I walked to town wrapped in the wool cape, my mind was filled with Grant. I worked on keeping my smile under control, but it was instantly erased when I arrived at the saloon and entered the kitchen.

Avery Singleton was holding Wong Kee by the front of his jacket. Warren and Rainbow were against the wall, clinging to each other. Bertha was beside Singleton endeavoring to quiet his anger. She was saying, "Now, Avery, I know the kids didn't mean no harm. Wong Kee is a special friend of theirs."

"I told you before, Bertha, those kids of yours gotta keep out of my way. And I won't have this heathen layin' his hands on me or tryin' to stop me!"

Bertha pleaded, "Honey, I know you had a bad night with the cards. I told these kids over and over that they're not to bother you. Wong Kee shouldn't butt in the way he did!"

She turned to the children and yelled, "You kids get yourselves upstairs and into our room, and I don't want to hear a thing from you for the rest of the day!" The children raced out the door.

Wong Kee had a large bruise on one cheek. Singleton had hit

him in the face, and as I watched, horrified, he raised his arm for another blow. Without thinking, I picked up a large cleaver from the wooden worktable and held it up high.

"Singleton," I yelled, "let that man go or I'll put this cleaver in the middle of your worthless head!"

Slowly he turned to face me as he released Wong Kee. Then both of his hands turned to fists.

"It's not enough that you brutalize children," I said, "but you hit a man that you know won't fight back."

I still held the cleaver high and could hear Bertha behind me screaming, "Leave him be! Leave him be!"

Just then Corby and Elmo rushed through the door, surveyed the situation, then moved to stand on each side of me. Corby said quietly, "You folks havin' a problem here? We can hear you clear in the saloon."

Without a word Singleton straightened the sleeves of his coat, glared at me, then stalked out the door. Bertha followed quickly on his heels.

Corby shook his head. "That man sure has a mean disposition. We've seen it ever since he got here. Don't know how good a gambler he may be, but he's a bit short on manners."

Trembling, I returned the cleaver to the worktable and went to Wong Kee. "Are you all right? How badly did he hurt you?"

Slowly Wong Kee straightened his back and once more was the man of dignity. "Bad man. He hurt children. I try protect. Make him angry."

He turned away to moisten a rag with water and began to wash the trickle of blood from his mouth and cheek. Suddenly I had to sit down. My knees were shaking.

"Corby," I said, "I didn't know what I was doing, but I couldn't stand by and watch him hit Wong Kee. Someone had to do something!" Briefly I told him what had happened and how the children and Wong Kee were being treated.

"You could've been hurt, Mis' Samantha. And Orrin will blame the whole thing on you! Bertha's been sweet on that fellow ever since he swaggered in here. It's a shame she doesn't take better care of her kids."

When they were sure Wong Kee and I were all right, Corby and Elmo returned to their work. I checked the damage on Wong Kee's face.

"Are you all right? What will you do when he comes in here again?"

He said sadly, "He not to hit children. He hurts, I must stop."

"But those are awful bruises on your face. That man is dangerous!"

With a shadow of a smile, Wong Kee replied, "Not my job to be pretty. Just cook!"

I could not help but laugh out loud.

Abigail entered the kitchen, finger on her lips. "Got a minute, Mis' Samantha. Heard what happened, and it's just awful. Bertha likes that scoundrel a whole lot and won't stand up for her kids. Us girls hate the way he treats 'em and Wong Kee. But let me tell you somethin' real quick before Orrin comes back."

She drew me over to the far side of the kitchen, then began talking quietly. "Us girls have been talkin' about the list you gave us and decided we want to give it to Orrin Saturday night. We like the demands just the way they are, and we're all gonna sign the paper or make our mark, including the Hurdy-gurdy Girls."

"Don't rush into this," I cautioned. "There may be consequences. Everyone must be sure that this is what they want to do."

"We're sure, all right. We want things to change around here real soon. We decided to do it quick before Zola and Bertha find out and ruin everything." She headed back to the door. "Can't stay longer. We just wanted you to know we made up our minds."

Wong Kee brought me a cup of coffee, and I observed, "It looks like you and I will have to protect those children the best we can. This is not a very happy life for them."

He nodded wisely. "I do what I can. It be better when you help." He lowered his voice and, with a glint in his eyes, said, "I keep knife sharp, ready for you!"

I roared with laughter. "Wong Kee, I never realized what a wonderful sense of humor you have. No wonder we get along so well."

As I went out to the saloon floor, I noted that many of the tables were filled with men playing cards or sitting with their drinks, talking and waiting for me to play. Not a terribly large crowd, but not bad. As I climbed the stairs to the piano on the stage, I saw that Corby or Elmo had placed a large beer stein on the floor next to the piano. It was sitting on top of a small box and someone had written in black paint on the side, TIPS.

I began the program for the day — I don't remember if it was Gershwin or Berlin—but as usual I enjoyed the music and the memories it brought. As I played, more people came through the door and began to fill the chairs around the stage. Not bad at all, I thought.

Willis joined me for the last half hour, and we played some of the new duets, which went over very well. His attitude was becoming more confident, and he seemed to enjoy the duets. He was smiling more, and even reminded me to take a bow with him at the end of the concert.

I waved good night to Corby and Elmo and thanked them for coming to my aid in the kitchen. It was there I found Grant, deep in conversation with Wong Kee. He looked at me oddly. "What's this I've been hearing about you? From what Wong Kee is telling me, it might be more appropriate to call you Lizzie Borden!"

I ignored his remark, put on my cape and said hurriedly, "I'll tell you all about it over dinner."

Going to Wong Kee, I said, "How are the children? Have they had anything to eat?"

"They fine. Waiter Girls take food. Not to worry. We watch them good."

I breathed a sigh of relief. "Thank goodness. I was quite concerned about them while I was playing."

When Grant helped me into the buggy, I whispered, "I missed you. Haven't seen you around all afternoon."

As he climbed next to me, he shook his head. "My dear lady, I do have a business to tend to now and then. It needed some attention today, but all is well. And now, I have a surprise for you. Rather than going to Norton's for dinner, I ordered some take-out, though I didn't use that term. It seems that Della Norton had a huge pot of beef stew on the stove, so I managed to get a small container full, plus some of her special biscuits. Is that all right?"

"Grant, that was inspired. We can go right to Hattie's."

"Besides," he said wickedly, "I wanted to have you all to myself. No telling when Hattie will be back. With her traveling clear to Sacramento in the covered wagon and the good weather, we may only have tonight and tomorrow night. She could be back as early as Saturday or Sunday. There is so much to talk about, we'll have to make the most of the time we have."

At Hattie's, Grant left the horse and buggy in back while I brought the food to the stove to heat. When he entered the kitchen, I felt his arms slip around my waist and he began to kiss the back of my neck.

"I've been thinking all day about doing this. It's even better than I imagined."

"My dear sir," I teased as I turned to face him, "dinner should come first, don't you think?"

"Dinner by all means, my lady, but I was thinking about

something in the way of hors d'oeuvres!" Looking up at the ceiling, toward the bedroom, he tipped his head to one side and waited for me to respond.

I frowned and stepped back. "Grant, everything is happening so fast. I've never been swept away like this, and it's all new to me. This kind of thing happens over and over on TV, but not to me. Just look what's happened in these past two, almost three weeks. Zip … I'm in Boone Valley and it's 1852! Zip … I meet two wonderful children. Zip … I'm taken in by Hattie. Zip … I meet a villain and soon I'm playing piano in his saloon. Zip … I challenge a man to a duel. Zip … you come into my life like a tornado and everything changes. Give me a moment, please, to keep my balance!"

He looked at me with love and understanding. "Of course. I didn't think to look at things from your perspective. I've had several years to make the transition and become comfortable with this lifestyle. But you've been confronted with major challenges, one right after another, and I admire you so much for the way you've handled them."

We were sitting at the kitchen table facing each other. Grant reached for my hand and covered it with both of his. "You must know by now that I not only feel great love for you, but I'm so very proud of how you have dealt with everything."

"But look at the outlandish things I've been doing — confronting Orrin, challenging Willis to a duel, and this morning I go after that gambler with a meat cleaver, for heaven's sakes! I need time to adjust! I am rising to these occasions like a wounded bear. Where did all of this come from, Grant? This isn't like the old me, not at all."

Grant chuckled and touched my face. "My guess is that it's always been there, my love. The guts, the strong sense of right and wrong, the rising to confront injustice rather than turn away. That strong inner core you've been carrying around all these years has finally come out and you're free to act as you feel, without restraints or fear of criticism. My regard for you grows tremendously each time I see you in action."

He took my hand and kissed it tenderly, his eyes looking deeply into mine. He continued, "I know it's early in the game, but my strongest wish at this moment is for us to be married ... soon. I want us to be united, not only body and soul as we are now, but I want to show the world that we are together in all that we do, that our connection is intertwined with the regard and respect we have for each other. How about it, Sam? Is this what you want as well?" I couldn't stop the tears from coming. I was touched so deeply I could not speak. Everything was happening so fast.

Grant once more wiped the tears from my cheeks and kissed my temples. "From the water works I will assume that I have struck a nerve — a happy one, I hope."

He came to my chair, pulled me into his arms once more, and held me until the tears subsided and I could speak at last. Finally, I was able to whisper, "Grant."

"Yes, my love."

"If you don't mind," I said softly, "I do believe it's time for the hors d'oeuvres."

He smiled and, without saying a word, took my hand and led me up the stairs to the bedroom.

Chapter Twenty

Hours later, lying quietly together, arms and legs intertwined, comfortably and glowingly connected, I had to ask, "How much is 60 pounds of gold worth?"

Grant chuckled. "You sure know how to make a guy feel good! After a wonderful night of making fantastic love, all you can think about is Ol' George and his strike!"

I hid my face in embarrassment as we laughed together. "Yes, because my mind has been bouncing on a lot of things, but it stopped on Ol' George. Tell me, will it be enough to take him to Nebraska and live for the rest of his life?"

"Well, let's figure it out. Sixty pounds, times 12 troy ounces to the pound, times $20 an ounce more or less, which is what gold is worth these days. If I had my handy-dandy calculator, I could tell you immediately. But I'd guess it would be in the neighborhood of maybe $14,000."

"Is that enough to last for the rest of his life?"

"Oh, easily. Remember, these days a family can live on $300 or $400 a year. They can buy a house for close to that figure. If Ol' George gets back home with at least $12,000, he can live quite comfortably for the next 24 years. If he makes a few investments, or gets interest from a good bank, he could enlarge that figure."

"What about us, Grant? Will we have enough money to do the things we're planning?"

He playfully squeezed the end of my nose. "You forget, my dear, I'm the beer tycoon of Boone Valley. Since setting up the brewery, I've managed to put away over $20,000. Substantial money will be added by the time the rush for gold is over and the saloons close down."

I added, "And don't forget what I'm making at the Majestic in salary and tips. I've no idea what it amounts to by this time. I've got several leather bags filled with gold dust and nuggets in my room, plus the back pay. It may help pay for the mortgage on the old homestead."

Grant hugged me. "Realistically there are other things to consider."

"Such as?"

"Some lucky miners have found large pockets of gold. But now the big companies are getting into the act. I heard the other day that hydraulic mining will soon begin in the Nevada City area, also extensive underground mining. Once begun, it will spread south throughout this area and the individual miners will be forced out. Some of them, I fear, will end up working in the mines for a few dollars a day just to make ends meet."

"Then this is the end of the Gold Rush?"

"No. I believe there are still large areas of gold to be discovered and fortunes yet to be made. But if I remember what little I've read on the subject, this year will be the peak of the gold activities in California. In time, the surface gold will be played out, and miners who haven't made it will have to search for gold — or silver — in Nevada, Colorado, Canada, and eventually Alaska."

I sighed. "I'm so glad Ol' George made it, and I dearly hope Barnaby will do well with his claim. He's been working so hard. Maybe one day he'll find enough to take back to Missouri before he's too old and worn out."

With Grant nibbling on my ear, I became distracted. Conversation terminated. The economics of the California Gold Rush left my mind and I tended to the immediate business at hand. Hours later, closer to midnight, we reluctantly drew apart and Grant tended to the stove to heat the beef stew and biscuits. As we ate, the conversation came back on track.

"Keep in mind, Sam," Grant explained, "there's a down side to hydraulic mining. The process causes hills and mountains to be washed away, rivers rerouted and, as long as it's used, the rivers themselves are polluted with dirt and debris. Much of this area will never again look the way God created it."

I shook my head sadly. "I'm getting the feeling that this part of the gold rush won't be easy to watch."

Grant explained, "During the next five or more years, fortunes will be made, but many claims will fail, and it will be a time of extreme hardship for many. I only hope Ol' George will be smart enough to sell his claim and pull out now. Above all, I hope he doesn't squander his newfound fortune in San Francisco. There'll be plenty of vultures there waiting to take it away from him."

We finished dinner, and I put the dishes aside and poured the coffee. "You'll just have to warn him of what's ahead and show him how to take care of his fortune."

"How can I do that without letting on that I have special information? Which brings up another point, Sam. Will there ever be a time when we'll tell our story to anyone? Where we really came from, or how we got here?"

"Grant, no one would believe us. It's not in the realm of their understanding. They'll surely think we're either lunatics or liars."

"Our first order of business, my dear, is to make it clear that your husband is no longer of this world, which is a fact. You've been telling everyone you were separated from your husband and two sons during your trip here. How can we make it clear you are a recent widow? After misplacing you, did he search desperately until his health and funds ran out; or did he lose his money in a poker game in San Francisco and was therefore dispatched by an angry gambler when he couldn't pay his debt? After witnessing the hectic and decadent life in San Francisco, did he take your two sons and head back home, leaving word that he no longer had the time or patience to search for you any further? Does any of this sound reasonable to you?"

I sighed. "Not really. Would you buy these stories?"

"You must realize, Sam, during these years people got lost, robbed or done away with. Many went alone into the mountains looking for gold and were never heard from again. And if they went too far south, the Indians or Mexicans robbed and killed them."

"All this sounds horrid," I said. "Let's not think about it. Somehow we're going to find a way."

He came around to my side of the table. "You can bet on it, my lady." His face filled with concern. "I hope and pray that the time factor we're dealing with is not like a rubber band, stretched out from here to where we were, and that one fine day it will snap one or both of us back into the 20th Century. That doesn't sound very scientific, but who knows what forces are at work where we're concerned?"

He pulled me to my feet and kissed me soundly. "Time to go on my way, and I leave you most reluctantly. Tomorrow and Saturday will be busy days for both of us. When we're not thinking of each other, let's give more thought to how we can clear the decks for our future. Besides, I think we both could use a good night's sleep."

"You're right. My head's like a wheel in a squirrel cage." Looking into his warm brown eyes, I said, "Let's think only about the miracle of our coming together, and let our saints and angels work on the problem while we sleep. Heaven knows, they're better qualified."

He raised an eyebrow. "I don't know where you get your information, but you seem to know who's on our side and it sounds right to me. Good night, my darling Sam."

"Good night, my darling Grant. Sleep well."

He made a face at me, then went through the door.

Upon waking the next morning, I looked from the bedroom window to find dark clouds covering the sky. I could feel a chill forcing its way through the closed window. During the night a light rain had left moisture on the windows. From the many visits to Rocky Crest, I knew well winter and snowfall would soon come to this mountainous area.

As I finished breakfast, there was a hesitant knock on the kitchen door. I opened it to find a man in his 60s with a sweet smile. He was holding a basket filled with vegetables. This must be Hector, Hattie's neighbor.

"I live next door," he said haltingly. "I take care of the gardens for Mrs. McKee. I hurry to pick the vegetables so a heavy rain won't hurt them. You give them to her, please?"

"Of course," I answered. "I'm sure she'll appreciate your thoughtfulness." I put the basket on the kitchen table. It was heavy with a bounty of carrots, potatoes, peas, green beans and other treasures.

The dirt road to town was marked with numerous ruts left by the carts and wagons. As I walked, I felt the surface of the road giving way beneath my feet. The cold, damp wind found its way through the wool cape. If rougher weather is soon upon us, I'll be needing warmer clothes and heavier shoes. I made a mental note to purchase some winter gear at Hattie's store. Meanwhile, I made it to the saloon without too much damage to my dress and shoes.

All seemed quiet and in good order in the saloon's kitchen. Wong Kee was busy, and several of the tables held an assortment of people. Corby was sitting at a far table with Warren and Rainbow. After greeting Wong Kee, I joined them, and the smiles that greeted me indicated that for now the climate indoors was agreeable.

"Howdy, Mis' Samantha," Corby said. "We're mighty glad to see you. These youngsters here have been sharing a special secret with me." Rainbow looked pleased as punch.

"What's up, my little one?" I asked.

"I told Corby my new name. He likes it and said that's what he'll call me from now on!

Corby remarked, "Don't let anyone tell her it's silly. If that's what she wants and it makes her happy, what's the harm?"

"Speaking of harm, have Orrin and Avery Singleton had their heads together? Any sparks flying that you can see?" I asked.

Corby shook his head. "Not that I can see."

"How about you, Wong Kee? Everything all right in here? Has anybody been giving you a bad time?"

"Everything quiet. But dragon's breath near."

"You mean that something is about to happen?"

He shrugged his shoulders and moved his head sadly from side to side.

A sense of concern passed over me and I began to dread the uncertain future. Corby joined me as I headed for the saloon. Something had changed. My piano had been moved back to its original location — under the balcony near the front entrance. Whether this was done for convenience, spite or anger, I didn't know, but I guessed the latter.

Elmo was working nearby, and I leaned over to ask, "Who moved the piano?"

"Coupla hours ago, three men came, took it off the stage, and put it back where Orrin told 'em. Didn't see or hear nothin' else."

Most of the tables around the piano were already filled. The Waiter Girls were moving back and forth, and each one of the four conspirators gave me a nod or a wink. The faces of the men in the saloon reflected the hard life of this period. They were care worn, burned by the sun, wrinkled and damaged by constant exposure to the elements. I smiled at all assembled and thanked them for coming, then turned to sit down.

Just then Elmo appeared, placed a large beer stein on top of the piano, then looked pointedly at the audience.

The relocation of the piano did not lessen the number of people who came that day or their response to the music. So whatever point Orrin wanted to make by moving the piano was not yet clear. When Willis joined me for the last half hour, he shrugged his shoulders and said, "Who knows?"

It was an easy afternoon. Most of the men knew me by now and enjoyed the music, and I was completely relaxed. They were less shy with their comments, and we connected in a very nice way. When I played "Little Brown Jug," they sang and clapped their hands in time. By the time the program came to an end, all of the tables were full and a few people were standing along the sides of the room.

Willis and I put our heads together and decided to end with a bang, so we did a few minutes playing a spirited "Turkey in the Straw." We were a hit, and without a doubt I would get the bonus for the week. I'd have to fight for it, but there were plenty of witnesses to verify the large and happy audience that applauded and cheered.

There was no sign of Orrin or Avery Singleton, though I entered the kitchen cautiously in case I would find one or the other there. Of course my dear Grant was waiting. Something wonderful was on the stove, and I walked over to look into the large pot.

Grant stood beside me. "Another surprise for dinner. Wong Kee has concocted this gourmet meal of chicken and Chinese noodles and offered some for our dinner. He'll dish some out and then we'd better get out before Orrin catches us."

"Oh, it does smell delicious. Grab the evidence and let's hit the road. Thank you, thank you, Wong Kee!"

We made our escape into the waiting carriage, and soon

were in Hattie's kitchen hungrily devouring the meal.

"Just think, Grant. Pasta in this time and place. Who would have believed it? I hope you tipped Wong Kee."

"Of course, I slipped him something. But what we need is a cup of tea to finish it off."

We settled into the parlor with the hot tea, contented with the day and each other. Grant leaned over and kissed me on the cheek, then his lips traveled slowly to my neck.

"Mind your manners, sir," I said with mock seriousness.

He straightened up and with a diabolical grin said, "I'll continue that project a little later. For now we must discuss how, when and where we'll dispose of your husband. It almost sounds like an Alfred Hitchcock movie. Or how about, 'Perry Mason and the Case of the Unnecessary Husband'?"

I confessed, "I can't help but feel we're doing something illegal or dastardly. I know in time Harland will consider me dead and probably remarry, that is if Mother Malcolm gives her approval. So what I have here is a misplaced husband, or am I the one who's been misplaced? How do we explain there's been no word or rumor that he may be searching for me? If such a thing had actually happened to me, I would have been searching along the trail we were supposedly traveling. In this time and place, a woman would probably wait several years before accepting the fact that her husband was indeed lost, and then marry again."

Grant agreed. "That follows the social customs here. But I've had a thought, and see if you agree. The one true friend I've made these past years is Andrew Locke, a lawyer. I took you to his office when we first got together. I could talk with him about this, but in return I may have to tell him our stories. If he refuses to believe our situation, he'll be lost to us."

"A good possibility. Why don't you give it a try, and if he finds it hard to accept, call me in. You have the contents of your wallet, and I have enough proof in my backpack to convince him."

Grant hastened to add, "In fact, this would be the best time to talk with him. His office is closed and no one will be around to overhear." He stood up. "If you don't mind, my dear, I'll scoot over to his house before it gets any later. Let's see if we can get this thing moving in some way before Hattie returns. All right with you?"

I stood and placed my hands on his shoulders. "Of course. I'm very anxious to get all this resolved."

He smiled. "If it's not too late, I'll come back and report. Otherwise, my dear Sam, I'll see you tomorrow. Sleep tight, my love."

And after one lovely, lingering kiss, he was on his way.

About 9:30 the next morning, Grant arrived at the doorstep, tired but smiling.

"You poor dear," I said. "Come in, have some coffee, then tell me everything."

As soon as he was seated at the kitchen table, the words poured out.

"Andrew and I have been talking all night. It took me hours to convince him that our stories are true. Then once he understood, he insisted on knowing everything about our time. I ended up drawing pictures to illustrate things like computers and cars and super jets. He was so dazzled, it was hard to keep him focused on our dilemma. When he finally settled down, he promised to give it some serious thought."

He massaged his eyes and ran fingers through his hair. "That's all I can tell you right now. I was hoping to bring you a few answers, but that's the best I could do. Andrew's a good man, and when he settles down, I'm sure he'll have something to give us."

After eating the quick breakfast I provided, Grant was so tired that it didn't take much persuasion to send him home for a nap and a change of clothes.

So, we still had no plan, but now we had taken someone into our confidence.

I walked through the drizzle an hour early that morning and stopped at Hattie's store for winter gear. There wasn't much variety, but I did find heavy boots. The women's wool coats were cut to be tight at the waist with narrow sleeves. Instead I selected a small man's coat that would allow room for bulky sweaters, and I bought two of the latter. To this I added a long wool scarf and a man's felt hat with a narrow brim. These clothes were far from fashionable, but they would serve me well in the cold days to come.

I took my purchases to Jim Bidwell to charge to my account and put aside for me to pick up later. He mentioned that Hattie should be returning either today or tomorrow. So much had happened since she began her journey. There was more for Grant and me to discuss, and this lady, I am sure, would be shrewd enough to determine that something had happened in her absence!

I didn't have long to think about it when I entered the side door of the saloon and found Orrin standing in the hallway.

"Well, there she is. The lady with the cleaver. You listen to me, you bitch. You're only a woman and you damned well better learn your place. Mind your manners, mind what you say to people, and your own damned business!"

His hands were two tight fists in front of his chest, and his face was mottled with rage.

I attempted to explain. "But Avery was threatening the children and beating Wong Kee."

"That don't give you no right to butt into Avery's business. Behave yourself, and do only what I pay you to do. I don't care how much the men like your piano playin'. I can kick your ass right out the door if you don't remember your place!"

He turned abruptly and I made my way into the kitchen. On seeing Wong Kee, I asked, "Did you hear Orrin just now?"

He nodded. "Heard dragon's roar. He not done. More to come."

No one else was in the kitchen, so I accepted a mug of coffee and spent a few minutes chatting.

"Wong Kee, you're always here when I come and go. Do you ever go home? Where do you sleep?"

"Where many Chinee men stay. When weather bad, I go to shack on mountain. Chinee men go there."

"Do you get enough rest after the long days you put in?"

"Can rest eyes and hands."

"And where do you get all of the meat and vegetables you cook each day? Are they delivered?"

"Chinee men bring meat, wood they cut, vegetables they grow."

The door opened and, after looking around carefully, Abigail slipped in. Her usually happy face was filled with concern. "It's all decided. After work tonight, Maggie'll give Orrin our list of demands. Me and the others aren't brave enough, but she's the strong one and says there ain't no need to wait. Besides," and she looked at the door fearfully, "Zola and Bertha have been havin' at us, sayin' somethin's up, and being real nasty."

She looked pale and frightened, and cut a sad figure in her well-worn velvet dress with tattered lace trim. I could not help but put an arm about her shoulders and hold her close.

"Please have faith that things will get better for all of you," I said. "You're entitled to a better life. You work very hard for Orrin, and he should at least listen to what you have to say. Did all of the Hurdy-gurdy Girls sign the paper?"

"They sure did, and we're all ready. Wish us luck!"

"Would you like me to be around when you talk to Orrin? I'd be happy to be here to give you some support."

"No, ma'am. It's too late for you to stay up. We usually finish work about three in the mornin', so us girls will be there with Maggie. We'll be fine."

"Well, I wish you great luck and success, and I'll work on some very powerful prayers tonight before I go to sleep." I gave her a quick hug, and she slipped through the door.

Wong Kee continued his busy work, but he said quite firmly, "This not be good. Mistah Smithas not like when women speak. If he not like what they say, he hits or hurts. He not want girls change for better."

"Surely not in front of all the other girls," I protested.

"Nothing stop him when he mad. I afraid for girls." And his head moved from side to side.

This sent a pang of fear through the pit of my stomach and I began to feel responsible, and at the same time helpless, that I may have encouraged this confrontation and would be unable to stop it. As I played the concert that afternoon, my thoughts were on the girls and what was ahead. The feeling of dread sat like a block of ice in the center of my chest.

That night Grant and I discussed the coming confrontation and shared dark feelings of helplessness. My sense of responsibility and guilt weighed heavily on my mind.

"Sam, you described to these unhappy girls what was possible. The fact that they took this information and decided to improve an unsatisfactory work situation shows how much you opened their minds. You should be very proud of them."

"Oh, I am, I am. But I don't want them to be hurt in the process. It would break my heart."

Grant put a hand on my shoulder and rubbed it gently. "They know all the risks and feel it's worth it."

We spent the rest of the evening talking quietly in Hattie's parlor. Since we knew she might return at any time, we made sure that everything would be in proper order. But I was concerned.

"Grant, how can we hide our feelings from Hattie? How much can we tell her about our situation?"

His smile was reassuring. "I'm having a helluva time keeping myself from grinning like an idiot for no reason. I look in your lovely face and see you're having the same problem. But look at it this way. We're not exactly teenagers with our first crush, and it's pretty terrific we can feel this way at this time in our lives. We've both been married with two children each, and still we're capable of these deep and powerful feelings like we've never felt before. And we'd better not see too much of each other for the time being, only from a distance. You'll be busy when Hattie returns, and she'll be anxious to tell you all about her trip. Meanwhile, I'll get Andrew down to the hard and workable facts of legally disposing of your husband. So, my dear, we'll have to play it cool for a while."

It was a hard decision, but necessary. We said a warm and lingering good night, and I prepared for sleep. Before slipping into bed, however, I spent a few moments sending love, energy and prayers to the girls. Just then Connor and Casey came to mind which triggered a flood of tears. My dear boys, I did miss them so and tried to imagine how their lives would be without me. I could remember every detail of their faces. On the other hand, it became more and more difficult to recall Harland's face, his expressions, the things I loved about him when we first married. Now I could barely make out his outline, but this was not deliberate on my part. Try as I may, I could not visualize the look of Harland. I fell asleep without finishing the thought.

I awoke suddenly to loud pounding noises. It took me a moment to realize that I was not home, but in Hattie's bedroom and the battering noises were coming from the front door. A voice was calling my name.

Rushing down the stairs, I flung open the door to find Naomi standing there, cold and shaking, her hair bedraggled and dripping with water. Quickly I brought her inside and found an afghan to throw about her shoulders, covering the gaudy costume she had worn for work that night.

"You gotta come quick, Mis' Samantha. Maggie's been hurt real bad." She shivered and drew the knitted blanket about her.

"What on earth happened?"

"We got together with Orrin after work and Maggie gave him the paper with the list of changes we're askin' for. He laughed, then he got real mad and yelled, then tore it up. He grabbed Maggie, pulled her into her room, closed the door and beat her up somethin' awful. We could hear her screamin' and cryin', and couldn't do nothin' to help her!"

"What about the night bartenders, or the customers downstairs?"

"Some of 'em came upstairs and stood with us outside the door, but all they did was yell at Orrin, tellin' him to stop! Didn't do no good. After a while he came out, yelled at us to get outta his way, then he left."

"How's Maggie doing now?"

"She's real bad, all bruised and bloody, and she ain't talkin' at all. The girls are with her now, but they don't know what to do. Please, please come and help us!"

Quickly I threw on my blue jeans, sweater and new rain gear, then grabbed the wool cape for Naomi to wear on our rush back to town.

My God, what had I done? Here I came with my grand ideas about the Bill of Rights. I should have realized that while the concept would be acceptable to the saloon girls, the men in 1852 would be far from accepting. Frantically I searched my brain and Hattie's house for anything I could use to tend to Maggie's wounds, but all I could find was a bottle of aspirin in my backpack. On the chance that Hattie might be returning in my absence, I wrote a quick note, told her of the crisis and that I would be at the saloon. That done, I closed the house and took Naomi by the arm. Together we rushed through the cold, misty morning toward town.

Chapter Twenty-One

Dashing through the front entrance of the saloon, I approached one of the night bartenders. I discovered later his name was Abner Swenson, and he reflected strong Swedish stock with a sturdy body, blond hair getting a little thin on top, and an open, sunny smile.

"What's going on?" I asked, pointing to the rooms upstairs.

His smile changed to a frown. "A real brawl, from what I heard. Orrin lost his temper again, for sure. All the girls were screamin', then he ran outta here like his tail was on fire. All I could find out was that Maggie was hurt bad. Some of the girls are up there, but no one seems to know what to do."

"Is Wong Kee still here?"

"No, ma'am, he's gone for the night."

I leaned over the bar and asked, "Will you please do me a favor? Could you or someone find Grant Douglas and let him know what has happened?"

"Yes, ma'am. I'll have Kip here watch over things and I'll do what I can to find Mr. Douglas." He grabbed a coat and disappeared through the front entrance. I worked my way through the people gathered on the staircase. They stepped aside as I headed for the crowded doorway. I entered the room to find the girls standing around the bed, a small cot really, where Maggie was lying. The floor was bare except for a well worn rug next to the bed where I could see what looked like spots of blood. The only light in the room was from a kerosene lamp on a box.

Taking Maggie's hand, I leaned over to look into her ravaged and bloody face. There were bruises around her neck and on her arms, her lip was torn, and blood was running from her nose onto her gown. Her blackened eyes were closed, but mercifully she seemed unconscious.

Abigail was beside me, crying. "We couldn't make him stop. He just kept hittin' and hittin' her!"

"What's been done for her? Did you send for a doctor?"

"We don't have none this side of town, and didn't know who to get. What can we do, Mis' Samantha?"

"First, Abigail, go heat some water and bring it up here with some soap. Next, find rags, sheets, towels—anything we can use to clean her. Next, have someone get word to Wong Kee that he's needed."

Without a word, Abigail hurried through the crowded door. I motioned Flower and Naomi into the room then closed the door. The room was quite small, which left barely enough space to move around. The only other furniture was a table with a metal pitcher and basin, and beside them a comb and brush, a small mirror, and a few other items. Several nails in the wall held all the clothing Maggie owned.

"Let's try to make her comfortable. Flower, you ease off her shoes and stockings. Naomi, help me take off her clothes, and let's be very careful while we do it. We'll cut them off if we have to. And what can we put over her?"

Looking at the bare cot, I could see the rumpled, grayish sheet and a blanket made of layered flannel. Flower finished removing Maggie's shoes and stockings, so I sent her for a warm blanket from another room while Naomi and I removed the torn and dirty clothes. I found that Maggie was wearing only long panties and a shift under the garish and wrinkled dress. Her poor body was covered with scratches and bruises. Even her arms were badly bruised where she had lifted them in an effort to protect her face.

When the hot water arrived, we used the ragged sheets and

towels to sponge the dirt and blood away. I ran my hands over her arms and legs to see if anything had been broken. Her right arm felt like it might have been fractured during the fierce beating.

Stepping outside, I reported her condition then asked every-one, except the Hurdy-gurdy Girls, to go back downstairs. The girls gathered about me, their faces reflecting the pain and shock we were all feeling. I told them how terribly sorry I was that Orrin reacted to their demands by attacking the messenger. Zola and Bertha did nothing to help but stood to one side watching.

Shrugging her shoulders, Zola said, "Well, she asked for it. You're dumb as a bunch of mules if you thought Orrin would act any different." And looking at me she snickered, "Miss Know-it-all, makin' all kinds of trouble with your hoity-toity ideas. When Orrin comes back, he'll set you straight, just like he did with that stupid Maggie."

Bertha was beside her, nodding her head. "Yeah, Orrin's gonna take care of you for sure."

I burst out, "If you two can't think of any way to help, then get your nasty butts out of here and leave us to take care of Maggie. Git!"

Gathering their shabby wrappers about them, they raised their noses in the air and left.

Flower, Naomi and Abigail were anxiously leaning over the bed when I came through the door. Abigail looked up. "She's been moaning and movin' a little, but she ain't opened her eyes."

"That's a blessing. Let's keep her quiet and comfortable until someone comes who knows what to do."

There was a firm knock on the door. Grant was standing there, his face full of concern. "Is everyone all right?"

"What a relief to see you. We're all fine except Maggie who received the full blast of Orrin's anger. She's been badly beaten. I think her right arm may be broken, and she's been semi-conscious ever since it happened. Do you know of a doctor who will come?"

"Got a horse and buggy and dashed over to get Doc Boyle, who's about the only good doctor in town. His wife says he's at one of the camps where cholera was reported last week, and she has no idea when he'll be hack. We just have to do the best we can for now."

"If Wong Kee can be found, I'm sure he'll bring some of his Chinese medicines, or at least do something to make her comfortable. I don't know what else we can do."

"Where's Orrin?"

"He ran out the door when he was done."

"He's probably at one of the other saloons, looking for sympathy and pats on the back for putting this girl in her place."

Maggie stirred and moaned. I kneeled beside the cot and took her hand. "Maggie, it's all right, my dear. We're all here to help, and we'll take good care of you. Orrin won't get away with this."

She opened her eyes a slit, moved her head slightly, then slid back into semiconsciousness.

Grant nodded. "That's good — she's out of it for now." Turning to the other girls in the room he asked, "How about you? Did Orrin hurt any of you?"

Their negative answers satisfied him. For the next three hours we all watched over Maggie, soothing her when she was restless, keeping her warm. The sun came up and flooded the room with more light so we were able to extinguish the lamp.

Responding to a soft knock on the door, we found Wong Kee with his arms filled with bundles. Grant drew him into the room where he quietly looked over Maggie, then nodded.

"I bring good Chinese medicine. Someone go to kitchen and bring hot water. Four bowls for mixing herbs."

Grant stated, "We think her right arm is broken. Can you treat that in any way?"

"Will try."

Naomi headed for the door. "I'll take care of things in the kitchen. Soon as the water's hot, I'll bring it up." She stepped outside the room, hesitated, then motioned for me to join her. I closed the door then turned to look across the saloon to where she was pointing.

The crowd of onlookers had swelled to at least 40 or more. The Hurdy-gurdy Girls sat near the stage waiting for further word of Maggie's condition. I followed Naomi down the stairs and paused to face the crowd.

"I assume you're all here because you heard what has happened. If you're just curious, please don't stay. But if you are concerned about Maggie, I'll tell you how she is."

There was a shuffling of feet, then everyone waited quietly.

"As you may know, Maggie was brutally beaten early this morning, and we think she may have a broken arm. She's still unconscious. I'll let you know when there's any change."

The men took the news quietly, shaking their heads. Some approached the Hurdy-gurdy Girls, removed their hats, and I assumed were expressing their regrets.

Clara, one of the Hurdy-gurdy Girls, approached. "We're feelin' mighty bad, Mis' Samantha. Didn't think Orrin would act that mean with all us lookin' on. Poor Maggie," she said and began to cry. "The men are askin' us all sorts of questions. What will we tell 'em?"

I didn't hesitate. "Tell everyone exactly what happened. You girls were asking for better working conditions, and this was the way Orrin answered. Wong Kee is up there now with his Chinese medicines to treat those terrible cuts and bruises. Until a doctor comes, we're doing all we can."

Her face was angry. "I'll tell everyone the whole story, I will!"

When I returned to Maggie's room, Wong Kee was treating the bruises on her arms and legs, then covering them tenderly with what looked like rice paper. When I looked at Grant, he nodded as if he approved.

We were busy the next few hours assisting Wong Kee. He filled the soup bowls with different herbs and formulas. Then Wong Kee and Grant stepped outside while Naomi, Flower and I wiped the mixtures to the various wounds on Maggie's body. The extent of the damage was horrendous, so bad that Flower crept into a corner and quietly wept.

When we finished, the men returned to the room and noted that Maggie seemed quieter and breathing easier. Wong Kee had given her a small amount of opium so she could sleep without pain for the next few hours.

Grant noted, "This room is cold. Is there a better blanket or quilt we can put over her?"

Naomi started for the door. "I'll get the one off my bed."

"Better yet," Grant suggested, "get the one from Orrin's bed. I'll bet it's nice and warm."

She hesitated, nodded, then went out the door.

Grant walked over to me to whisper, "Can you believe the awful living conditions these girls have? Not a chair, and the bed clothes are a disgrace. Imagine coming in here to rest after the long hours on their feet. No wonder they were so anxious to improve their lives, and look where it got them!"

I said quietly, "You know very well how women were treated during these years. There's a great demand for women to entertain, but as you can see, their living and working conditions are appalling."

He nodded thoughtfully. The girls were watching us curiously, so he walked over beside Maggie. Wong Kee picked up his packages and bowed. "Go now to kitchen. Make coffee."

I could see Naomi, Flower and Abigail were exhausted after this long and terrible night. All three were huddled on the wooden floor about the bed. Flower was holding Maggie's hand, and Abigail was sitting so her head was resting near Maggie's shoulder.

I said, "Why don't you girls get some sleep. Maggie will be fine for the next few hours, then we all can take turns watching her." Flower and Abigail stood, but Naomi didn't stir. "I'll stay just a little while longer, then I'll turn in."

Grant turned to me. "Okay. I'll keep her company if you'll bring us some coffee. We all could use it about now."

Nodding, I went through the door and down the stairs. The crowd had shrunk a little but not by much. Three of the Hurdy-gurdy Girls were still holding vigil with a few men sitting with them. Customers were scattered at different tables drinking. All looked up expectantly as I approached and announced that Maggie had been treated, was now resting quietly, and that we would be watching her condition. This report seemed to comfort the Hurdy-gurdy Girls, who stood up, stretched tiredly, then headed through the front entrance for their homes.

The coffee was not quite ready, so I sat at one of the tables to wait. The next thing I knew, Wong Kee nudged my arm to wake me, then presented a tray holding three mugs. When taking it through the door to the saloon, I stopped at the bar to thank Abner for finding Wong Kee. He didn't answer but gestured over toward the stage.

Orrin was at one of the far tables, listening carefully to what the men were saying, and men at the other tables were moving closer to hear. As I watched, I could tell from his body language that he was becoming more and more agitated. When he turned around, it was clear he was furious. Oh, now what? I was too tired to deal with him.

He made eye contact, then walked toward me slowly, deliberately. Everyone in the room froze, and all eyes were fixed on the two of us.

The words burst from him. "It's all your fault, you meddling slut. Once more you put your damn nose where it didn't belong. And thanks to you those fool girls insisted on giving me their stupid list of demands." He screamed at me, "You've gone too far, do you hear?"

I answered in a voice loud enough for everyone to hear. "Orrin, those girls aren't slaves. It's within their rights to have decent working conditions."

His answer was fierce. "In my saloon they have no rights. They do what they're told to do or I kick 'em out."

I was tired, but managed to answer in a voice that was strong and authoritative. "Let me put it this way so you can understand. If you don't agree to sit down and talk seriously about their concerns, they're determined to walk out — all of them, including me."

Orrin snorted, "They don't have to walk out, I'll throw 'em out, every one!"

"Who will serve the drinks or dance with the men? Women are scarce in this area, Orrin, and after what you've done this morning, no girl will want to work for you."

He snarled, "You ain't got me over no barrel, you bitch. There are plenty of girls in San Francisco who'd be glad to come here to work for me."

"But how long will it take you to find that many and bring them here? Two weeks, a month? You'll be without at least twenty girls. And I won't be here to play in the afternoons. How much will that cost you?"

I could see Orrin's rage accelerating, and he came at me, fists clenched.

I backed away saying, "Is this the way you solve your problems, Orrin? You're very good when it comes to battering helpless women and children."

He walked more quickly toward me, fists clenched at his sides. Without thinking, I responded by picking up the tray of coffee mugs and throwing it at him. It landed on the floor at his feet and the hot coffee splashed up and onto his pants. With a yell he reached down and slapped at his trousers. He looked up, his face distorted with anger. His eyes were wild and fixed, and once more he walked toward me with deadly purpose.

"You're nothin' but a damned woman," he said furiously. "I'll show you how I deal with people who cross me!"

With my left arm on the bar, I began backing away and watched with dread as he came to the far end and reached under the polished surface. When he straightened up, there was a heavy wooden club in his hand. Watching me, he raised the club and slapped it onto his other hand in a deliberate, threatening manner. Several of the men standing behind him raised their voices in protest, but no one offered to come to my assistance. I was on my own.

I was now retreating toward the front entrance, my mind frantically searching for ways to escape such a beating. Then I felt the end of the long wooden bar. Abner was there and I caught his eye and whispered, "Where's the gun?"

Without moving, he looked down and under that end of the bar, then back at me. A few quick steps brought me to where my hand could go under the bar until I felt the hard steel of the Colt Walker .44 that Corby had shown me that first day. Clumsily I pulled out the 4-pound gun and pointed it at Orrin. The weight of it, plus the nine-inch barrel, caused my hand to wobble and I struggled to get it under control.

Orrin stopped, then with a burst of laughter said, "Who the hell do you think you are, a sharpshooter? Gun or not, you're sure gonna get what's comin' to you."

His comments gave me enough accumulated anger to raise my left hand to support the right one, Clint Eastwood style. The gun was not steady but I managed to aim at the middle of Orrin's fancy vest. His angry face reflected surprise and once more he paused. The onlookers, now on their feet, watched silently.

Speaking so all could hear, I said, "Orrin, if you don't stay away from me, I'll have to shoot you. But if you're determined, keep on coming." As he hesitated, I continued, "Come on. Make my day!"

I heard a loud burst of laughter from the stairway, but didn't dare look to find the source.

Orrin took two more steps, and I could see his rage building to operatic levels. His face was red and his eyebrows came together in a fierce expression.

I slowly lowered the barrel of the gun until it was pointed below his belt.

The room went deathly quiet.

Using both thumbs, I pulled back the hammer of the gun and the loud click echoed through the room. My hands were tiring from the weight of it, but I didn't dare show it. Speaking so only he could hear, I said, "One more step, Orrin, and you'll be singing soprano the rest of your life! Is this how you build good will and respect in Boone Valley? Do you want to look like a monster to all these people, or do you want to be a hero and announce that you'll consider what the girls are asking for?"

The rage seemed to drain from him like steam from a teakettle. He lowered the wooden club and looked at me in astonishment. After some deep thought, he turned to the waiting crowd, shrugged his shoulders and said, "I really wasn't goin' to hurt this … lady, and she really wasn't gonna shoot me. We just had a disagreement that we're gonna clear up one of these days. So, free drinks all around and no more talk about this nonsense."

There was a collective sigh of relief from everyone, followed by a rush to the bar. Without a word, Orrin turned away, handed the wooden club to Kip, then joined the onlookers, who shook his hand and slapped him on the back. It must have dawned on him that he could come out of this smelling like a rose, in spite of everything. Even he could understand this.

But I could not. As I watched this scene of male bonding, I became monumentally angry. Nothing had been resolved, and I was furious! It was a knee-jerk reaction that made me point the barrel of the gun at the floor and pull the trigger. It scared the hell out of me — and the sudden roar of the gun brought the festivities to an end. All eyes were once more focused on me and the room was suddenly quiet.

My voice was close to screaming when I said, "Damn it to hell, Orrin, stop this nonsense. There's a lovely girl lying in that lousy bed upstairs, bruised and bleeding and with a broken arm because you beat her until she was unconscious." I pointed the gun toward her room. "Is that something to celebrate?"

Orrin turned away from me and looked at the men surrounding him for comment or support.

"So tell me, Orrin," I said forcefully, "what are you going to do to make this lousy situation better? What are you going to say to those girls who have been working their hearts out for you? You've injured one of them badly, and in the process you've shattered their hopes and dreams. What reason can you give them to stay here and work for you?"

Orrin was still rooted to the spot, but the men who had been partaking of his bounty of beer and whiskey began to back away, leaving him to stand alone.

With great effort Orrin stood up straight and said in a voice that was none too steady, "I ain't really a hard man. I'm willin' to talk with the girls another time when things settle down. I'll let them know when I'm ready to listen to what they have to say."

"That's exactly what they want, Orrin. I'll certainly pass the word that you've agreed to meet with them, when — within the next five days?"

Orrin was uncomfortable being cornered, but to terminate the discussion he said, "That sounds about right." And he turned his back.

The crowd of onlookers expelled a second audible sigh of relief, and once more they joined Orrin at the bar. There was no rejoicing this time, but quiet comments and conversation.

I could feel Grant beside me, whistling under his breath as he reached over and took the gun from my hands. "Samantha," he whispered as he handed the gun to Abner, "Clint Eastwood would be proud of you. I can't believe the way you turned this whole messy situation around!"

Delayed reaction set in and I leaned weakly against him, my arms and legs shaking. "I did it again, didn't I? I don't know what comes over me. I only know that I really didn't want a beating, and Orrin had to face what he'd done. It won't help Maggie a bit, but now the girls will have a chance to work things out with him."

Grant leaned over and said, "Doctor Boyle just came in. Why don't you take him up to Maggie's room and I'll keep an eye on things down here."

I turned to see a round little man dressed in black with a chubby, cheerful face, carrying a black bag. I rushed to lead him upstairs to Maggie's room.

Efficiently he examined her, then said, "Who treated her with these salves and medicines?"

"We really didn't know how to help her, so we called on Wong Kee, the Chinese cook, who kindly brought some of his medicines. They did help to make her comfortable until you were able to come."

He frowned and commented, "I don't believe in these foreign medicines, but I'll allow that she's resting reasonably well after what she's been through. We won't really know how badly these injuries will affect her — there are several nasty bumps on her head — but the longer she can rest and sleep, the better. I'll set her arm with your help, then we'll keep an eye on her for the next few days."

I turned to Naomi. "You've been up all night. Please go and get some sleep. We'll wake you if there's any change. All right?"

"Oh yes, I'm very tired." She smiled weakly and went to her room.

When Maggie's arm rested in a sling made from torn bed sheets, she roused just enough to weakly ask, "Where am I?"

Dr. Boyle patted her shoulder. "You're in your own room, little lady, and you've had quite a bad time of it. You're going to be just fine in no time at all. You must stay quiet now and rest all you can."

Maggie nodded faintly, noted that I was there holding her hand, then closed her eyes. Soon she was once more asleep.

I roused Abigail to watch over Maggie while I walked Dr. Boyle to the front entrance. She offered to take over and insisted that it was time for me to go home and rest. I gratefully accepted.

As I walked Dr. Boyle to the door, he said, "I've never seen a woman beaten so badly, and it's a shame. But she'll come through it in time. I only hope the man who did it will pay in some way. Why did he do it?"

"She was the spokesman for the girls who were asking for better working conditions. The man became angry and took it out on her."

He said dryly, "You don't have to tell me who that was. These ladies have a hard enough time of it in their young lives. Perhaps after this things will be better for them."

I said firmly, "If I have anything to say about it, things will definitely improve!"

He nodded, tipped his hat and went out the door. Grant was beside me saying, "There's hot coffee in the kitchen, but it's time for you to get some rest yourself."

As we walked into the kitchen he commented, "Through all of the trauma of this morning and your confrontation, did you realize that what you're wearing is not of this century?"

I looked down and gasped. There I was in my blue jeans, oversized sweater, and athletic shoes! "Oh, dear, I just threw them on quickly, not thinking. Grant, please get my raincoat and hat from Maggie's room. I've got to get out of here and back to Hattie's."

Grant returned with my coat and hat, bundled me up and led me to the waiting horse and buggy. Leaning back in the stiff seat of the buggy, I said, "Thank God it's Sunday. No way could I go back there and play pretty music after what the girls and I have been through. Now I would dearly love a bubble bath and a nap, but that's not possible. What about you? Can I fix you some breakfast before you head for home?"

He reached over, patted my cheek and smiled. "I'd sure appreciate your kind hospitality, Mis' Samantha."

I returned his smile and the ride home was silent while we shared a warm and peaceful togetherness.

Chapter Twenty-Two

We devoured scrambled eggs, bacon and coffee and ended up standing, holding each other tightly and sharing a kiss that so far had lasted a few minutes. Then we heard the front door open. A blast of cold air came through the house, and Hattie walked into the kitchen looking tired, bedraggled and rather damp. Dropping onto one of the kitchen chairs, she said, "We've been traveling in that old wagon since dawn and I'm sure tired to my bones. I must be getting soft."

She stopped and looked us over, the two of us standing awkwardly by the table. "Well, what's this, may I ask? You two having breakfast at this hour, here in my kitchen?"

Grant regained his composure and was able to answer, "Hattie, my dear, we are recovering from a very rough night. Wait until we tell you what's been happening."

I was able to say, "And I'll fix your breakfast while you listen."

An hour later Hattie finished breakfast and had heard our account of the unhappy events at the Majestic. She shook her head. "I hate what Orrin did and I hate him for not even listening to what the girls had to say."

Then her bright eyes focused on me. "And you, Samantha. Wherever did you get it in your head to go toe to toe with Orrin? He could have beaten you awful bad just like he did Maggie."

"Hattie, I just lost my head. Having all those people looking on helped, because everyone would know him for the terrible brute he was if he laid a hand on me."

Grant was laughing. "Hattie, she looked like an avenging

angel. You should have seen her holding that gun and forcing him to agree to meet with the girls."

"Didn't anyone try to help her when he picked up the club?" Hattie asked.

Grant hastened to say, "We didn't have a chance. She was taking Orrin to task all by herself. I only saw the last of it, but this lady had everything under control!"

Hattie yawned. "Well, you haven't even heard about my trip, and I'm too tired to start the telling. It's a terrible story what's happening in Sacramento. They're having a cholera epidemic, and so many of those dear people are dying. We took care of business quick as we could and headed back. It's mighty sad that those folks traveled all this way, only to die of the fever. And this isn't the first time that a terrible sickness has come through that area."

Even through my exhaustion I could feel the impact of her news and my eyes filled with tears. "My God, what a tragedy. All those poor people."

Shaking his head, Grant stood, ready to go. "That truly is heartbreaking news, Hattie. Tell us all about it tomorrow when we're not so tired. Get some rest now, the two of you, and I'll check later to see how you're recovering from your unfortunate experiences. Good morning, ladies." And after settling his brown Stetson forward just above the eyebrows, he went on his way.

Hattie also stood. "I'm off to bed. We'll talk more later."

"Me, too," I said. "I'll sleep a few hours, then go back to check on Maggie. Do you have a spare blanket I can take for her? I'll replace it when your store opens tomorrow. We had to use Maggie's sad blanket to clean her up, and she should be kept warm while she's recovering."

Hattie paused by the door and gave me a tired smile. "Look in the wooden chest at the foot of your bed. Take whatever you find that will help that poor girl."

"Thank you so much. We'll talk tomorrow about blankets, sheets and proper bedding for all of those girls. Orrin is going to pay for them, that's a fact."

Hattie waved a hand over her shoulder and headed for the stairs. I took a moment to clean up the kitchen, then headed for bed myself.

After three hours of sleep, I dressed, selected a warm blanket from the chest at the foot of my bed, and found my way through the cloudy and overcast day to the saloon. I found Flower, her thin face pale and concerned, sitting on the floor in that sad bedroom, holding Maggie's hand.

Flower said the girls had insisted that someone be with Maggie at all times. In response to this first group request, Orrin reluctantly agreed that they could go, one at a time, for an hour each. In this way the evening trade could be served and Maggie would always have someone with her. This one concession was a hopeful sign that there would be more to come. Despite all that had happened, the girls still wanted to meet with Orrin again. Flower asked me to talk to him.

Upon leaving, I passed by a table where Orrin was talking with four men. Smiling, I said pleasantly for all to hear, "Excuse me for interrupting, but may I suggest that early Monday morning would be a good time to meet with the girls. They have some good ideas that would help your business."

I left before he could respond, but what I heard seemed to indicate the onlookers thought it was a fine idea. A quick look showed me that there wasn't anything Orrin could do but nod.

Later that day I fixed a welcome home dinner for Hattie who was still sleeping upstairs. With the fresh vegetables picked from the garden, I created a reasonable chicken pie. The chicken, by the way, was dispatched, defeathered and degutted by the same kindly neighbor. When I spotted him tending Hattie's garden, I waved him over and asked for assistance, although he was rather puzzled by a woman who was unable to do such a simple chore. With flour, lard and other items found in the kitchen, I was pleased that the pie came together quite well. Finding a can of peaches in the larder, I built a fairly presentable peach cobbler, keeping in mind the teachings of many talented TV cooks.

Hattie joined me looking refreshed, dressed in a pretty dark-blue calico dress. "That nap did me a world of good, Samantha, I'm ready to get going. What smells so good?"

I brought out the chicken pie and peach cobbler and filled our plates. She began the saga of her journey to Sacramento, and as I listened I couldn't help but compare in my mind her journey of several days over the rough terrain of those mountains, to the enjoyable four hours it used to take Harland to drive from our home to Rocky Crest.

"Everything's fine at the farm. It's in the Central Valley, so they don't get much of the real cold weather. The rain hasn't been bad enough to spoil the crops, and the animals are fine. Business is good 'cause the Vernons not only send supplies to Rev. Norton for his café, but they sell what's left to the miners and travelers passing by. Tom Vernon, his wife and three boys are good, hard-working people and reliable. His oldest boy, Daniel, brings supplies up here every three or four days. In fact, he'll be bringing us fresh milk and butter in the next day or two."

"Sounds like an excellent arrangement, for you and for them. But tell me more about what you found in Sacramento."

"I want to cry whenever I think about it. Cholera has been running through that area for the past two weeks, and so many dear people were desperately trying to care for all those sick people, not to mention the dead and dying, bless their poor souls. All those men and women, and the dear children. It broke my heart. Martin and I saw much of this on the trail coming here, and now this sickness affects the whole town. We learned on the trail not to touch any strange food or water, and it was pure luck that I thought to bring a barrel of water and food on the wagon. Thank goodness I was able to do my business in one day, then Frank and I got right out of there."

"I heard Doctor Boyle has been treating the sickness at one of the camps near here," I said, "and he came back yesterday in time to treat Maggie. I didn't think to ask him for details. The fact he returned so soon might mean it wasn't as bad there as it was in Sacramento."

"Oh my, yes. We don't want anything like that coming to this town. Not at all."

Just then Grant knocked on the kitchen door, smiling and looking rested. "May I join you ladies? If you can spare a cup of coffee, I'll give you some news."

We waited eagerly while Grant sipped the coffee Hattie put before him.

"Maggie's narrow, uncomfortable cot has been bothering me. I've decided to build some decent beds for all the Waiter Girls. Then we'll get them decent sheets, blankets, pillows and mattresses. In fact, I came by Ida Penny's this afternoon and told her my idea. She offered to make calico curtains for all the rooms, and matching pieces to go on their tables."

I was overjoyed. "The girls will be so pleased!"

"The best part is Orrin can pay for all this. It can be part of the new agreement. He charges them for rent, laundry and food, so he should stand the cost for decent living quarters."

Hattie loved the idea. "You can get all the wood you need from my lumber mill. It shouldn't take that much for six beds."

"Not really. Once I design the bed and start building five more from the model, it'll go fast."

I told them how I coerced Orrin into meeting with the girls

Monday morning so the bargaining could start then.

"However," I inserted, "there's the proposed uniforms for the Waiter Girls and the overskirts for the Hurdy-gurdy Girls. My thought is that the girls should pay for them since this was their idea. Orrin won't agree to take on those costs as well."

"Probably not," Grant agreed. "Let's see what can be worked out at tomorrow's meeting. It's a good concession for the bargaining process. After what Orrin did to Maggie, the girls will have the determination to hold their ground."

Hattie, Grant and I developed a working list of demands so the girls would be clear on what they wanted. Hattie and I volunteered to see the girls first thing in the morning to review everything before the meeting. The three of us developed a final draft of the earlier list of demands.

1. The Waiter Girls and Hurdy-gurdy Girls will always be well mannered, and they agree to serve and dance with all customers with smiles and good grace. It will be understood that no other services will be asked of them.

2. Waiter Girls will wear uniforms consisting of a black skirt, white blouse, and an apron, necktie and hair bows made of the same material.

3. Hurdy-gurdy Girls will wear costumes consisting of colorful calico overskirts to cover their usual white muslin dresses. Short jackets and hair bows will be made of the same material.

4. Comfortable beds will be provided for the Waiter Girls, in addition to sheets, pillow cases, pillows, mattresses and warm blankets.

5. Each girl will be allowed two days a month for rest or sick leave.

6. The rule of the house will be that all girls

are to be treated with respect and not to be touched below the neck except what is customary for dancing.

7. Drunks who cannot sit or walk straight, or who loudly pester the girls, will be asked to leave or be taken out.

8. Customers who are loud and abusive will be asked to leave.

9. Foul language, and verbal and physical abuse will not be tolerated. Individuals who persist will be asked to leave and then be physically escorted out the door.

I inserted number five for obvious reasons, and Hattie added the last condition and was pleased with the final list. "It sure looks fair to me," she said. "We all know that Orrin won't give in easily, and he'll probably yell like a stuck pig. But look what he'll be getting — girls who are nicely dressed and working well with his customers. Heaven knows they'll be much happier."

"Don't forget," Grant noted, "Orrin's future treatment of the girls will be watched very carefully by everyone who knows what's been happening. Either he can come across as a narrow-minded, nasty man who mistreats his girls, or he can appear to be their benefactor and look the better for it."

The next morning Hattie and I assembled the girls in the empty card room (except for Zola and Bertha). We went over the list, then gave a rousing pep talk to bolster their confidence. Still uneasy about meeting with Orrin, they asked Hattie to join them since she owned a business and would be a strong addition to their team. She agreed, so Orrin would be in a room with 19 determined girls (Maggie was in no shape to join them), plus Hattie.

After taking Hattie to the saloon for the meeting, Grant and I returned to the house. We used the time to exchange long hugs, some luscious kisses, and discuss our own plans.

I caught my breath to ask, "Has Andrew Locke given you any ideas on how to dispose of my, um, late husband?"

"Haven't seen him, so we'll assume he's working on it. Have you had any further thoughts?"

"Yes, I do. After listening to Hattie report on her trip, we may have an answer. You know about the terrible cholera epidemic in Sacramento."

Grant frowned. "Oh, yes. First news of it came up here several weeks ago. They've had more than one plague sweep through that area. I understand that fifteen percent of the people in Sacramento died during that last one. That's the tragedy of this time and place. Terrible illnesses and no way to treat them."

"Do they have hospitals in that area, and if so, would they keep records?"

"I see what you're getting at. Andrew could make inquiries and discover that your husband and boys may have been victims."

I caught my breath and felt the tears coming at the thought. "Oh Grant. I know it's only for the record, but if such news was circulated, I'd be devastated even though I knew it wasn't true."

Grant came to comfort me. "Easy now. You and I both know that your husband and two sons are, or will be, alive and well in 1996. Also, this part of your life here must be wrapped up. Do you think you'll be able to go through with it? It'll be rough."

I tried hard to hold back a few tears at this point. Hastily I said, "It's getting late, and I must get ready for work. I should get there early enough to hear what Hattie has to say about the meeting."

"I'll drive you, then go on to Andrew's. I'll mention the sickness in Sacramento. He'll know what can be done and how to go about it."

As it happened, Grant drove me to the side entrance of the saloon just as Hattie was leaving. Her face was grim but determined.

"It wasn't easy," she started. "Orrin was hard-nosed about the uniforms and at first absolutely would not allow them. He said that was not what the men came to see. I finally suggested the girls get the uniforms and wear them for two weeks. If the customers do not like the change, they would go back to the old dresses. When I mentioned the girls would pay for the uniforms, he reluctantly agreed."

"How about the new beds and fixing up the rooms?" Grant asked.

"He was bullheaded about that as well. Said what they had was good enough, but when I reminded him that Mr. Douglas would do the work and the lumber would be free, he softened. He was stubborn about paying for the bedding until I offered to sell those to him at cost."

"That's wonderful. The meeting was a success, then."

"Not quite. Orrin insisted that the last four items were not worth discussing. He would not tell his patrons how to act. If they want to get drunk and make a fuss, it was their right. As for touching the girls improperly, he said it was up to the girls to handle it as long as they didn't end up making the customers angry. That was the best we could do. Sorry, Samantha."

"And what about item five. Did he allow that?"

"That was a hard one. The girls were embarrassed, and Orrin sputtered and finally said there would be no days off unless the girls were deathly ill and unable to move. So, that's as far as we got with that."

"You did what you could, Hattie. It's a start, and the girls and I will subtly work on everything else they want to improve."

"That'll have to do," she said firmly. "Now, Mr. Douglas, if you'll kindly drive me over to my store, I'll be beholden to you. After my trip, I've got lots of work to catch up on. See you at dinner, Samantha."

The next four weeks were busy ones for all of us. When they weren't working, the girls congregated at Ida Penny's shop selecting and agreeing on the materials for the new uniforms. Ida began a flurry of activity, cutting and sewing. That dear lady put in long hours to complete four black skirts and four white blouses. Hattie and I helped with the production of the four aprons, neckties and hair bows.

Within two weeks Maggie was on her feet, but the arm was still healing so she was still unable to work. Nothing more was said about her injuries, and she was paid each week just as the other girls were. The cuts and bruises were almost gone, but Dr. Boyle reported her arm would need another few weeks to heal. When the first bed was delivered to her room with the colorful curtains and bedding added, she soon became her confident and cheerful self.

Of course, Zola and Bertha also benefited from these improvements, and they accepted them all without comment or appreciation. Bertha gave only a shrug when Grant delivered a special bunk bed and placed it in a corner. Rainbow and Warren were delighted and Warren commandeered the upper bunk with its own ladder.

At last the stitching and sewing were complete. The girls decided to wear the uniforms the following Monday. That Sunday morning we all congregated at Hattie's. I volunteered to trim and style their hair. The girls were reluctant to have their long hair cut, but by the time I finished with Maggie, making pretty bangs over her forehead and soft curls on each side of her face, they were more than agreeable.

My surprise, with Hattie's help, was to provide makeup and show the girls how to apply it sparingly so they would look prettier and not so garish. Hattie had obtained rouge, powder and mascara. By showing how to use them lightly, the girls looked quite nice.

Once the makeup and hairstyles were completed, they all retired upstairs to change. When ready, they came down the stairs, one by one, in their new working outfits.

"You're all so beautiful," Ida Penny said, almost in tears. "Those men won't be able to treat you with anything but respect. Just you wait and see."

Hattie was overcome. "I had no idea it would make such a difference. I betcha when all the other saloons in town see what you've done, they'll want uniforms for their girls."

As for Zola and Bertha, they criticized and bitched about the whole project and refused to take part. In order to keep them on his side, Orrin bought each of them two new gowns. He was still far from happy about the agreements, and tended to act like a bear with a sore paw. Bertha, of course, was happy to have the new dresses to show off to her love, Avery. He barely paid attention when she strutted before him.

During this time Andrew Locke was considering the cholera epidemic story for the sham disposal of my family. In time he came up with a better solution. Just after I came to town, a ship ran aground and burned on the river that emptied into San Francisco Bay. Ships were busy taking mail, supplies and passengers to and from Stockton and Sacramento, which were gateways to the Mother Lode. The resulting traffic and competition for the lucrative trips caused the crews to fill the river and channels with their ships, pushing one another aside in order to be the first to dock at those ports. One tragic night a ship, the Mary Jane, exploded in flames with tragic loss of life. The more recent event was the sinking of the Annie Laurie under similar circumstances. Since passenger lists were sometimes available, Andy determined this type of incident could be the instrument to remove the shadow presence of my husband and two boys. Grant and I were waiting to hear from him.

Meanwhile, Grant and I were hard at work maintaining a

polite and friendly relationship. We dared not look at each other too often, nor could we be seen talking together. Then, one rainy evening Andrew came to call. He soberly sat Hattie and me down in the parlor, gave me a searching look, then placed a large envelope in my hand. This was the first time we had met since he learned of the amazing history that Grant and I shared.

He cleared his throat. "Sadly, Mrs. Malcolm, I must present this to you. Through Mr. Douglas, you have charged me with the search and location of your lost husband and two sons. My investigations have come to an end and there's evidence that they were aboard the Annie Laurie, which ran aground with great loss of life. It pains me to surmise, even though many of the bodies were burned and not recovered, that your family was lost in that tragic event."

Though I knew that this was untrue, I still went into shock. "When did this happen?" I gasped.

"About a week after you arrived in Boone Valley," he answered.

The tears began to fall in an aching sorrow when I realized that my sons were truly lost to me in this lifetime. My memory filled with the look of them, the sound of them, the hugs that were given so freely. All of that was now erased from an entity to a shadow.

Unable to speak, I excused myself and went to my room to sit on the bed. Of course I knew his news was untrue, but I was deeply saddened. I could not help but weep. Hattie came into the room to sit beside me in quiet sympathy. Making her an unknowing party to this charade stabbed my conscience.

As she gently held my hand, I was able to say truthfully, "Hattie, I do miss my boys so much, and it's terribly hard to realize that I'll never see them or my husband again."

She was a true, dear friend, and in the days following she did all she could to console and reassure me. She was not pleased when

I continued playing at the saloon, but I convinced her it would help me work through my grief.

During this four-week period, Barnaby began to appear on a regular basis at both the saloon and Hattie's front door. Through determined work on his claim, he began to uncover encouraging discoveries of gold nuggets and dust, which raised his confidence notably. Hattie, in turn, began to look forward to his visits. In fact, one Sunday afternoon she asked me to style her hair. The softer, less severe hairdo made her look younger and the bangs brought out her pretty, deep blue eyes.

That day Grant nudged me and pointed to Hattie and Barnaby deep in conversation in the parlor. He whispered, "Look how cute those two are together. Their faces are just shining with happiness." And it was true.

Another afternoon, when talking about his work on the claim, Barnaby said he was having difficulty removing a large deposit of rich ore. "It's a hard one to pull out. It's just plain stubborn and doesn't want to move. But I'll keep a workin' at it. You bet I will."

Grant came to call on those Sunday afternoons and briefly during the week. Our conversations in front of Hattie were polite and cordial, but nothing more. It was several weeks since receiving the news from Andy, but I was dealing with a continued sense of emptiness in my heart that didn't seem to lessen.

During this time, Rev. Norton was kind enough to call and sympathize. His visits and spiritual support helped me through my inner turmoil, and in time I was able to deal with the real and unreal. I finally accepted that my boys had lives that would exist in another century, and I would be content knowing they were a part of me that would endure.

Chapter Twenty-Three

Monday, October 9th, finally arrived; the day when the Waiter Girls would wear the new uniforms. We kept most of the details under wraps, so to speak, though Zola and Bertha were still scratching for information. They had been flaunting their new dresses, vainly confident that the other girls would look less attractive by comparison, but the other four secretly enjoyed their posturing and grandstanding.

On the day of the unveiling, I had just started my program when the upstairs doors began to open and, one by one, the Waiter Girls came down the stairs. I could not help myself — I began playing, "A Pretty Girl Is Like a Melody." Too bad the full MGM orchestra could not join me in a lush arrangement. The event rated such an outburst of music, and I was only sorry Grant was not there to enjoy the irony and humor of the occasion.

First came Naomi, her light brown hair arranged in curls on the top of her head, the hair bow just in back of the curls. She had never looked prettier.

Flower was next, her pale blonde hair in a braid down her back, the bright bow perched on the back of her head. The slight bit of makeup added flattering color to her pale face and showed what a truly pretty young girl she was.

Abigail came next, her round, happy face just beaming. Her frizzy, strawberry-blonde hair was soft around her face, then contained in a hairnet in the back. The bow was perched on the very top of her head.

Maggie came hesitantly at the last, not sure how she would be accepted, and painfully aware that most of the men knew how badly she had been beaten. She allowed me to cut some inches from her hair, and the length was then braided and arranged like a coronet around her head with the bow just in front of it. The visible bruises and scars were covered with makeup, and her lovely complexion was glowing.

Once the men in the saloon caught on to what was happening, they began to cheer. As the girls began circulating throughout the lower floor of the saloon, the large room was buzzing with outpourings of approval.

Zola and Bertha, on the other hand, were wearing their bright velvet gowns. In comparison they looked as if they had dressed up for the wrong party, and their makeup seemed bright and overdone. They went about their work visibly peeved.

During my break, Corby and Elmo expressed their delight, saying the uniforms brought a new atmosphere to the saloon. The men seemed quieter, more respectful, and almost gentlemanly. As promised, the girls were well-mannered, pleasant and smiling. The once rowdy atmosphere had subtly changed to one of well-ordered enjoyment.

Corby commented, "Orrin's lookin' surprised and puzzled. Guess he doesn't know what to think, but from the remarks the fellows are makin', they sure like what they're seein'. Elmo and I agree the Waiter Girls look mighty pretty."

"Just wait until the Hurdy-gurdy Girls come in tonight," I said. "Bet you anything the reaction will be the same. Tell me all the details tomorrow, will you?"

They laughed and nodded as they went back to work. It was Maggie's first day after her injuries,, and it was evident that carrying the heavy trays of drinks would be difficult. By carrying fewer orders at a time, she was functioning nicely and the regular customers were most happy to see her.

When Willis joined me at the piano for the last half hour, he didn't know how to respond when I asked for his reaction.

"Ain't seen nothin' like this afore 'cept for the waitresses you see at them big hotels in San Francisco and New Orleans, only better. Hard to tell if Orrin's goin' to like all this. He sure looks puzzled, but I ain't heard him yell yet. Maybe it's a good sign."

From all accounts, the Hurdy-gurdy Girls were met with the same wonder and enthusiasm. The flashing bright ribbons in their hair whirled as they danced and seemed to bring more gaiety and celebration to the evening. Clearly the message was that the new look was in and Orrin would have to accept the approval of his customers.

One interesting development emerged. I had not realized that Corby was showing special feelings for Maggie. I heard later that he was furious beyond words when Orrin beat her so brutally, so much so he could not decide at first whether to shoot Orrin or just walk out the door for good. In the end he wisely kept his temper. Getting hung for a shooting couldn't help Maggie, and as long as she was working at the saloon, he wanted to be there as well.

Once Maggie had healed and dressed in the new uniform with her beauty coming to the surface, Corby could be silent no longer. The special looks and smiles the two shared began to build until it was there for all to see.

One day, when they were both in the kitchen, Orrin made the mistake of raising their feelings as a public issue. He said roughly to Corby, "I been watching you making eyes at Maggie lately. I don't want no nonsense getting in the way of your work."

Corby, a strong man with a good sense of values, would have none of it. He stopped what he was doing and said firmly, "Orrin, whether or not Miss Maggie and I are taking a liking to each other is none of your damn business. She does her work, I make the drinks. Do you have any complaints about my work or hers? If you do, or if I hear about any nasty remarks you might be making around here, you're going to be short one, and maybe two, bartenders."

Elmo, the other day bartender, was standing nearby and nodding in agreement. I knew Elmo was a married man and quite the romantic himself. He approved heartily that his unmarried partner had developed a fondness for Maggie. Orrin was wise enough to back off that day, but I noticed him watching the two men after that. None of the changes in the saloon were lost on Rainbow and Warren. Once Warren made the mistake of asking his mother why she wasn't dressed like the other girls. She slapped his face and said, "All the other girls are dressed like whores, and only me and Zola are dressed right."

This was sadly relayed to me one day by Wong Kee, who was still one of the few constant influences in the lives of the children. He quietly indicated his approval of the changes, but I sensed his own troubles were continuing because of the demands and criticisms from Orrin and the difficult treatment and racial slurs from the gamblers. Yet he maintained his usual quiet and inner calm.

When I mentioned that I had received notice about the loss of my husband and two sons, he stopped his work, looked at me searchingly, head to one side, but said nothing.

"Wong Kee," I observed, "you never ask questions or have much to say, but I feel you see and know just about everything that goes on. I see how caring you are with the children and Waiter Girls, and you have given me support and encouragement when it was really needed. Would you say that we are special friends, just like Hattie and I are special friends? I would be honored if it were true."

He paused, then spoke. "We far from world we know, we are friends. You have secret garden. You grow pretty flowers. You help children, Waiter Girls. You speak when there is wrong. Not many this strong."

Taking a chance, I came closer to him and said, "Wong Kee,

your wisdom is from your ancestors, and I understand this. Whatever I have is from the future where I really belong. I don't know
how I came here, but this is where I must live out my life. This I am
learning. Just as you are learning and accepting the life you have
here. Does this surprise you?"

He looked deeply into my eyes, and we regarded each other
with knowing and understanding. At last he spoke, his face bright
with awareness.

"You speak truth. You shine for ones you touch. You know
this where you come from?"

"Sadly there is still greed, hunger, brutality, war, dishon-
esty." I answered. "But there are many who are working to create a
fellowship of human beings who love and respect each other. It may
take a few more centuries to come about."

He answered, "My country is hard, belief strong. Gives
strength. Is more than search for gold. Many good ones we see. I not
be here to see world you describe."

"Do you believe in life after death, being reborn to live again
with new tasks to perform, new lessons to learn? What we do not
accomplish in this life, we can go on and work with in the next. This
is the hope we have."

There was a silence between us until Grant opened the door
and saw us. He felt the tension, the electricity in the air.

As he approached, he said softly, "Is everything all right
here?"

"Grant," I said, "this fine man has a great understanding of
many things. He knows that I am a stranger here."

Grant put an arm around me, looked closely at Wong Kee,
then nodded.

"Wong Kee," I found myself saying, "Grant Douglas is also
from the future and knows all that I know."

Wong Kee bowed his head in honor, as if to acknowledge

- 303 -

what he already knew. Grant in turn reached out and quietly shook his hand. I reached for Wong Kee's other hand and for a moment the three of us stood together in quiet communion and acceptance.

Now it was approaching mid-October and winter was flexing its icy fingers as the weather made its way through the cold, wet, and snow. Boone Valley was at an elevation where the grip of winter was continuing and the sun did not show itself for many days. Work on the claims slowed. Many miners struggled merely to stay dry and warm. It was a hard time for men who barely had a tent or lean-to for protection.

As for Boone Valley, life activities continued haltingly during the rainstorms and bitter cold. Those who had a small stake of gold spent as many days as they could afford at the saloons scattered throughout the valley, seeking the warmth and companionship that was lacking at the diggings. The hotels and every structure with a roof were greatly over-crowded. The lobbies were filled with rows of men sleeping on the floor, and the rooms themselves were packed with as many men lying side by side as multilevel benches would allow.

Luke Norton and his wife responded to the heavy demand by loading their stove with huge vats of wholesome stews and soups, which they served in large bowls with thick slices of bread at only $1 for each bowl.

Deep snow locked up the passes and trails; just finding shelter and enduring was the basic life issue. How easy it had been for Harland to drive the boys and me over the highways cleared of snow to Rocky Crest. We enjoyed weekends of skiing and playing in the snow, sitting in front of a roaring fire, then returning home in ease and comfort. Now I could see firsthand the bone-chilling, soul-trying, back-breaking existence that challenged every individual who had chosen to dig in and endure at any cost.

Attendance at the saloon dropped off and Orrin was sorely

aggravated by men who ordered one beer and then nursed it for hours in order to stay where it was warm. Life settled into a routine for all of us — the Waiter Girls, Hurdy-gurdy Girls, my concerts, Grant's activities at the brewery, and Hattie at her store. With the money they had managed to save, the girls bought heavy underwear and extra blankets for their new beds. I convinced Orrin to reduce my schedule to every other day. Of course, he agreed, knowing my salary also would be reduced very nicely. However, I was happy to stay indoors at Hattie's, away from the storms that made my trips to and from the saloon such an ordeal.

The arrangement worked well in another area. Warren and Rainbow were still forbidden to hang around the saloon during the day. With Hattie's permission, Grant brought them to the house where I began their very first schooling. The shelves at Hattie's store included a selection of books for teaching young children. Warren and Rainbow were attentive and eager, and we had great times telling stories, singing the ABC's and other songs. On the days I worked, Hattie allowed them to sit by the potbellied stove in her store, their chairs to one side, away from the store's activities.

During this time Warren showed what a bright and helpful lad he could be. Little by little he became acquainted with the variety of goods on the shelves, as well as the inventory in the store-rooms. In time, Hattie or the clerks could call, "Warren, go fetch some blankets." Or, "See if there are any more coffeepots in the back." He'd jump to his feet, run into the storage area and quickly deliver everything with a broad and happy smile. He also proved to be useful in delivering goods and supplies to the shops along the street, as well to the houses and shacks close by.

One night Hattie commented, "Samantha, I had no idea what an asset that boy could be to my business. No matter what we ask him to do, he does it quickly and then pops back into his chair and waits, ready to take on whatever else comes up. Really, I hadn't noticed what an agreeable child he is, and it bothers me all the more the way his mother neglects him and his little sister."

She continued. "And little Rainbow is also growing and learning. The other day, to keep her busy, I got out some wool yarn and knitting needles and showed her how to knit. She's taking to it amazingly well, and if she gets real good she can knit wool scarves that I can sell at the store. I can even pay her a little for each one. She's a bright little tyke, and I'm growing very fond of both of those youngsters."

One long and blustery day Wong Kee and I put our heads together in the kitchen. I was describing how well Rev. Norton was doing at his café serving simple meals to the miners. He raised his eyebrows. "In China we make cakes full of meat, vegetables. Easy to do."

Catching the idea, I said, "Do you think Orrin would be interested in selling snacks to the men who don't have enough money for a large meal and don't want to go out in the middle of the storm? It would be a good way for Orrin to make some money, and whatever you put together should be worth something to you."

He indicated his acceptance of this concept by nodding, then turned to his worktable to assemble vegetables and other ingredients. Later, when I finished my program, I walked into the kitchen and found him standing proudly beside a dish filled with white dumplings the size of tennis balls. Grant was sitting at one of the tables, a small plate before him.

"Samantha, come try these. They're great!"

I bit into one to find it filled with minced meat and vegetables, seasoned with a combination of salt, pepper, and flavors I could not identify.

"This is luscious, Wong Kee, very tasty. Is this your own recipe? Do you steam them?"

He confirmed with a nod.

Sitting next to Grant, I asked Wong Kee, "Could you cook up a hundred of these every day? And could you find the ingredients to produce that many?"

"Can do. Use meat here, chicken, beef, pork, deer."

I added, "Something occurred to me — see what you think. How would it be to flatten the dumplings almost like a small pie, and then bake them? Most of the men come in with dirty hands. These dumplings are lovely and white, but they'd be covered with dirt before they're entirely eaten."

"I try. We see," Wong Kee replied.

Grant asked, "And what shall we call them? A meat pie, vegetable pie, a tasty pie?"

I chimed in with, "They're not quite cookies, but why not call them Wonkees, after their creator?"

Grant and I turned to Wong Kee for his reaction. "Good," he said quietly, going on with his work.

Grant and I clapped our hands and laughed, then Orrin walked in. Taking in the scene, he demanded, "What the hell is going on in here?"

Grant motioned him to a chair at the table. "Orrin, Wong Kee has put together these wonderful dumplings. Here, try one." He passed over a plate that held three of the dumplings. Orrin looked at them suspiciously, lifted one to sniff it, then took a tentative bite. He bristled with suspicion, but by taking one small bite at a time he consumed the dumpling without comment.

"What do you say, Orrin? Was it good?" Grant asked.

Orrin casually put one arm over the back of his chair. "Not bad."

Grant warmed to his presentation, probably reminiscent of his days as a high-powered executive. "These dumplings would be ideal to serve here with the drinks. These miners come into town for drinks and to get out of the storms. Just like Rev. Norton serving soups and stews at his café, you could serve these. Wong Kee could get them out by the hundreds. You could charge 50 cents for each one, or three for a dollar, and make a dandy profit while you're at it."

The range of expressions on Orrin's face ran from suspicion, to interest, to rapt attention when he realized the profit that would come to him. He allowed himself a smile, like a cat approaching a bowl of milk.

Grant added one condition to his presentation. "Of course, since Wong Kee's talent created these tasty treats, and he'll be making them in great quantities, he should be paid a commission of at least 4 cents each."

The smile left Orrin's face. "Why should I pay him? He's paid to work in my kitchen and that's enough. Why should I pay him more?"

"Because you're a businessman who knows the value of a good employee. Wong Kee works long hours in this kitchen, he puts out good food and excellent coffee, day or night, and he's been constant and dependable in his work." Grant was on an executive roll.

"Besides, it's an incentive for him to work harder."

Orrin looked down at the dumplings still on the plate and pondered the issue. Absently he reached for another and chewed it thoughtfully.

He nodded at Wong Kee. "Make it 3 cents and start makin' 'em as soon as you can." And having said that, he walked from the kitchen with an air of triumph.

Grant and I burst into laughter, and in his own restrained manner, Wong Kee looked quite pleased and said, "Is good."

Grant declared, "Looks like you're in business, Wong Kee. You've got lots of planning to do — supplies, ingredients, whatever. Think you can do it?"

"Can do. I bring in another cook. Can do."

Just before the heavy rains and snows hit Boone Valley, a new employee had arrived at the Wells Fargo office, whose stage coaches were busily transporting passengers, gold and mail to and from San Francisco. To the already established telegraph and other services, they added banking in the sturdy brick building with the heavy metal shutters. The new man was Robert Heath, and Grant brought him over to the saloon late one afternoon and announced that Robert would serve as bank clerk and that Josiah Stevenson would act as bank manager.

Robert Heath was a studious-looking young man, serious and quiet in his demeanor and shy with the ladies. He barely made eye contact when Grant introduced us, but his brief smile lit up his face like a spotlight. He had light brown curly hair that covered his forehead. His brown eyes seemed rather sad behind gold-rimmed spectacles. I could see why Grant had taken him under his wing.

As Grant and I talked briefly, Robert's attention had moved from our conversation to what was happening around us. He watched fascinated as the Waiter Girls moved quickly about the room. Then Flower rushed by with a tray filled with drinks and he was completely captivated. He stood, rooted to the spot, watching her every move. When Grant noted what was happening, he winked at me.

"Is this your first trip to the gold country?" I asked politely. He did not reply, or perhaps was incapable of answering. Grant gently took his arm. "Robert, why don't you sit down for a moment and have a drink?"

When there was no answer, Grant tightened his grip and repeated the question. Robert looked at him as if he had awakened from a dream, and said gratefully, "Oh yes, that would be very nice." He dropped into the nearest chair and continued to watch Flower.

Grant and I settled into our chairs, then he waved to Flower.

She came over and stood waiting for Grant to order. He leaned over to Robert and said, "How about a beer, young fellow?"

Robert could only nod. Grant ordered two beers and a sarsaparilla for me. Mesmerized, Robert watched Flower move to the bar, then brought his attention back to our table. Patting his arm, I said, "Her name is Flower and she's just as sweet in nature as she looks. Shall I introduce you?"

At this he lowered his eyes. To ease his discomfort, I told him about the girls' uniforms and how they came about. Grant said he had heard that girls in at least one saloon on the far end of town were demanding similar uniforms. Robert settled down and listened with interest.

Flower served our drinks, and Grant paid her. "Flower, this young man is new in town. He'll be the bank clerk at the Wells Fargo office. Let me introduce Mr. Robert Heath."

At this, Robert awkwardly rose to his feet, made a slight bow and said, "It is an honor to meet you, Miss Flower." Flower replied softly, "Very nice to meet you, Mr. Heath," and with a smile she returned to her duties.

To cover the awkward moment, Grant announced, "Let's make a toast to welcome Robert Heath to Boone Valley and wish him well in his future career."

Grant and I raised our glasses, clinked them together, then raised them to Robert. He sat a little taller in his seat, gave us a sweet smile, and clinked his glass with ours. "You are both very kind, and I am most grateful for your welcome."

The conversation was more relaxed after that and Robert was able to tell us about his background.

"I was born in Cincinnati, Ohio, got my schooling there, and when I reached 15 I was apprenticed to a bank. I lived there until my mother died of pneumonia. That was when my father and uncle decided to come to the gold country and try their luck. They got passage for the three of us on a ship heading for San Francisco."

I commented, "That must have been a big adventure for a young man like you. That's a long voyage."

Robert said quietly, "Not exactly, ma'am. My father died of dysentery that went all through the vessel. They buried him at sea."

Grant patted his shoulder. "We're very sorry you had such a sad experience. But you and your uncle did eventually arrive in San Francisco, is that right?"

"Yes sir."

"And what happened then?"

"Sorry to say, sir, my uncle began gambling and soon lost whatever money was left. I never did know the exact amount."

"And then?" Grant asked.

Robert hesitated before answering. "One night my uncle was killed in a disagreement with a gambler. This left me on my own, but I managed to find a position as a clerk with Wells Fargo. Then they offered me the opportunity to come to Boone Valley. It seemed that by coming here it would end the journey that I began with my father and uncle."

He told his story without commentary or blame. He was indeed a fine young man, sad and lonely perhaps, but with a true heart. I liked him.

One day shortly after that, Grant and I were able to visit alone. "Grant, I no longer think of myself as a stranger in a strange land. I'm so involved in the daily life of Boone Valley that I consider myself a citizen rather than an interloper. Haven't you noticed that we rarely speak about the San Francisco and California that we knew? Is this what happened to you after you first settled in here?"

"In time, yes. Of course, the nights were bad since there was so much time to remember the details of the life I left behind. And I had no one to talk with and share those feelings. But you're right.

I hardly ever think of how things were; I'm too involved in what is happening here and now."

The opportunities where we could be alone were very few, but those moments were filled with quick embraces and whispered plans for our future. I couldn't help but giggle when Grant remarked one day, "Sam, I feel like a teenager stealing kisses behind the stadium bleachers. Here we are in our 40s, acting like youngsters in love for the first time."

"But Grant, how wonderful to be able to feel such joy. This is light years away from how I felt when Harland was courting me. Perhaps the years of maturing and dealing with marriage and raising our children allows us to fully comprehend this gift we've been given."

And with these thoughts, we were able to rest contentedly in each other's arms whenever time allowed.

Chapter Twenty-Four

A few days later trays of Wonkees appeared on each end of the brightly polished bar, and in no time they were part of every order.

"Bring me a beer, girlie, and a couple of them Wonkees." Patrons devoured the baked dumplings in such quantities that Wong Kee did indeed bring in a young Chinese lad who deftly assisted the production line. The kitchen became a busy, bustling place where, in addition to the usual activities, a constant supply of Wonkees emerged from the hot oven. Wong Kee's assistant delivered them to the bar, and the Waiter Girls whisked them off to the waiting patrons before they had a chance to cool. Those who were not served sipped their drinks and waited impatiently for the next batch.

The winter storms brought with them a few side effects that were new to me. First was when the men came through the front door dripping or covered with snow. The coats were put to one side, but once warmed by the heat of the saloon, they began to smell like wet puppies. Miners avoided washing themselves and their clothes in the icy cold streams, so there were high levels of unhappy odors. Next, the weather confined men to their shacks and tents, either alone or with one or two others. This closeness festered into anger and frustration. Conversation was exhausted early, food was not plentiful nor varied, and when they had whiskey, the men turned to it to dull the anger.

Corby was describing this to me one day in the kitchen. "These men come in here pretty well dog-tired of their bunk mates. You don't see 'em, Mis' Samantha, but there are down-and-dirty fights here just about every night. These men get so sick of each other, they just want to kill the one that annoys 'em the most, or else they just stand at the bar and drink 'til they're flat out on the floor." Elmo joined in the conversation. "We can't count the fights we hafta break up, or the critters we carry through the door. When they pass out, all we can do is pick 'em up and lay 'em on the boardwalk outside."

Early in the winter Orrin installed new gambling devices in the large room across from the kitchen. The room could hold about seven tables, and to four of them he added chuck-a-luck, poker dice and bird cages. The miners, bored by the weather and confinement, looked for diversions and so were easily attracted to the newness of the games. That these games were designed to relieve them of their hard-won gold and coins did not matter. For a short time they were entertained and the cold and wet were forgotten. The remaining three tables still offered poker and blackjack, and were usually filled days and into each night. Winter or not, Orrin still profited.

Bertha made it a point to work in this room just to be near Avery Singleton. Orrin told her more than once to serve the drinks and get the hell out, but she lingered, hovering near Avery, one hand on his shoulder. Since Avery had come onto the scene, there was little or no protest from her concerning the time the children spent with me or at Hattie's store. Her attention and concern were focused elsewhere.

While tutoring Rainbow and Warren one very cold winter day, I could see the little girl was not well. Her forehead felt warm and she was developing a slight cough. I gave her one aspirin from my backpack and cautioned her to keep warm and drink all the water she could.

When I stopped by Hattie's store the next day, I expected to see the children sitting by the warm fire. They were not to be seen.

Hattie was busy, but came over when I entered. "The children aren't here, and I've been hoping they're all right. Haven't had time to check on them at the saloon."

"I'll take it from here, Hattie." On the way to the saloon, I spotted Grant driving the horse and buggy and flagged him down. "Let's get over to the saloon right away. The children didn't show up today and they're not at Hattie's."

Grant quickly turned the buggy around and headed for the side door of the saloon. We found Warren in the kitchen having a serious talk with Wong Kee. His small face reflected concern and worry. "My sister's real sick. Momma Bertha didn't come in at all last night, and Rainbow's been coughin' real bad. I been tellin' Wong Kee we gotta do somethin'."

I put my coat aside. "Warren, why don't we go right up and check on her." We quickly mounted the stairs and entered Bertha's room. Rainbow was on the bottom bunk, feverish, her little body shaking with a racking cough. When the spasm passed, she lay back weakly and closed her eyes.

"We're here, little Rainbow. You must be feeling terrible, and we're going to take good care of you."

Warren stood beside me, patting the small shoulder as I felt the feverish brow, which I estimated to be over 100 degrees. "Warren" I said, "there's little we can do for her here. Let's get her to Hattie's house where she can have better care."

His eyes widened. "Momma Bertha will get real mad."

"Don't worry. Grant and I will talk to Bertha when the time comes. Now, help me wrap your sister in this blanket so she'll be nice and warm."

I carried Rainbow into the kitchen and laid her on a table. When Wong Kee came over, I reported urgently, "She has a high fever and a terrible cough. What can it be — flu, pneumonia, what?" Wong Kee checked her over and shook his head. "I go now get medicines. You watch, keep warm, give water." And he left the kitchen.

Grant leaned over and made sure Rainbow was comfortable while I found a clean rag, rinsed it in cool water from a jug on the sink, and brushed it over her forehead. Warren looked on anxiously. Now and then Rainbow opened her eyes and smiled, but the smiles were wiped away by the convulsive cough.

Grant noted, "The cough seems to be in her chest, or the lungs. Sam, use your most powerful prayer that it's not pneumonia, since medicines to treat it aren't even available." His face was filled with concern. Then he barked, "Where the hell is Bertha? Why isn't she with this child?"

"Where else," I said wearily. "With her lover, Avery. I had no idea that she was neglecting the children this way. It seems she often leaves them on their own with only Wong Kee and the Waiter Girls to feed and care for them. She should be shot!"

Warren spoke up. "Please don't say that, Mis' Samantha. Momma Bertha is all the family we got. Rainbow and me take care of each other pretty good. Now you're teachin' us to read and write, and we're doin' fine."

Grant and Warren cared for Rainbow, wiping her brow with the cool cloth and soothing her when she opened her eyes. When hungry people came through the door, I tended to the hot stove, keeping a supply of hot coffee, and whipping up eggs and bacon when ordered. Wong Kee's young assistant arrived, and without a word became busily engrossed in the business of making Wonkees.

Grant, Warren and I took a quiet moment to make a lunch of Wonkees and coffee. Within the hour Wong Kee returned, arms filled with packages. Taking hot water from the stove, he filled a cup, added a combination of herbs and mixed it well. Lifting Rainbow gently, he had me feed her a teaspoon at a time. She wrinkled her nose at the taste, but when I assured her that it would help her feel better, she gamely took as much as she could. Wong Kee soaked a cloth with hot water, wrung it almost dry, added an odd-smelling oil, then placed it carefully on her tiny chest.

"This help. Give hot drink every four hours. Keep cloth on chest. Send Warren and I come."

After a short conference, we moved Rainbow to Hattie's where we could care for her. Orrin was nowhere to be seen, so I left word with Willis and Corby that I would not be playing that day. Soon Rainbow was comfortably settled on the sofa in the parlor next to a crackling fire. Warren was set up on the settee across the room.

For three days we cared for Rainbow, and to our great relief the fever broke. Grant and I guessed from the symptoms that she had bronchitis, and Wong Kee's treatment worked a miracle. Soon our girl became bright and sassy once more.

As for Bertha, once she learned we had moved the children to Hattie's, she came storming over ready for war. When it was clear that Rainbow was quite ill and needed constant care, she retreated, saying that she didn't have the time or knowledge to care for a sick child; and besides, she had to work every night. She then announced most emphatically that she could take care of her children quite well if she had the time. After patting Rainbow and Warren on their heads, and threatening to retaliate if we didn't take proper care of them, she left hastily.

During the days that Rainbow was recovering, the children, Hattie, Grant and I had a jolly time talking, reading, laughing, playing games and teasing each other. In a loving and nourishing environment, they opened like flowers in the sun.

Something else was blooming at this time. Maggie and Corby could no longer hide their feelings for each other, and Willis reported to me an interesting conversation between Corby and Orrin. Corby cornered Orrin early one day and sat him down on the stairs leading to the stage.

"Orrin," he began, "I got somethin' to tell you 'bout me and

Maggie."

"Do tell," Orrin said sarcastically. "I been watching you two moonin' over each other and I'm ready to call you on it. I think it's gone far enough."

"You got nothin' to say about it, Orrin. I'm here to tell you that me and Maggie are goin' to get married, and soon."

Orrin snorted. "Well, now, I don't know if I want to lose one of my Waiter Girls at this time. Business is too good, and Maggie won't have time to be married, she's got too much to do here. Besides, how do you think she'll take to sittin' in your little shack waitin' for you to come home at night? And where would I find me another girl?"

"That ain't how it's goin' to be, Orrin. Maggie and me plan to be married around Christmas and we'll keep on workin' here so we can be together as much as we can. We'll both stay here until midnight, then we'll go home together. After what you did to her, she still needs to take it easy. Ten hours a day is all we want to work. You can find other people to fill in."

According to Willis, Orrin roared, swore and waved his hands. Corby waited patiently until the storm subsided. Then he said quietly, "We'll be glad to stay with this understandin', or we can move on to one of the other saloons. We decided we'll work for you, but we'll live our own lives and decide when we'll put down our aprons and go out the door. Take it or leave it, Orrin."

Typically, Orrin burst into anger. "I won't have you two makin' eyes at each other while you work for me. Won't have it at all. No sir, not at all."

Corby was firm. "Maggie and me work hard and do our jobs real good, just like we've been doin' for the years we've been here. You ain't had no complaints before and you won't have none after we're married."

Orrin probably didn't get much sleep that night, but he went for it! He must have spent the hours figuring how to benefit from the situation. Two days later he approached Corby and announced he would allow them to get married, and that he would provide the wedding celebration at the saloon and invite everybody. This was a little more than the couple had in mind, but making their marriage a special event was something they could not resist.

Shortly after, Corby and Grant were talking in the kitchen and Corby confided, "I sure hate to take Maggie to the one-room shack where I live. She deserves better than what she's had in her life."

As a result of that concern, the two men put their heads together and my dear Grant made a dream come true. He and Corby designed a small home for the newlyweds. Two rooms — a nice bedroom with a window, a kitchen and small living room with a fireplace.

Once the plan was completed, construction began almost immediately, with Grant supervising. He found several capable men in town who badly needed money. When the weather allowed, work began. He spent many a chilly day cutting and erecting the walls, finding stones for the fireplace, and the heavy pieces for a sturdy door. He assured me it was a fun project. I could tell this was a fact by the way his eyes sparkled when he described the daily progress.

Everyone was involved in the project, and Maggie was not to know until her wedding day. Hattie worked with the Waiter and Hurdy-gurdy Girls to find suitable chairs and began sewing the material to cover the seats and backs. Ida Penny would sew the curtains as soon as the walls and roof were in place. In the meantime, she and some of the girls began work on a fluffy and colorful quilt. Hattie and I worked with Ida to make a special dress for Maggie. She found a handsome blue wool suit for Corby in her store, and added a white shirt and tie.

When Hattie and I were lunching at Norton's Café one day,

we brought Della Norton out of her busy kitchen to ask if she could bake special wedding cakes. She was delighted.

"You ladies just don't know how tired I am of cooking the same old meals every day. A wedding cake would be such a treat for me. And confidentially, the Reverend told me that conducting the ceremony in the saloon would be like a new adventure for him, but please don't tell him I told you!"

There was excitement in the air as the wedding day approached. Most of the girls were happy for Maggie and showed it at every opportunity. Zola and Bertha, on the other hand, shot off bitter remarks every chance they had.

"You'd think they were royalty," sneered Zola, "the way everybody's takin' on. He's just a bartender and she's a beat-up waitress puttin' on airs."

Bertha shot a few arrows herself, but her unhappiness and envy showed in the pinched expression on her face. Only the time she managed to coax from Avery maintained her shaky self-confidence. Even though Avery clearly showed his disdain for her, he did not hesitate to bring her to his room many nights to satisfy his sexual appetite. We all knew the dynamics of that relationship and could not help but feel sorry for Bertha, but it was the life she'd chosen and it sustained her in some joyless way.

Zola, in the meantime, was promoted to the dubious position of Orrin's bed partner of choice. While this brought great relief to the other girls, her attitude made it clear she was, without question, the top lady in Orrin's world.

One afternoon Grant and I discussed the fact that several people we knew were coming together two by two. Corby and Maggie, Hattie and Barnaby, Robert and Flower, Grant and me. Love was blooming that winter.

Warren and Rainbow were so proud when Maggie asked them to be part of her ceremony. Warren would be the ring bearer (the ring for Maggie was fashioned from a gold nugget contributed by Barnaby), and Rainbow would be the flower girl. It was mid-winter and there were no flowers, but Hattie found the solution. For years Martin had tucked a supply of pink wrapping paper on a far shelf in the storeroom. It had no practical use, so there it had remained. Why not, Hattie suggested, cut flower petals from it so Rainbow could scatter them down the aisle? The Hurdy-gurdy Girls agreed to work with Rainbow, and from then until Christmas day scissors were busy and the pile of pink flowers grew.

About the same time, Hattie began to pick up on Grant and me. No matter how careful we were, it was not possible to hide our pleasure when we were together. One day Grant and I were deep in conversation and no doubt not as polite and restrained as we should have been. As the discussion came to a close, we gave each other a warm smile before going our separate ways. At dinner that night Hattie questioned me.

"Samantha, girl, what's this going on with you and Grant?"

"Why Hattie, Grant has become a special friend."

"Well, for a widow lady, your conversations seem rather informal. After Martin died, it was almost a year before I could warm up to anyone other than being civil and polite. Things may be different where you come from, but you only got word about your family a few months back, and you haven't even been wearing black. Being the way you are and speaking your mind the way you do, it seems all right. Even playing the piano so regular without taking time off to mourn. Of course, I had to keep a strong hand at the store after Martin died. Wasn't nothing else I could do. But there's something about you two that doesn't seem quite proper."

"But Hattie," I protested, "Boone Valley is nothing like a small town in Missouri where everyone knew everyone else and they lived by the same set of rules. Here practically every man and woman is behaving differently in order to fit in and get along with so many new people."

"All right, Samantha, I'll allow that may be true. Certainly you do have a unique way of talking with people, different than any lady I've known before."

"I'll tell you something, Hattie. Where I come from, men and women can become very good friends, so much so that when they greet each other, they share a warm hug. It's like saying to them, 'I like and respect you as a person'."

"Land sakes, I can't see myself hugging the people I see at church, or the people who come in my store. I see some of the ladies hugging when they meet, but they're usually related or old friends."

"Remember, Grant and I have been through a lot. We both came here all by ourselves, disoriented and lonely. We have shared some of our feelings, our fears and concerns, and it has helped us to feel less alienated from our past."

With a sly smile, Hattie asked, "Answer me this, little lady. Have you ever hugged each other?"

"Truthfully?"

"Truthfully," she insisted.

Looking deep in her eyes, I could see concern, but also a woman wanting to share the richness of life with another. I took a deep breath, then answered softly, "Whenever we're sure nobody's looking!"

She clapped her hands and laughed. "If that don't beat all. Even though your husband's been dead about four months, I reckon you wouldn't be human if you didn't have a strong and loving heart still beating in you. And you've got a lot of good, loving years left." Then she sighed and looked down at her hands and confessed, "I guess those loving years aren't there for me any more. But I tell you, Samantha, I would delight in having a loving man to share my bed these cold nights."

She clasped her hands and looked up at the ceiling. "If

Martin could hear me talking this way, he'd surely send down a thunderbolt to set me straight!"

Our laughter filled the room like our warm friendship. "Hattie, I'd bet my prettiest gown that you have never talked to another woman this way. I'm proud of you, and I'm also going to make a prediction. Believe it or not, wishes do come true, and somehow I just know that yours will, and that there will be a loving man in your future."

Her eyes widened. "Do you really think so? Really?"

"Be patient, and keep that special wish in mind. Then we shall see what happens," I said mysteriously.

After that conversation, Hattie seemed happier and more loving in her outlook on life. Whenever Grant and I were together, no matter how innocent the meeting, she smiled slyly. Grant commented on the change, so I reported the lovely exchange I had with her and he was delighted.

"Let's teach her how to ask the Universe for help!" he laughed.

Chapter Twenty-Five

Christmas Day came bright and shining. A light snow, just enough to cover the mountains and trees, had fallen the night before. The air was crisp and cool, but not too cold.

The wedding was scheduled for 2 o'clock, and all details were covered. Reverend Norton would deliver the wedding cake to the kitchen when he came to perform the ceremony. The Hurdy-gurdy Girls were in charge of the basket of paper flower petals and seeing that Rainbow and Warren were dressed and ready. Ida would give Warren the satin-covered pillow that she had made to hold the ring. The Waiter Girls were in charge of Maggie — to see she was dressed and looked her prettiest when she came down the stairs to meet her husband-to-be. Wong Kee and his young helper were busy in the kitchen, as they had been most of the night, preparing the food that Orrin ordered.

Willis and I would provide the wedding march and appropriate music, and I would ad lib background music during the ceremony. This wedding meant more to me than the one I shared with Harland. I couldn't have been more excited.

At Hattie's invitation, Grant and Barnaby would join us for lunch before the ceremony.

At 10 o'clock Grant and Barnaby arrived at Hattie's with a horse and buggy so the four of us could inspect Maggie and Corby's new home and make sure all was well. Grant was bursting with pride when he opened the door and motioned for us to enter. We could not have been more pleased; everything was so beautifully executed. The furniture was in place and there were calico curtains at the window. The fireplace was filled with logs ready to be ignited.

Hattie and I opened the bedroom door to see the well-crafted bed Grant had made. The fluffy quilt covering the bed was a riot of blues and greens. The curtains at the small window echoed the same colors.

I couldn't help but give Grant a hug. "You've done a wonderful thing here, my dear. Maggie and Corby will be very happy in such a sweet environment. What a wonderful way to begin their married life."

Taken aback at the public hug, Hattie mumbled, "Barnaby, let's check the kitchen and see if everything is where it should be." And they hastily left the room.

Grant kissed my forehead. "Dear Sam," he whispered, "you've put as much into this wedding as I have. Our enjoyment will be in knowing they will live here happy and contented."

Hattie came to the door and cleared her throat. "We'd better be getting back to the house. I still have some cooking to do."

Back in her kitchen, the wonderful aroma of roast chicken rose from the stove. As she finished preparing the meal, Grant and I admired Barnaby's new outfit. He stood uncomfortably decked out in a new shirt and pants and a warm wool jacket. His hair was slicked down, but it had grown considerably during his absence. After lunch, with his permission, I gave him a quick trim while Grant looked on, amused.

"If I had known you were so capable, Mis' Samantha, I would have asked you to apply your talented scissors to my shaggy hair."

"Any time, Mr. Douglas," I laughed. "My appointment book is open."

Lunch was delicious and filled with laughter and good conversation. Barnaby brought us up to date on the work at his claim, which was deep in the side of the mountain. His efforts continued far into the mine.

"I'm still workin' away at that solid hunk of rock that don't seem to want to break up. It's stubborn like me, but I'm gonna pull it out yet!"

Grant teased, "I betcha there's a miner on the other side of your mountain who's working just as hard trying to pull it out his way. When you finally get it out, he'll be holding on like crazy!"

Barnaby was not amused. "I sure hope not. After all my work, I hate to think that someone else has a claim on it."

At 1:30 we piled into the buggy and headed for the saloon. Grant was dressed smartly in the tailored outfit he was wearing when we first met, with the tan Stetson placed firmly on his head. Hattie was dressed in a pretty blue dress and matching hat. I wore the dark blue gown Ida designed, and she found several yards of soft blue wool that she'd fashioned into a voluminous stole to drape about my shoulders.

We hastened into the warmth of the saloon's kitchen, where Wong Kee and his assistant were hard at work.

We went to the door leading to the main floor and peeked through. People were milling about, helping here and there. Someone had wrapped tree branches about the stair railings. To this had been added large bows made from the pink wrapping paper. A small table was placed in the center of the room, and it too was covered with the pink paper. On this were two lovely candelabras holding a total of six candles. Chairs and tables were arranged in a circle about the area where the ceremony would take place.

As I looked about, Willis walked over. "How does everything look, Mis' Samantha? Me and the bartenders have been working all morning on everything."

"It looks just wonderful, Willis."

Looking toward the bar, I could see that only Elmo was on duty. Corby was probably in one of the other rooms getting dressed. People were coming through the front entrance, and the chairs were beginning to fill. Around the central area, nicely dressed couples were seated and quietly waiting. The seating from there to the front entrance was almost completely filled by the usual patrons of the saloon, an odd assortment of miners. Some had managed a clean shirt and a comb through their shaggy hair. The rest, however, came in their usual worn and torn clothes still covered by the red earth and exuding the odors resulting from their efforts. Many of them were in animated conversations interrupted by loud bursts of laughter.

This bothered me at the time, but left my mind when I stopped by the bar to ask Elmo, "How's the best man doing today? Ready to do your duty and support the groom?"

"You bet, Mis' Samantha. The night bartenders will take over anytime now, then I'll be ready, sure enough." He pointed his thumb toward the front entrance. "Look at Orrin over there, greetin' everybody as if he's the father of the bride. You'd think it was his day, not Corby and Maggie's." He shook his head sadly.

Returning to the kitchen, I suggested to Grant that he, Barnaby and Hattie find seats near the altar before all the chairs were filled. Grant offered his arm to Hattie, and the two of them walked grandly to their seats.

I hung up the wool stole and left the kitchen. Working my way to the stage, I caught Willis' eye and pointed to the piano. He nodded, then walked through the crowd to join me. He had already positioned two chairs at the keyboard, so we sat and waited.

Within minutes the Waiter Girls appeared, each one looking lovely. They stood against the wall of the staircase, waiting with happy expectation. The Hurdy-gurdy Girls, escorted by their husbands and gentlemen friends, settled in seats close to the stage. These ladies, happily smiling, were dressed in their finery. Zola and Bertha were not to be seen.

To cover the lateness of the ceremony, I began playing "I Love You Truly." Soon Willis nudged me and pointed to the stairs where Naomi was waving and nodding. Time to begin. Willis and I began The Wedding March. As we were playing, I was able to glance at the staircase.

Warren, hair slicked back and wearing new dark-blue pants and a matching shirt, came to the top of the stairs and began to carefully step down. He frowned as he carried the satin pillow bearing the wedding ring. He moved to stand beside Corby who patted him on the shoulder and nodded. Then Clara brought Rainbow, dressed in a long pink calico dress with streaming pink ribbons in her curly red hair, to the stairs. She held the basket filled almost to overflowing with the paper petals and listened intently as Clara whispered to her. With a nod and a smile, she slowly came down the stairs, throwing petals with every step. At the bottom, she stood next to Warren.

All eyes were focused on the top of the stairs where Maggie stood, looking frightened but very happy. Her dress was pale blue polished cotton with white lace about the neck and three-quarter sleeves. Her brown curly hair was brushed up into a braided coronet with blue ribbons woven through. She carried a bouquet of short, green sprigs of pine with a profusion of multicolored ribbons and bows cascading from the sides. Her makeup was lovely, and she was indeed a glowing bride.

Rev. Norton's strong voice filled the saloon as he began the ritual.

"We are gathered together, dear friends, to witness the marriage of these two fine people, Maggie and Corby. God in his loving kindness has brought them together to share their lives, their fortunes, and their futures in this place and time."

All was quiet as those assembled hung on every word. I added soft music to the background. Rainbow did not fidget but paid close attention to every word. On cue, Warren proudly presented the pillow with the ring. When Rev. Norton finally declared,

"I now pronounce you man and wife," there were loud whoops and cheering throughout the room, and the bride and groom were immediately surrounded by well-wishers. Quickly, Clara led Rainbow and Warren away from the crush of people.

Della Norton's luscious wedding cake with pink frosting was displayed at the end of the bar. She had thoughtfully provided three smaller cakes decorated with short branches, just in case the larger cake could not serve everyone. All along the bar were huge platters of Wonkees and sliced vegetables.

Gradually Maggie and Corby moved to the bar where Orrin made himself part of the festivities. "Ladies and gentlemen," he began, "I'm sure we're all happy for the bride and groom and wish them well as they share these magnificent wedding cakes and other tasty bits provided for this occasion by the management of this saloon." (What a bald-faced lie!) "You are all invited to join them in this celebration. I ask that you notice the large beer steins placed along the bar. In these, I might suggest that you contribute whatever coins or nuggets you can spare to help this happy couple begin their new life together, and to cover the cost of our grand celebration on this special occasion."

I couldn't believe what I was hearing, and I looked about for Grant, Rev. Norton, Hattie and Barnaby. We all stood with mouths open. Shocked. But Orrin was not finished.

Holding up his arm for silence, he continued. "I am happy to report that beer and other refreshments are also available." And smiling as if he had just made a magnificent gesture, he grandly escorted the bride and groom to the wedding cakes.

It is hard to describe the reactions of those of us who had put this occasion together. Maggie and Corby looked puzzled, but they gamely moved toward the wedding cakes and went about the custom of the cutting the pieces amid the cheering crowd.

Grant, Hattie, Barnaby and I retired to the kitchen. We were not surprised at Orrin's lies, and his blatant effort to profit from the wedding, but we were greatly disappointed. We didn't have long to feel sorry for ourselves, though.

Naomi soon came in with a worried look. "Everything's goin' crazy out there, and Maggie looks like she's ready to cry. Lots of people came up to wish them well, and most of the men with their wives went right home. But the miners are still there drinkin', diving in the food and lookin' for a good time. What can we do?"

Then we realized that we had abandoned the wedding. Grant suddenly got to his feet and said firmly, "Barnaby, take the horse and buggy and drive Mrs. McKee, Mrs. Malcolm, Rainbow and Warren to the new house. Then come back here with the buggy and wait."

He turned to Naomi. "If there is any wedding cake left, get a big piece of it and bring it back in here."

To me he said, "You and Hattie light the fire at the house, make a big pot of coffee and lay out some plates. We'll just give Maggie and Corby a happier, warmer reception — just friends sitting around sharing their wedding day away from the saloon."

I kissed his cheek. "I do like the way your mind works, my friend. Let's go, Barnaby."

Just then Naomi came in with Rainbow and Warren, who were looking rather confused. I took their hands. "Come with me, my little friends. We're going to have our own party for Maggie and Corby and we want you to be a part of it." And off we went to the new home.

Thirty minutes after Barnaby dropped us off, he ushered Maggie and Corby through the door. Ida Penny came next. Grant followed, carrying a good-sized parcel that turned out to be one of the smaller wedding cakes which he set carefully on the table.

Maggie was bright with happiness as Corby showed her the house that was built just for her. When they joined us in the kitchen,

Maggie was wiping her eyes and Corby had his arm about her shoulders. He was finding it difficult to speak, but he managed to say, "There ain't no way we can thank you for all this. There ain't enough words. Maggie and I agree that right now is the very best time of our lives and we're beholden to you all."

Maggie nodded, still wiping away the tears.

There was a knock on the door and Elmo and his wife, Mary, joined the celebration. A thin, frail lady with a sweet face, she was dressed in a black cape and bonnet. It was touchingly clear she could not hide her pride as she looked from her husband to others in the room. This couple was lovingly connected.

By now there was a fire blazing in the fireplace, and dishes and forks were set out on the table. Maggie sat down, and Corby stood protectively at her side, not sure what to do. He burst out, "Blast that Orrin! He just had to use our wedding to fill his pockets. When I told him we were getting married, he offered to take care of everything and invite all our friends. How was I to know what he had in mind?" He patted Maggie's shoulder to comfort her.

Elmo brought out two bottles of wine from his heavy overcoat. "This comes from Orrin's secret stock, and it's a pleasure to add them to your celebration!" He passed the bottles to Grant, who opened them and poured the contents into the teacups and glasses on the table. Once everyone had been served, Grant spoke to the couple. "Maggie and Corby, there's no need to be downhearted. Here you are in your new home, surrounded by friends, and we'll have us a proper celebration."

Maggie raised her head and smiled, and Grant went on.

"This house was made especially for you two to live in love and happiness. A lot of special wishes went into the making, and it will be here for you when you come home at night. Who cares about Orrin and his tricks? He won't change. Let him be the coarse, thoughtless man he's always been. We should feel pity for him because he will never, ever have what you two have and will always have — everlasting love and a wonderful life together."

He drew a breath, then raised his teacup. "My dear Maggie and Corby, you have the warm regard of your friends, and you can always count on us." He raised his teacup higher and stated, "So, let us share this toast to wish this couple joy in their life together. May the years ahead bring them happiness that knows no bounds. To Maggie and Corby!"

Everyone raised their cups. Grant had put a teaspoon of wine into the cups held by Warren and Rainbow. They smiled broadly as they sipped it, clearly delighted to be part of the ritual.

Still holding Maggie's hand, Corby declared, "Your good wishes are makin' this day all Maggie and I hoped it would be. Thank you so much, Mr. Douglas."

Maggie got to her feet to stand beside Corby. "We sure are lucky to have such fine people on our side. We'll always be beholden to you for makin' this day so happy."

Just then Rainbow raised her hand and jumped up and down. "Can we have some wedding cake now? It sure looks good!"

Everyone burst into laughter. Maggie found a knife and cut slices into the waiting dishes.

Grant cleared his throat, and all eyes turned to him once more. "Everyone, we must acknowledge one part of the ceremony that was beautifully executed. We must agree that Rainbow made a beautiful flower girl, dropping flower petals as she came down the stairs with grace and style. And Warren, you will agree, carried the ring on the pillow without a flaw. No one could have done it as well." Everyone broke into applause while the two children laughed with delight.

It was a wonderful party. We laughed, told stories and spoke of the future until the fire began to die and Warren and Rainbow were drooping in their chairs. I stood and said to Grant, "Why don't we get these youngsters over to Wong Kee for dinner, then hustle them into bed. They've had a big day."

Hattie stood to say, "I'll help you, then Grant and Barnaby can take us home before I get as sleepy as the children."

I hugged Maggie and whispered in her ear, "You know you have all my good wishes for your future together. I'm so very happy for you."

She hugged me back and said, "Mis' Samantha, things haven't been the same since you came to Boone Valley. Us Waiter Girls were talkin' about you the other day, and sayin' how you helped to change things for our own good."

"But to get these changes you were badly hurt in the process. My mind has been terribly uneasy because I was responsible for what happened," I responded.

Taking my hand, Maggie said, "That's all behind us now so let's not think of it. We're all so pleased you're here. If there is anything any of us girls can do for you, just say the word."

"There is something you can do," I said.

"Anything," she replied.

"Allow me to give your handsome husband a good luck hug. Is it all right?"

She laughed. "Just one, now. I want him to save the rest for me!"

Corby looked up as we walked over, then raised his eyebrows when he saw the smiles on our faces.

Maggie said, "I just told Mis' Samantha she could give you a good luck hug, but just one. Is that all right? It's all right with me."

Laughing, Corby embraced me, his arms strong. "You know that I wish a bright and happy future for you two," I whispered.

"I do thank you, ma'am," he replied. "And while I'm at it, Maggie, I may as well have good luck hugs from the other ladies — Miss Hattie, Miss Ida, Mary and Rainbow."

Grant and Barnaby got into the action and managed to exchange hugs with all of the ladies, and on this happy note we went on our way. With Wong Kee's help, the children ate, then Hattie and I tucked them into their bunks. Bertha was nowhere to be seen, so all went smoothly.

The Hurdy-gurdy and Waiter Girls were not around when we came down the stairs. We found later they jointly decided not to work that night. I don't know how Orrin took the news, but the crowd in the saloon had diminished. We could see the wedding cakes had been completely devoured, as had the platters of food, with only crumbs and frosting remaining on the floor.

Grant drove Hattie, Barnaby and me back to Hattie's where we sank into the comfortable seats in the parlor and spoke in quiet voices. On impulse, I went to the piano and played "You'll Never Walk Alone."

Grant said quietly, "What a perfect way to end the day. That was just right. I've missed it. "

"Such lovely music," Hattie observed. "Is this the kind of music they have where you two came from?"

"Oh yes," Grant answered. "And it's like giving water to a thirsty man to hear it once more."

A few moments later Grant stood and motioned to Barnaby. "Come on, old man, let's go on our way and let these ladies get some rest. It's been a long day. You can bunk at my place. I've got a cot you can use." Barnaby quickly got to his feet and gave us a smile as he awkwardly bowed and said good night.

Once they were gone, Hattie and I ascended the stairs. About halfway up she stopped and looked into my eyes. "You might as well face it, my girl. It's no secret how you and Mr. Douglas feel about each other. So, what are you going to do about it?"

"Hattie, can you accept that Grant and I have strong feelings for each other and hope to marry someday? How do you think people in Boone Valley will react when they find out?"

Hattie observed, "Let's face it. People do pretty much what they want around here because they come from different towns, different rules. Those who do make a fuss aren't important."

She stopped and pointed a finger at me. "Listen to me! Before you came, I was straitlaced, prim and proper like I just knew how things should be. But look what you've done to me! I'm talking and thinking different than when I was in Missouri. And you're to blame!"

I put an arm around her shoulders. "Hattie, my dear, you have such humor and great fun under the surface, it's been a pleasure to watch it come out. Thank you for accepting the feelings that Grant and I have for each other. We don't know just when or how, but someday we'll find a future together and that will be a great day for us."

With a contented sigh, we mounted the stairs, ready for a good night's rest.

Chapter Twenty-Six

Our lives in Boone Valley resumed with few adjustments, but well on course. Hattie and I decided to have a New Year's gathering, and as the last minutes of 1852 ticked away, we were in the warm company of Maggie and Corby, Barnaby, Grant, Andrew Locke and Ida Penny. Between us, Grant and I managed to mix a huge bowl of eggnog, and somehow he obtained a bottle of excellent brandy for the final ingredient. It was to be a festive occasion, with special meaning for Grant and me. We were moving one year closer to the future we'd left behind, though well aware that we would never catch up.

Of greater significance were the stolen moments Grant and I managed between Christmas and New Year's. My love for this extraordinary man was growing stronger each day, and neither the life I'd left behind nor the husband and sons dwelling there could alter the emotions that were sweeping over me. I could tell Grant felt the same. As he drove me home over the snow-covered road just two days before New Year's, he brought the buggy to a halt and turned to me. Bless his heart, he even removed his hat before he spoke.

"My dear, it looks like our Universe is going to leave us where we are, here in the past. So far we haven't felt a tug or rumble of thunder that would zap us back to our other lives. It's obvious we're not going anywhere except into 1853, and maybe this is where we're supposed to be. I can't wait any longer. I want to be with you every day — to see your funny face the first thing in the morning and the last thing at night. I want to be able to hold you close every fantastic night that is given to us. I don't know or care what the rules are — here or anywhere else in time. We're here now, and I'll just bust if you don't say you'll marry me, and as soon as possible."

All I could do was look at the love in his wonderful face. I held back so long that he burst out, "Well, how about it? I just made the greatest speech of my life and there's no reaction, not even applause or a cheer."

Finally I was able to say, "It has occurred to me that the Universe didn't dump us here in the 1850s to live alone. Adam and Eve were not created to live alone. Obviously they were meant to be together, just as we seem to be, and I am so terribly grateful."

I held up an index finger to indicate that I needed another moment to collect my thoughts, then answered. "The thought of spending the rest of my life with you, to see you, to work with you, to share our special secret through the years, is like a gift wrapped in gold ribbon. Our life together promises such richness in so many ways that I can't wait for it to begin. Yes, yes, my darling. We must be together for always, and it had better be soon!"

Not caring if there were people or wagons on the road, Grant pulled me to him, enveloped me in his arms, and placed a series of magnificent, bonding kisses all over my face. When his arms relaxed, we sat there, holding hands and talking quietly about what we should do.

"If you agree, my wife-to-be, why don't we announce our engagement at the New Year's party. Our dear friends will be there, and it'll be a blast to watch their reactions. And then we can finally show everybody just how we feel. If you want, we can put an ad in the paper or shout it through the streets. I want everyone to know that I, Grant Sheridan Douglas, am terribly in love with Samantha Malcolm, and, wonder of wonders, she's in love with me!" He laughed with joy as he gathered me in his arms once more.

During the last stretch of road to Hattie's house, we decided that Grant would make the announcement just after midnight. There were tears in my eyes as I grabbed his hand and held it against my cheek. I had no more words.

A few days after their wedding, Maggie and Corby decided to return to the saloon for the time being, and resumed their duties. This was done smoothly without comment, and Orrin seemed to accept that the full staff would be on duty all evening up to and after midnight. Maggie and Corby held their ground, then left at nine o'clock, a benefit they had given themselves after their wedding. They seemed unworried about any repercussions there might be when they would resumed their duties on New Year's Day.

On New Year's Eve I played during the usual afternoon hours, while Orrin skulked about making noises that my services would be needed into the evening. I smiled and shook my head as I concentrated on the keyboard, and he soon left in an 1850's version of a snit.

That night we all came together at Hattie's. Grant and I agreed to sit apart and be polite to each other until midnight. Meanwhile, he made sure that all the cups were filled with eggnog when it came time for the announcement. Maggie and Corby arrived just in time to join in.

As midnight approached, I suggested that each person describe what they would like the new year to bring. With a loving smile, Corby took Maggie's hand. "We want the coming year to be just as fine as the time we have had together this past year, to enjoy our new home and our friends. As far as we're concerned, life is as good as it can be right now." Maggie smiled in agreement.

Barnaby was next. Shy about expressing himself, he dropped his head, looked at his work-worn hands and said, "I want my claim to pay off this year so I'll have enough money to go back home to Missouri. I'm tired of diggin' away at that durn mountain. It's been long enough, and I just want to go home." Then he sat back in relief.

Ida Penny was next, and she hesitated before speaking in a quiet voice. "Some of you may remember that my brother Timothy and I came from Ohio to California two years ago. We got as far as Sacramento where he got the fever and died. I was alone, and scared, and not sure what to do, but there was some money left and I heard about Boone Valley. I came here hoping to start a small business. It's been lonely, but I managed all right. The people here have been most kind and friendly, and I've been doing pretty well with my shop and feel rather happy." She looked down at her hands, then finished. "My wish for this year is to keep on as before with my work and my friends for many years to come."

Andrew was next. He stood, held his coat lapels, then cleared his throat as if preparing to speak in a courtroom. "It seems that coming to Boone Valley has been extremely fortuitous for me. To review, my brother, Adam, and I both studied law in Pennsylvania as my parents wished us to do, and in time we shared a practice, just as my parents decreed. However, my brother proved to be more successful, more flamboyant, and more in demand than I. My parents clearly showed their disappointment, and I found it difficult to carry on in such an atmosphere. I announced my plans to come to California, which promised change and great opportunities. Through an opportunity with the new Wells Fargo Company, I moved to the gold country, which has proved to be most beneficial." He paused as he pondered a suitable closing statement. "I am hopeful that this new year will bring me greater growth in my career and, in time, a lovely young lady to share my life."

He cleared his throat, embarrassed that he had exposed so much of himself, but the comments and encouragement from his friends put him at ease.

We all turned to Hattie who seemed a bit flustered. She wasn't accustomed to revealing her life to a group of people, but she managed a smile and began.

"Land sakes, it's hard for me to know what to say. This past year has been pretty good. Business at the store has been just fine. Naturally I still miss my Martin and my Rosalie." Her voice broke here, and we waited in sympathetic silence.

Then she sat up straight, pointed at me, and in a stronger voice continued. "But one good thing was when that young lady over there knocked on my door. Things haven't been the same since!" All eyes turned toward me and there was a great round of laughter.

Barnaby added, "That's for darn sure!"

Hattie went on. "That young lady brought music and laughter into this house, and changed my life. There's been fun, surprises, and a few sad times, but I hope very much that this coming year will be more of the same!"

Everyone smiled and nodded, then turned their attention to me. I pointed to Grant, saying, "Perhaps Mr. Douglas would like to be next."

Just then the small clock in the parlor began to chime. It was midnight. Glancing at me, Grant stood up.

"You all know me and some of my history. I arrived here without funds, but I was able to accumulate and borrow enough to start my brewery. Life has been good to me ever since. This past year has been remarkable in several ways. As we listen to the chimes mark the last moments of 1852, let us raise our glasses to toast the coming year, and also mark the announcement I am about to make."

Taking a deep breath, he stood, raised his cup of eggnog, and with a shining smile on his face, declared, "Ladies and gentlemen, it is my great, no, not great, it is my stupendous pleasure to announce that Samantha Malcolm has consented to give me her hand in marriage." He walked over, took my hand, and brought me to my feet to stand beside him. He then planted a lovely kiss on my cheek.

After a shocked silence, everyone rose to their feet voicing their approval. Together they raised their cups to toast us and the new year to come. There was a flurry of questions: how long had this been going on, and when will the wedding be? Laughing, we answered as best we could.

Andrew came to my side, kissed me on the cheek and whispered, "I had an idea this would happen, and it's clear that you two really, really belong together. Your future happiness should be extraordinary, and I shall look forward to watching it happen."

I gave him a wink and a hug.

Hattie came to take my hand. "Even though it's been less than a year since you lost your family, life must go on, as we both know. You two are so happy together and I'm happy for you."

Ida Penny was standing beside her, and she said softly, "Samantha, I'm so very, very happy for you. I always thought Mr. Douglas was a special gentleman, and it's just wonderful that you two will be together. You make such a lovely couple." I kissed her on the cheek in reply.

Maggie was next, and the others moved away. "Now you have a fine gentleman of your own. The other Waiter Girls will be so excited when they hear the news. And Orrin, won't he just have a fit when he hears! Will you go on working for him?"

"For the time being, I guess. But, yes, you're right. I believe my days of working at the Majestic are numbered."

Maggie shook her head. "Things won't be the same when you leave. You've been such a good friend to all of us, helpin' us through the bad times."

"But that won't change," I assured her. "We will always be friends. All of us will work to get the best of Orrin, no matter where I am."

Her face was beaming as I gave her a hug.

Grant was standing to one side talking to the men, and then he raised his voice. "Listen, everyone. Right now Sam and I have no plans when or where our wedding will be, or even if we'll stay in Boone Valley. But be assured you will know as soon as we make some major decisions."

He walked over to join me, put his arm about my waist and finished, "And to make it official, I now wish to present this lady with the symbol of our engagement." And he reached into his coat pocket and withdrew a gold ring, which he put on my finger. It just fit, and why not. It was the same gold ring that Harland had made from nuggets found on his rock hunting expeditions! I gasped. I could see that Grant's face was questioning. "Don't you like it? What's wrong?"

I leaned over and said softly, "I just love it, and I'll tell you later." And I held up my hand so everyone could see the ring. Hattie thought it was lovely and most appropriate, not remembering that she was with me when I took it into the Assay Office to sell.

Hours after midnight the evening came to a close and one by one our friends said their good nights. Andrew Locke loaded his rented buggy with Maggie, Corby and Ida Penny. Barnaby would be staying at Grant's house rather than riding his mule, already comfortably bedded down at the livery stable, back to his claim. While he was saying goodbye to Hattie, Grant and I talked quietly in the parlor.

He seemed deeply concerned when he asked, "What's the story on the ring?"

"Where on earth did you find it?"

"I spotted it at the Assay Office when I was talking to Aaron Ross. What about it?"

"My dear," I began, "I sold this ring to Aaron Ross my second day here for money to live on. It was the only thing I had to sell that didn't advertise the 20th Century. You see, Harland had it made from nuggets from his rock hunting expeditions."

"Well, what's your feeling on it? Do you want to keep it?"

I shook my head. "No, I want nothing that reminds me of my workaholic, disapproving, self-absorbed former husband. I'd rather wear a brass or iron ring, thank you."

Taking the ring from my finger, Grant gave me a quick kiss and said, "Don't worry. I'll find something much nicer and more suitable."

I could not contain a sigh of relief. "I'm so pleased you don't mind. But what will we tell everyone? They all had a good look at it."

"We'll tell them the ring had sharp edges that caught on your dress, and was also rather heavy to wear. That should do it."

With a sigh I said, "It's late and you must be on your way."

"My lady, a proper good night kiss from you will send me happily into the night." He swept me into his arms until we heard Hattie say, "Tsk, tsk. What a way to carry on. From the look of things, you two better get to a preacher right away. Samantha, come say good night to Barnaby before he goes."

Smiling, I took Barnaby's hand. "We're so pleased you could be with us tonight and share our happy news. You and Hattie have been our special friends, and that's the way it will always be." Grant added, "Even if … no, when you find a pile of gold and move to Missouri, we'll be connected regardless of the distance."

Hattie and I saw them to the door and waved as the horse and buggy pulled away from the house.

As we entered the kitchen and saw the pile of dishes waiting to be washed, Hattie said, "No, I just can't face these dishes right now. Let's just leave 'em and wash up in the morning when we're fresh. I told Jim Bidwell and the other clerks to open the store at noon so they could sleep in. And what about you? Are you going to work today?"

I yawned. "I'd rather not. It would be a good day to relax and work on my priorities."

"I'm not sure what all that means, but there's work for me to do. People are still coming through town, looking for claims and needing supplies. And there'll be men at the saloon wanting an easy day listening to your music."

As we headed for the stairs, I commented, "You're right, Hattie. We're working ladies and we've got work to do. But now and then, let's take a whole day off and mellow out, play some cards, sing some songs, and do only what comes easily and naturally."

Hattie looked at me quizzically. "Well, you'll have to show me how to do that sometime, but tomorrow is not the day. There's too much to do." She kissed me on the cheek. "So, good night to you, engaged lady. The people in Boone Valley are going to have lots to talk about, but who cares? You have a good man there, and he's a very lucky fellow. We'll have a nice little talk about it over breakfast."

She yawned as she reached the top of the stairs and entered her bedroom. Once comfortably in my nightgown, I found myself kneeling by the bed, my face buried in my hands. Yes, it was certainly time for a prayer as one part of my life was closing and another was about to begin.

"My dear Father in Heaven," I began. "There is so much to be thankful for, especially my unexpected journey to this place. What began as a calamity has now become a new existence in a new world. How many months has it been since I was dumped into this new life? Four? Five? And now my life has meaning, purpose, direction, friends, love, a totally new existence, a completely different way to look at the world around me and the courage to deal with it. Thank you for answering my prayer that night on the mountain. You have my everlasting gratitude. Please be with me in the years to come, and help me to be worthy of this gift and cherish it with love and acceptance, as You would wish me to do. Help me to do the best I can and be the best I can in Thy name. Amen."

As I snuggled into bed, my mind was a kaleidoscope of scenes from my past and present, and best of all, my future with Grant. My new life has allowed me to act freely without limitation or censure. My instincts for right and wrong can function without restriction, and I have been able to reach out and connect with people on a very human level. What a wonderful world the Universe has given me. Then I smiled as sleep captured my active brain.

Hattie was so full of questions the next morning, I hardly had a chance to eat buckwheat cakes and drink my coffee.

"I knew you two had feelings for each other, but it was still a surprise when Grant made the announcement. Tell me now, how long have you two been sweet on each other?"

I had to think, then replied, "Well, we met just before the piano duel, and it sort of grew from there. When you went to Sacramento, we had plenty of time to talk and get to know each other. Then when Orrin brutalized Maggie so badly and we worked together to help her, our feelings for each other became stronger. Oh, Hattie, he's the finest, handsomest, sweetest man I've ever known. He was a great support during my grieving period. He's very caring, and we connect in such a loving way."

"As good as you had with your first husband?"

"Actually better, much better. Grant and I can talk about just anything and everything. Harland wanted only to talk about the things that were important to him. He barely listened to anything I wanted to share. His life became focused on his stores, golf and his rock hunting. Oh, I was a good wife and mother, and the perfect hostess when he entertained at home. But I never felt I was an equal, a partner in the marriage. That may be the reason I ran away."

"Ran away? You never told me this," Hattie exclaimed.

"When did this happen?"

I'd said too much, revealed much more than I wanted. "I'll tell you all about it later, Hattie. Now is not the time."

She looked disappointed that I would not share that part of my life with her.

"Hattie, you know you are my dearest friend and I've told you more about myself than almost any other person in my life. When the time is right, I promise I'll tell you everything there is to know. Can you please wait until then?"

She nodded slowly, and then we discussed the night before.

"Were they really surprised, everyone except you, about Grant and me?"

"They were flabbergasted, and that's a word I haven't used in years," she said.

Thoughtfully I said, "I was surprised and touched the way everyone was sharing with us — Ida, Andrew, and most of all, Barnaby. I had no idea he had such a longing to go home to Missouri. Many men in these mountains must feel the same. It's rather sad when you think about it. I can't help but wonder what will become of them when the rush for gold is over."

"Over! What makes you think it'll be over?"

I flushed at this second slip and explained, "The surface claims will be played out in time, hydraulic mining is coming this way, and soon the big companies will come in and take over the gold production. The only thing that will be left to the miners will be working for those companies or moving on to Colorado or Alaska."

"How do you know all this, Samantha? This is all new to me."

"Oh, I pick it up in snatches of conversations. There is a lot of talk at the saloon, and Grant and I have also talked about it."

Hattie grew solemn and sighed. "I must admit that I'd surely hate to see Barnaby go back to Missouri. I'd miss him."

I sympathized. "Yes, he's been a good friend. We can only hope he does well at his mine since that's his dream. Heaven knows he's a determined man."

She straightened her back and demanded, "And what about you, young lady? There's going to be a wedding, but when? And where will you settle down? You're not going to leave me right away, are you?"

"All of that is undecided. There will be time to talk it out now that Grant and I can be seen together. And do you know what? I'm anxious to get Orrin's reaction, which should be most interesting." I stood and stretched. "Well, my friend, this is New Year's Day, which should be a holiday for everyone. But it's also Monday, so I guess I'll go to work."

"Me, too. There are records to check and things to see to at the store. So whenever you're ready, we'll walk to town." She peered out the window. "Last night's snow is on the ground, but it looks like the clouds are breaking up. It should be a nice day."

There was a knock on the kitchen door and there stood Grant and Barnaby wearing bright smiles. Grant announced, "Over breakfast at Norton's Café, which was very crowded this morning, Barnaby and I decided we should observe New Year's Day and continue the festivities. The horse and buggy are waiting, so how about a ride in the country while it's so nice. What is your pleasure, ladies?"

Hattie shook her head. "Gentlemen, Samantha and I just now decided we should see to our work. I'll check on things at the store and she'll be playing as usual this afternoon."

The men looked disappointed.

"How about this?" I proposed. "Since it's only about 9:30, maybe Hattie and I can spare an hour or two so you could show me about town. Since arriving here, I've seen very little of Boone Valley, and I'd enjoy a tour."

Grant said dryly, "Well, the high spots are the shacks and

houses on the sides of the mountain that we can see from here. But yes, Boone Valley does extend beyond Hattie's store, the church, Norton's Café, Ida's shop and the saloon. All right, ladies, put on your coats and bonnets and away we'll go!"

We were escorted to the buggy by a delighted Barnaby and playful Grant. I sat in front with Grant, and Hattie seemed thrilled to share the back with Barnaby. Then our tour began.

Grant began explaining the sights. "On your right, ladies and gentlemen, is the palatial home of one of the city's outstanding citizens, Mrs. Hattie McKee. On down the road is the very functional black-smith's shop, which seems to be shut down for the day."

He turned down a badly rutted dirt road with wooden buildings on both sides. "On the left we have the world famous gourmet restaurant, Norton's Café, and across the road is the home of the long arm of the law for this thriving city, the sheriff's office, and jail designed to accommodate four residents, so they tell me."

The tour continued farther away from the center of town, past the newspaper office, lumber yard, sawmill, leather shop, a boot and shoemaker's shop, and Grant's brewery. There we stopped for a short walk through the vats, clouds of steam and noise. Grant explained, "Everyone here was willing to work the full day, but there was plenty of stock on hand. I offered a half-day for a full day's pay, either the morning or afternoon. They chose to work the morning shift, mainly so they could spend the afternoon and evening with their families. So everything worked out quite well."

The workers stopped and tipped their hats as Grant ushered us through. Then he showed us a very tidy, well-organized office where two men sat at desks working with pen and ink on the records of Grant's thriving business. Grant introduced them, saying his business could not function without their capable assistance.

He resumed the tour to include five of the saloons in town —some small, tidy and worn down; some with gaudy signs; others with doors wide open to show the bar and activities within. One had a balcony where several under-dressed and overly painted ladies beckoned to us as we passed by.

I commented to Grant, "After seeing some of those beauties, Orrin's place seems to be the best in town."

He nodded. "Yes, he wasn't the first, but he came with enough money to build a larger, more attractive facility. It's just about the best in town, and the only one with girls who will dance with the men every night. Some of the others have gambling where the cards are marked. Others have the girls upstairs — sad, scrawny, unhappy girls. It would break your heart to see them."

I suggested, "Perhaps I should go over and have a talk with those girls, just as I did with the Waiter Girls."

Grant's laugh was bitter. "You wouldn't be able to get close to them. Number one, once inside the door, you might never be seen again. And number two, word has spread about the outlandish things you've been preaching to the girls at the Majestic. The men running the saloons aren't about to let you turn their fearful, docile women into questioning, thinking females."

"There must be a way …"

"Don't even think about it, Samantha. You have enough to handle right now. What you've accomplished at Orrin's will spread through town, and perhaps some of that will seep through to the girls in the other saloons. Only time will tell."

I sighed and nodded.

The tour continued with a look at Grant's house, a well-built structure, much like the one he built for Maggie and Corby. Ida Penny's shop was next, and the fact we stopped by during our tour pleased her greatly.

The tour ended with a stop at the Wells Fargo office and a quick hello to Andrew Locke. The next stop was the Majestic. Some miners were lounging on the outside benches, and we could see

Warren and Rainbow sitting on the wooden steps in the sunshine. We called them over.

Grant asked, "Little friends, do you realize what day this is?"

Warren shrugged his shoulders, then listened with interest when Grant told them the story of Father Time and the celebration when the last day of one year ended and a new one began. "You close one year," Grant explained, "and then look forward to a new and happier year to come." One could see that Warren took this information seriously.

I took his hand. "What would you like to see happen in this new year, Warren, for yourself and Rainbow?"

His reply was serious. "I'd like to see us learn to read and write real good. We'd like Momma Bertha to want to be with us, to sit 'round the fire and talk in the evenin's like we did at Mrs. McKee's when Rainbow was gettin' better. We want you and Mr. Douglas and Mrs. McKee to be our friends, even though Momma Bertha don't like us to be."

We were silent until Grant answered, "You're a good man, Warren, and you deserve a much better life. You just keep in mind all the things that you want the new year to bring you. Maybe it all might come true, okay?"

Warren raised his head and nodded with a hopeful smile.

As we drove back to Hattie's, Grant said in a burst of anger, "I don't know about the rest of you, but I'm going to do everything that's humanly possible to bring a better future to those kids. They deserve better than what they've got."

I took his hand and squeezed it in agreement. "As I've said before, Mr. Douglas, I love the way your mind works and I'm with you all the way. We have work to do." I turned to Hattie and Barnaby. "Are you two with us in this endeavor, dear friends?"

Barnaby and Hattie leaned forward to rest their hands on our shoulders. "We're with you wherever you want to go with this," Hattie pledged.

And speaking more strongly and forthrightly than we had ever heard before, Barnaby wrapped up the moment with a heart-felt, "And may God bless them children. Amen!"

Chapter Twenty-Seven

When I returned to play on New Year's Day, the men in attendance listened quietly. Many were grinning as if they shared a secret. Grant and I had hoped to keep our engagement quiet, but word must have spread through this part of Boone Valley like a forest fire. As I began, I could see Orrin standing to one side and frowning. The next time I looked, he had disappeared.

A few minutes before my gig was over, I noticed Grant standing by the front entrance, smiling. I couldn't resist. I had not been singing as often, choosing only to play the melodies I had learned over the years. But now I broke into a song for this occasion: "People, people who love people, are the luckiest people in the world." After the last triumphant note, the applause began with a roar as Grant walked over and kissed me on the cheek. We faced the rowdy audience and their congratulations. Grant leaned over to whisper, "You sure know how to make a great exit."

After waving to the crowd, we made our way out, pausing to greet Corby and Elmo, then gratefully reached the quiet of the kitchen and the calm presence of Wong Kee.

Grant smiled and asked, "Well, my friend, have you heard the news?"

Wong Kee nodded. "Engagement mean to marry like Miss Maggie and Corby? I very happy it is so. You have history. Make your future rich, not like others." And he bowed low to us, with respect.

Wong Kee was our special friend in the months to come. We came to draw on his wisdom and traditions. On the days when Orrin was elsewhere, we shared cups of his hot tea and meaningful conversation. Grant quietly informed him that the gold rush would end within a few more years and Boone Valley would decline in population by more than half. Wong Kee nodded as if this was something he could foresee. What were his plans? He did not know, but was accepting the changes to come with equanimity. He was so calm and centered that we were drawn to him while our future plans began to formulate.

Spring came early in April. The snow remaining on the surrounding mountains and fields sparkled under the clouded skies. The air was cool and crisp, but the warming sun heralded the near ending of the harsh and difficult winter.

The new year saw a settling of our different lives into comfortable routines. Maggie and Corby's habit was to conclude their day's work no later than 9 o'clock, then enjoy their new home away from the clamor and dusty odors of the saloon. Their faces radiated a contentment that caused some to display their envy. Zola and Bertha continued to toss verbal arrows and flippant criticisms at Maggie. The serenity in her face inflamed them all the more. Corby was ready to make an issue of the behavior, but Maggie assured him that their comments could not bother her.

During this time the Waiter Girls, with Hattie's blessing, moved their savings from the safe in her home to the Wells Fargo bank, which was just down the street from the saloon. Flower was often there, hoping to see the handsome Robert Heath. There was no doubt he was smitten, but so far their romance hadn't gone beyond smiles and glances. The couple never had time to be together, since he worked days and she worked nights. Maggie and the other girls decided that something had to be done.

The warmer weather allowed Barnaby to ride his mule Biscuit into town on Sunday mornings to join Hattie, Grant and me at church. In time it became a custom to retire to Hattie's for lunch and relax in the parlor for pleasant conversation and music. Barnaby was always slicked up, his clothes as clean as scrubbing in the river would allow.

One Sunday, Hattie declared that since they were partners, she would "do up" his laundry if he brought it in. He beamed as if he had been given a great gift. Grant and I watched with pleasure as these two gentle people came together.

During those Sunday afternoons Grant and I began developing plans for the wedding. The date? Mid-June seemed the best, giving Ida Penny time to design and sew a dress for me and one for Hattie. Also, Grant wanted to renovate his small home to make room for a wife and all the female items that came with her. We even designed an outhouse with a weather vane on top and two small windows with brightly painted shutters. It would have a covered walkway from the house. Hattie and Barnaby could not understand why the design was so ornate, nor why Grant and I laughed so much over its construction. In fact, she was rather shocked that we made such an issue of an ordinary, functional outhouse.

Work began, and Ida and I had several conferences regarding a voluminous nightgown and matching robe, complete with yards of lace and embroidery. She declared she had never seen anything like it, but once begun, we had a wonderful time putting it together. Meanwhile, Hattie and I compiled the guest list and planned the reception.

Warren and Rainbow still spent the cold days before the pot-bellied stove in Hattie's store, and I continued tutoring them at the house three mornings a week. It was our custom to walk together to the saloon when weather permitted. On rainy days, Grant brought the horse and buggy to the house for the trip to town. We all settled down into a rather pleasant routine.

April ended, and after a day here and there of rain, early May brought more sunshine, which was a blessing for the miners. The search for gold resumed with great energy. The muddy roads were crowded with wagons, horses and stages, all bringing eager newcomers into the area.

Then one day Barnaby burst into the saloon just as I finished playing for the day, and it was obvious he was terribly anxious to tell me something. Curious bystanders began to gather, so I drew him into the kitchen and Wong Kee put a mug of hot coffee before him.

"What's happened, Barnaby? Are you all right?"

He took a sip of coffee. "Everything's more than all right. After fussing at that darned rock in the tunnel of my claim, I finally got it out in one big piece. Almost broke my leg! But here it came, sparkling like the pot under a rainbow. Mis' Samantha, I wasn't sure what it was, but I pulled it out and after some doin' put it on Biscuit's back. He wasn't very happy 'bout it, but he let me tie it on with a rope, then cover it with a blanket jus' so people wouldn't think it was what I thought it was."

"Which was what?" I asked.

"A nugget, a real gold nugget this big." And he spread his arms to show me the size.

I gasped, "Barnaby, what did you do then?"

"Biscuit and I brought it all the way here and I managed to carry it into the Assay Office so Mr. Ross could see it. And do you know what he told me after he looked it over?" He waited impatiently for me to answer.

"No, please tell me quick."

"It sure enough is a gold nugget, and he even weighed it for me. It weighed 76 pounds, Mis' Samantha! Seventy-six pounds!" He sat back in his chair and went on. "By golly, how about that? After all these years of diggin', I just can't believe it." Suddenly he stood up and headed for the door. "I gotta tell Mrs. McKee; I want her to know!"

He stopped at the door when Grant walked in, and behind

him were many faces looking in and demanding, "What's happenin' in there?"

Grant closed the door and ushered Barnaby back to the table. "I thought I might find you here. I was riding by the Assay Office and could see something interesting was going on. Your discovery is on display, and I must say it is impressive. Congratulations, old man. That's some great piece of rock you found."

Barnaby beamed, speechless but happy.

Grant added, "Aaron also introduced me to a gentleman who just came into town, Mr. Sted Hoffman. He represents a syndicate interested in purchasing promising gold claims, and he would like to look at yours and see what it could be worth."

Barnaby was in a daze and shook his head. "I dunno, Mr. Douglas. I just dunno what to do right now."

Grant took command. "Let's go to Hattie's and have a quiet dinner, then you can decide what to do now that your ship has come in."

We headed through the kitchen door, and found the hallway filled with bodies. All were impatient to hear the news.

"Did your claim pay off? Did you strike it rich, man?"

There were also angry voices. "Winners always buy drinks for everyone when they make a strike. Are you goin' to buy us some drinks, Barnaby?"

Grant held up his hand to quiet the crowd. "Barnaby needs some time to himself right now. After he's able to think things through, then he'll be back today or tomorrow to celebrate." Then he ushered Barnaby and me out the door to the buggy. There were complaints and angry comments as we left, but they didn't stop our hasty exit from the saloon.

As we drove away, Barnaby protested. "Biscuit, we can't leave Biscuit!" The mule was waiting patiently the by rail outside the saloon. Grant quickly tied the animal to the back of the buggy, then drove on before another crowd could gather.

We stopped to pick up Hattie at the store, and on the way we shared the news of Barnaby's strike. She was very happy for him and insisted on every detail. Once in the house, Grant and Barnaby settled in the parlor, sipping on the last of the brandy remaining from New Year's Eve. Hattie and I went to the kitchen to fix a quick dinner of boiled potatoes, leftover corned beef, and vegetables from her garden.

After dinner we relaxed over coffee and I asked Grant, "What's the value of Barnaby's nugget? Is it pure gold?"

Grant stated, "We're talking about troy ounces, or 12 ounces to each pound of gold. So, 76 pounds multiplied by 12 troy ounces equals ... roughly 912 ounces. Gold is going for about $20 an ounce, so 20 times 912 ounces would come — to a little over $18,000! You're a rich man, Barnaby!"

Barnaby sat back in his chair, unable to speak. We were all quiet until Hattie said sadly, "You got your wish, Mr. Barnaby. Now you can go back to Missouri, just like you were telling us on New Year's Eve."

Barnaby said softly, "Lord above, I can't believe it. I can go home now, just like I wanted."

I said, "We're all so happy for you, Barnaby, but we'll miss you if and when you go."

After a quiet moment, Grant said, "Well, that won't happen for a while. Barnaby must first decide what he wants to do. Why don't you show your claim to Mr. Hoffman tomorrow and see what he has to offer, then go from there?"

Barnaby nodded, still unable to talk. Grant patted him on the shoulder, then offered, "Would you like me to go with you when you talk to Mr. Hoffman?"

Barnaby was relieved. "I sure would appreciate it. Looks like there's lots of thinkin' to be done, and havin' someone to talk it over with me would ease my mind."

We talked quietly the rest of the evening, but Barnaby's head was so full of the turn his life had taken that he barely said anything until he bid us a good night.

The next day Hattie and I were on pins and needles, dying to know what was happening, hoping all was going well for Barnaby. At the end of the day, we had a big dinner ready. At last we heard the neighing of a horse and a mule complaining, then footsteps and a knock on the door. Grant and Barnaby came in, dirty, tired and very hungry. As they ate, Grant described their busy day.

"I was able to catch Mr. Hoffman at the hotel first thing this morning. We rented horses and rode up to the claim. Mr. Hoffman brought his assistant, a geologist, who looked over the claim and took some measurements and samples. At one point Mr. Hoffman came over and said to Barnaby, 'Mr. Tinker, did you examine what was behind the nugget?' Barnaby said he was so busy getting that nugget out and into town, it didn't occur to him."

Barnaby took over, excitedly. "And Mr. Hoffman told me the darndest thing ever. Where that nugget was they found a vein of pure gold! There's more gold in there than I ever could imagine. We got back just now, and Mr. Hoffman says he'll talk with his partner, then let me know tomorrow what he thinks my claim is worth!"

Hattie patted him on the shoulder. "Well, just you settle down and rest now. You had a big day, and it looks like tomorrow may be even more exciting. We're very happy that fortune has finally smiled on all your hard work. I even made a cake just in case, so we'll have ourselves a real celebration!"

After Grant took Barnaby back to his house for a good night's rest, Hattie and I cleaned up the kitchen. She stopped and looked at me sadly, "If Barnaby goes back to Missouri, I'll sure hate to see him go."

"If he does, why don't you ask him to visit your people and

tell them how well you're doing? He can write you all about it and that way you can keep in touch."

"I guess so," she sighed, "but it won't be the same."

Midmorning the next day, Grant and Barnaby were knocking at the back door, and over coffee told us the news.

Grant began by saying, "Mr. Hoffman came to see Barnaby first thing this morning. He and his man went over their findings most of the night, and they are offering to buy the claim outright for $17,000 dollars. Or, they would pay him $10,000 and a percentage of the profits from all of the gold his company pulls out of there."

Hattie put a hand over her heart. "My heavens, that's a great deal of money. Whatever did you decide to do, Mr. Barnaby? That's a hard decision you'll be making."

Barnaby shook his head. "It's more than I can figure. Mr. Douglas fixed it so those two men are now talkin' to his friend, Lawyer Locke. He feels the three of them can work out the best possible deal for me."

Grant then said, "Tell the ladies about your transaction at the Assay Office."

Barnaby smiled and said proudly, "Mr. Douglas fixed it with Mr. Ross to give me $200 as first payment on the nugget. I'll take 100 of it to the Majestic, and give it to Corby for free drinks 'til the money runs out. We'll have us a party like the men have been askin' for. First we're goin' to Mrs. McKee's store to get me some new clothes, then we'll have us a party as soon as you're done playin', Mis' Samantha, so we won't bother you."

All that afternoon there was an undercurrent of excitement. During my turn at the piano the buzz of conversation continued until 6 o'clock when Grant and the new Barnaby came through the front door. Dressed in dark blue trousers, white shirt and black string tie, a brocaded vest and cutaway jacket, Barnaby looked like a man of the world. He held his head high, and on it there was a black felt hat, similar to the one Grant wore. The assembled crowd cheered as they entered and settled at a table near Willis' piano below the stage. The celebration began, and in time, Mr. Hoffman and his partner joined them to share a bottle of fine brandy. Corby had been given a hundred dollar bill, and he and Elmo were dispensing beer and whiskey at a fast rate.

I watched all this from the kitchen door, and was soon joined by Wong Kee and Andrew Locke, who confided that Barnaby would be 'well taken care of' through the agreement with Sted Hoffman. Barnaby would get a payment of $18,000, and 5% of all profits made from the development of his claim. All papers would be signed in the morning, and Barnaby would be free to return to Missouri whenever he was ready.

Of course, Orrin was in the background, overseeing the distribution of drinks, and hustling the Waiter Girls to serve the men at the tables and keep the drinks coming. At one point the gamblers came out and invited Barnaby to join them for a "friendly game of cards." Barnaby was too busy, and Grant sent the not-too-happy men away.

The celebration was still at a high level when I fetched my coat from the kitchen and said good night to Wong Kee before picking up Hattie at the store.

The next morning Grant and Barnaby joined us at the breakfast table. Even though it was short notice, Hattie and I served breakfast while we waited impatiently for a report on the evening's celebration.

Shaking my head, I remarked, "I will assume that the party, well financed by Barnaby, was a great success. How long did the $100 last?"

Grant laughed. "It was a blast. Singing and celebration like you never heard before. Willis was there playing his heart out, and I don't believe the poor Waiter Girls had a minute to sit down and rest. And when the Hurdy-gurdy Girls came, the place went wild. Things got so out of hand that the girls refused to dance after the first hour and went home. The $100 was gone by 11 o'clock, and Barnaby slipped another $50 to Corby. The Waiter Girls did the best they could, and by midnight they went to their rooms and the men were serving themselves at the bar."

Looking at Barnaby, I commented, "I'd say it was a rip-roaring celebration. Were you happy with it?"

He sadly moved his head from side to side. "It sure was noisy, and everyone was actin' like they was crazy. I'm glad we left when we did. All that noise made me tired."

Hattie stood. "You just sit yourself down in the parlor, Mr. Barnaby, and rest. You've had a very busy two days, and before you know it, time will come for you to go home to Missouri." As they slowly walked toward the parlor, Grant and I stayed at the table and had a few quite moments to talk.

"How is he really doing, Grant? For a quiet man, he's had an awful lot to deal with these past few days. Has he been able to keep his balance so far?"

Grant smiled and played with his fork. "He's been just fine through all the madness. But do you know the best part?"

I shook my head.

"He's slowly beginning to realize that he's a rich man. He'll take about $30,000 back to Missouri — enough to last him and his family for the rest of their lives. We talked about it last night, and I innocently commented that he would now be able to think about getting married and settling down, and was there any lady in Missouri he would consider?"

"You didn't!"

"Yes I did, and it got him to thinking that marriage could be part of his plans, and not necessarily in Missouri. Can you see where this is leading?"

"Did he mention Hattie?"

"Of course. You two were busy at the stove fixing breakfast, but he couldn't keep his eyes off Hattie as she moved about the kitchen. He truly admires that lady and even commented that she was a fine specimen of a woman — strong, levelheaded and handsome. I'll venture a guess that within the week he may find the nerve to, as they say in the novels of the day, declare his intentions."

I clapped my hands with happiness. "Oh, I do hope so. Then maybe we can make it a double wedding. Would you like that?"

Grant was delighted. "It'll be a great day if it happens that way."

We joined the couple in the parlor and found Hattie smiling shyly as Barnaby tried to describe his home and family in Missouri. Hattie announced, "Mr. Barnaby was just telling me about his family's farm just outside of Hannibal. It must be a big one, from what he says."

"Not too big," Barnaby hastened to explain. "Big enough for several crops, some horses, cows, sheep, geese and chickens. But it's been years since I been there and I ain't sure what's been happening to my kin. I'll have a time trying to find all of 'em."

"What do you think you'll do once you return to Missouri?" I asked.

"Oh, I dunno right now. Maybe build a house and settle down."

Grant cautioned, "Try to be careful with your money, my friend. Don't let slick and dishonest people try to take it from you. Wait until you get home, then put it in a safe, dependable bank at good interest, or maybe find an investment or two, like railroad stock or coal mines. Ask Andrew or Mr. Hoffman about it before you leave. They may have some good advice for you."

"Thanks a lot, Mr. Douglas. I sure appreciate what you're sayin'."

"And let's do one thing starting tonight. From now on everybody will call me Grant, we'll all call you Barnaby. And perhaps the ladies will allow us to use their first names. The four of us have been through a lot together, so let's not be so formal. All right with you, Hattie?"

"Sure is, Grant, and I don't know why we didn't think of it before. How about you, Barnaby?"

"It's just fine, ma'am, I mean Hattie. I ain't had a true friend to call by name for the many years I've been moving about and workin' all my claims. And now I have three!"

We responded with laughter that continued through the evening. After Grant and I said a loving good night, we joined Hattie and Barnaby at the front door. He was holding her hand, but dropped it and bowed to say a hasty good night and go through the door.

I teased Hattie as we went to our rooms that night. "Barnaby seems rather taken with you, Hattie. Is something going on that I should know about?"

"Land sakes, no. Isn't that what friends do? Shake hands hello and goodbye?"

I smiled and said, "If you say so, my friend. If you say so!"

Chapter Twenty-Eight

Things were never quite the same after that. Just when Grant and I thought life was settling down to a quiet pace, something else brought us up short. For the next few months we had more than our share of happy surprises and painful tragedies. Of course, such things happened in the 20th Century, but Grant and I seemed to become more involved than ever before in the harshness of life in the 1850s.

One of the sweetest things was that Flower and Robert, with the secretive assistance of the Waiter Girls, began meeting 'just by chance' at Hattie's store, then walking on to attend services at Rev. Norton's church. After services, they would lunch at Norton's Café, then Robert walked her back to the Mercantile Store to say a reluctant farewell as she returned to the saloon.

Orrin had long disapproved of the Waiter Girls having alliances away from the Majestic. He feared these relationships would turn into the loss, either by marriage or escape of some kind, of one or more of his regular girls. Following Maggie's marriage, Orrin jealously watched all the girls and had no patience with any behavior out of the ordinary.

The Hurdy-gurdy Girls weren't as much of a worry. Their husbands or lovers quickly possessed the earnings as soon as the money was brought to them. The girls dutifully returned the following week to assure the ongoing happiness of the men in their lives.

Of course, Orrin's affair with Zola was beside the point. That was the privilege of the lord of the manor. Bertha's attachment to Avery Singleton was also disregarded since Orrin needed to keep his best and slickest gambler satisfied.

I continued to work six afternoons a week, earning my salary, plus the $5 bonus (big deal!) that Orrin reluctantly added when my program filled every chair in the saloon. Also, the tips kept appearing in the beer mugs on top of the piano. These were added to the leather bags supplied by Barnaby and Grant, then safely stored in Hattie's bedroom safe.

Grant continued the renovations at his small house. His attention was also focused on overseeing the brewery. Ida Penny was busy with my wedding dress and trousseau. Then one night Hattie invited Grant and me to a special dinner. We assumed that it was a pre-wedding celebration. I waited at Grant's house while he finished installing a new kitchen shelf, then we went to Hattie's.

The house was filled with delicious aromas. Hattie's table was set with the best china and crystal, and she had scattered candles about the room.

"Everything looks so festive," I said. "What are we celebrating?"

"Sit down, have some wine, and you'll find out," she said mysteriously. Barnaby, dressed in one of his new suits, came in from the parlor and served the wine.

Hattie nodded to Barnaby. "You'd better tell 'em."

Barnaby stood erect, took a proud stance, then announced, "It is my pleasure to tell you that my dear Hattie has consented to become my wife. We will be married here, then leave for Missouri shortly after, where we will settle down."

Grant and I exploded. "It's about time, Barnaby," Grant said. "We've been waiting for this good news, and now you've finally done it. Nothing could make us happier."

I kissed Hattie on the cheek, and then gave Barnaby a huge hug. "When did you decide, and when will you be married?"

"Sit down and have some wine," Hattie replied, "and we'll

tell you all about it."

We toasted the couple, then Hattie patted Barnaby on the arm. "You both know that Barnaby's rather shy. Now that he's told you the news, let me tell you the rest. First of all, we want to be married in July, which will give us time to pack and wrap up everything here. We hesitate to ask, but would you two mind if we made it a double wedding? We could all be married together!"

Grant slapped his knee. "I can't stand all of this good news! Sam and I thought something like this would happen. We were talking earlier about how great a double wedding would be. We would be delighted to move our date to July."

Hattie continued. "Ida Penny is already making me a pretty dress for your wedding, Samantha, so that's taken care of. Now there is more. Shall I tell them everything, Barnaby?" Barnaby smiled and nodded contentedly and she went on.

"First of all, we made some mighty big decisions and most of them concern you two."

"Really?" Grant asked. "In what way?"

Hattie pointed to the table. "Food's getting cold. We'll tell you while we eat."

Barnaby agreed. "Whatever you say, my dear. I'll begin while you put the food on the table."

"Yes, Barnaby," she said shyly, and turned to the stove.

Barnaby turned to face me. The fact that he was now a man of means was beginning to show in his demeanor, and it was delightful to see the changes taking place.

"My dear Samantha, you came here to Boone Valley and things began to change. I never even spoke to my dear Hattie until you started workin' at the saloon and I walked you home. You and my friend Grant have been very kind to me ever since. When you and Hattie became my partners, I decided to make good at my claim or die tryin', and look what happened! We'll all profit from my strike. So, as my partner you're entitled to one-third of everything I got."

"Not one-third, Barnaby. That's too much."

Barnaby pointed to Hattie who was now sitting beside him. "You tell her the rest, my dear. You can do it much better."

Hattie motioned for us to start eating, then began. "We've been talking about packing and moving back to Missouri, what we'll take with us and what we'll leave behind. It's a big step for both of us and we had to make some major decisions."

Grant and I put down our forks and gave her our full attention.

"My dear Samantha, would you take, as your share in Barnaby's mine, my Mercantile Store? Rather than pack and move all that or worry about it at all, we thought it would be easier for you to take over. That way you don't have to work for Orrin anymore. The three men working for me are good people and I've never had a bit of worry from them. All you have to do is the ordering and keeping the books. I can teach you all that before we go. As you may have guessed by now, it brings in pretty good money — just like having a gold mine of your own."

Grant and I were speechless. He took my hand and said to Hattie, "What a wonderful, sweet thing for you to do." Turning to me he said, "How does it strike you, Sam, to be the proprietor of your very own store, a woman of substance?"

For once I was unable to speak. What an unselfish, genuine gift from this wonderful couple. Before I could speak, Hattie had more to say. "That's not all. This house was another puzzle. Why take everything with us in a wagon when we can buy whatever we need, and more, when we get to Missouri? That's when we made another decision."

Grant's grip on my hand tightened as we waited for Hattie's next pronouncement. Barnaby was beaming as if he had just won the lottery. "Tell them, my dear. They'll really be surprised!"

"Outside of a few things I brought with me or sentimental stuff, Barnaby and I," and she looked at him proudly, "want you to have this house as a wedding present!"

This time both Grant and I sat in stunned silence, until he was able to say, "Well, you two have really been busy. It'll take a while for Sam and me to realize how absolutely dear you both are, and how your kindness will greatly add to our future happiness. You've been incredibly generous, especially you, dear Hattie. It seems like too much."

"But remember," she cautioned, "it will really ease my mind to know that my store and this house will be well taken care of. Besides, I could never thank my dear Sam enough for all she has brought to me."

For the rest of our dinner, we laughed and teased each other about being newlyweds within a few months. I had never seen Barnaby so relaxed and happy, comfortable in his new station in life and very much in love with his lady. Life was good for him, and he had truly earned this happiness.

After dinner, Hattie and Barnaby settled in the parlor. Grant took my arm. "I'm going to take my lady to the porch for some air where we can recover from all this good news. We'll be back in a few moments."

He guided me out the front door and over to the far side of the porch. I whispered, "What's up?"

"Sam, so many great things are happening for us. You'll soon be the owner of a thriving business, and this lovely home will be ours. How lucky can we be? Tell me, my lovely Sam, is this what your Universe planned for us from the very beginning? Compared to presenting you with a life filled with meaning, this is like Disneyland!"

We hugged each other and laughed with absolute joy until,

as we caught our breaths, it ended in a super-wonderful kiss. Grant drew away, held my hands before him, then looked at me sternly.

"Do you realize that we have a problem, something that we must do before these two take off for Missouri?"

"What problem is that?"

"Hattie and Barnaby can't go home in July. Remember your history, dear lady. Does the year 1861 ring a bell?"

"The Civil War. Oh my God!"

"Even before the Civil War began, there was fighting between pro- and antislavery groups in Missouri. Hattie and Barnaby are going to be right in the middle of it. There will be great loss of life and property in those raids. What will happen if we don't warn them before they leave? Barnaby mentioned Hannibal, which is right on the border between Missouri and Illinois. Could they settle there and be safe?"

"Heaven above," I breathed. This hadn't occurred to me. "We've got to tell them what they'll be up against. They must find somewhere to be safe during those years. What can we do?"

Grant said firmly, "We have no choice but to tell them who we are and why we know these things. Whether it's now or just before they leave, we must tell them. It should be soon, though, so we can answer any questions and they'll be clear on what's ahead."

"When shall we tell them?"

"What about right now?"

"No, this is their evening," I said. "What we must tell them will be quite a shock, and we can't spoil their happiness tonight."

Having made this difficult decision, we returned to the parlor. Hattie looked alarmed. "What's wrong? You two look like you just heard some terrible news."

I reassured her, "Not at all. We're overwhelmed by all of the good things ahead of us. Why are we so lucky? I'll tell you why. It's because we're all special people and we deserve every bit of it!"

"Hear, hear," Grant agreed. "I'll get what's left of the wine so we can celebrate a lovely evening."

We spent the rest of the night planning the double wedding, whom to invite, the reception, what we all would wear, and the wedding rings. There was laughter, and some tears of joy and sadness. The warmth and sharing of that night would be with us always, wherever we might be in the years ahead.

All too soon, in the midst of this happiness, calamity visited and changed our lives again.

One Friday afternoon I was playing the last few selections of my program. Willis had just joined me for the closing duets. We were having great fun playing a series of songs popular with the miners when we heard two shots from the game room. Grant and Barnaby were standing at the bar. They ran, with many others, to see what had happened. A crowd soon filled the hallway leading to the game room. Voices were yelling and there was the sound of boots dragging along the floor. The area then cleared and four men, holding tightly to Avery Singleton, wrestled their way through the saloon toward the front entrance. As they rushed by, we could hear Avery protesting frantically, "I didn't mean to do it! It was an accident, I swear. That silly woman just got in the way!"

Some men were yelling, "Find some rope and let's have us a hangin'!" Others called out, "Get Sheriff Parkins!"

Some followed through the door. Others settled at the empty tables and bar for drinks, animated conversation and speculation. This enabled the Waiter Girls to go into the game room. Orrin came rushing through the entrance after seeing Avery under restraint and the crowd that was gathering in the street. He disappeared into the game room.

A few moments later Naomi brought Flower from that room, an arm protectively around her. Flower was close to hysterics. They sat at the first empty table where I joined them.

"My God! What on earth happened in there? Was anyone hurt!"

Flower was unable speak, but Naomi gasped, "She's dead. It happened so quick, and now she's dead. That Avery shot her." She held back a sob. "Bertha's dead."

"Oh my God, no," I said. "Are you sure? Isn't there something we could do for her?"

They both shook their heads. "I dunno," said Naomi. "It just seemed to happen, and everyone says she's dead."

I was in shock. Warren and Rainbow, those poor children! There had been so much misery in their lives, and now to lose their mother!

Grant and Corby emerged from the game room and joined us. I grabbed Grant's hand and asked, "Is it true that Bertha has been shot? Is there anything that can be done for her? Send for a doctor?"

Grant shook his head in disbelief. "It's too late for that. Evidently Avery got sloppy and was caught cheating, no doubt about it, and one of the players protested. Avery always carries a gun, and the man who challenged him got to his feet and pulled out his gun. Avery shot first, but it went wild, so he tried to get in another quick shot. Bertha was there as usual, standing next to Avery. She saw the other man point his gun at Avery, and in an odd and misguided impulse, she reached out to stop him just as Avery fired his second bullet — which hit her." He shook his head. "It happened very quickly, and there's no doubt about it. She's dead."

Corby added, "That Avery is a mean man, and he just had to have his way. He had to get all the money he could — any way he could. Well, it won't do him no good now." He sighed, then got to his feet. "Guess I better get back to the bar. Maggie's in the room with Abigail doin' what they can for Bertha."

I looked at Grant in alarm. "The children! Dear God, they're still at Hattie's store, and they'd be shattered if some idiot tells everyone what happened. We must get them away from this terrible mess."

Grant stood quickly and gripped my shoulder. "I'll find them. But where shall I take them? Hattie's house or my place?"

"Take them to Hattie's. I'll see what I can do to help with Bertha, then join you as soon as I can."

And with a quick kiss he was on his way.

Naomi was still soothing Flower when Abigail joined us. "Orrin got some men to carry Bertha to her room, so they'll be comin' through here. He wants to get her out of the way so the card room and bar can get back to business like nothin' happened."

Just then four men emerged carrying Bertha as gently as they could. Her head was to one side and her blue velvet gown was covered with blood. They quickly moved their burden up the stairs, followed by Abigail and Zola. For the time being, nothing more could be done. A constant buzz of comments and speculation filled the bar.

Then Barnaby came through the door. "Just saw Grant outside and he said to tell you what's happenin'. There's lots of people in the street, and they're talkin' about lynchin' Singleton right away. Sheriff Parkins came and told 'em to hold off 'cause it just wasn't proper. He said they'd have a trial all legal and find out just exactly what Avery did, and then hang him. The sheriff took him off to jail and everyone's mighty disappointed. They're all goin' to be at that trial."

Barnaby offered to see me through the crowds in the street to Hattie's house. As it turned out, when word spread through the street, Hattie had immediately gathered up the children and walked them to her house where she settled them in the parlor with some picture books.

Hattie, Barnaby and I had a quiet conference in the kitchen on when and how to break the news to Warren and Rainbow. My heart ached with concern for them.

Grant joined us half an hour later. "I talked to Orrin to see what he would do about a funeral and decent burial for Bertha. He refuses to do anything. Nothing would change his mind. I was so furious I walked away. Corby said that last year the regulars donated money for the burial of a miner who died at his claim. He thought they would probably do the same for Bertha. He'll get things started tonight and collect the money."

"He's a good man, that Corby," Hattie said. "But what about the funeral?"

"I took that on and talked to Sam Cable, the undertaker. He promised to see to the coffin and bring Bertha over to his place. One of us can work out the funeral and burial details with him. I think between the collection at the saloon and all of us here, we can cover the costs."

Everyone agreed.

"And who is going to tell those dear children?" Hattie asked.

Grant responded sadly, "Why don't you leave it to Sam and me. Is that all right, Sam?"

I nodded.

He took my arm. "Let's not put it off. Those kids have the right to know what has happened to their mother."

Warren and Rainbow were in the parlor looking through Hattie's picture book. They looked up as we entered.

"Let's have a talk, little friends," Grant said gently as he knelt before the sofa where the children sat.

Warren, young as he was, stood up and faced Grant squarely. "Somethin's happened. Somethin' bad. We been feelin' it ever since people were whisperin' to each other when they saw us. You better tell us right off what it is."

Grant took each one by the hand. "All right, my young friends. It is bad news."

Warren lifted his head and put a protective arm about Rainbow, who leaned against him, eyes wide and frightened. "Is it about Momma Bertha?" he asked.

"Yes, it is. You know how some people get awful mad at times when they don't get their way? They want to hit someone, or even worse. You know about that, don't you?"

Warren nodded his head slowly. "We know all that."

"Well, there was a fight in the card room at the saloon and two men got awful mad at each other and pulled out their guns. Shots were fired, and one of them hit your momma by mistake."

Warren stood there, silently holding Rainbow tighter while taking in the words and their meanings. Finally he softly asked, "Is our Momma Bertha dead?"

Grant answered as kindly as he could, "I am so very sorry to tell you. Yes, your momma is dead."

I moved over to the sofa, sat down and took Rainbow on my lap. Her body went limp as I held her close and rocked back and forth. She did not cry, but with each breath she whimpered softly to herself.

Grant put an arm about Warren's shoulder. "It's all right if you want to cry. Sam and I will probably cry with you because we feel so bad for you, Rainbow and your momma. We're here for you and we're not going away."

I whispered to Rainbow, "Little one, we'll stay with you as long as you want. But for now, just rest easy and remember your momma."

Grant and I sat with the children until they were exhausted and fell asleep. We made them comfortable on the sofa, covered them with an afghan, then joined Hattie in the kitchen. She asked, "How are those dear children? How did they take the news?"

Grant shook his head. "They've had so much calamity in their young lives, this is just another bad break. What are we going to do for them? Where will they stay?"

"Well, right here, of course," Hattie said firmly. "They can't go back to that saloon. Who'd take care of them? No, they'll stay right here until we can figure out something else."

The next day Singleton had his trial. Sheriff Parkins hastily called upon a judge in nearby Volcano, the Honorable Roscoe Spencer, to preside over the legalities. During the proceedings, it was clear to all that the violence was deliberate and senseless. Several men testified that Avery was indeed caught cheating, and had drawn a gun to shoot his challenger. His first shot missed, and when he quickly fired another bullet, it hit and killed Bertha, the Waiter Girl who worked at the saloon. He was found guilty and immediately taken out to a sturdy tree on the outskirts of town and hung. To the end Avery was surly and arrogant, and as a result few, if any, were sorry to see him so dispatched.

I decided not to witness his punishment. It may have been part of life in this time and place, but I chose to focus on Warren and Rainbow and their needs.

The next day we sadly walked to the barren cemetery where Rev. Norton said some beautiful words over Bertha. Everyone in the crowd assured the children that their many friends loved and cared about them. All of the girls, and some of the saloon regulars attended. About 40 people were there to say goodbye to Bertha, which brought some comfort to the children.

From that day on Hattie's house was their home. Rainbow slept with me in my big bed, and Warren slept on the sofa downstairs. At night as we lay in bed preparing to sleep, Rainbow would ask questions.

"Mis' Samantha, where is Momma Bertha now?"

"Why, she's in heaven in God's arms, dear."

"Is she happy up there?"

"You can be sure she is. She can rest on a fluffy white cloud and never have to work in a saloon again."

It was during those evenings that I taught Rainbow her nightly prayers. She loved the part about blessing her mother and the girls at the saloon. She even included Biscuit, Barnaby's mule. Barnaby brought Biscuit over to cheer her, and allowed her to ride him. Her brightest smiles were when she was allowed to ride Biscuit all by herself.

So Rainbow and Warren slipped into the new routine — eating, sleeping, classes at Hattie's house, and helping at the store several days a week. This routine gave them goals and responsibilities, and they grew mentally as well as physically as a result.

Hattie, Barnaby, Grant and I were stretching ourselves to make sure that one of us would always be at the house to feed and care for them. One happy day Hattie found a solution that she shared with us at dinner.

"Rev. Norton came in today, and I was telling him how we felt the need to be with the children during the day. He came up with an idea that might be just what we need."

Grant, Barnaby and I were eager to hear more.

"He told me about a young lady who comes to services. Her name is Myra Collins, and she's having a bad time of it. She came here with her husband and little baby, and she hasn't heard a word from him since he went off a year ago looking for gold. She and her two-year-old baby are living in a drafty old shack not far from here, and they're just barely making out. Mrs. Norton has been bringing her food from the café. The Reverend thought perhaps Myra could help out here at the house during the day and watch over the children. That way the four of us can go on with our own work and pay something for her time."

"A perfect solution," I said right away. "She could help clean the house and maybe have some dinner ready by the time we get home. Sounds great to me. How about you, Hattie?"

"Well, I'm not used to having strangers taking care of my house. I've done it myself for years, but it's been a chore when I'm tired at the end of the day."

Rainbow chimed in. "Warren and me could play with the baby and help take care of it. We never got to be close to any new babies before."

It appeared to be unanimous.

The next Sunday there was a knock on the door and there stood a painfully thin, sad-looking woman dressed in a long calico dress badly worn from frequent washings, a ragged shawl, and a straw hat on her brown hair. Her large brown eyes mirrored her struggle to survive. She had beside her a solemn child with yellow curls. Once they were invited into the house, Rainbow and Warren immediately took charge of the baby. This was Myra Collins and she managed a lovely smile that showed the strong spirit within her.

"Rev. Norton told me to come over after services and talk to you all. Can you use someone to help out here?" Her voice was filled with earnest hope as if she had been living with disappointment a very long time.

Heaven must have sent Myra Collins and her baby, Charlie. She fit our little group like a hand in a glove. From the first day she took over, all three children were lovingly cared for, and the small chores about the house became little games where everyone could help. Even little Charlie enjoyed going into the hen house with Warren to gather the eggs and put them into the waiting basket. Hattie and I came home each evening to a sparkling house and a tasty dinner. It was a happy arrangement for all.

After the first week, the six of us were remarking over dinner what a great help Myra had been. Grant interrupted, "Have you seen that shack where they live? It's a wonder that she and Charlie survived the winter. I'd like to take a couple of men and some of your lumber over there, Hattie, and see if we can make that place more livable."

"By all means," Hattie said. "Take all the lumber you need. That sweet lady has never once complained about the hard time she's had this past year waiting for her husband to show up. Shame on him for neglecting her and the baby this way!"

Grant observed, "Maybe he's been hurt, or fallen off a mountain, or is even dead by now."

Hattie added, "She's truly been a godsend to all of us, and we should be helping her in return. It's the Christian thing to do. Samantha, you find out what she needs in the way of bedding, blankets, kitchen things and let's do all we can. And from the looks of her, she and Charlie could use some new clothes."

Within a week Myra's eyes were no longer sad, and her smile was growing brighter every day. Both she and Charlie were dressed in warm and serviceable clothing, and their faces were shining with pleasure and confidence.

At dinner several days later, we could not help but compare our comfortable lives to the struggle Myra and Charlie were having. Although Grant had done what he could to improve the shack, it was still rugged housing for a mother and child.

Looking quite serious, Grant spoke. "I have a proposal to make. I haven't told Sam about it yet because it just occurred to me."

We waited patiently for his announcement.

"After we're all nicely married and Sam, Rainbow, Warren and I settle into this house, what would you say if I let Myra and Charlie move into my house, rent free? A lady with such a gallant spirit deserves all we can do for her. Do I have everyone's approval?"

I leaned over to kiss him. "I've said it before, and I'll say it again. I love the way your mind works. Your idea is sweet and generous, and I am absolutely delighted that you will soon be my husband."

His loving smile was brighter than the candles burning on the table, and it filled my heart with such joy that I felt it would bubble over.

Hattie, Barnaby, Warren and Rainbow were quite responsive to the proposal, and Operation Myra became a happy project in which we all participated. Eventually one other player came into our project, which later proved to be a wonderful surprise.

Chapter Twenty-Nine

The following week Grant proudly showed me the completed improvements on his house.

I sighed. "I'm rather sorry we won't be living here after all your effort. I love everything you've done, and I was looking forward to quiet evenings before the fire, and — whatever."

Grant laughed. "It's the 'whatever' that I'm looking forward to, but you must be a proper lady and stay at Hattie's until the wedding. We'll have a few days here after the wedding until Hattie and Barnaby leave for Missouri."

With a wicked smile he looked deep in my eyes and whispered, "Maybe we'll work on the 'proper lady' title another time." He gently directed me to the bedroom. As I sank onto his bed he said, "It's a good thing there's no Boone Valley edition of 'The Intruder' to worry about."

"Who cares," I breathed as I responded to his eager hands. It had been many weeks since we'd had time together, and our intense and heated embraces made up beautifully for the lost time.

As we lay back, relaxed and enjoying the afterglow, Grant said, "Miss Samantha, I do believe that you've missed me a whole bunch."

I moved closer to him and responded, "You ask if this is what the Universe has intended for us. If it is, it's more beautiful and fulfilling than anything I could have prayed for on that mountaintop. You've blessed my life, my dear."

We lay there quietly until Grant, looking rather serious, began to talk.

"I've been thinking, my dear," he began.

"Is that good or bad?" I teased.

"I'm hoping you'll like what my busy brain has come up with."

I snuggled down and got comfortable. "I'm listening."

"All right. You know we've been talking about moving to the Central Valley once the gold in this area has played out. We're at the crest of the Gold Rush years right now, and each day more and more people are pouring into California."

"Too true," I agreed.

"This would be an ideal time to check into the valley south of Sacramento and see what's available, what it would cost, what water is available, and the best weather for farming. I could take Andrew with me to see to the legal aspects just in case we find something too good to pass up. Also, I'm thinking about taking Wong Kee, or one of his capable friends, to scout for the best soil for farming and what crops would prosper there. The great fruits and vegetables he brings into the kitchen — the Chinese grow them in the fields near their little community. Just think of rows of apple, peach and orange trees growing in the sun! Maybe some of those fellows would like to build a settlement of their own near our ranch. They could set up the planting and harvesting program, and take care of that part of the property entirely. It would be beneficial to all of us."

I sat up in bed and listened closely as he enthusiastically described our future home.

"The way I see it, we have more than enough money to not only buy the land, but start construction this year. It will take time to find lumber, tools, dependable workers, and all of the other details, but with luck, we could move in the next year or two. Then we could either sell the brewery and your store, or hand them over to others to run for us as long as Boone Valley is still standing. How does it sound so far?"

"Mr. Douglas, I'm totally impressed by your foresight. What you're describing sounds like the 1800's version of Wonderland. I've never planted a tree or worked a bed of flowers, but from the way you describe it, I can hardly wait. What about money? Do we have enough?"

"Probably. I have over $25,000 put aside, which is more than enough for the land and buildings. What about your nest egg?"

"Golly, I have no idea what's put away in Hattie's safe. Everything's in the leather bags you and Barnaby gave me. We can take them to the Assay Office in the morning and see what's there."

"Good idea. We probably have more than enough, but it'll be good to know how far your nest egg will go when the building starts."

The next morning after Myra and Charlie checked in, I gathered up my nine well-packed, heavy leather bags and Grant drove me to the Assay Office. We laid the bags on the counter before Aaron Ross who then weighed the contents while we watched.

At one point Aaron peered at me over the glasses resting on his nose. "Where did you get all this? You been out diggin' on your own claim?"

"No, Mr. Ross. You know very well that I play piano at the Majestic, and these are the tips the men were kind enough to leave on the piano after each program."

"Did you know there were several 20-dollar gold pieces in here as well?"

"I had no idea, Mr. Ross."

Aaron sorted, weighed and figured everything and finally lifted his head. "Young lady, your tips — gold dust, nuggets, gold coins and other coins — add up to $4,415."

Grant whistled and pushed his hat back on his head. "That's a nice bit of petty cash, Samantha. That could easily finance a barn, some horses and cows, and maybe a fancy carriage. I'd say between the two of us we have enough to build a pretty comfortable estate down there in the valley."

We immediately rode on to the Wells Fargo facility and opened an account to hold my fortune. Andrew was there, and we spent an hour in his office laying out our plans and the role he was expected to play. Soon he was as excited as we were. We would bring Hattie and Barnaby into our plans the next time we all met.

It was about time to go to work, so Grant delivered me to the saloon, kissed me on the cheek and said, "Play pretty for the people, my dear. And while you're busy, I'll be having a long talk with Wong Kee. He should be impressed with our grand plan, and I'll see if I can ruffle that calm exterior of his. See you later."

The first order of business and daily routine was to report on Rainbow and Warren, first to Corby and Elmo, and then to the Waiter Girls one by one. The children were sorely missed, but their friends at the saloon were happy to know they were well cared for. Each day I passed messages and good wishes back and forth. Rainbow and Warren were happy to know their friends still cared about them.

When my program was over, finishing as usual with duets with Willis, I rushed to the kitchen to see how Wong Kee reacted to our news, and if he would allow himself a small smile or a quiet "whoopee!"

As I entered, Orrin was there, fuming. Oh, dear. Now what!

"Well," he sneered, "if there's somethin' sneaky goin' on, you're always right in the middle of it. I came into my kitchen and found your man Grant and my man Wong Kee with their heads together. Sure looked like they're cookin' up somethin'. This stupid Chinee won't say a word about what they're talkin' about."

"Orrin," I said dryly, "they're friends, and friends do talk together now and then."

"Not like this," he insisted. "They're plannin' something, I can tell. Do I have to remind you, this is my kitchen and my saloon, and I won't have nothin' goin' on that I don't know about. If I find there's a plot of some kind, believe me there will be hell to pay. Do you understand, you dumb slut?"

And turning to Wong Kee, he said, "And is that clear, you stupid Chinaman?"

Wong Kee said nothing, but continued his work at the wooden chopping board. Orrin let out a string of profanity, then left the kitchen in disgust.

Wong Kee seemed a little shaken by the confrontation. "Are you all right?" I asked.

He nodded, going on with his work.

"Did you and Grant have a chance to talk?"

He nodded once more, then stopped his work and faced me. "Is good to happen what he say."

"It'll happen, my friend. Just be patient and we'll all talk later. Now I'd better scoot out of here before Orrin comes back." He bowed and I went on my way.

The next day was Sunday and Maggie and Corby had invited Rainbow and Warren to spend the day with them. It seemed to be the most propitious and uninterrupted time for our long delayed talk with Hattie and Barnaby. During an early Sunday dinner, Grant described our plans for acquiring the land and settling in the valley.

"As we see it, it will be a combination working ranch and a productive farm. We plan to recruit some of the Chinese farmers, those who raise the excellent produce we've been seeing here in Boone Valley. They will have their own settlement and be totally in charge of the crops. The ranch house will be roomy and we'll have plenty of space for Rainbow and Warren, and even Myra and Charlie if they want to come."

Hattie and Barnaby were delighted with the news, but Hattie began to frown and shake her head back and forth. "But what will happen to the store and this house when you leave? It sounds as if you'll leave Boone Valley as soon as you can."

Grant hastily assured her. "Dear Hattie, once we get the property, it may take at least three or four years to build everything. The store and this house are our foundations. When the time comes, we may be able to split our time between the two places. But that is far in the future, and we'll tell you every detail as it develops."

She seemed satisfied and commented, "How pleased you must be to have such a happy future ahead of you. Barnaby and I are thrilled about all your wonderful plans. I never knew people who planned their lives with such detail, except that's what Barnaby and me have been trying to do."

She made eye contact with Barnaby, who nodded as she went on. "We've been thinking about the children, and the way we figure is, if they want to come with us, we could give them a good home and schooling away from the hustle and bustle of Boone Valley. They need peace of mind and order, and we'd dearly love to have them with us."

There was a silence as the four of us studied each other. This brought me to a dead stop.

"This had not occurred to us. We just assumed they would stay here," I said. "How long have you been thinking about this?" I was getting a little uncomfortable.

"Ever since Barnaby and I been talking about settling in Missouri," Hattie explained. "We just assumed you two would be so busy with your brewery and my store, you'd be hard pressed to give them the time and attention they need."

Hands resting on his chest, fingers intertwined, Barnaby nodded in agreement.

Grant and I exchanged glances, then he shook his head. "Sam, I think the time has come."

Hattie and Barnaby seemed puzzled, but quietly waited for

us to go on.

Grant stood. "Let's take our coffee into the parlor. There is much to say to you today and much for you to understand."

The four of us settled into chairs, then Grant began. "Dear friends, we have quite a story to tell. Sam and I have been waiting for just the right moment, and I guess this is it. Please be assured that everything, everything you hear tonight is the absolute truth and it must be held in confidence."

Barnaby took Hattie's hand and patted it in a comforting manner. They waited for what was to come next.

Grant began slowly. "It all started when I arrived in Boone Valley four years ago. I was disoriented and confused. I had no money, no horse, no possessions. Do you remember when we first met, Hattie?"

"Sure do. You were a sad looking feller when Martin found you, but he got you and Titus Boone together. You started working for Titus right away."

"That's right. Titus gave me my first meal in three days. He got me on my feet and to work so I could earn my way." Grant paused, then continued, speaking slowly and clearly. "The day before arriving here, I was living in San Francisco in the year 1992. I was born and lived my life in the 20th Century. The next day, without my planning it, I found myself here in Boone Valley in 1848."

Again he stopped and waited for the couple to assimilate the information. As far as I could see, there was no reaction. Grant looked at me and shook his head. "You take it from here, Sam."

"Hattie? Barnaby? My arrival here was also unplanned. My husband and I were vacationing in our summer home in these mountains. That was 1996. One day I was feeling frustrated and unhappy and took off on my own. I hardly knew where I was going. Later in the day I was totally lost and somehow stumbled into Boone Valley which, at that time, was a ghost town. Do you understand? Not a soul was to be seen, and all the buildings were empty and rotted. By nightfall I was exhausted, without food and water. I fell asleep on the wooden stairs leading to one of the ruined buildings. The next morning I woke up where Warren and Rainbow found me, and I discovered to my surprise that the year was 1852."

Hattie shook her head as she struggled with what she was hearing. She finally spoke. "How can this be? Such things don't happen."

Grant responded, "We would agree with you, dear Hattie, but they did happen. We think that unexplained forces of the Universe sent us back in time. Perhaps we were meant to be together at this time and place. It's something we cannot explain to you or to each other."

Hattie and Barnaby exchanged glances and raised their eyebrows in disbelief. On an impulse I went to my bedroom to get my backpack.

Grant remarked as I returned, "They're still thinking it over and it's clear they don't know what to say."

I stood before them. "Can you understand any of this? Do you have any questions? There's more to come, but we want to be sure you understand and accept what we've told you so far." When they did not respond, I asked, "Would it help if I gave you some proof that what we've told you is absolutely true?"

Hattie found her voice. "Yes, indeed, Samantha."

I reached into the backpack and pulled out the digital wristwatch and looked at it fondly. It still faithfully showed the time, second by second. It didn't matter if the year was 1996 or 1852. It was a constant that was comforting to see.

I placed it in Hattie's hand then waited for her reaction. She turned it over and over, examining every side. She looked up. "It's such a tiny clock. How do you wind it?"

Grant explained, "It's called a digital watch and we wore them on our wrists to know the time of day whenever we liked. You don't wind it. It has a tiny battery, a source of energy, that keeps it running for months and months until it wears out and is replaced by another battery."

Hattie handed the watch to Barnaby who looked it over. "Never seen nothin' like this before. I had a pocket watch once, much bigger than this, but it got broke."

Grant explained, "These watches are shockproof and water-proof and were an important part of our lives before we came here. They replaced the large pocket watches like the one you had, Barnaby."

Hattie was fascinated by the numbers and watched as they reported the time second by second. Then she silently handed the watch back to me.

Next I brought out my wallet. I removed the plastic driver's license and offered it to Hattie, who slowly read the information it contained. She compared me to the picture. Like most driver's licenses, the picture was not flattering, but she could tell it was me.

"In the late 1900s, Hattie, we did not have horses. We drove automobiles, motorized buggies, and we were required to carry a license like this. Look in the upper right-hand corner. It tells you the date of my birth and the date when the license expires and must be renewed."

It took some time for Hattie, then Barnaby, to examine the plastic card and digest what they were seeing. When they returned it to me, Grant asked, "Can you make any sense of what we've been telling you?"

Hattie shook her head. "I just knew you two weren't like anybody else. It was your attitudes, the way you talked and used the language. Oh, you both fit in with everyone here in Boone Valley, except when Samantha went head to head with Orrin more than once."

Grant added, "We both are well educated. Starting from age

five, many of the children of our generation attended school, up through college. Sam and I were most fortunate in that regard."

Grant described his life, his progress through college, earning an MBA, then working for the largest and most successful brewery on the West Coast. Which is why, he explained, he was able to build and launch a successful brewery in Boone Valley. He mentioned he had been married, had two daughters, and was divorced.

I told them my history — parents, education and extensive piano studies. I described briefly my 20-year marriage, my two fine sons and the unhappiness I felt in the last five years with Harland, which led me to escape from our mountain home and end up in Boone Valley.

Hattie and Barnaby listened without comment. Then she spoke, "That's quite a tale you two are telling us, and a hard one to swallow. But you said these were the facts and the truth, so that must be the way of it. But why are you telling us now? Seems like there's more to come."

Grant took a moment before he answered. "My friends, this is merely the tip of the iceberg. There are some things you must know before you settle in Missouri."

Looking at Hattie, I said, "Coming from the future we know what will happen in the years ahead. To us it is history we learned in school; to you it is coming events that will dramatically affect your lives."

Grant faced Barnaby. "How do you feel, my friend? Do you want to hear more of what we have to tell you, or would you rather wait until later?"

Barnaby frowned, rubbed his forehead in frustration. "Grant, me 'n' Hattie came a long way. Both of us have seen droughts, floods and hard times. We went through all that just to get here. We saw men, women and children fall by the wayside, and the sickness that killed many of them. I seen miners that got hurt at their claims or terrible sick, then crawled to their shacks to die. It ain't been that easy, but we made it this far. I think my lady and I can take anything more you want to tell us. Isn't that right, my dear?"

She patted his hand lovingly. "Yes, Barnaby, you speak for both of us."

Grant looked at me, then took a deep breath. "You may have heard there is growing unrest in the states back East. They are divided between those who are pro-slavery and those who object to human beings being used as property. It's a controversy that will not go away, and in no time it will cause a great rift in our country. Southern states will secede from the Union and form their own slaveholding nation, the Confederate States of America. Thus will begin what history will call the Civil War, or the War Between the States. The North and South will be in a full-scale war by 1861, and there will be a terrible loss of property and lives before it's over."

"Good Lord in heaven," Hattie said fiercely. "What's to become of this country?"

"Now this is the hard part," Grant continued. "Within the next two years, by 1855, the troubles will turn violent, and people migrating into Kansas from Missouri will cause it. Raiders will recklessly destroy whoever and whatever gets in their way, burning homes and even whole towns in the process. From then on the people in Missouri will be split down the middle — those who are sympathetic to the South and those who are not. There will be skirmishes within the state. The governor, because of his pro-slavery sympathies, will make no effort to maintain order."

When Grant paused, I went on. "Our concern is for your safety, should you settle in areas in the path of these early skirmishes, not to mention the war that will cover many of the northern and southern states, or the financial hardships that will result. There is nothing that could be done to stop it. All you can do is make your home somewhere farther north or west, well removed from the battles and raids."

Grant continued the thought. "As I remember my history, you would do well to consider settling in either Nebraska, Wisconsin, northern Illinois, Ohio or Iowa. The latter would be the most desirable. You and the money you worked so hard for should be safe there. Then after the war ends in 1865, you could return to Missouri if you wish. But what will remain will not be pretty.

Barnaby shook his head sadly while Hattie leaned against him and wept quietly. Finally he raised his head and asked, "Who will win this war, the North or the South?"

"The North," Grant said sadly, "and the South will never be the same. The rebel armies will surrender, and the federal government will be wise enough not to persecute them. There will be many hard years as the South rebuilds."

We all sat quietly, lost in our own thoughts. Grant put a protective arm about me and kissed my temple. We could not help but feel an oppressive sadness about the burden of information we had just given to our friends. Their acceptance could influence their lives over the next 10 years, or more.

Hattie sat up suddenly and looked at us sternly. "Who else have you told about all this?"

"Just my friend, Andrew Locke," Grant answered. "There was a time when it was necessary to bring him in. But beyond that, just you two. And I must caution you again. The information we have given you tonight must not go beyond this room. You must realize the panic it would cause."

"Is there more to tell?" Barnaby asked. His face was sad as he comforted Hattie who was leaning on his shoulder. "What is to become of my family in Hannibal, or my dear Hattie's family?"

"We will discuss all of that, and more, when you're ready. You must first think carefully about the course that will be best for you."

Hattie rose to her feet, drying her eyes. "This is quite enough for tonight, don't you agree, Barnaby?"

He nodded.

She said briskly, "We've got lots of talking and thinking to do and we need someplace quiet." She hesitated, then said firmly, "Sam, will you and Grant stay here until the children come home? Feed them some of the leftovers from dinner if they're still hungry. Then get them to bed. The best place for Barnaby and me right now is at Rev. Norton's church where we can talk to the Lord and each other. It'll be quiet there and we can stay as long as we want. Is that all right with you?"

"Of course," I assured her.

Barnaby carefully guided Hattie from the kitchen and out the front door. Grant and I sat in the silent house and shared our thoughts.

"Grant, those dear people. We've shattered their happy plans for the future. And what will become of the children? I always thought they would stay with us, but we never really talked about it. How do you feel about that?"

"Sam, it would be hard to let them go. I can't help but love them. There's so much we could give them — a fine education, our insights into the future, and the tools of thought and behavior that would help them become good citizens of this growing nation. They're both so bright and loving, I'd like to be the father they never had."

I answered, "In spite of their early years of neglect, they have come through with their spirits bright and endearing. If they go with Hattie and Barnaby, we would have no way to know what perils they may face. It will be enough of a challenge for Hattie and Barnaby to settle somewhere that would be safe and secure."

Grant said aloud what we both dreaded. "The bottom line is, we must let those children decide where they want to be, and with whom they want to be."

I nodded sadly.

Grant took me into his arms. "For now, my darling, we'll wait for Hattie and Barnaby to determine their own path. That will help make clear the course for all of us."

Two hours later the children came bursting through the door with Maggie and Corby. Warren was bubbling over. "Corby hired a buggy and we went for a nice ride far away from here, and he let me drive it all the way back. I did good, didn't I, Corby?"

Grinning, Corby patted Warren on the head. "This young man drove that horse like he was born to it."

After exchanging farewells with Maggie and Corby, the children said they already had dinner, so we shared music and bedtime stories until their young eyes began to droop from the excitement of the day.

We had just settled them in their beds when Hattie and Barnaby came through the front door. Their faces were grim and determined, but also there was an air of completion.

Hattie announced, "We had a good, long talk at the church about everything you been telling us and what we decided. Let's make some coffee and talk."

And that was how this lovely couple resolved the future, and how they decided to face it armed with the knowledge that Grant and I gave them that evening.

Chapter Thirty

"Samantha and Grant," Hattie began, "it's been real hard for me and Barnaby to understand and accept what you've been telling us. We know you two have no reason to make up such stories just to give us pain, and no way around it. It's been mighty painful to hear your facts about what's going to happen to this country." She paused while Barnaby took her hand.

"We must be the only folks in this here country who know for sure what's ahead, and if it's a blessing, we intend to treat it that way!"

Barnaby nodded as she went on. "What we're gonna do is this. We'll pack our things and head for Missouri just as we planned. Tell them what we'll do next, Barnaby."

Still holding Hattie's hand, Barnaby said, "We think it's best to leave as soon as we can, 'cause there's lots for us to do. Travelin' back to Missouri, findin' and visitin' with her family, goin' on to Hannibal to visit with my family, then findin' the best place for us to settle in. We think it's best to get to San Francisco, take a ship to Panama, then cross over to that ocean on the other side. We'll get a riverboat up the Mississippi to St. Louis."

Hattie took over. "We'll talk to all those folks, and what we see and hear will show us how things are going, and maybe we'll have an idea of what to do next."

"That's right," Barnaby agreed. "After we've had our fill of talkin' with our kinfolk, we should know pretty well where to go. If, like you say, folks are gettin' steamed up over this North and South thing, we hope to be clear on what to do for ourselves."

Going to the piano, I picked up an item I'd placed there

earlier, feeling it could be part of their information at this point. It was a $5 bill, and I handed it to Hattie.

"This is some of the paper money Grant and I used where we came from. The man you see pictured is Abraham Lincoln. Have you ever heard of him?"

They shook their heads.

"This man will be one of the greatest presidents this country will ever know. You'll be hearing his name more and more when you return to Missouri. In 1860 he will be elected President of the United States and inaugurated in 1861. This man would not be popular in the South, however."

Grant began to pace about the room. He continued my thought. "This man's election as President, as well as the result of a court case known as the Dred Scott Decision, will be two of the issues that will cause a great resistance in the southern states and bring about the first skirmishes of the Civil War. Some of the southern states will secede from the Union and the lines will be drawn. One of the first will be the firing on Fort Sumter by the southern forces shortly after Lincoln's inauguration."

"Look at the $5 bill, Hattie," Grant directed. "Mr. Lincoln's picture is on it in our time, even though in 1853 he was not a candidate for the presidency. One of his greatest actions as president will be the Emancipation Proclamation, which will legally free the slaves throughout the country. Yes, my friends, you'll be hearing a lot about this gentleman when you return to Missouri."

He paused, then continued. "One last thought. Be careful where you put your money once you arrive. Don't be tempted to invest in anything involving Confederate money, or Southern banks, companies, lands and so forth. That would be very risky."

The night wore on as Grant and I described the war, the battles, events, and the names that would shine through history. With a broad grin, Grant said. "My father was interested in military history and had great regard for some of these men. I was named Grant after General Grant, who later becomes president, and Sheridan after a cavalry commander who distinguished himself in many battles."

Hattie stood up. "It's late and my head is spinning with everything you've been telling us. Give Barnaby and me a few days and I'm sure we'll have many questions."

Barnaby stood and put his arm about her. "We're beholden to the two of you for trustin' us with your story. We'll have a time sorting it all out, but we'll do our best to use it carefully. Right, my dear?"

She patted his cheek and said, "You said just the right thing, Barnaby."

On the way to bed that night, Hattie commented, "Samantha, it must have been hard for you and Grant to know these things and not be able to tell anyone. There were times I felt that you were carrying a big, big secret."

"You're very wise, dear Hattie. Tomorrow morning over breakfast I'll tell you how far women came during the 20th Century. It'll do your heart good. For now, let's both get some rest."

And after a hug, we retired to our bedrooms.

Monday morning was filled with our new routine — waking, dressing and feeding Rainbow and Warren. Then Myra and Charlie arrived, and the children went to the front porch to play with the wooden toys Grant had made for them. Myra went upstairs to make the beds and sweep and clean the bedrooms and stairs.

Hattie and I lingered over coffee, and she admitted that she had not slept well. However, she was eager for more information. I told her about Louisa May Alcott, Clara Barton, Eleanor Roosevelt, Susan B. Anthony, and other women who became doctors, scientists, lawyers, members of Congress and the House of Representatives. I told her women would become officers in large corporations and own their own businesses.

Hattie put a hand over her heart. "My heavens, that is certainly a busy world you are describing. But for me, right now, Boone Valley and even Missouri sound more to my liking."

"You're absolutely right, Hattie. By comparison, life in Boone Valley is simpler, and I'm enjoying it all the more for that reason. My main concern with 1853 is that men treat women like belongings, as if women have no feelings or brain power. Women are to do as they are told, without question or complaint, and never have opinions or ideas of their own. But, little by little, they are coming into their own. Some, like you, Hattie, are forced into new roles by hardship. Now you own a store, and heading toward a second and very happy marriage. Others will take on new roles by choice."

Hattie slapped her knees. "Well, I say good for those ladies, and for me, too, while we're at it!"

Later Hattie and I walked to her store, discussing quietly what I had shared with her. The air was crisp and clear, the blue sky was sprinkled with fluffy white clouds, and the trees on the surrounding mountains were a brilliant green. The worst of winter had passed and spring was in full bloom.

When we reached her store, Hattie whispered, "My head is sure enough bursting with all you've been telling me. Don't know how I'll keep my mind on business today, but it pleasures me to know that I'll be carrying a mighty big secret inside. I'll bet my dear Barnaby is feeling the same way."

The following Sunday morning Warren and Rainbow were whisked off to Maggie and Corby's house for a happy reunion with the Waiter Girls, Ida Penny, Willis and others from the saloon. For our lunch, Hattie and I concocted an enormous chicken pie for the four of us, and Andrew Locke. Since Andrew was familiar with our history, we brought him into our circle where the conversation was open and unlimited.

As we ate, Andrew motioned with his fork. "Grant, did you tell Hattie and Barnaby about subways and super jets, the telephone and television? I find it a wonder that things like that will be a normal part of life, just as we accept the horse and buggy."

Grant shook his head. "We haven't had time to go into all that. Hattie and Barnaby will have their own questions."

Andrew persisted, "So, is your mind in a whirl, Barnaby? Have you worked through all these marvels you've been hearing about? I know how it is. It took me more than a week to sort through everything. Makes me want to travel to their time just like they traveled to ours."

Barnaby shook his head. "I ain't clear about a lot of it. They told us what will be happenin' in the next ten years, which was enough of a shock. When they describe how it will be over a hundred years from now, my poor brain just can't picture it."

Andrew continued. "What they have to say about traveling from place to place is amazing. For instance, Grant, when you came here from San Francisco in your auto, how long did it take?"

"About four hours. At that time there were four bridges connecting San Francisco with the mainland."

"Just think of that," Andrew marveled. "It takes us at least three or four days to make our way to the Bay, and more to go to San Francisco, unless we take a boat from Sacramento or Stockton. Grant tells me there'll be automobiles, trains and buses that can cross this country in just a few days. He says they can fly there in just a few hours. Just think how many men, women and children could have survived that trip to California if such wonders had existed."

The curiosity of our audience was endless, especially spurred on by Andrew's enthusiasm. Finally, Grant put up his hands in surrender. "Sam and I have given you more than enough to think about. Remember, though, that none of us will live long enough to see much of this happen. After the Civil War, railroads will span the continent, and in time the United States will build a canal at Panama to enable ships to pass from the Pacific Ocean to the Gulf of Mexico, and then to the Atlantic, rather than sailing around South America. There will also be — already is — something called the Industrial Revolution which will make possible the manufacture of much that is done by hand these days. My advice to you is to invest in such companies and make yourself a small fortune. Or, take what you have and find a lovely place where you can live in peace and quiet. The bottom line is to concentrate on the quality of your lives and what will make you happy."

"But whatever you do," I cautioned, "guard this information very carefully. We have shared this much to help you understand who we are and what we have brought with us from the future. To pass this information on to others would cause repercussions that would be difficult to imagine. Do we all understand that this secret must be guarded for the rest of our lives?"

All sitting around the table solemnly agreed.

Afterwards, Grant and I felt that trusting our friends to such an extent was risky, but they seemed to understand that they had been honored by our faith in them. If someone had offered to tell us about the 21st Century, we would be just as dazzled and anxious for details.

Two days later Grant, Andrew, and Ho Shen, a countryman of Wong Kee's, made ready a wagon for their trip to scout for land in the Central Valley. At the last minute Barnaby indicated he would be pleased to join them, and he wore a happy grin when he was accepted. He drove the wagon loaded with food, tools and supplies, and Ho Shen sat beside him. Grant and Andrew rode two strong horses rented from the livery stable. Hattie and I could not help but giggle as we waved farewell to four men who looked like children off on an adventure.

Seven days later the three explorers returned, weary, covered with dust and dirt, and wearing crooked smiles of victory. After seeing their condition, I put a pot of coffee on the stove while Hattie started frying bacon and whipped up a huge batch of johnnycakes. As the men ate with gusto, Grant looked over at Andrew.

"Where shall we start?"

Washing down a mouthful with coffee, Andrew urged, "Start where we arrived in Sacramento and the people we called on."

"Right," Grant agreed. "First of all, Sacramento is back to normal, and there are no signs of the plague and the tragic loss of lives and property. Thank God all of that has past."

It was a sad reminder of how mankind was at the mercy of such diseases in those years.

Grant continued. "As we rode by the first buildings in Sacramento, we saw a sign that said, 'Land For Sale.' We went right in and talked to a man who turned out to be a shyster, an opportunist who thought he was dealing with someone fresh from the East. We went on to a bank, which seemed to be the most logical place to inquire since bank presidents get to know practically everyone in town." Andrew nodded in agreement and continued eating.

Grant laughed and went on. "Well, now, when this man, his name is Horatio Albright, heard that Andrew was my attorney and that I was in the market for prime land in the valley, he couldn't say or do enough to give us the lay of the land. You should have seen him, Sam, a ringer for W.C. Fields. He was bald, red cheeks, a stomach out to here covered by a red brocaded vest, and wearing a heavy gold watch and chain."

"That's hilarious," I laughed.

Grant continued, "And while I was there, Sam, I put half of my savings into that bank. I didn't want anyone to know I was carrying that much, but we made it to the bank okay and now it's in a savings account drawing interest."

Andrew took over the narrative. "Well, from then on that gentleman treated Grant like he was the King of Siam and I was his adviser. He immediately gave us the name of a land agent he absolutely guaranteed was honest and knowledgeable about the land south of Sacramento. His name is Oliver J. Lundy, and we went right on down the street to his office. Nice fellow, couldn't do enough for us. He arranged to take us out the very next morning to look around. Even provided lunch and a small keg of beer. That man really knew how to treat prospective investors."

Grant laughed, then took up the story. "Lundy knew all about the Spanish Grants available in California and we traveled miles and miles and saw the most beautiful land you can imagine."

Barnaby added, "And I was mighty pleased to see all of that land and I didn't have to put a pick and shovel to any part of it unless I wanted to!"

Grant went on. "The most amazing thing of all was Ho Shen. First of all, he had us all in stitches when he sang 'Oh, Susannah' as we traveled. He loves that song and sang it in Chinese and a little English. When we got to one particular piece of land, he examined it like it was full of diamonds. He looked it over, rubbed the dirt between his hands, smelled it and, most remarkable of all, tasted it before he indicated it was the best possible land for our ranch and growing of all kinds of fruits and vegetables. And Sam, it's in a beautiful location. You can see the range of mountains to the east, and it's not far from a river."

"It sounds perfectly wonderful. Did you buy it?" I asked eagerly.

"On the spot! My dear, we are now the proud owners of 600 acres of prime land in the valley about 15 miles south of Sacramento. I know just where to put the ranch house, and Ho Shen pointed out a perfect area for a farm and Chinese settlement.

Oliver promised he'd have a man stake out the boundaries of our property, and he knows of a man who uses a divining rod to find water. He'll identify all of these things on the map he'll have for me on my next trip."

"And the land is really and truly ours now?"

"Sam, it's really and truly ours, and here's another news flash. That land is selling for 50 cents an acre! Fifty cents! Almost like robbery, in fact I felt just a little guilty when I gave him the money. Three hundred dollars!"

All I could say was, "I can't believe it. When Harland bought land in these mountains about five years ago, he paid a thousand dollars an acre and felt he could only afford to buy five acres at that price! Later he felt it was worthwhile when he found bits of gold while rock hunting."

Grant sat back in the chair and shook his head. "We are blessed, Sam. Our new home will be a wonder. And Oliver promised to line up reliable men to begin construction just as soon as we have plans to show them. First of all, my dear, we'll plan and build the barn and corral so the workmen will have a place to live and store lumber and tools. Then we'll plan just how we want our house to look. The front porch, kitchen, bedrooms, everything."

I reminded him, "Don't forget a family room, laundry room, fireplace. Oh, my, Grant, this will be our very first for-real home."

He answered with his very best John Wayne imitation, "You'd better believe it, pilgrim!"

The exhausted men soon left for their homes, but the excitement lingered in the kitchen.

"Land sakes," Hattie commented, "you'd think those fellows found gold, the way they've been carrying on."

"In a sense they have, Hattie. That land represents our future. We'll live here and at the ranch until the Civil War ends. Then we'll decide whether to stay at our homestead or move east to a larger city. We'll know when the time is right."

"You really have thought this through.

"Just as you and Barnaby have. Deciding the kind of life that will make you happy is a bit scary and overwhelming, but it's also exciting. I really don't know if I'll make a good farmer's wife, but I'm willing to give it a good old college try."

Hattie shook her head. "You do say the strangest things, but it sure is pleasing to listen to you. It'll be hard to leave you and Grant behind, but I promise to write often, and you promise to do the same."

"I promise to answer every letter immediately."

Hattie was silent for a second, then asked. "But what about the children? That hasn't been decided. Have they said anything to you?"

"Not yet. Grant and I feel we all should talk to them, explain what we have in mind. You and Barnaby going East, Grant and I staying here. Although they are very young, they still can decide what will make them happy."

She nodded her head. "You're right. We shouldn't tell them where they should go. After what they've been through, they deserve the best possible life any of us could give them."

Ida Penny sent word she had finished the gowns for Hattie and me, and the more intimate items were in the final stages. Hattie blushed and fussed that she was too old for such pretty nightgowns and other beribboned pieces, but Ida and I had no trouble emphasizing that she deserved all the pampering she could get. She shyly agreed.

That Wednesday when I entered the kitchen, Orrin was there, giving Wong Kee a hard time about something. From what I could hear, it was all storm and smoke, but he went on and on. In order to take the heat off Wong Kee, I approached Orrin to say, "I'm glad you're here because it's time we had a talk."

Orrin transferred his fury from Wong Kee to me. "Well, what the hell do you want? Now that things are beginning to settle down around here, you want to talk?"

I motioned to one of the tables at the far end of the kitchen. "Let's sit down. I have something to tell you."

Grumbling, he took a chair and then faced me, bristling with anger and aggravation.

"Orrin, you may have heard by now that on the first Sunday in July Grant and I will be married."

"A ridiculous twosome if ever there was one," he sneered.

I refused to let him get to me. "The Friday before that Sunday will be the last day I'll be working here. I'm giving you plenty of notice so you can find a replacement, if you choose to continue these programs."

He sat there for a moment, trying to decide what it would mean to him. I should have expected the lightning and thunder that followed.

"Well, damn you to hell for doing this to me. Now that the men are gettin' used to you playing your silly tunes. What am I supposed to give them now?"

"Why not bring in someone from San Francisco — a singer, a dancer or someone to play the piano. What with the weather improving, this would be an excellent time to go and see what's available. Crowds of people, including entertainers, are pouring into San Francisco every day, though the more talented ones would require more money than you've been paying me."

"I don't need you to tell me what to do." He pushed back the chair and stood up. "I'll be just fine and I'll have no trouble replacing you!" He stalked from the kitchen with a full head of steam.

I moved to Wong Kee and said, "Well, that seemed to ruffle his feathers a bit."

Wong Kee shook his head. "Good you go. Many miss you.

Mistah Smithas say more, you bet."

"That's for sure," I said as I headed for the saloon.

During my break that afternoon, I took Willis aside and broke the news.

He frowned. "No need to tell you that I'll miss you and the fun we've had with the duets. So will the men who come here every day just to hear you. Things will never be the same, I'm afraid."

"Why don't you help Orrin find a replacement, someone easy to get along with, and you can teach him or her the duets we've been playing, and even make up some of your own?"

"I'd sure be pleased to do that. Thank you."

I couldn't help commenting, "Willis, we've come a long way since the first day I began working here."

He lowered his head in embarrassment. "I sure was wrong, Mis' Samantha, and you've been very nice to me in spite of everything. And I learned a few things, didn't I?"

"We both did," I laughed. "From now on until I leave we'll just have fun playing the music we like best."

A huge grin filled his narrow face as he nodded his head.

And that afternoon I had a jolly time playing an interesting selection of music: "Bridge Over Troubled Waters," "A Hard Day's Night," "Cockeyed Optimist," "Bye, Bye Blackbird," "I'm Gonna Wash That Man Right Outta My Hair." As soon as I played one, laughing to myself, another tune with double meaning came to mind. Grant was there for the last hour and also enjoyed my humor. I had a ball saying goodbye to that part of my life in my own way. As Grant walked me out the door, I said, "I gave Orrin notice today that I would be leaving the Friday before the wedding."

"That's great. Wish I could have seen it. How did he take it?"

"I don't think he's quite decided, but these next few weeks should be very interesting."

On our way to Hattie's we had a great time trying to imagine how Orrin would react and what he would say. Unfortunately, we underestimated him. We were thinking of him as a fool rather than the devious, calculating man that he was.

Chapter Thirty-One

That night we had a festive dinner with everyone talking at once. Rainbow and Warren were still full of the happy Sunday they spent with Maggie, Corby and the others from the saloon. Ida Penny brought Rainbow a charming new dress for spring. The blues and greens of the calico were most flattering to her curly red hair. It was a joy to see how pretty she was becoming.

Warren was sporting a new cotton shirt and blue overalls, also from Ida's skillful hands. With the haircut I worked in before dinner, he looked like a boy on the edge of maturity. These days were happy ones for the children and they fairly blossomed under the love and attention they received.

One evening after dinner we headed for the parlor. Grant led the way by saying, "My little friends, so much good is coming into your lives, all of us are very happy for you. Now it's time for us to have a very serious talk."

Warren and Rainbow settled on the settee, looking a bit uneasy.

"Don't be frightened," Grant reassured them. "This won't hurt a bit. First we'll talk about the double wedding we'll be having in five weeks. You both know that Hattie and Barnaby will be married, and so will Samantha and I. You two did such a good job as flower girl and ring bearer for Maggie and Corby that we'd like you to do the same for us. Would you like to stand with us when we all get married?"

Warren relaxed a bit. "Sure thing. Me 'n' Rainbow will be glad to be there."

Carefully Grant paved the way. "But what comes after the

wedding is what we want to talk about. When two people get married, they make plans about their future and where they want to live. We want to tell you what we have planned. After you hear and understand everything, you can tell us what you think."

Warren said carefully, "Everything's fine just the way it is. Ain't that right?"

Rainbow moved closer to him and nodded.

Grant continued. "You two are very young, but already you've had to learn that changes, good and bad, happen in all our lives. Well, now is the time for good changes for all of us, and we want you to be part of them."

Grant nodded to Barnaby who rubbed his hands together, then began. "After we're married, Hattie and me'll be packin' up and movin' east to Missouri where we both have family. We plan to take a ship from San Francisco, then a riverboat up the Mississippi to Missouri. When we find a likely place to settle down, we'll build a new home, a big house with a fancy staircase and large bedrooms. We might even have some chickens, ducks, and maybe a barn with horses to ride. We're lookin' forward to havin' a fine new life when we settle down." He then nodded to Grant who moved to stand beside my chair.

"Samantha and I have somewhat different ideas. We'll stay in Boone Valley for at least another three or four years. You've heard us talk about our trip to California to look at some land. Well, we found a wonderful place in the Sacramento Valley where we'll build a house, grow lots of good food, and live quietly away from the hustle and bustle of Boone Valley. Wong Kee and some of his friends will come with us to help, and they'll be living nearby in their own settlement. It will be a completely different life than what we have here, but we're really looking forward to it."

There were several minutes of silence as we waited for the children to react to the news.

Hattie then came to the point. "What we're saying here, youngsters, is that after the wedding we'll be going in different directions. However, we'd like you both to be part of our new lives. What we're asking you now is — would you like to move East with Barnaby and me, or stay here with Samantha and Grant, and then move from the mountains to the valley?"

Rainbow and Warren were two bewildered children. Once more their lives were being upset, and it would take time for their inexperienced minds to realize what the two separate lifestyles might mean. Right now it was difficult for them to understand what was expected of them, how to answer.

I moved to the settee and put my arms around Rainbow. "Don't be afraid, little one. Nothing has to be decided right now. You two think about it, talk it over, and if you have any questions, come and ask any of us. Just keep in mind that no matter what you decide, Hattie, Barnaby, Grant, and I love you very much. We only want you to decide which of the two changes would make you happier."

Warren suddenly suggested, "Why don't we all live together?"

I answered, "Because we all have different lives. Barnaby and Hattie have families in the East that they haven't seen in years. It's important to them to visit their people once more. Now that Barnaby has found the gold he's been searching for all these years, he can go home. Isn't that wonderful? On the other hand, Grant and I have no one else in this world who are kin to us. Our lives will go on from here."

Warren wrinkled his brow. Rainbow could only watch us with eyes wide and puzzled.

Grant broke the silence. "Nothing has to be decided tonight, so let's just relax and enjoy ourselves. Samantha, why don't you play something? I'd like some of the golden oldies I haven't heard in years. How about "Chasing Rainbows"?

I moved to the piano and began the melody.

Grant moved to Rainbow and bowed. "May I have this dance, my lady?"

Rainbow did not move, so Grant took her hand and brought her to her feet. Bending over, he put one arm about her waist, then began guiding her feet back and forth in time to the music. He sang the lyrics as they moved from side to side. Rainbow's face became radiant. For the moment her fears and concerns were forgotten and she was being treated like a real young lady.

Hattie went to Warren and held out her hand. "It's been years since I danced with anyone, but let's show those two we're just as good."

Warren was cautious as he joined Hattie, took her outstretched hand and they began their own dance. It was such a beautiful scene that I played on and on. Barnaby looked like a very contented man, and he winked when I caught his eye.

When Rainbow began to yawn, it was time for the evening and dancing to end. Grant made Warren comfortable on his cot in the parlor, and I helped Rainbow into a nightie, then tucked her into our bed. After our prayers, I said, "It's been quite a day, young lady, and you and Warren have lots to talk about."

She nodded as she settled under the covers and yawned again. "Warren will tell me all about it tomorrow."

"Don't worry about it now. You two can talk it over, and be sure to tell Warren how you feel about everything and what changes would make you happy." I kissed her goodnight.

In the kitchen Grant said, "It'll be hard for those two to think clearly about what could be ahead for them. All we can do is answer their questions as simply as possible, make clear their options, and let them work it out."

Two days later, Grant met me after work. "On such a fine day, my lady, I'm here to walk you home. We both could use the exercise and time to ourselves."

I teased, "Shall we put on our sweats and jog back to Hattie's?"

Grant let out a hoot. "I wish we could. For today, let's just take an old-fashioned walk."

We worked our way through the crowds and wagons on the road, then left the bustle of town behind and walked hand in hand down the quieter road.

"Madam," Grant began, "have you noticed that spring is in the air, the flowers are blooming, and the birds are singing happily in the trees?"

I looked at him closely. "Does this mean that you have a major case of spring fever?"

"To a degree," he said with a sly smile. "But there are others who have been smitten, and two of them have confided to me that they are seriously in love."

"Who, who? Tell me quick!"

"Robert and Flower. The fact that we'll be married soon is bringing them closer to making the same decision. Robert is so much in love he can't stand it. He wants to marry Flower, get her away from the saloon and into a home of their own. Flower feels the same, but she has the dark cloud of Orrin hanging over her. It would be difficult, if not dangerous. You know how Orrin keeps a tight grip on anything that his girls want to do."

"Robert and Flower deserve to be together. They've had more than their share of misery in their young lives. Mr. Douglas, we'll just have to put our exceptional minds together and do all we can to help their dreams come true."

"Just what I had in mind, so where do we start?"

"We'll cover that later. You said there were others with spring fever."

Grant stopped in the road just in front of Hattie's house, and with a big smile, announced, "Andrew Locke has serious feelings for Myra, and he's become very attached to little Charlie. I have no idea when it began or how far it's gone. I doubt if Myra is even aware of his feelings."

I thought about this combination for a moment. "Well, now, I hadn't thought of it myself, but what a wonderful match. We must see what we can do to encourage this one as well!"

Inside the house, Myra was ready to head home, and Warren and Rainbow were saying goodbye to Charlie.

Grant volunteered, "It will be my pleasure to walk you home. You must be tired, and Warren and I can take turns carrying Charlie."

Myra hesitated. "We wouldn't want to put you out, Mr. Douglas. It isn't too far and we can go slow."

"Not at all," my gallant knight insisted. "It will be dark soon, so let Warren and me deliver you safely home."

With a shy smile of appreciation, Myra went out the door with Warren following. Grant picked up Charlie, turned to blow me a kiss, and off they went.

Rainbow and I could smell a wonderful aroma coming from the kitchen. "Well, look here, Rainbow. Myra has already fixed our dinner. What a nice lady."

"I helped her," said Rainbow. "I got the potatoes and peeled one. I even got to cut them up. I cut my finger just a little bit. See?" She held up her hand where I could see a red line on one finger.

"Oh, my, does it hurt?"

"Nah. Myra washed it good with soap 'n' water and it's jus' fine."

We made a game of setting the table. It wasn't long before Grant and Warren burst through the door telling us how quickly they went up the hill to Myra's shack, the people they saw on the way, and the funny little dog that barked at them. Hattie and Barnaby arrived a few moments later, and we all sat down to share a delicious dinner.

Under my guidance, Rainbow and Warren had been taking turns saying a short grace before meals. Tonight was Rainbow's turn.

"Dear God up there in heaven, bless these vittles that Myra and I made today with our own hands. We hope they taste good, and that it will make everyone happy. Amen."

Later Grant and I discussed Myra's situation. "When I walked Myra home, she told me her husband left for the gold fields the day after they arrived, and she's had no letter or report on him in 18 months. How can a man take off like that and leave a wife and baby behind to survive the best they can? He left her no money or supplies. He just packed his bag and took off. Either he's a thought-less, uncaring man, or he's dead. However, he could drag in here one day, worn down to a nub and a shadow of himself, without a nugget in his pocket. So, even if Andrew and Myra find that they do indeed have feelings for each other, there isn't much they can do."

"But I was in the same situation, remember? We found a way out."

"In your case a man could be reported dead and that's that. In Myra's case, her husband could still show up months, even years from now."

We discussed Robert and Flower. The main problem was Orrin and his attitude. With the loss of Bertha, there were only five Waiter Girls. So far Orrin had not made a move to bring in another girl. The long hours and extra work seem to leave the girls exhausted.

It came to a head a few days later when I arrived for work. Orrin came storming over and ordered me into the kitchen.

"What's this damned business with Flower and that empty-headed clerk from Wells Fargo? Zola tells me Flower's makin' noises like she wants to get married. I'll have none of it! I allowed Maggie and Corby to get hitched, but I won't have my girls not payin' attention to their work."

"Orrin, you might as well get used to the idea that just as Maggie married, Flower is certainly free to do the same and, if she chooses, to move the hell out of here!" Never before had I lost my temper enough to swear at someone.

His smile was evil. "Tell you what I been thinkin' lately, Missy. Other saloons in the valley have been doin' it and makin' a fine profit. I'm goin' to have the girls take the fellas upstairs for some pleasurin'. That will be part of their duties and there ain't nothin' you or anyone can do to stop me. You be clear on that, you meddling bitch, or I'll make it part of your job as well!"

My anger was such that my knees began to shake, but I shot back, "Don't even think about it, Orrin. If I get a hint that you have such plans for any of the girls, we'll all be out that door before you can finish a sentence."

We glared at each other until Orrin snorted and stormed out of the kitchen.

My music that day was full of anger and despair. Over dinner I exploded in a fury of helplessness. When I managed to calm down, I reported my conversation with Orrin. Hattie was horrified and Barnaby did his best to calm her. Grant's face darkened, then began to clear. He asked with a grin, "Hattie, does your store provide the Majestic Saloon with supplies?"

"Sure does, lots of them. We have orders coming up from Sacramento for Orrin almost every other week." Then her face brightened. "Why, yes, of course. Orrin depends on my store for many things."

Grant turned to me. "Samantha, I'll take you to work a little early tomorrow so we can have a heart-to-heart with Orrin. He's overdue for an attitude adjustment, and the two of us will help him see the light."

We arrived an hour before my program. I settled in the

kitchen with a mug of Wong Kee's fine coffee and Grant went to find Orrin. When he returned with him in tow, Orrin already was sputtering and swearing.

"Who the hell do you think you are, demanding that I come in here to talk to you and this slut you're goin' to marry?"

Grant sat down and said quite calmly, "Because we have something of importance to discuss, I will not take the time to knock you on your rear end for that remark. But if I ever again hear you talk to or about Samantha in such an insulting manner, there will be hell to pay such as you've never seen before. Do you understand me, Orrin?"

Orrin raised his eyebrows and folded his arms, trying to look nonchalant.

"Orrin, we need to discuss the Waiter Girls and your hold over them, not to mention your threat to force them to service your customers upstairs."

"No one tells Orrin Smithers what to do, and I won't allow that dummy, Flower, to marry and leave her obligation to me."

Orrin was acting as if he was holding all the cards.

Grant had a determined look as he said, coldly, "Orrin, who do you depend on for the many supplies you order and receive regularly?"

Orrin smugly replied, "McKee's Mercantile, of course. Hattie and I have done a lot of business together."

"Next question," Grant said calmly. "Who supplies the beer that you serve to your customers every night?"

Looking disgusted by the obvious questions and answers, Orrin answered tiredly, "You do, of course."

Grant moved in for the kill. "Then listen very carefully, Orrin, because I've got a bulletin for you. Are you ready to listen?"

"Let's get this bullshit over and done with," Orrin burst out. "I'm tired of this stupid game!"

"All right," Grant continued in a reasonable voice. "First bulletin. In a matter of weeks Hattie McKee, soon to be Tinker, will be leaving for the East. And who will be the new proprietor of McKee's Mercantile? Have you any idea?"

Orrin just shrugged his shoulders.

"All right, sir. Let me inform you that the new owner and director of all transactions through that store will be the lady who is sitting at this table."

Orrin began to look a bit uncomfortable.

"Surprise, surprise," I confirmed, smiling brightly.

"Ready for the second bulletin, Orrin? As the owner of the largest brewery in this part of California, I am considering reviewing and adjusting the output and delivery to the many saloons that I service. I may not find it worthwhile to include your orders in the near future. How does that grab you?"

Orrin was irate. "Why you son of a bitch! You can't do that to me! I've been a good customer. You know damned well it'll wreck my business if those deliveries don't come in on time. What the hell are you trying to do to me?"

Grant switched to a firm but reasonable tone. "Merely to adjust your thinking in certain areas. First, it might be wise to rethink your ruling forbidding the girls in your employ to make their own personal decisions. Second, it would not be very nice to force them to go upstairs with the men unless the ladies choose to do so. To offer entertainment of that kind, go to San Francisco and recruit girls who are in the business. And while you're at it, think about getting one or two more Waiter Girls. We also suggest that you reconsider Flower's desire to marry Robert if, indeed, that's what she really wants to do."

Orrin was snarling. "You and this — woman of yours think you have me over a barrel, don't you?"

Grant was smooth. "Over a beer barrel, you might say. But

as far as the arrangements you have with my brewery and Hattie's store, they could easily continue as they have been. It's all up to you, Orrin. I have nothing more to say." He looked at me. "Do you have anything to add, my dear bride-to-be?"

"No, husband-to-be. You've covered everything quite well. I do admire the grasp you have on difficult but correctable situations. And now, if you will excuse me, I will now go to my work." And with a smile and a kiss for Grant, I sauntered from the kitchen.

Grant had much to report when we met after work. He was sensing that Orrin might have a deeper, darker side than we had seen before. "After you left, Sam, Orrin yelled, threatened and blustered about the kitchen for some time. Then suddenly he calmed down and quietly agreed to everything we suggested."

"I'm concerned," Grant stated. "One moment Orrin was out of his mind with anger, and the next he sat there quietly. His eyes narrowed and he seemed a little too benign. He came around, but he was silky smooth. Does that make sense? We'd better watch him carefully from now on. We may have pushed him too far."

For the rest of the week, we watched Orrin closely. But from all reports, he was his usual horrid self.

Meanwhile, Grant passed the word to Robert and Flower that there should be no obstruction to their marriage.

That Sunday morning as we were preparing to leave for church, we found Robert and Flower, hand in hand, at Hattie's front door. He asked to speak with Grant. As the others went on, Grant took the couple into the parlor. Within a few minutes he called me to join them.

Robert and Flower sat side by side on the settee. Without parents or friends to guide them, they had come to Grant. Robert was explaining that Flower was able to accompany him since Orrin was in San Francisco on business, perhaps the business that Grant had so strongly recommended.

Grant explained to me, "This young couple want to be married and they're not quite sure how to go about it."

"That should be easy," I answered. "Why can't they be married with us in July? Never heard of a triple wedding before, but there's nothing to say it can't be done."

They both shook their heads solemnly. Robert explained, "That's your day, the four of you, and we wouldn't want to intrude. We were thinking of something very simple, quiet. Where do we start?"

"Well, do you know who you would like to invite?"

"Just you and Mrs. Malcolm. In fact, we would like you to stand up with us."

Grant and I smiled. "We would be honored. And have you decided where you would like to live?"

Robert put a protective arm about Flower. "I'm determined to get her away from that saloon as soon as possible. I've been looking all over for somewhere we could live. I have only a very small room, and so far I haven't found a thing. Every house, shack and room is taken. Besides, prices are so high and my salary is all we'll have. We don't know where to go or what to do next." He sounded forlorn, and Flower leaned her head against him and sighed.

Grant took a positive tone. "Now look here. All is not lost. If there are any answers out there, Samantha and I will find them. You two just concentrate on each other and try not to be downhearted. Give us a few days and maybe we'll have some news for you. All right?"

The young couple smiled their thanks as they left, and Grant and I hurried to church. Afterward we went to Norton's Café with Ida Penny and Andrew Locke. When we described the dilemma Robert and Flower were facing, Ida shyly offered, "I have just a small place with two large rooms. Wish I had an extra room for them, at least until they get on their feet."

We were quiet with our own thoughts as she continued. "Maybe we could put a curtain over one corner of the room where they could sleep." Then she added mournfully, "You know I lost my only brother and have no other kin left. If I could make room for this lovely couple, it would be like they were my own family and I wouldn't have to be alone so much."

Grant suddenly held up a finger for attention. "I think I've found the perfect solution." With a broad grin he looked around the table, taking a moment to build the suspense. "I know your house, Ida. In fact, I worked with Titus to build it. He had a crush on you, did you know that? He wanted you to have the best house we could possibly build. Now, if you mean what you say, the solution could benefit both you and this young couple."

Ida joyfully clapped her hands. "Oh, I dearly hope you have found a way."

Grant was clearly pleased with himself, and his eyes sparkled as he laid out his plan.

"We can add another room to your house, Ida. There's a blank wall on the north side. A door would go there nicely and leading to a good-sized room, say 12 by 12, with a couple of windows. It wouldn't take long. Now that I think about it, I recall that wall connects to the kitchen where we could add a few more feet and make room for a pantry and larger dining area."

Bless him. He had found a way, and Ida was shedding happy tears. "It sounds too good to be true," she gasped.

Grant was beaming. "I amaze myself, I am so brilliant!"

Andrew cautioned, "Don't get carried away. It sounds fine but how much will it cost, and how soon can we start?"

I added to Grant's plan. "With Hattie's help, we can manage the lumber as well as nails, hammers, and other things. I'll be glad to contribute some of the extra money that's come my way."

"And I'll give you all the time and money I can spare,"

Andrew offered. "Robert is a good man and he's doing a fine job for us at Wells Fargo."

Ida added, "And later, if they're short of money, Flower can help at my shop. These have been busy days for me. Men are coming here without any womenfolk, so they need help with their mending or for strong, sturdy shirts to wear in the mountains."

That was the day that Operation Dream Come True was launched, and as it grew it seemed to take on a happy life of its own.

Chapter Thirty-Two

That afternoon the plans for Operation Dream Come True moved ahead briskly. Hattie was all for it. "What do we do first?"

Grant laid out the details as we listened. "First we need drawings and measurements of Ida's house. Andrew is there now looking it over. Next we'll get the lumber, tools and labor, and by next week construction should be well under way. Andrew will tell Robert that we're working on a solution and they should go ahead with their plans. We won't say another word until everything's ready."

I was caught up in the project. "We'll be busy, Hattie, gathering the things they'll need — sheets, pillows, pillow cases, blankets, curtains. We can be Flower's fairy godmothers. We'll help Ida with the wedding dress and trousseau just like Flower was our very own daughter."

This brought Hattie close to tears. "I wasn't able to do this for my dear daughter, Rosalie, before she ran away. I'll just give my help and affection to Flower who, poor dear, has had so little in her life."

Meanwhile back at the saloon, Willis and I continued to work on duets. Without his knowing, I tried to keep the music in the 1800s, songs like "Red River Valley" and others. As we worked on the melody, he was saying how much he would miss me and the music we played together. He had changed from the sullen, vindictive person I first met, to a man of pride whose face often brightened with a smile. I was delighted when he shared the news that he might have found my replacement.

"She plays piano at the Wild Rose, and she's not very happy

there. It sure would be nice if she could get away and come here. Her name is Marina. She's from Europe and she studied music just like you. She plays mostly classical music, and I really like the way she plays. She could take over Bertha's old room if Orrin let's her come. Right now she looks like she don't get enough food and sleep, but maybe comin' over here would be just the thing, in spite of the fact she'd be workin' for Orrin."

That afternoon I convinced Grant to drive me to the Wild Rose to hear Marina play.

"You really don't want to go inside that place, Sam. You won't like what you'll see."

"I'm a big girl now, remember? With you as my protector, we'll just step inside the front door and listen. Don't you deliver beer to the Wild Rose?"

"We do, but I haven't become bosom buddies with any of the guys there. We'll go inside just long enough to hear this lady play, then we're outta there. Okay?"

"You got it, my hero!"

Well, the visit wasn't as easy as planned. As we entered the double doors, I was almost overcome by the odors. The air was thick with smoke and the smell of stale whiskey and beer. Together with the smell of unwashed bodies, it was bad enough to make you choke.

"What a shame that air conditioning won't be invented for a hundred years," I muttered.

As our eyes became accustomed to the darkness, we could see men milling about, and many of those seated had scantily clad girls sitting on their laps. A very drunk miner stumbled by, then stopped to look at me closely.

"Well if it ain't the little lady that plays the piano. Come to play a tune for us? That gal over there's too high-falutin' for me. Come on, play us some good music!" He leaned against me so close it seemed I could get drunk from his breath.

Grant moved between us and towered over the little man by a good six inches. The man stepped back and mumbled, "On the other hand, never mind," and stumbled on his way.

Over the noise of the crowd I could hear the faint sounds of a piano, and by stepping deeper into the building we found where it originated. We could see a slight figure sitting at an upright piano, playing Mozart for a crowd totally unaware of the skill she was demonstrating. The rendition was masterful, but wasted on people who could not appreciate the composer nor the interpretation.

Grant and I stood to one side, apart from the stream of people moving about. As we drew closer to the piano, we could see a very slim girl with long delicate fingers playing the last chords of the melody. She looked up to reveal a face framed by black curly hair that fell just to her shoulders, pale olive skin, and dark eyes surrounded by tired smudges. Her eyes reflected trial, unhappiness and the loss of hope.

Leaning close to her, I said, "I love the way you play Mozart, it's outstanding. Can you take a break and come outside so we can talk?"

She looked about fearfully, then nodded. We started for the door but were stopped by a large, muscular man. "Where do y'think you're goin', Marina? You ain't through for the day."

Grant recognized the man. "Mike, we just want to take this lady outside for a little air and chat with her. You know me, I own the brewery."

Mike hesitated. "I guess it's all right." Then he spoke roughly to the girl. "And you come right back and get to work, d'ya hear me?"

She lowered her head then followed us through the crowd and out the double doors to where the air was fresh and the noise subdued.

I introduced myself. "Marina, I'm Samantha Malcolm. I play piano at the Majestic, but nothing close to the skill and training you show. Where are you from?"

She answered in a deep monotone, "I come to this country from Roma with my father and three brothers. My mother, she is dead. Before she die, she wanted to make sure my studies at the Conservatory in Roma will go on, but my father said there was no money left."

"Where is your family now?"

"My father says we must come to this country for new life. We take boat to New York. He not find work yet but he find a lady also from Italy he likes very much. When my brothers say they want to come here to find gold, he says they can go and I must go also to take care of them."

"But where are your brothers now?" Grant asked.

"They go into mountains to look for gold. They leave me here to wait for them."

I said bitterly, "So they left you here to take care of yourself the best way you could." I looked at Grant. "We've heard that song before, haven't we?"

He shook his head sadly.

"If it were at all possible," I began, "would you be willing to replace me at the Majestic when I leave in July?"

She shook her head. "Is not possible. Since I begin work here, they watch me at all times."

"But would you come if it could be done? This gentleman is Grant Douglas, and he has ways to convince certain saloon owners to change their minds."

"Very true," Grant agreed.

She raised her sad face to us. "It is what I pray for every night. If you do this, I would be so grateful."

I cautioned, "Say nothing for now, and we'll try to clear the way. Meanwhile, keep your spirits up and believe with all your heart that it can happen."

She gave us a shadow of a smile just as Mike came out the door, held it open, and motioned for her to return. She disappeared into that dark, ugly environment as Grant and I got into the buggy. "Oh, Grant. She's like a flower wilting in the darkness. We must do all we can to get her out of there."

He sighed. "It looks like I'll have to have a heart-to-heart with another saloon owner. You know, I'm convinced you must have been a Girl Scout in your other life."

"How did you guess?"

Willis was pleased with the possibilities when I told him about our visit with Marina. He was full of ideas of how they could work together, and perhaps learn a few duets. He said, "I do hope you can get her out of that terrible place. Who would have believed that moving over here to work for Orrin would be an improvement!"

As for Operation Dream Come True, the lumber was delivered and stacked behind Ida's house. Andrew's layout was completed and, with a few alterations by Grant, provided the blueprint for the work to be done. He found four men capable of building the new bedroom. Their need for money was critical, so he had no doubt they would see the project through to the end. Grant adjusted his working day in order to oversee their labor.

After Andrew notified Robert that a solution was taking shape, the couple made plans to be married privately by Rev. Norton on the same day as our double wedding. We invited them to be part of our reception afterwards.

Meanwhile, Orrin returned from San Francisco, puffed up like a peacock and bragging that the girls there were clamoring to work at the Majestic. Though he threatened to look for prostitutes to add to the saloon's entertainment, he brought instead two rather plain country girls wearing the garish clothes he had provided. He made it clear they would not be forced to wear the uniforms chosen by the Waiter Girls."

There was also a man who had traveled from San Francisco with Orrin. Corby confided that this man moved about the saloon but kept to himself except for short, guarded conversations with Orrin. Like a note on a piano that is not in tune with the others, this man brought a dark energy that caused all of us to be wary.

Zola had already approached the two girls in an effort to bring them under her wing. As it turned out, the girls were sisters — Genna and Sarah Grayson — and not as innocent as they seemed. Lessons learned since landing in San Francisco made them wise when it came to Orrin. They were given Maggie and Bertha's rooms, and settled in.

Zola immediately called on them to lay out the pecking order of the Waiter Girls. She also made it clear that she was Orrin's woman and not to make any moves on him. Having met and traveled with Orrin, the girls had no argument with that. Little by little they watched how things really were, and wisely fit in very well from their first day.

They were having lunch in the kitchen a few days later when I arrived for work, so I introduced myself and we had a short visit. Sarah was the most outspoken. "Our farm's in Indiana. Daddy and Momma live there with our three brothers. They didn't like it much when Genna and me said we wanted to see the world outside of Indiana. But with all those mouths to feed, they let us go. Daddy talked for hours about the bad things we would find away from home. We knew it wouldn't be easy, but it just seemed like the thing for us to do."

"That's the way of it," Genna said.

"Well, we sure learned, and by the time we got to San Francisco we were a lot smarter. The men on the wagon train would look us over when their wives weren't around."

"You seem terribly young to be out on your own like this. What are your ages?"

Sarah pointed a thumb at her sister. "She's 14, I'm 17."

"So young and so confident. Good for you! Then what happened when you got to San Francisco?"

Sarah smiled. "Lot's more to learn there, but we caught on when we talked to other girls at the bars where we were workin'. With Genna and me having each other, we made out all right."

I couldn't help but ask. "But why did you come all this way to Boone Valley?"

"The men in San Francisco were just there for a good time. We figured the men up here would be busy workin' the mines, tryin' to find gold. Hard workin' men. We're both lookin' for strong men with character, sorta like our daddy, but with some gold in their pockets."

I thought to myself that the possibilities in this area might not be what they had in mind. It was something they would have to learn on their own, but they seemed equal to the task. This was clear when, once they had met the Waiter Girls and heard the history of the uniforms, they secretly had uniforms made to match the others. When completed, they wore them bravely, in spite of growling complaints from Orrin.

Genna said with a lopsided smile, "Sarah and me found out right away that there was a difference in the way the miners treat the Waiter Girls. Girls wearin' the uniforms are treated nice, but Zola, in her fancy dresses, gets treated just like the bar girls in San Francisco, like trash."

When I asked about their trip here from San Francisco, Sarah made a face. "That Orrin ain't a barrel of laughs, we know that. But what he told us about this saloon seemed better than what we were gettin', so we decided to take a chance. But that feller what came with us, he's a scary one. Always frowning, didn't say a word, not a good mornin' or howdy, but just spent his time sharpenin' that knife he carries, or talkin' with Orrin. Strange man."

Sarah and Genna liked to sing and, as it turned out, had lovely voices. I took them to the piano that afternoon and found a song they were familiar with, and they took off like a rocket. Their song, "Bringing in the Sheaves," sung in harmony, was delightful and, judging from the reaction of that afternoon's audience, they would be a popular feature from then on. Orrin stood to one side, frowning like a thunder cloud.

Willis was pleased, and he found the girls pleasant companions as they developed the songs they would use to entertain the miners.

Also, we discovered the girls displayed high spirits and humor as they worked. The miners joked with them, laughed heartily at their salty comments, and soon developed a growing respect. All this set them apart from Orrin and foiled his tendency to control all his girls. A new age had come to the Majestic!

One day Orrin chastised the girls for not serving the drinks fast enough. Genna replied saucily, "Keep your bloomers on, Mr. Smithers! Your customers will get their drinks as fast as us girls can bring 'em to the tables. You don't see anybody with their tongues hangin' out from thirst, d'ya?"

Everyone seated in that immediate area roared with laughter. From then on, the men waited to hear the sassy remarks that came from the sisters.

The man Orrin brought from San Francisco remained a black cloud, however. He was dressed as a gambler, though his clothes were worn and shabby. His face was long and bony with deep lines on the forehead and both cheeks. His one vanity seemed to be a black mustache and goatee.

Corby filled me in one day. "His name is Morgan Holly, and

he don't seem to talk to no one but Orrin." He leaned over the bar, then said quietly, "Watch his eyes, Mis' Samantha. They're always goin' from side to side, watchin' everything and everyone. As far as Elmo and me can make out, he don't do no work. He just hangs around, watchin' us pour out the drinks and handle the gold dust and nuggets. He watches the Waiter Girls real close when they're servin' drinks and how long they gab with the customers. He really seems interested in you, Mis' Samantha, when you're playin', and Grant when he's around waitin' for you, and even when you're talkin' with Wong Kee. It seems he's doin' all the watchin' that Orrin used to do, then later I see them with their heads together. We don't know what to make of it, but we're doin' our work real careful just like we always do."

That day I became more aware of Holly moving about the room, watching me closely, then the Grayson girls as they sang and went about their work. Corby was right. His eyes seemed to be everywhere. We became accustomed to his dark presence and life went on as usual. Orrin, on the other hand, seemed more relaxed, chatting with the customers and roaming about the saloon like he was lord of the manor.

That night, as Rainbow and Warren helped Hattie and Barnaby clear the table, Grant led me out to the porch where he sat me down on one of the steps. It was a beautiful evening, the moon was peeking around the fluffy white clouds, and there was a slight breeze. He placed one arm firmly about my shoulders.

"My dear Samantha," he began, "have you noticed how very nicely we fit together? We work well together, our thinking is synchronized, and we have yet to have an argument or difference of opinion."

"I know. It's remarkable that we can say anything to each other — any thought, any feeling — and it is always accepted and respected."

He touched my cheek. "Promise that we'll always be honest with each other. Let's be free to discuss everything openly and frankly. Our past marriages clearly demonstrated how damaging hidden feelings and silent hurts can be. Knowing all this, we can build a new and better life for each other."

"Dear, dear Grant, that's a promise, and it's something we can teach Rainbow and Warren as they grow up."

"And what about them?" Grant asked. "Have they indicated where they want to go — with Hattie and Barnaby, or stay with us? Let's ask them tonight if they have any questions. Maybe they're hesitating because they don't want to hurt our feelings."

We sat there quietly, enjoying the delicious closeness until Grant stood and held out his hand. "Now is the time to ask them. Whatever they've decided, we'll accept and work from there. Let's make them comfortable with their opinions and, if they're ready, their decision."

We found kitchen duty was about finished. Grant pointed to the parlor. "Let's all go in and talk about what's ahead for all of us. There will be happy changes in all our lives, and let's share the possibilities."

We came together in the parlor, then looked to Grant for further word. He addressed the children.

"Little friends, we know you're old enough to understand there will be different roads ahead for all of us. Have you had enough time to think about everything, talk it over, or at least have an idea of what you want in your young lives?"

Warren found the watching eyes of the adults rather daunting, but he pulled his 10-year-old back up straight and faced us. Rainbow leaned against him and hid her face in his jacket. Finally he spoke.

"Y'all been extra-special nice to us. When Rainbow was so sick, you brought us here and made her well. And when Momma

Bertha died, we came here to stay. We just don't want nobody to feel bad. We talked on it, but we can't make up our minds."

Grant moved over and sat on the floor before them. "We just want you to decide what you really, really would like. Every one of us has choices. It's like going down a road, and suddenly you see it's going in two directions, one to the right and one to the left. So what do you do? You say to yourself, 'Well, that road on the right looks nice. It's smooth with a few trees. I might take that road.' Then you look at the other road and you think, 'On the other hand, that road leads to those green hills over there and I might like what's on the other side.' That's when you have to make a choice by paying attention to what you see, what you think, and what you feel inside."

Warren's eyes were large as he repeated, "We don't want nobody to feel bad. Besides, we'd miss being with the ones we don't pick."

I joined Grant on the carpet before them. "Warren, please understand that won't happen. Wherever Hattie and Barnaby go, or wherever Grant and I settle, we will always be in touch with each other. No way would we let go of the wonderful friendship we have. And if you decide to go with Hattie and Barnaby, you could come out here and visit us. Before you're too much older, there will be a railroad that comes all the way to California. Traveling here would be as easy as pie."

Grant took over. "Or, if you decide to stay with us, you can take that train in the other direction and have a lovely visit with Hattie and Barnaby wherever they are. We'll always be good friends, the six of us. When you're older, you can travel all by yourself whenever you want to."

Warren solemnly studied us, then his face brightened with relief. "You see, Rainbow? We wouldn't be losing nobody, we'll just be a few miles apart!"

Rainbow leaned over and whispered in his ear, and he in turn whispered in hers. This quiet conversation went back and forth until they faced us once more.

"The Waiter Girls and some of the people at the saloon, like Corby and Elmo, Willis and Wong Kee, have been good to us since we were little. We want to be with them before you two (indicating Grant and me) go to your farm. If we can go see Hattie and Barnaby at their new home, that makes everything all right. Right, Rainbow?"

Rainbow shook her head so rapidly that her red curls flew through the air.

Grant turned to Hattie and Barnaby, "How does this sound to you? It seems to me like they know what they want."

Hattie burst out, "Of course it's all right with us, isn't it Barnaby?" Barnaby agreed. "Leave it to these youngsters to find just the right answer, and they seem happy about it. That's all we ever wanted."

Rainbow said shyly, "Will we have to go back to the saloon for a while?"

Hattie scoffed, "No way, little angel! Guess you haven't heard that when Barnaby and I leave for Missouri, Samantha and Grant will be living here with you. This will be your home for a long time."

I got to my feet, and spread my arms. "Let's have a nice round of hugs to celebrate! Everyone on your feet!"

Smiles and hugs were exchanged, more than a few.

With the determination of that part of our lives, we all turned our focus to the details of our immediate future. The weddings, reception, packing, transfer of the Mercantile Store to me, and settling the two households gave us plenty to deal with. It didn't occur to us that others were not concerned with our happiness, rather just the opposite.

In the middle of my program the next day, several miners

burst through the front entrance and began yelling, "Fire, fire! There's a big fire on the other side of town!"

Everything stopped and we rushed into the street. To the south at the far end of town, just before the slope of the hills began, we could see great clouds of black smoke rising into the sky. Wagons, carts, men on mules, horseback and on foot, rushed like an army in that direction. Their hands were filled with buckets, shovels and blankets.

Willis was beside me and I asked, "Don't you have a fire department here, or men organized to help when this happens?"

"It never happened, though they talked about it from time to time. Everyone knows that if we don't pitch in right away when there's a fire, this whole town could burn to the ground. 'Scuse me, Mis' Samantha. I'll run over and see what I can do to help."

I stood on the boardwalk in front of the saloon, looking anxiously at the billowing smoke. Corby and Elmo joined me, watching the frenzy of the crowd as they rushed toward the fire. When I looked over at them, they said, "We can't go, Mis' Samantha. Orrin swears he'll kick our butts out the door if we go off for something like this and leave the bar and all that liquor." They shrugged their shoulders and shook their heads. Maggie and Flower joined us on the boardwalk.

I was so tempted to join the crowd, rush to the fire and help in some way. But what could I do, in the middle of a crowd of men frantically working to smother the flames?

We watched anxiously until within a half hour, to our relief, the mass of smoke began to lessen, then was reduced to just faint wisps in the air.

Elmo went back inside, but Corby, Flower, Maggie and I watched as the people began to straggle back to our part of town. Their clothes and faces were smeared with soot and water. Oddly, many of them were smiling. Corby called out to one that he knew.

"Where was the fire, and is it all out now?"

The man came to the steps, threw his jacket over one shoulder and rested a water soaked boot on the bottom step. "We got it all out, and had us a treat in the doing of it. Of all places to catch on fire. The brewery! It started in the offices, but there was all them barrels and vats filled with water and beer. So we all pitched in, and what we didn't throw on the fire, we drank down our throats which were gettin' pretty dry."

"The brewery!" My body went cold and my heart beat anxiously. "Was anyone hurt? Did you see Grant Douglas? Is he all right?"

"No one hurt that I could tell. Douglas was out there with all of us, throwing all that beer on the flames. And he was yellin' to us, 'Drink up boys, but leave some for the fire!' Well, we all worked mighty hard after that, and in no time it was done and we saved most of the building."

"Thank God," I said to myself. But I was still fearful and resisted the impulse to run to the brewery to see for myself. I was unable to move or speak as I waited an eternity for Grant to return. Anxiously I watched the stream of people returning to this part of town. One wagon passed by loaded with men, and as it came close, Andrew jumped off. I rushed to him, grabbed his damp and smoky sleeve.

"Is he all right?"

"Samantha, he's just fine, just fine. A little worse for wear, with a brewery that will need some fixing up, but it really isn't too bad."

I was so relieved that I rested my head on his shoulder.

"Now, don't you worry, the worst is over. He's out a couple of vats of beer and a barrel or two, but he'll recover." He lowered his voice. "Sam, this wasn't an accident. Someone deliberately started the fire."

"My God, no!"

"I was in the office talking to Grant when we heard a smash like something hitting the wall outside, then the whole side of the building was on fire. We managed to carry out the ledgers and records before the flames filled the room. Grant and some of his crew brought huge buckets filled with water and beer to throw on the fire. From what I could see, the large vats and the barrels, empty and full, were mostly untouched."

"And is Grant all right?"

"As right as rain as far as I can tell. He's busy now checking the damage and figuring out how much rebuilding needs to be done. He said to tell you he's all right, though he'll be busy with the repairs for a while. But he said to be sure to tell you that Operation Dream Come True will go ahead as planned."

"Well, bless him for knowing that would be my second question. I'm so relieved."

Though I was still shaking, I went back inside to finish my program. The response of the audience wasn't quite there, but I didn't mind. I amused myself by playing "Too Darn Hot" and "Having a Heat Wave." When it was over, I rushed to Hattie's store.

She remarked, "Fires that start anywhere in this town are enough to make your hair turn white. These wood structures are all close together, so a fire gone wild could sweep this place clean. We've had a few close calls in the past, but nothing that couldn't be fixed."

By 10 o'clock the children were snug in their beds. Hattie had retired, and I was awake and waiting, hoping Grant would come by. He did, reeking of smoke, his clothes covered with dirt and soot. After a hello kiss that left streaks of black on my face, I sat him down and served coffee and a large sandwich from the leftover pot roast. In between bites he talked.

"It was deliberate, Sam. Someone started the fire to burn

down my business or kill me, or maybe both. On the ground outside the office, I found what was left of a kerosene lamp that evidently had been thrown against the wall. The wood was soaked, and whoever threw it stayed long enough to set a match to it. That's why the fire was going full force before I even knew what happened."

He finished his sandwich and sat back in his chair. All was quiet until I just had to say the obvious: "Do you think it was Orrin?"

Grant looked at me thoughtfully. "Sam, I don't know for sure, but we must face the fact that somebody deliberately tried to hurt me today and, since I've survived, we must be on guard. It was aimed at me, not you, but promise me you will be very, very careful from now on. I'm afraid we've gotten a little too pleased with ourselves, solving other people's problems, helping everyone with our 20th Century arrogance."

I added, "Remember that Orrin was not happy when I coached the Waiter Girls about their rights under the Constitution. I know I've come on pretty strong, never hesitating to express myself openly, never accepting a situation, like women are supposed to do these days. These men, other than you, want their women to be docile and not muddy the waters." Grant nodded in agreement.

I finished my thought. "If this is part of the problem, my dear, then I'm in big trouble, right along with you!"

Chapter Thirty-Three

The following week Grant was fully involved, not only with the repairs on the brewery, but also with the continued production and delivery of beer. He apologized that it was taking most of his waking hours to deal with the many details, which meant there was little time for us.

We did connect briefly. I found that Operation Dream Come True had come to a halt and every effort was transferred to the brewery.

"I had to do it, Sam. The work on the brewery is more immediate, but it should be completed within five or six days. We still have time to finish the work at Ida's. Don't worry, everything should be done by the first of July."

My work at the saloon continued and became more enjoyable since each day brought me closer to Grant and our dreams. Nothing bothered me — not Orrin's frequent glares, nor the jealous and biting presence of Zola, nor the dark and ever-watchful presence of Morgan Holly. He moved about the saloon like a referee watching a fight.

That afternoon Grant waited for me with a horse and buggy when I left the saloon. "There was a break in the work, and I missed you. I gotta have a Samantha fix before I can go on."

"You read my mind. I've been missing you something fierce myself." I settled close to him.

"How was your day?" I asked. "How much more work is there left to do on the brewery?"

"Well, the walls are in and we've started on the interior. I'm adding a couple of small offices so the two clerks can work more comfortably. I'll have a larger, more secure place for my work, with room for a small safe."

The closing hours of the day were beautiful. The air was still and cool, the white clouds turned pink tinged with gold. I was filled with contentment. "As far as I'm concerned, Mr. Douglas, all is well with the world."

"I'll second that, my dear."

Putting my arms about his arm, I settled my head on his shoulder. We rode that way in quiet togetherness.

Suddenly the sound of a gunshot split the air, then another. Grant grabbed his shoulder, then fought to hold the reins with his right hand as the horse jumped in fright. When the horse bolted sharply forward, I was thrown from the buggy. Dazed and in pain, I lay on the ground. If I tried to move, the pain in my left shoulder was enough to threaten my consciousness. Waves of pain also came from my left knee and hip.

People who gathered around were ready to move me, but I begged them not to until the extent of my injuries was determined. I asked them to see to Grant and help him bring back the buggy. It was hard to deal with the pain and remain conscious. Then I heard Grant's voice.

"Samantha, dear God. Are you all right? Where are you hurt?"

His dear face was before me. I smiled weakly. "You, what about you? Are you all right?"

He made a face. "I seem to have a bullet in my left shoulder. I managed to get the reins in my right hand to turn the buggy around and bring it back."

I managed to say, "I guess we can't call 911 and the paramedics, and there's no hospital here. What do we do now?"

"I sent a man to fetch Dr. Boyle. Just hold on, sweetheart. Try to relax, breathe deep and deal with the pain."

I closed my eyes and drifted away until I felt someone touch my shoulder. I managed to say, "Stop what you're doing! Don't touch me!"

A hand patted my other shoulder lightly and I heard a soothing voice say, "Just be quiet, little lady, and we'll find out just how badly you've been hurt."

Grant was there. "It's Dr. Boyle, Sam. He'll take good care of us."

Within a short time many helpful hands brought us to Hattie's where I evidently passed out. Next I heard Hattie's voice come through the fog. I was in my bed and she was sponging the dirt from my body.

"Don't you move now, Samantha. Just let me do the work and get you cleaned up so Dr. Boyle can look you over. He's in the parlor with Grant."

"What's wrong ... Grant?" I was barely able to form the words.

"Shush, Grant will be fine. He was shot in the shoulder, but the bullet went straight through. Soon as the doctor's through with him, he'll come up to see you."

"And me — what's wrong?"

"Doc says the fall from the buggy broke your collar bone. Your hip and knee are injured. We don't know how bad yet. Try not to worry and remember that things could be worse."

"But what happened? Shots ..."

Hattie said sternly, "Samantha, it looks like someone was trying to shoot you and Grant. Andrew's out looking around now to see who could have done it. He'll talk to Sheriff Parkins and get help. As soon as they figure out what happened, he'll be back."

I allowed myself to sink back into the painful darkness. My eyes closed and I rested until I felt a heavy bandage being wrapped about my left shoulder and chest. Dr. Boyle put a cup to my lips.

"Drink some of this, little lady, and it'll help dull the pain. The shoulder's in good shape, just a broken collar bone, and now I must check your knees and hip."

I clenched my teeth as he moved my left leg and pelvic area. Finally he stopped. "There doesn't seem to be any broken bones, but you wrenched those muscles pretty bad. It should only take a week or two to get you back on your feet. Meanwhile you'll have to stay in bed until your body heals."

"What about Grant?"

He patted my cheek. "Not to worry, little lady. That bullet went right through the flesh and missed the bones. Couldn't have been better if the shooter had tried."

Grant saw the doctor to the door, then rushed back to me. "You're the one I'm worried about. I'll be all right. My shoulder is a bit chewed up and painful. Walking around is no problem, though I won't be able to pitch for the Yankees this year." We traded smiles.

For the next week I was confined to bed, unable to walk and one arm out of commission. Hattie plied me with chicken soup and endless advice like a mother hen. With the wedding just four weeks away, she was concerned I wouldn't be able to stand for the ceremony.

"I'll make it," I said grimly, "even if someone has to carry me to the altar!"

One morning Grant and I had a moment alone. "Have you and Andrew found anything at all? What about Sheriff Parkins?"

He shook his head. "Parkins is the Barney Fife type of sheriff. Not too anxious to jump into action. He's good at putting the bad guys in jail and a hanging now and then, but he's a bit short on detective work. Andrew and I found out a few things by asking around." He frowned.

"Sam, if you think about it, who would be the instrument to get us out of the way?"

"The obvious answer is Orrin, but he's not the 'shoot 'em and get 'em out of my hair' type. It's clear now that he brought in Morgan Holly to remove any and all annoyances from his life."

"Just what Andrew and I decided. People say they've seen Morgan Holly roaming about town, away from his duties at the saloon. And just yesterday, Corby told me that the Colt .44 they keep behind the bar, I think you're familiar with that item, is missing. As far as Andrew is concerned, the case is closed, but we're not out of the woods."

I felt a spasm of fear. "We're being hunted. Someone has tried twice to harm us, and if it's Morgan Holly, then he's in as much trouble as we are. His work has not been done to Orrin's satisfaction. What can we do to protect ourselves?"

Grant knelt by the bed and took my hand. "My darling, we haven't come this far to have calamity take away our future. No way! I asked Parkins for help. He has a deputy who will stay here at the house during the day. We'll have to pay him something so he'll be enthusiastic about his assignment, but it's worth it. He'll be downstairs with his shotgun. Then Barnaby and I will take over and watch at night."

"And what about you? Who will look after you?"

"Barnaby has volunteered, also Andrew. So I'll have someone with me during the day."

As we were talking, Myra knocked on the bedroom door and announced, "There's a lady from the saloon who wants to talk to you."

After a moment, Maggie appeared at the door, fearful and concerned. "Us girls are so sorry 'bout what happened to you. Orrin'll kill me if he knows I'm here. I told everybody I was goin' to Hattie's to get some yardage. But Corby and I thought there was somethin' you should know. I'm so glad Mr. Douglas is here."

I patted a place on the bed. "Come, sit down and tell us what you know."

"Orrin's acting funny. He tried to tell Corby and me how bad he felt about your accident but it never seemed to come out right. And that Morgan person is still around, but we don't see 'em talking together. Corby said that yesterday Sheriff Parkins and Mr. Locke came in and had a secret talk with Orrin. Afterwards, when Corby was behind the saloon emptying some trash, he saw Orrin and Mr. Holly talkin' together. They weren't yellin', but they was pointin' fingers at each other and very angry. Corby got away real quick, but he wanted you to know."

It was another piece to add to the puzzle, and we were grateful for it. That evening Andrew arrived and we had a conference in my bedroom while he told us of his meeting with Orrin.

"Grant and I both talked to Sheriff Parkins and laid out our suspicions. Then Parkins came to see me, saying he thought I should be there, me being a lawyer and all. Actually, he was afraid to approach Orrin by himself, so I went along to back him up."

Grant made a disgusted noise. "How did it go?"

"You know Orrin," Andrew laughed, "smooth as glass and in control. He didn't quite put a hand over his heart and swear he had nothing to do with the fire at the brewery or the attempt on your lives. He claimed that Holly was in the saloon all those days and into the night, and why would he want to do such a thing? Parkins was willing to accept his story, but I made sure Orrin could see in my attitude that I did not believe him. Now Orrin knows what we know — that Morgan Holly is suspected, and that Orrin may have given the order. After we left the saloon, I made this clear to Parkins in case he didn't catch on. He said he or a deputy will drop by the saloon now and then to let Orrin know that he hasn't been forgotten."

Grant slapped his knee. "Well done! Orrin has been confronted and the next move is up to him. Still, Sam and I will be on our guard from now on."

After the first week, I was able to stand but not too steadily
. Some of my progress was due to Wong Kee and the herbs and
potions he sent with the Waiter Girls when they came to visit. With
the help of Myra and Hattie, his hot packs were applied to my knee
and hip morning and evening. Also, another potion, mixed with
water, enabled me to sleep comfortably each night.

The next bulletin came from Willis who stopped Grant on
the street. Orrin was seen outside the rear door to the saloon in a
heated argument with Morgan Holly. He was handing him money
and pointing the way out of town. It seems Orrin had to pay him,
not for the failed assignments for which he was brought from San
Francisco, but to absent himself from Boone Valley where questions
about the incident were still being whispered.

Willis also gleefully described the disappointment of the
saloon regulars who came to hear me play. Willis, plus the Grayson
sisters and their lovely voices, filled the bill. After hours they put
their heads together and practiced an acceptable program of songs,
then offered them each afternoon. The customers loved them, and
Orrin had no choice but to accept the changes.

Rainbow and Warren were watching all of this. That they
might have lost two major people in their lives frightened them.
They followed Hattie and Myra about the house, asking over and
over if Grant and I would be all right. The answers were soothing
and consoling and the children became part of the Samantha and
Grant get-well team.

Myra's daily presence kept the household running smoothly,
even though my care and comfort added to her duties. The children
helped by bringing meals to my room, then sitting on the bed as I
ate and told them stories. They assisted Myra and Hattie whenever
asked, and brought me bouquets of blooming spring flowers as they
found them.

Grant reported one evening that Operation Dream Come

True was resuming and would be ready within a week. He rubbed his left shoulder and said, "I'm not much use except for pointing to the work or holding one end of a board. The men I found are working well. They did a fine job on the brewery, and they're determined to make our deadline."

Within two weeks I was able to walk carefully, and the use of my left arm was slowly reviving. Grant assisted my first trip down the stairs to the kitchen. Later that night we had a celebration. Andrew, Myra, Charlie, Barnaby, Warren, Rainbow and Ida Penny were there. Hattie fixed a wonderful dinner. Andrew brought wine for us and sarsaparilla for the children. There were toasts all around. The conversation that night was animated. During a break, Ida said, "Remind me to measure the children for their wedding outfits. Don't know if they'll fit into the ones I made for Maggie and Corby's wedding. They're sproutin' up like weeds!"

"So they are," Grant admitted and turned to the children. "How old are you now, youngsters? Your birthdays must have slipped by us this past year. When were you born?"

Rainbow and Warren sadly shook their heads. Warren muttered, "Don't have no birthdays, never did. We're not exactly sure when we were born."

This drew expressions of surprise and disappointment from everyone. Barnaby said, "I'm a-guessin' that Rainbow is 7 years old — and Warren is a big boy of 10."

I chimed in with, "Why don't we give them a birthday party right now! Then they can each pick a date and we'll know when to celebrate next year."

Grant turned to the children. "How about it, partners? Out of 365 days in the year, which one would you like to be especially yours?"

The children were confused. Selecting a date on such short notice was asking much of them, and they frowned, concentrating.

Everyone at the table was silent. Then Warren raised his head and smiled.

"I would like my day to be the one when we found Mis' Samantha on the stairs, sound asleep. That was ...," then he looked at me in confusion.

"As I remember, my dear, that date was the 20th of August."

His face brightened. "That's right. That's the one I want. August 20th! I remember that day real good, Mis' Samantha, and you've been extra special nice to us ever since." He sat back, satisfied with his decision. Everyone applauded, and I began to wipe the tears that filled my eyes.

"I'm very honored, dear Warren."

Hattie also wiped away a few tears at that exchange. Grant kissed me on the cheek and whispered, "That would have been my choice too!"

All eyes then went to Rainbow who was still deep in thought. The expression on her face suddenly brightened. "I know what day I want." She cocked her head to one side. "What is the first day of the year called?"

Grant gave the answer the dignity and assurance she needed.

"That, my dear Rainbow, is called New Year's Day, or the first day of the year. January first."

Rainbow beamed. "I like that day 'cause that's when you can start a whole new year, and you get to tell of the good things you want to happen."

We all congratulated her thoughtful choice. Just then Hattie arrived with a cake bearing one candle in the middle. "I made this for dessert, but now it seems it will serve a better purpose." And we all sang Happy Birthday and watched the two children blow the candle out together.

Grant took the cue, got to his feet. "We officially declare that Rainbow and Warren now have their very own birth dates. May each year's celebration bring happiness as they, and their loved ones, come together."

Hattie solemnly lit the candle as I leaned close to Grant to say, "Wouldn't it be wonderful to be with them 25 years from now, to know them as adults with their families ?"

He clasped my hand firmly and said, "If we have any faith in your Universe, I pray it will indeed be so."

Later that night Andrew stopped by, hoping to spend some time with Myra. Their chance meetings were developing into comfortable exchanges. When his attention finally turned to me, he looked concerned. "Things are not going well at the saloon. Morgan Holly is out of the picture, but now the girls have new concerns."

He told me about Orrin's new form of retribution and how disturbing it was to the girls. It seems that Orrin was on a new tack. During whispered conversations one night with men seated at various tables, he intimated that he had bedded all of his Waiter Girls, especially Flower whom he described as a "dainty little dish."

This caused the pleasant verbal sparring between customers and the girls to change, and now they were the targets of slurs and bawdy remarks. Needless to say, morale had fallen and tempers risen. The girls served the drinks silently and somberly, and the joy and fun of their jobs was now totally absent. Corby told us later that the girls were often close to tears when they picked up drinks from the bar. Flower was devastated and feared that Robert would hear the trashy things that were said about her.

During our conversation I asked Corby to give the girls a message from me.

"Tell them to treat all of this like it's not important. They should smile and serve the customers like always, and when anyone made an improper remark, have the girls reply pleasantly, 'Sounds to me like you've been listening to fairy tales,' or 'You really shouldn't believe such nonsense,' or 'My, my, I never heard of anything so silly.' Then they should walk away. If they don't react to those rude remarks, the fun will be gone and things should get back to normal."

Later I asked Andrew how Willis and the sisters were doing with the afternoon programs. "Just wonderful. You're missed, of course, but the three of them manage to keep things lively in the afternoons. And what about you? When do you think you'll be able to play again?"

"Well, my shoulder is sore but my fingers are fine, so I should be able to come back next Monday. Would you mind telling Orrin?"

"I'd be delighted!" he said. "He'll have mixed feelings about your return."

The next morning I found Grant's reaction to my returning to work was far from enthusiastic, but he knew it was time. I could tell he had news, and I waited patiently.

"Sam, it's time for another quick trip to Sacramento to check the work on the property. Barnaby and I will go by horseback, which will be faster than a wagon. We'll leave tomorrow morning and be back in four or five days, Thursday at the very latest. The deputy will see that you get to and from the saloon safely, then Andrew will be here in the evenings until I return."

I was worried, but how could I have stopped him? He was juggling work on the brewery, Operation Dream Come True, and the details at the ranch. All of his experience as an executive gave him the tools and planning skills that allowed this. I know he had considered all aspects and it was a high-level challenge he seemed to thrive on. Then he reminded me, "There's some business that should be taken care of before I leave. I'll go over to the Wild Rose and clear the way for Marina. We lost some time when we were injured, so I'll take care of this right away."

He gave me a kiss, taking care not to embrace my left shoulder, then left saying, "I'll come back in a flash with the cash!"

Myra came to the bedroom to ask if I needed anything. I requested some hot tea, then asked, "Is the deputy downstairs and is he watching over everything as he should?"

"If sittin' in the parlor all day and eating us out of house and home is watching over us, then he's doing a good job. I feed that man when he comes in the morning, then before I even finish making lunch for everyone, he's digging into it. It's a wonder there's anythin' left for the rest of us."

I shook my head. "That man is being paid to keep us safe, and sitting in one room, and stuffing himself isn't the way to do it. Make sure that he stays where he is until Grant returns. Tell him that Mr. Douglas wants to have a talk with him. As soon as Grant comes, take him aside and tell him what you have just told me."

Myra smiled. "That I'll be pleased to do!"

Grant returned two hours later and had much to tell me. But I had the first question. "Did Myra fill you in on the lack of vigilance offered by our special guard?"

"That she did, and our protector and I had quite a talk. Rather, I talked and he listened. He's probably never been brought up short and given the word as thoroughly as I gave it to him."

"Good for you! Tell me more."

"He was informed that in order to earn the money we will pay him, he is to patrol the outside of the house every half hour, and while inside, he is to check the area through the downstairs windows every hour. Then, and only when this is done as scheduled, he will be fed when the food is prepared, not before or after."

"How did he take your instructions?"

"I think it was hard for him to swallow, but he got the message."

"And what about seeing Tom Maloney at the Wild Rose about bringing Marina over here?

"That was another interesting meeting, and here's what happened."

Chapter Thirty-Four

Grant's report on his meeting with Tom Maloney at the Wild Rose was factual, except for Maloney's heavy use of cuss words, which he took care to edit. The bargaining back and forth took some time. Maloney was shrewd and determined to gain what Grant was willing to offer, then double it to his advantage.

Like most saloon owners, he felt the girls were his property and a large percentage of his business. Grant pointed out that Marina was not one of the girls, but merely played background music. She provided no income, but Maloney was not about to let her go easily. The bargaining tool was barrels of beer, the mainstay of Maloney's business, and he demanded that three barrels of beer be delivered, without charge to him, each week for a year.

"It took some horse trading, but I finally got him down to three barrels a week for six months, plus one gallon of good bourbon each month, which is hard to get in any quantity these days. Maloney has had trouble finding a reliable source."

I asked, "Do you have some hidden away?"

Grant looked pleased with himself. "No, but I know a fellow in San Francisco who offered me bourbon at $2.50 a gallon. I bought one and it wasn't bad. It's not as available as whiskey or rye, but I'll have him send me a wagon load, and what I don't trade with Maloney, I can easily sell to other saloons, or give to my crew at the brewery for Christmas."

"So the deal was made, but it sounds like you'll be paying a rather high price."

"Not so. Once the repairs are done at the brewery, I can produce the additional beer with no trouble. There is space for two new vats. I've been wanting to increase the output anyway."

"Well, good for you, fella. And how about Marina? When will Maloney let her go?"

"She'll be free the Monday before the wedding, so you'll have a week to train her. And one more thing. Maloney has demonstrated more than once that he has a vicious temper. I made it clear that if we find any bruises or marks on Marina, the deal is off. He didn't take kindly to that condition, but he shrugged his shoulders and we shook on it."

We spent the rest of that day together. First Grant wanted to give Chet his orders. When we entered the parlor, Chet was spread out on the settee, feet crossed, hands behind his head, and his rifle leaning against the velvet covering. His sandy hair was disheveled; the flannel shirt, tan vest and pants were dusty and wrinkled. On seeing Grant, Chet jumped to his feet and stood awkwardly before us.

"Hard on the job, I see," Grant said dryly.

"Sorry, Mr. Douglas. I was just takin' a rest."

"And do you rest very often when you're on the job?"

Chet looked down at the floor and shuffled his feet in embarrassment. "No, sir."

Grant shook his head then got down to business. "Here are your instructions for this coming week. Do you think you can handle them?"

"Sure can, Mr. Douglas."

"Starting Monday you are to help Mrs. Malcolm down the stairs for breakfast, and then see that she gets to the saloon by noon. Mr. Locke will be here with a buggy to drive you both there. Is that clear so far?"

"Oh yes, Mr. Douglas."

"All right. Once she enters the saloon, you are to watch her every minute until Mr. Locke comes for her at 6 o'clock to bring her back here. Then you'll be done for the day. Have you got it?"

"Yes, sir. I'll take good care of her."

Grant looked at him for a second, then sighed. "Chet, if you take extra good care of Mrs. Malcolm in the coming weeks, there might be a small bonus in it for you. Will that help to give her your full protection?"

Chet enthusiastically responded, "You bet, Mr. Douglas. I'll take real good care of her."

"All right. I'm depending on you. I'll take over now and you can go until Monday morning."

Chet was out of the door like a shot. By the time he said, "Yes sir, Mr. Douglas," he was out of sight.

Hattie, Rainbow and Warren retired, and Grant and I spent the night sitting quietly in the parlor. Other than the time he spent checking the doors and windows, these were precious moments until Barnaby came to the kitchen door at 5 a.m.

Barnaby was holding the reins of two robust, handsome horses. He was smiling, eager to be off. Hattie was beside me, yawning. "Look at Barnaby and Grant. They're like a couple of kids going out into the world!" We smiled and waved until they were out of sight, then Hattie helped me to my room to join Rainbow in my bed for some sleep.

Sunday was a day of rest and time with the children. We had fun singing songs, telling stories, and discussing the weddings, which was a special, happy event for them. Little by little we were slipping into parent/child relationships. They accepted our guidance and training, and in turn did all they could to help. Rainbow had been sleeping in Hattie's bed while I was bedridden, but now she wanted to return to that quiet time in my bed when we shared so many secrets.

Her prayers were filled with concern for Grant and me. Her view of life was no longer just Warren and herself, but included everyone around her. She happily shared herself, her observations and discoveries. We found she also shared her time with Charlie, who didn't fully understand all she was trying to teach him, but he loved the attention. It was a good time for all three children. No darkness, no interruptions. Just a quiet, orderly household.

After Sunday service, Hattie and I met with Della Norton to discuss the wedding reception. Della was quick to suggest, "Why not have everyone come right over here after the wedding. We can serve much easier right from the kitchen. The tables and chairs can be arranged so there'll be plenty of room. Anyway, Luke and me decided to close the café most of the day because we're so busy with all three weddings. The reception here could last until three, then we'll put everything back and get ready for the dinner business."

Another problem solved. Things were working out just as if that wedding day was really meant to happen. Could it be that the Universe or our angels were stepping in to make our dreams come true, in spite of setbacks or physical limitations?

Ida arrived at Hattie's with our lovely wedding gowns. My dress was a deep rose silk with ecru lace covering the high collar and around the three-quarter sleeves. Rosettes of the lace were scattered about the full skirt. I stood quietly as Ida did a final fitting. Hattie remarked, "Samantha, wearing that dress, you're going to be the prettiest bride this town has ever seen, and that's a fact."

"They'll be busy admiring you, Hattie. Those colors are so flattering." Hattie's dress was a soft blue velvet with black lace across the shoulders and down the full sleeves. Ida's creations were as stylish as anything whipped up in the Parisian fashion houses, if they existed in 1853.

The colorful dress Rainbow wore for Maggie's wedding was let out and the hem lowered. The ribbons would once more adorn her pretty red hair. Warren, on the other hand, had grown so much he would need a new white shirt and black tie, and long black pants befitting a soon-to-be young man.

"I can do all this in no time," Ida declared. "Also I saved the satin pillow for Warren to carry the rings, and the basket to hold the flower petals for Rainbow to scatter." Since it was summer, we assured Rainbow there would be an abundance of wild flowers on the surrounding hills to fill her basket.

Monday morning Chet reported to work just as Myra and Charlie arrived. His hair was nicely combed for a change, and his clothes much improved — clean and orderly. After breakfast, he patrolled the outside of the house, then inspected the downstairs to make sure all was well. As planned, Andrew arrived with the buggy just before noon to transport me to the saloon. He allowed himself time to have a cup of coffee while Myra worked about the kitchen. "Andrew," I asked, "how did Orrin take the news that I would be returning to work today?"

"He's a strange man. He just looked at me without a word, trying to decide what to say."

"And what notable words did he finally utter?"

"Ready for this? He just said, 'It's about time,' and walked away. That man never has a pleasant word to say about anything, at least within my hearing."

At 11:30 I made my way, with Chet's clumsy assistance, into the saloon kitchen. It was not easy using a cane with a full skirt. I motioned to Chet to sit at one of the tables and wait. He shrugged his shoulders and sat.

Wong Kee turned from his work to greet me, almost smiling. He bowed with respect. "You use stick. You better now?" We talked quietly.

"Almost," I answered. "My shoulder is healing and I can play again, but the knee and hip are still painful. At least I can walk. And that young man over there will guard me until things get better."

"Fine you here. Bad things behind you."

"And what about you, Wong Kee? Are you all right? Is there any news?"

He glanced at the door. "Everything good. I find nice young man for when I go. Teach him cooking. He be ready."

"When will you tell Orrin you'll be leaving his fine saloon?"

"Maybe day before. Then show him young Chinese boy can cook. He no like, too bad!"

For the first time the corners of his mouth turned up ever so slightly. I clapped my hands and laughed with him.

"You are coming to the wedding, aren't you?"

His smile was gone and he was back to his calm and stoic exterior. "Mistah Smithas be mad."

"You're probably right. Grant and I will tell you all about it. "We'll even save you a piece of wedding cake. Once we get to our new home, we'll be able to say and do what we want without Orrin watching us."

"That be good. Very happy time. Yes!"

"It may be a year or more before we all can leave Boone Valley for the farm, but that really will be a happy time."

"My people patient. Can wait for good to come. You and Mistah Douglas bring much happiness." He bowed again.

"It's a day we're all looking forward to, my friend."

Just then Orrin came through the door, ready to argue or harass. "Well, are you going to get your butt out there and get to work? People are waitin' and here you are jawing with this heathen." His long arm and bony finger pointed at the kitchen door. "Git!"

I smiled sweetly and pointed to Chet. "This young man is a sheriff's deputy who will guard me from now on. Don't be surprised if he's in here for coffee, or a drink or two from the bar. I hope this meets with your approval."

Orrin had nothing to say, but I did. "By the way, Orrin, my

replacement, Marina, will report for work the Monday before I leave. I hope there will be room for her by that time, and that this, too, will meet with your approval."

His look of exasperation was a work of art, but he did not answer.

"And now I will do as you bid, oh great master. I go now to play for your customers, for which I am handsomely paid."

Even with a cane, I made a regal exit.

My self-esteem was vastly improved when Chet opened the door leading to the saloon and I was met by cheers and applause. Corby rushed to grab my right arm and guide me through the crowded tables.

"They been waitin' for you to come back."

"But how did they know I was coming today?"

Corby smiled his crooked smile. "Oh, I dunno. Word must've got around."

Taking his role seriously, Chet placed a chair close to the piano, then sat, arms folded and looking important.

I stood to greet the smiling men. Raising my right arm to quiet them, I was able to say, "Thank you, thank you so much for coming today. I'm very happy to be back."

There was more applause as I awkwardly sat before the piano ready to play. What would be appropriate for such a special day in my life? I hadn't touched a keyboard since the accident, so I took a moment to massage my stiff hands and fingers until my memory presented the perfect choice. I raised my hands to the keyboard to play and sing:

"I've got the world on a string,
Sittin' on a rainbow,
Got the string around my finger.
Lucky me, can't you see, I'm in love."

It felt good playing and singing those happy words. I had played that particular song only once, but I found joy in developing the chords, changing keys. Like a kid in a sandbox, I let the notes sift through my fingers. A kaleidoscope of emotions went through my mind. In spite of the fire at the brewery, the attack on Grant and me, the pain and discomfort we were enduring, I could take heart in the wedding, the wonderful days to come, and the new life that was waiting.

I didn't remember ever having such a warm sweep of emotions. I felt strong and ready to accept all that had happened. These must be some of the many lessons I was destined to learn. I had survived so far, and was ready for whatever additional lessons the Universe still had in store for me.

All of this was going through my mind as I played that day. I ended the program with, what else, "Send in the Clowns." Orrin entered the room as if on cue!

During the halfway break, I stood at the bar talking with Willis and Corby. I filled them in on Marina's arrival date. They quietly assured me that Morgan Holly seemed to be far from Boone Valley. Upon learning that Chet would be guarding me for as long as necessary, Corby grabbed a beer stein, filled it to the top and handed it to Chet.

"You take good care of this lady, d'ya hear me? We think a lot of her and don't want nothin' else to happen to her."

Chet, gulping down the cool beer, nodded and managed to say, "Yes, sir, I sure will. You can bet on it!"

After the concert, Andrew took us back to Hattie's where Warren, Rainbow and Hattie were anxious to hear about the day. Chet went on his way, and Andrew was persuaded to stay to dinner. Myra helped in the kitchen and then cleaned up. Andrew loved the excuse to see her again, and to escort her and Charlie safely to their shack.

After their departure, I was free to describe to Hattie and the children how everyone except Orrin was happy to see me. Hattie asked me to play "World on a String" Rainbow loved the song, especially the part about the rainbow. As I finished, she begged, "Play it again, please.," And I did, but after the third chorus, I begged off and very slowly made my way up the stairs to bed. I was still rather sore and it had been a long day.

And so the days slowly passed. Wednesday came and went without incident, and Thursday. The programs were well attended since it was known that I would leave at the end of the month. Willis passed the word that my replacement was extremely talented, and Corby and Elmo did the same when Orrin wasn't around. I dearly wanted Marina to be warmly accepted.

Thursday night, after the children were settled in their beds, Hattie and I relaxed in the parlor. There was a series of rapid knocks on the front door that persisted until Hattie opened the door. There stood two very tired, bedraggled but smiling men.

"Open the door, woman. Your weary travelers have returned from their crusade and we're demanding food and drink to revive us!" Grant rushed through the door, then covered me in a strong and smelly hug. Barnaby was occupied administering a similar enthusiastic greeting to Hattie. He had never before openly demonstrated his affection, but he was getting the hang of it and Hattie thoroughly enjoyed this new side of him.

I joined in the revelry. "Welcome, weary travelers, and tell us what dangers you faced along the way. Were you attacked by bandits, and did you fight them off? You look and smell like you had dealings with hungry bears or aggravated skunks. Tell us everything as we bring you food and drink."

The men drew water from the pump at the kitchen sink and began to wash away some of the dirt from their travels. Hattie put on a huge pot of coffee, and I began making sandwiches.

"Tell us, kind travelers," I said, "did you rescue any maidens on your journey, or fight off varlets anxious to steal your purse? What adventures did you share?"

Grant was laughing as he took a seat at the kitchen table. "Be not alarmed, dear ladies. There was hand-to-hand combat but we fought them off bravely. These we will tell you about later. First, the purpose of our journey."

"Yes," I laughed. "Enough of this nonsense. Let's get down to facts. How did it go?"

Between bites, Grant began. "We checked in with Oliver Lundy, the land agent, who told us the land markers outlining the property are in place, and wells have been located. Lumber and tools have been set out so construction on the buildings and wind-mills can begin. He found four qualified men, totally broke after arriving in San Francisco by ship. Oliver arranged to pay them in full when the work was completed, so that way they'll see the pro-ject through to the end before moving on."

He took a large bite from his sandwich, sipped some coffee, then smiled at me. "Sam, you'll never guess what I've done!"

"Do I have to guess, or will you just tell me right away?"

"I think it's marvelous. Oliver took me right out to the prop-erty and insisted on showing me another plot of land adjacent to ours that runs all the way north to the river. It's 400 acres of rich soil, beautiful, filled with trees, and for only $200. Now, how could I turn it down?"

"Of course you couldn't." I was as excited as he was. "We can go there in the summer for picnics, and swim and fish. It sounds wonderful and I do approve very, very much." And I gave him a kiss of appreciation.

Hattie turned to Barnaby. "And you, my dear, what happened to you?"

He looked guilty. "I admit, my dear, that buying land in such a fine location was tempting. But it seemed to me that we can find good property wherever we settle. We really haven't talked about what kind of a homestead we would like, or even where, have we?"

"That's true enough, my dear."

"But what would you want? A stylish house, or something similar to what Sam and Grant are planning? Would you like a farm, or ranch, or place in town?"

Hattie patted his arm. "My dear, we both have had plenty of years of hard work. We grew up doing all those chores, milking cows, tending the chickens. You worked plenty hard all these years on your claims, and I've had my share working at the stores in Missouri and here. I think I'm ready to just relax in a pretty house, just doing what's comfortable."

Barnaby added, "Then let's wait till we get to Missouri and see how our kin are doing. Then we should look around Missouri or other states to find just the right location."

Hattie nodded. "That sounds right to me, Barnaby. No telling what we'll be wanting until we've been there awhile."

I couldn't help but comment, "Isn't it wonderful you two have reached a point in your lives where money is no worry and you can settle anywhere you like."

Barnaby sighed, "That's exactly what I been dreamin' about all those years I was diggin' for gold." And looking fondly at Hattie, he declared, "And I sure struck gold in more ways than I ever dreamed of!"

Chapter Thirty-Five

The work on Ida's house was almost finished. All the workers were true to their oaths of silence. One day Grant came to dinner a bit dirty and exhausted, but with good news.

"Today we completed the exterior work. The finishing touches on the interior — shelves, window frames, and a wardrobe — will be done early next week."

Hattie slapped the table. "Well, that's gonna work out just fine. When you're done, my clerk, Jim, and Barnaby can take over what Samantha and I put aside. The sheets, blankets, pillows, towels, soap, and other things will be in place so Flower and Robert can move right in after their wedding. Think we can get it all done by Wednesday morning, Samantha?"

"Easily. However, we haven't been able to find one important item — a mattress. Hattie's store hasn't had any for months, so where do we find one? We'll have to do better than a canvas bag filled with straw."

Grant raised his eyebrows in thought. "I have a few resources. Let me see what I can do."

Barnaby commented, "Grant sure knows his way around town. He'll come up with somethin', for sure."

Grant's shoulder was almost healed, but twinges in my collar bone were a constant reminder of that injury. As for my knee and hip, there were still remnants of pain and discomfort. However, my mobility was improving and I could now get about without the cane. Grant and I hoped our march down the aisle would be smooth and easy. At this point it wasn't clear.

Sunday after church, Grant and I, with Hattie and Barnaby,

reviewed the details of our wedding day with Rev. Norton. The vows he suggested were loving and thoughtfully woven into the ceremony. Grant and I agreed they were just right. The ceremony I once shared with Harland was far from my memory and I could not recall them nor my feelings at that time. It was just as well.

Early Wednesday, Hattie and I went to Ida's to check on Operation Dream Come True. The four-poster bed Grant put together was already in place. Soon after, Grant and Barnaby arrived at the front door, holding a mattress and looking quite pleased with themselves.

"Where on earth did you find that?" I asked.

As they placed the mattress on the bed, Grant answered, "Well, where do you find mattresses these days? At a hotel! I ran into Dave Bannon yesterday and a light went on in my head. I asked the right questions and he said he might have a few mattresses stored at his hotel. We did a little bargaining and I convinced him to find one for me. We met with him this morning and, by golly, we struck gold!"

"And how many barrels of beer did this cost you?"

"Sam, it was a gentleman's agreement, but the final negotiation included a gallon of bourbon, so you see things worked out just as they should."

Hattie and I covered the bed with fresh linens, a blanket and the new comforter. Barnaby put the colorful calico curtains from Ida over the windows. Grant donated two chairs and a small cabinet on which we put a matching calico covering. We added a shining blue-and-white china pitcher and basin, and a mirror on the wall just above it.

We stood together reviewing the final effort with pride. Hattie observed, "This turned out to be a mighty nice room, and those two youngsters should be very happy here."

I moved to hug Grant. "My dear, your brainstorm turned

out very nicely. What a wonderful way for Flower and Robert to start their new life together. And best of all, dear Ida will finally have a family of her own."

Barnaby added, "And they will have everything goin' right in their lives for a change." Hattie moved to give him a loving hug. "How does it feel," I asked her, "to be a fairy godmother and help make this dream come true?"

Hattie shook her head. "I never met up with one myself, but if they feel as fine as I do, I can see why they fly about doing good deeds."

The following Monday morning Grant and I drove to the Wild Rose. Leaving me in the buggy, he entered the saloon and within minutes assisted Marina through the door. Her hands were empty except for a Bible she carried close to her bosom, and she wore the same black dress as before. Her face was solemn and her body seemed clenched about the Bible. Grant gently guided her onto the buggy next to me.

"Where are her belongings, her luggage?"

Grant shook his head. "Maloney insisted that's how she came. Just the clothes on her back and nothing more. We know this was not the case, but I wasn't about to make an issue of it."

I put my arm around Marina's slim shoulders. "It's all right, my dear. Everything will get better from now on."

She replied softly, "I'm very grateful to leave there. Anything would be better, thank you."

We drove directly to Hattie's store where we bought a suitcase and quickly filled it with stockings, cotton undergarments and petticoats, shoes, a comb and brush set, soap and toilet water. Thank goodness we knew the proprietor who gave us a generous discount! She also elected to help us welcome Marina to her new life.

Grant dropped us at Ida's shop where Marina was greeted with Ida's usual warm manner. Once Marina was settled with a cup of tea, Ida darted into the storage area. Marina watched with wonder as Ida, with help from Hattie and me, reviewed the bolts of material she brought out. We chose two, but Marina protested. "For many years I wear the darker or black colors my mother chooses. We did not wear bright colors at our home."

Ida held up a soft green brocade next to Marina's pale face. "My dear, just look how this shade will bring more color into your lovely face. And this pink velveteen will be striking against your skin. You'll be lovely to look at when you're playing your beautiful music."

Marina stroked the rich materials with her slender white hands and sighed. "Never have I anything so pretty. But how can I repay you for such beautiful things?"

Hattie said kindly, "We can work that out later. For now Samantha and I want you to have everything you need for the new job ahead of you."

After taking Marina's measurements, Ida brought out a simple calico dress in a maroon and blue pattern. She eyed Marina's slight figure. "I'm sure this will fit you, and it's something to wear until your other clothes are ready. Please take it with my blessing."

Marina was overcome. "It is so pretty. I never have a dress with so many colors. You are a good woman, and I am grateful for your kindness."

Ida then brought out a lovely polished cotton gown with soft flowers of pink and rose all over. The simple collar and short, full puffed sleeves were trimmed with a delicate white lace.

"This is Flower's wedding gown," she said proudly. "She wanted something simple and plain, but that sweet girl truly deserves a wedding dress as pretty as she is. I do hope she is pleased with it."

What a sweet lady. "Ida, you have a beautiful and loving heart, and it is reflected in this dress. Flower cannot help but be very happy when she wears it."

Ida insisted that Marina spend the day with her. As she walked us outside her shop, she said, "Marina and I can get acquainted. And from the looks of her, I'll bet she'd like a nice hot bath before she tries on the new dress."

I kissed Ida's cheek. "You're such a thoughtful lady. It's just what Marina needs right now, to pamper herself, and to be in a quiet environment. I have a feeling you all will be good friends in no time." Ida's sweet smile sent me on my way.

It was only a five-minute walk from Ida's to the saloon, so we took it slow and easy with my sore hip. Following my concert, Grant and I headed for Hattie's. The house was flooded with beautiful music that could be heard even before we opened the front door. Marina was at the piano playing, and Barnaby, Ida, Myra and the children were sitting quietly, mesmerized by music they had never heard before. Resounding chords filled the room to bursting. I had forgotten that the classics could be so passionate. Quietly Grant and I found seats and listened until half an hour later when the concert came to a close.

Marina turned from the piano and was actually smiling. She was dressed in the new calico dress, her hair freshly washed and arranged, and she was truly a lovely young lady. Her body now reflected dignity and pride in her talent, which was enormous. The butterfly that she could be was evolving and, praise be, she could now go forward into happier existence.

Grant offered to let Marina stay at his place and he would bunk with Andrew until a room was provided for her at the Majestic. After dinner, I had a moment to talk with her before it was time for them to go.

"When you were studying in Rome, did you present any recitals on your own?"

She shook her head. "These were done with others to show

our progress. The teachers were very strict. We must play well in order to continue our studies. I was able to go forward until my father brought me here."

I acknowledged, "You must have worked very hard to do so well."

"My mother wanted me to do best I can, so I practice many long hours to please her."

"She must have been very proud of you."

Marina nodded sadly in reply.

The next morning, an hour before my time to play, I brought Marina to the saloon, introduced her to Wong Kee, then settled her at one of the tables in the kitchen. Chet, still my constant watchdog, sat at a nearby table with a cup of coffee while I went to find Orrin. He was leaning against the bar, talking with Corby. He stopped when he saw me and said in measured tones, "Why the hell are you so early?"

"I came early so you could meet Marina, the young lady who will replace me. Do you have a minute to come into the kitchen and talk with us?"

"What's on your busy mind now? Something to annoy me?"

"No, Orrin. On the contrary. I promise it won't hurt a bit."

Orrin followed me into the kitchen to the table where Marina was waiting. She rose to her feet as we approached.

"Orrin, this is Marina Riccardi from Italy. She's a very talented pianist and I think you'll be pleased with the music she can bring to the afternoon concerts. Marina, this is Orrin Smithers, owner of the Majestic."

Marina bowed her head and said softly, "It is an honor to meet you, Mr. Smithers."

Orrin was taken aback by her beauty and manners. He managed to say, "Pleased to meetcha, Miss Riccardi."

He sat at the table and gestured for us to join him.

I began. "Marina is available to begin the afternoon pro-grams. I would like to suggest that starting today, she be here while I play so people will get to know her. During my break she can introduce the music she plays so well. She can do that every day until Saturday, when she will present her first full program from noon to six. Does this meet with your approval?"

Orrin was almost speechless. He was being asked, nicely, for something, and he was so impressed by Marina that he only ges-tured with one hand.

"Ah, yes, you have my approval. Good idea."

Marina smiled shyly. "You are most kind."

I said, "Marina plays mostly classical music. Willis and I can work with her to develop a wider range of popular music. Then she can structure her programs in a way that would be most pleasing to the men who come to listen."

Orrin looked as if he were considering an important ques-tion, then agreed. "That sounds all right to me — for now. If there are any problems, we can talk it over."

Marina smiled, "That would be most kind of you."

Then I added, "And one more thing, Orrin."

Orrin stiffened, but I smiled and asked, "Will you have a room here where Miss Riccardi can live, or are they all filled right now? Could she take over Flower's room after her wedding on Sunday?"

Orrin was on the verge of expressing his displeasure with Flower's marriage and departure, but he wisely put it aside. "If Miss Riccardi has somewhere to stay until Sunday afternoon, I suppose she can have Flower's room."

Our meeting with Orrin ended with an air of harmonious agreement, and for once I watched him leave the kitchen in a mood different from the high dudgeons he did so well.

It was still 30 minutes before my program, so I guided Marina to the bar where I introduced her to Corby and Elmo. The men were their usual gallant selves and warmly welcomed her. Then one by one as the Waiter Girls picked up drinks at the bar, they met Marina and were pleased to add her to their group. During all this, Chet sat in a chair close to my piano and waited patiently.

Next I found Willis sitting at a table near the stage. As we approached, he rose from his chair.

"Marina, this is the man who first told me about you and how impressed he was with your talent. He set in motion the idea of your playing here at the Majestic. This is Willis Weatherby, and I'm sure you two will enjoy working together."

Marina extended her slender hand to Willis. "You were most kind to think of me and make it possible to leave the Wild Rose. A most unhappy place. Thank you!"

Willis shyly shook her hand. "It's our good luck that you'll be playing such fine music here."

I interrupted. "Excuse me while I go to work. I'm sure you have much to talk about. I predict you two will play the finest music ever to be found in these mountains. And Willis, Marina will play during my break today, so would you please escort her over to the piano when it's time?"

"I'd sure be glad to," he answered.

They were shyly, quietly conversing as I walked away.

At intermission, Marina joined me at the piano, and I stood to address the assembled crowd.

"Gentlemen, it is my great pleasure to introduce Marina Riccardi who will replace me starting this Saturday. What she will play for you will be quite different, but I guarantee it will be most enjoyable. Please give your full attention to Miss Riccardi as she plays her first selection for you."

With a slight bow, Marina sat at the piano and began. What she played was bright, happy, and filled with rippling runs and chords. The men had never heard anything quite like it and they listened with great interest. When she played the last chords, they responded with thunderous approval.

During the clamor, I spotted Orrin leaning against the bar and nodding his head faintly in agreement. At that moment he seemed pleased. Behind his back Corby and Elmo were signaling and applauding quietly. As Marina walked away from the piano, she was surrounded by the Waiter Girls who made clear their acceptance. All except Zola. Of course she kept her usual distance.

Everything went well those last few days before my departure. As a surprise for Friday's program, Marina and I worked on a duet to knock their socks off. We sat at Hattie's piano, giggling and experimenting with what we could play. Since I was not as proficient in playing the composers she knew so well, and the music I knew wasn't grand enough, we finally hit upon Schubert's "Ave Maria." Of course I played the easier upper keys, and Marina played the rolling chord pattern on the lower keys. We had great fun putting it together, and could hardly wait for Friday.

At one point during our rehearsals, she stopped. "Samantha, I just now realize it's been long time since I ever laugh like this. You have done so much for me since I leave the Wild Rose, but I just now think this is the best gift of all. You show me how to laugh again, and bring more happy into my life."

As she spoke my eyes filled with tears. "There is one more thing to teach you, Marina, and I hope you learn it well."

"What can it be, Samantha?"

"This," and I leaned over and gave her a gentle hug. "This is a hug, and you'll be getting a lot of them from now on. You'll get them from the children, and all of us who know you. And after a while, you'll be giving them without hesitating. There's a saying where I come from — everyone needs at least two hugs a day to keep you going, and at least two more to help you grow."

She laughed softly. "This I will try to do."

Each evening that week Marina came to Hattie's for dinner, then took over the piano to share the gift of her considerable talent. Bach, Beethoven, Mozart, Liszt — all the great piano masters were played for us.

On Friday every table and chair was filled with miners, shopkeepers, and others who had come many times to hear my music. They came to see the passing of the afternoon programs from one pianist to another. I couldn't have been more pleased as I walked out and took my place at the piano.

Before sitting down, I turned to the audience and announced, "It is an honor to see you all here for my last program. It has pleased me very much that you enjoyed the music I played for you. And to finish, Miss Riccardi and I have a surprise."

Then I sat at the piano and played what I thought would be an interesting program of goodbyes, but only Grant — who was standing at the bar with Barnaby and Andrew — truly appreciated the sentimental and ironic choices.

Playing the music only, I began with "Yesterday," followed by "Tenderly," "Over the Rainbow," "The Party's Over," "Sentimental Journey," "On a Clear Day," "Every Time We Say Goodbye," "After The Ball" and "Charade."

When I finished, the applause told me everything I needed to know. I gestured for Marina to join me at the piano where Willis had already placed a second chair. I winked, nodded my head, and we began.

Maria began slowly, playing the progressive chords that were the foundation of "Ave Maria," then I began the melody. We played it beautifully, respectfully. There wasn't a sound until the last beautiful chords faded away. As it ended, Marina looked at me and we smiled, and then laughed when we found both of us had tears in our eyes. Everyone was on their feet cheering, and we were surrounded by smiles, handshakes and applause. We were a hit, and I turned to give Marina a mighty hug!

Finally Marina and I were able to walk toward the side door where I knew Grant, Barnaby and Andrew would be waiting. I stopped, however, when Corby handed over a large beer stein filled to the brim with coins, gold dust and nuggets. "This is the only way the men know how to properly thank you for the very nice music you've been playin' these past months. This is their way to say goodbye and good luck." Once more I was moved to tears.

It was a silent ride to Hattie's that night. We were all tired but happy. On reaching the house, we found Hattie, Ida, Rainbow and Warren waiting for us with a festive dinner. The children made a point of showing us the flowers they brought in to decorate the table. Once seated, there was a burst of conversation while we ate. Everyone was giving their own interpretation of the duet and the response of the audience. Barnaby provided the wine, so we found many reasons to toast and praise the duet, and especially Marina's performance. She was almost overwhelmed by the celebration, the noise and the glowing compliments of her performance. This was probably the first real happiness that had come to her since the death of her mother. I was terribly happy for her.

Another segment of our lives was completed that evening, and the beautiful weddings we would share in two days promised to mark another new beginning. It was a beautiful celebration that went on until the late hours.

The next morning, not yet awake and still a bit tired from the night before, we had another great occasion before us. Hattie and I were to present ourselves at Ida's home for a shower in our honor. The small house was filled with Waiter Girls (except for Zola), most of the Hurdy-gurdy Girls, Elmo's wife and Hattie's friends. The kitchen table was covered with cakes, cookies, corn bread and other goodies. Flower was standing by Maggie, and she was lovelier than

I had ever seen her before. Her body was at ease and graceful. Her face was more relaxed and had taken on a lovely pink shade that darkened her pale blue eyes. Happiness, I told myself, that's what it looks like.

The room was filled with chatter, and I could not help but detach myself and observe everyone lovingly. Here I was, watching history and tradition as a spectator, but also as a participant. It was a blessing to be here with these friendly ladies dressed in their best and wearing their hair in plain but attractive styles of this era. Comfortable conversation filled the room. Going from one group to another, I found their dialogue sincere, simple and music to my ears.

Then one of the ladies said, "Ida, I smell fresh wood. Did you have some work done to your house? Is that a new door over there?"

Ida hesitated, then answered, "I did have some work done, but it's a surprise." Then she looked at me and raised her shoulders. The ladies had not only brought gifts for Hattie and me, but for a surprised Flower as well. We opened the plainly wrapped packages as they were presented. They contained a variety of embroidered handkerchiefs and pillow cases, knitted gloves and scarves, a cookbook for me, and lace and crocheted collars to be added to simple calico dresses. Once the packages and their thoughtful contents were revealed, Ida stepped forward.

"This has been a happy occasion, but there is more to come. We have a special surprise for one of our brides." Then she gestured. "Flower, my dear, will you come over here beside me?"

Hesitantly Flower moved to stand quietly next to Ida. Ida took her hand. "You all know that Flower and Robert will also be married tomorrow. Behind that new door is a very special wedding present for this fine young couple. Flower, will you open the door and see what's waiting there for you?"

Flower held her shoulders nervously, but after encouraging

motions from Ida, she put her hand on the doorknob and slowly opened the door and stepped inside.

Ida turned to the ladies to explain. "You all know that I live alone. Friends of Flower and Robert came together to build these new living quarters where they can begin their new life."

The ladies let out a chorus of approval and moved to cluster about the door. Flower was standing in the center of the room, looking about in disbelief. Turning to look back to Ida, she asked, "Is this really for Robert and me?"

Ida and I both answered with smiles and nods until Flower moved to sit on the bed, weeping softly.

I rushed to her side. "My dear, this is our loving gift for you and Robert. We do hope you both will like it, and if there is anything more we can add, please let us know."

Flower shook her head back and forth until she could speak. "It's our dream come true. I didn't know I could be so happy!" And tears continued to roll down her pretty face.

Through the excited conversation, we barely heard the knock at the front door. Grant and Andrew were standing there, holding Robert firmly between them. Grant said breathlessly, "We had quite a time getting this young man to come with us. He kept protesting that men didn't belong at a party for ladies."

The women stepped back from the bedroom door to make a path for Robert. He moved to look into the room and saw Flower in tears, still sitting on the bed. Rushing into the room, he sat beside her, saying loving words and caressing her hair. Without a word, the women stepped away from the door and Ida closed it firmly. "We sure had a fine celebration, ladies, but now we should give Flower and Robert some time to themselves."

Silently, as if they were leaving church, the women filed out of the house. Grant and I brought up the rear. Ida closed the door behind us, then turned to open her heart and her home to Flower and

Robert.

Our special day is tomorrow, and upon reflection I decided we all had been blessed. Blessings that Hattie, Grant, Barnaby and I never could have anticipated when we first met last August.

Now Hattie is entering into a second marriage with a fine and upstanding man. Barnaby's lonely years of working torturous hours on a gold claim were behind him, and his life would now be shared by a lady who would bring him love such as he had never known before. Neither of them would ever be lonely again.

Chapter Thirty-Six

Early that special Sunday morning, Hattie and I were busy with last minute details. Although traditionally grooms do not see their brides until they meet at the altar, Hattie and I decided to wear our wedding gowns for Flower and Robert's wedding.

As Hattie pointed out, "It wouldn't be right to stand up with those youngsters, then rush away and get ready for ours. We don't want to leave them to celebrate alone — it wouldn't be right."

Grant agreed. "I've brought a bottle of wine and glasses so we can properly toast the new bride and groom for a celebration that is rightfully theirs."

Then Hattie lifted an eyebrow and announced sternly, "Now is the time, gentlemen, to tell us what you'll be wearing today."

For weeks Grant and Barnaby had been secretive about their apparel. Within our hearing they would chat about canvas pants like the miners wore, topped by black stovepipe hats. They also considered straw hats and red bandannas about the neck like the stagecoach drivers wore. Hattie and I were not amused and found their comical viewpoint rather annoying.

Now they looked at each other and laughed. Grant explained, "Our attire calls for a few finishing touches, but we'll be two handsome dudes when you see us. Right, Barnaby?"

Barnaby smiled and looked at Hattie, who was frowning and shaking her head. He suppressed his smile, but eyed her like a pixie with a secret.

She had to smile and reached over to touch his hand. "You're not the man you were when we first met, my dear. Sam and I were saying the other day that you've turned into quite a nice fellow, and I'm mighty glad you'll be mine from now on. There are lots of ladies in this town who'd love to serve you tea in their parlors!"

"That's very true," I laughed.

After breakfast, Grant and I walked to the open front door for some fresh air. We found Warren sitting on the top step of the porch, elbows on his knees and two hands supporting his downcast head. Grant pointed to himself and then to Warren, and I nodded in agreement. It was time for a man-to-man talk.

Quietly Grant stepped onto the porch. Patting the small shoulder, he said, "Well, here's a good fellow deep in thought. Anything you want to talk about?"

Warren looked up into Grant's face. "Will I be your little boy, and Rainbow your little girl?"

"More than that, young man. You'll be my very special, ever-and-always son."

Warren's eyes were wide in wonder. "Will you be my Papa Grant?"

"Papa, father, daddy — whatever sounds right to you. And when we walk down the street and meet someone we know, I'll be proud to say, 'This is my son, Warren.' "

"And Mis' Samantha will be our momma?"

Grant laughed. "No doubt about that, and she's as happy about it as I am. In fact, it would make her very happy if you go in right now and give your new mother a hug."

At that, I moved quickly away from the door and joined Hattie, Barnaby and Rainbow in the kitchen. I cautioned them to be quiet and wait. Warren rushed into the room, came to me with arms open wide and said, "Papa Grant said to come in and give my new momma a hug."

Almost in tears, I gave him my best hug and rocked him in my arms. Turning to Rainbow, Warren prompted her. "Come here and give your new momma a hug. We're going to be a family and live in this here house together."

Rainbow ran over and I put my other arm around her. Hattie pulled out a handkerchief and began dabbing her eyes. "How lovely," she sniffed.

Barnaby in mock anger said, "Well, what about us. Don't we fit into this family?"

Wiping her eyes, Hattie said sternly, "You bet we do. We're not going to be left out."

Juggling the small bodies I was holding, I looked into those sweet faces and said, "I'll bet anything that you two never had an aunt or uncle of your own. Well, my new son and daughter, meet your Aunt Hattie and Uncle Barnaby. You never dreamed that you'd be part of a family of six, did you?"

Grant entered the room, scooped the children into his arms and waltzed around the table while we clapped our hands in time. Moments like this were never a part of my old life, and I shall cherish this life all the more.

Around 10 a.m. Grant and Barnaby left to get ready. As they had done for Maggie's wedding, the Waiter Girls took charge of Rainbow and Warren, their clothes, and arrival at the church . Corby rented a horse and wagon, filled it with the children and girls from the saloon, and drove into the foothills and meadows to divest the wild flowers of their colorful petals. When Rainbow's basket was full to the top, they went to Maggie's to dress for the ceremonies.

Back at the house, Hattie allowed me to arrange her hair with lovely soft bangs. With the new and contented smile now permanently on her face, Barnaby would find a lovely and glowing bride.

In turn, Hattie brushed my hair, which had become rather long, into a bun. I made soft tendrils of hair on my forehead and around my ears. From the rose silk remaining from my dress, Ida had made a long strip, which Hattie pinned to the bun. The long ends trailed down my back to the waist. We looked at each other nodding with approval, then declared ourselves ready to become married ladies.

When we heard a horse and buggy outside, we knew the grooms had arrived. Grant stuck his head just inside the door and ordered, "We want you ladies to close your eyes until we tell you to open them."

Hattie and I obliged, then heard shuffling footsteps. We waited quietly until Grant said, "Open your eyes. ladies, and behold your handsome husbands-to-be."

And there they were, standing proudly in a formal pose, shining black stovepipe hats sitting jauntily on their heads. Both were wearing well-fitted black trousers and long frock coats, right out of an Edwardian novel. Their shirts were glaring white, well tailored, with black ties bearing diamond stickpins. They had found a tailor in Sacramento who followed Grant's directions as to designs, and the suits were fitted during their trips to inspect our property. Now they stood before us, handsome in the completed outfits.

Barnaby was laughing. "Grant says we should wear our hats up to the altar and during the ceremony. He says that would be just the perfect touch."

Hattie made it very clear that this would not do.

Grant tapped Barnaby on his shoulder and declared, "What do we have here, Barnaby? Who are these two bewitching creatures standing before us?"

Hattie and I were beaming as the two men inspected us front and back. Grant found just the right words. "Good thing we can see them now because I tell you truly, Barnaby, if I had to wait until they were coming up the aisle, I couldn't stand there calmly. My dear Sam, you look enchanting, which is the right word because without a doubt you've cast a spell on me. What a delightful vision you are."

He took my hand and gently kissed it. Close to tears, I reached out and caressed his cheek.

As for Barnaby, he could barely speak, his eyes were so filled with love for his lady. "Hattie, dear, I'm the happiest, luckiest man in this world. Spending the future with you will be like going to heaven."

Placing her hands on his shoulders, Hattie gave him a soft kiss, followed by a hug they held for several minutes. With a loving smile she responded, "Barnaby, because of you I have everything I could ever want in my life. Living each day with you will be like a gift to treasure. Our years together will surely be filled with peace and happiness."

All too soon it was 10:45 and Hattie and I were escorted in style to Reverend Norton's church for the first part of our marvelous day.

Meanwhile, we knew that Andrew would be collecting Robert from his small rented room, then Flower and Ida from her nearby home. We all arrived about the same time at the small office at the rear of the church.

Flower was radiant, and I just had to hug her. "My dear," I whispered in her ear, "I've never seen you look so beautiful." Her cheeks were rose pink from the excitement, and her white-blonde hair was soft about her face and braided down the back. There was a perky bow on top of her head, just where the braiding began. She clung to Robert as they greeted us.

Moving to Ida, I commented, "Flower is absolutely lovely in the gown you made for her. I can see the love and happiness you put into it."

Ida was beaming. "Samantha, this is absolutely the happiest day of my life. Flower, Robert and I have become close already. We'll be very happy together in my house, I can feel it!"

Robert seemed ill at ease, but when the men shook his hand with friendly words of encouragement, he relaxed.

Rev. Norton arrived, and the men took a moment to discuss the ceremony. He arranged us before him, and then began the ritual for Flower and Robert. The room was still, and the morning sun shone through the window, giving a lovely glow of serenity.

The ceremony concluded with, "Do you take this young lady to be your lawfully wedded wife?" Rev. Norton asked Robert.

"Yes sir, I do!" said Robert emphatically.

"And Flower, do you take this man to be your lawfully wedded husband?"

Her face was radiant when she answered softly, "Yes sir, I really do."

Robert gave her a reverent and loving kiss as we all happily approved. Grant brought out the wine and, when all glasses were filled, directed us to lift them in a toast.

"This is a time of newness and change. Flower and Robert were blessed when they found each other, and now they will share a future filled with God's loving grace. Our wish for them is that their road will be clear and smooth, that the sun will shine kindly on them, and that God's love will always surround them in the years ahead. Let us toast to Flower and Robert. May they have all the goodness that life can bring."

Laughter and happy conversation occupied the next half hour. When asked if she had moved her things out of the saloon and into the new room at Ida's, Flower answered, "Yes, early this morning. Naomi and Abigail helped me pack and move."

"Orrin knew, of course, that you would be leaving the Majestic. Did you work last night? Did Orrin give you a bad time?"

"Mr. Smithers was watching me. Maybe he thought I'd take something of his. He didn't say one word then or later when we carried out my things."

"Did the men in the saloon know that you'd be married today?"

Flower smiled. "Oh yes, and they were so kind – wishing me luck, and handing me tips even when I didn't serve them. Naomi said they gave nuggets to her and Abigail, saying they were for me. We gave them to Corby, and he put them in a bottle behind the bar. I don't know how much is there. Robert and I can look at it later."

Barnaby added, "Everyone liked you a lot, Flower, and the men wanted you and Robert to have a good start after you're married."

Her face was shining. "Everything is so wonderful now. I've been so unhappy and afraid I would live my life working in saloons. Now I'm married to a man who is handsome and very kind to me." She was close to tears.

"Now, now," I cautioned, "This is a happy day and there will be nothing but smiles from now on!"

Hattie joined us, then I moved to surprise Robert with a hug and a kiss on his cheek. "Young man, there is no doubt in my mind that you'll bring love and happiness to your bride."

"You are most kind, Mis' Samantha. I've been trying to thank Mister Douglas and Mister Locke for the room they built for us, but they won't listen."

"Robert, just knowing you and Flower will live there happily is all the thanks they need."

I took his arm and we moved toward the others. Too soon Rev. Norton announced, "It's well past noon and there is more for us to do. Time now to move to the church."

Hattie, Grant, Barnaby and I walked to the front entrance while Andrew escorted Flower, Robert and Ida into the church. A peek inside showed many of our friends were already gathered.

Naomi and Abigail breathlessly brought Rainbow and

Warren to join us, then they hurried into the church. Rainbow was holding tight to a basket filled to overflowing with multicolored petals. I leaned over to say, "You really found a lot of pretty flowers for your basket. And you look so lovely, little one. Are you ready to walk down the aisle for me and Hattie, just like you did for Maggie?"

She nodded rapidly. "It'll be easy. No stairs."

Warren stood straight, holding the satin pillow before him like a young man with a serious mission. I kissed his cheek. "How handsome you are today. You'll do us proud." He nodded absently, thinking of the solo walk he would take up the aisle.

I moved to Hattie standing near the church door. "How are you doing? Are there nervous butterflies in your tummy?"

"Not at all, Samantha. I've never been so sure of anything in my life. It's like a gift from God that I never expected. My first marriage was rather stern and formal, but starting today there'll be nothing but quiet contentment. I'm ready. How about you?"

"Just like you, my friend. This is a gift from the Universe. Rather than nervous, my heart is open and ready to say those wonderful words so Grant and I can be together."

Just then Rev. Norton approached. "It is now time to begin. Is everyone ready?"

We all happily nodded.

He pointed to me. "I see you're still limping a little. Will you be able to walk to the altar without assistance?"

Hattie seized my arm. "She can hang on to me and we'll make it just fine!"

The procession went smoothly. After a wink at me, Grant nudged Barnaby's elbow and together they moved with great formality to join Rev. Norton at the altar. Warren was next, concentrating on the pillow and the two rings that were placed there. He walked stiffly as if he were carrying two eggs on a plate. Rainbow followed, totally absorbed with the business of sprinkling flowers evenly along the aisle.

After a slight pause, I turned to Hattie. "Time to go, Hattie. After this, we'll never be the same."

"I do hope not," she said dryly. "Now lean against me, and we'll walk to the altar like a couple of queens!"

I held on to Hattie as we slowly made our way up the aisle to the men waiting for us. My heart was nearly bursting with the love I felt.

The small church was not decorated with an abundance of candles or extravagant flower arrangements. The decor was simple, uncomplicated, and it connected me to the life that was waiting. I had never before felt such unrestricted joy.

Rev. Norton handled the details of the double ceremony smoothly. He began, "Dear friends, we are gathered today to bring together in the solemn ceremony of marriage four special people. Like many of us, Destiny brought them here, far from the homes and families that raised and nourished them. Everyone with us today heard and responded to the call that beckoned, telling us that this new frontier is where we should be. Like many of you, this adventure has brought us trials and rewards, enrichment of our souls and strength to our characters.

"And so the process has brought together the two couples now before us. Since arriving, they have found challenges, new experiences, faithful friends. They have also found love and happiness to share for a lifetime. Let us rejoice with them as they repeat the vows of marriage and commitment."

The minister turned to Barnaby and said, "Will you take Hattie to be your wife, to live together in God's will in the holy bond of marriage, and will you promise to love and comfort her, honor and cherish her, in sickness and in health, in prosperity and in adversity, forsaking all others, throughout your life together?"

Barnaby answered solemnly, "I will."

He then turned to Grant to say, "And Grant, will you take Samantha to be your wife, to live together in God's will in the holy bond of marriage, and will you promise to love and comfort her, honor and cherish her, in sickness and in health, in prosperity and adversity, forsaking all others, throughout your life together?"

Turning to gaze at me, Grant answered, "I will."

Rev. Norton then asked, "Hattie, will you take Barnaby to be your husband, to live together in God's will in the holy bond of marriage, and will you promise to love and comfort him, honor and cherish him, in sickness and in health, in prosperity and in adversity, forsaking all others, throughout your life together?"

I could tell that Hattie was finding it hard to speak, but she managed to say strongly, "Yes, I will."

Then it was my turn to listen to those lovely traditional vows, and to smile at Grant and say when I was asked, "I will."

Rev. Norton then asked of Barnaby, "What token do you offer in pledge of your vow?" When Barnaby took the ring from Warren's pillow, the Reverend directed him to say, "This ring is given in token and pledge of my constant faith and abiding love," and he placed it on Hattie's finger.

As directed, Grant lifted the ring from Warren's pillow, took my hand gently and said, "This ring is given in token and pledge of my constant faith and abiding love." Those words struck me as a shining bond to our love. I could see Warren was visibly relieved when the rings were removed from his pillow and put on our waiting fingers.

Rev. Norton closed by saying, "We praise Thee, our Father, for the sweetness of mortal love which reminds us of the love of God and Christ. We thank Thee for the deep love that draws these men and women together in the sacred bond of matrimony, causing them to cleave to one another and to establish a home where virtue, happiness and truth may abide. Help them ever to discern the true values of life, to keep fresh and unsullied the idealism, sobriety and spirituality of this hour. Sanctify both couples to Thy uses, and bless them in their love forever. Amen."

Rev. Norton spread his arms to embrace both couples, to say the traditional words: "Forasmuch as Barnaby and Hattie, and Grant and Samantha have solemnly pledged themselves to live together in the holy bonds of marriage, and have so declared before God and these witnesses, I now pronounce each couple husband and wife. What God hath joined together, let no man put asunder. And now, may God be with you and bless your marriages, sanctify your homes, and make fruitful all your righteous endeavors."

He then announced, "And now you may kiss your brides!"

This was nicely done by the grooms. There was an audible sigh from the witnesses.

Turning, the Reverend announced: "To all in the congregation, I now present to you Mr. and Mrs. Barnaby Tinker, and Mr. and Mrs. Grant Douglas." Then he motioned for us to walk back down the aisle to the door of the church.

Once outside, Grant kept a firm grip on my arm as we were surrounded by joyful well-wishers. We then moved to Norton's Café, which rapidly filled with our smiling and laughing friends. Della Norton had laid out a feast. Two huge cakes — one with pink frosting, one with white — were the centerpieces, and at the end was a large bowl of apple cider. The white tablecloths were covered with a variety of muffins, cookies, apple dumplings, corn bread, lemon biscuits, and other goodies.

The ecstatic girls from the saloon surrounded Flower and Robert. Marina stood with them, pleased to be part of the celebration. To one side were Elmo and his wife, with Maggie and Corby. Rainbow and Warren happily greeted many of their friends from the saloon. They had been missed, and the children jumped up and down as they greeted and hugged them all.

"Who's minding the store?" I teased. "It looks like everyone is here except the customers."

Corby and Elmo shook their heads. "Luckily Orrin wasn't there when we walked out the door. The night bartenders took over so we could come."

The clerks from Hattie's store were there, as well as most of the men from Grant's brewery.

Willis stood by Marina to help her feel at ease. He expressed his good wishes, and added, "Wish they had a piano or organ at the church. I would've been happy to play the wedding music for you. But everything was real nice anyway. And, if you don't mind, Genna and Sarah, the two new girls, have a surprise for you."

Willis hushed the crowd and the two girls began to sing. It was a beautiful love song I'd never heard before, full of sentiment and hearts joined together, and two lovers walking under a full moon. It was sweet and appropriate. When urged, they sang it again. There was an opportunity to ask Willis how Marina was fitting in. "She's doin' real good and we've been workin' on a few things together. She started Saturday, and is awful nervous about Monday and the rest of the week. I keep tellin' her she's goin' to work out just fine."

"Good for you, Willis. I know you'll help all you can until she's comfortable with the routine."

"She's such a nice lady, and I'll do my best to see that Orrin doesn't give her trouble."

Rev. Norton called for quiet. "You all probably know that we're honoring not two but three couples today. We want to recognize the first couple, Flower and Robert Heath, whom I had the pleasure of marrying this morning in my office. My wife Della made a special cake for them, and here it is!"

Della came from the kitchen carrying a smaller cake, beautifully decorated. She handed a knife to Robert and indicated he was to hold Flower's hand so they could jointly cut their cake. This thoughtful gift brought even more joy to their wedding day.

The rest of the day went by in a blur of food, sliced cakes, conversation, good wishes, and hugs. Three o'clock came all too soon and, following a closing toast and prayer, everyone went on their way.

By early evening, Flower and Robert were settled in their room in Ida's home, and Barnaby moved his belongings into Hattie's. The clothes I would be needing for the next several weeks were transferred to Grant's small house. It was a night for settling in, adjusting, and the first evening together for three couples very much in love.

Chapter Thirty-Seven

At last we were alone. We said our thanks and goodbyes to so many loving friends. We left hugs and kisses with Rainbow and Warren and saw them comfortably settled with Corby and Maggie. In the quiet shelter of his rustic but comfortable quarters, Grant and I now faced each other. The improvements we had planned were completed. The lamps were dimly lit, our packages and belongings set aside, and a few remnants of wedding cake were on the kitchen table.

We stood, just looking at each other, until Grant spoke. "We both know what it's like to be married and commit to a new life. But though this isn't the first time together for us, I feel we are just beginning. At this moment my love for you is tremendous, and what is amazing is that you love me back."

Resting my head on his shoulder, I whispered, "My dear, we've been given this gift of time from the Universe, so let's be thankful and cherish every moment."

We stood that way, quietly, until I stepped away to bring out the satin gown and matching robe Ida Penny made for me. Grant raised his eyebrows and smiled,

"I know, I know," I said, "but remember I'm a bride in 1853, and this is part of my preparation for the occasion. It may be momentary, but for now I intend to follow tradition."

"All right, my lady, if that's the way you want to play it."

Grant left the room and closed the door. This being our wedding night, I felt some sort of ritual was called for. At the small table, I lifted the pitcher of water and poured some into the basin. Then I began to cleanse my body, slowly and thoughtfully. Next, as

I covered myself with a sprinkling of lavender water, I said a small prayer for Grant and me, what we meant to each other, and the richness of the days we will share. Once done, I put on the lovely satin night wear, then sat on the bed to brush my hair, taking out the pins and ribbons. I called out, "Sir, I am ready. Are you?"

The door quickly opened and Grant marched in wearing boots, an old-fashioned nightshirt and a black Stetson hat set at a rakish angle. Striking a pose, he asked, "Is this what every dashing bridegroom is wearing this year?"

Laughter poured from me, and Grant joined me on the bed as we relished the delicious humor and irony of our situation. Where else in time could such a scene be duplicated?

He took me into his strong embrace, and said quite seriously, "Sweetheart, I have so much love for you. What we have tonight is just the beginning for us, not only now, but always."

Bringing me even closer, he began to kiss me, starting gently, then more deeply as his tongue explored my mouth, gently touching my teeth and tongue. Overwhelmed, I went with the feelings that blossomed.

It was never like this with Harland, not even on our wedding night. For him, making love was an exercise, not a romantic adventure. We were married for 20 years, but he was never good with emotions, keeping everything bottled up inside. With Grant, everything was new, intense and special.

Grant's kisses went on and on, not frantic, but long lasting ecstasy. Without a thought, my tongue met his. I could feel him untying the satin ribbons that held my robe together. The ribbons of my gown were released, then it slipped from my shoulders to the floor. The Stetson, nightshirt, and boots followed.

His kisses went around my ears, down the sides of my throat, and then slowly traveled to my shoulders. One of my hands was raised and the back covered with kisses until Grant turned it over. His tongue slowly traced the life lines on my palm, then every finger, one by one. One finger was captured by his mouth and gently explored and kissed. My body was reacting in unexpected ways. Never before had I felt such a rush of excitement. A symphony of new feelings exploded within me as Grant's mouth traveled from my lips to my breasts, then even lower.

I opened myself totally to the surge of feelings that were rising within me.

Our bodies moved in perfect rhythm as if we had been made for one another. Grant's intensity raised to such a high level that our throbbing bodies came together quickly, eager to climax the love we gave to each other. He reached around to firmly hold the roundness of my hips, then pulled me closer to join with him for a thundering climax that left us both stunned and breathless. It was like we had never been together before. The peak of ecstasy seemed to last forever. It was the blending of two souls, the commitment of a lifetime. It was not only the loving sensations of our bodies, but this night our hearts and minds became one.

We lay there in the afterglow, quiet, unable to speak. Then Grant said softly, "Remember how Hemingway described the love-making by two main characters in one of his books? He wrote that 'the earth moved'? Well, lady, as far as I'm concerned, the whole Universe just moved, with a few shooting stars and comets thrown in!"

I laughed heartily. "Well said, my dear, well said."

A peacefulness came over us and, arms and legs entwined, we fell into a lovely sleep. The first glimmer of light was coming through the window when I woke and found Grant, one arm supporting his head, watching me.

"This is what I've been waiting for, my darling. Waking in the morning to find you beside me, never having to rush away but to wake gently together. And, I might add, having the time to take care of some unfinished business."

"What?" I responded. "Do you think you forgot something?"

He smiled and moved closer and over me, catching my lips in a passionate kiss. Even though the lovemaking of the night before had taken some of the charge out of my sexual energy, the powerful longing to join once more with my husband quickly revived. By the time he entered me and began, ever so slowly, to move with the rhythm of our breathing, the beautiful love I felt for him responded sweetly. It was as if the music of our bodies had been tuned to a heavenly chord, waiting to be played again and again.

Never before had I known such passion could be given, and received, with such perfection. We had become deliciously in tune with one another.

Much later that day we met with Hattie and Barnaby for dinner. Hattie and I were busy in the kitchen while the men were teasing Rainbow and Warren about their part in the weddings. We could hear laughing as the children described how they walked down the aisle to the altar, all eyes upon them. Rainbow was scared, but Warren was bragging that he had made the trip just fine.

Stepping closer to Hattie, I said, "My dear friend, I'm noticing there is an air of contentment about you that wasn't there before. You look like a totally happy bride, and it's very becoming! I am assuming your wedding night was beautiful."

She was flustered and blushing. "Now Samantha, we just don't talk about such things."

"But you are my dear friend and we have been able to talk about everything. And what I am seeing is a lady very much in love, and greatly loved in return."

A soft smile came to her face. It continued to grow until she could no longer contain it. She was radiant. "It was beautiful, Samantha. Barnaby and I are both shy by nature, but we are learning to share our happy, loving feelings with each other." She stopped, took a breath, then stated firmly, "And that's all I'm going to say about that, young lady!"

Those were beautiful days, that summer of 1853. A progression of clear blue skies, light winds — the most tranquil days I had ever known. Each one was as energizing as the one before. Even with the gathering of a few clouds now and then and a smattering of rain, they pleased the senses so that it was a joy to rise in the morning and partake of another day.

Following the weddings, the pleasant and gradual transitions began. Barnaby and Hattie were busy packing, sorting and planning. They brought Warren into the process of fetching, some packing, and part of the decision making. Rainbow had the care and entertainment of Charlie while Myra was busy elsewhere. There was a constant bustle of activity, voices called up the stairs to those working above, or yelled to those in the downstairs rooms. In other words, a happy household.

Flower and Robert settled blissfully into their love nest. Each day Flower sent Robert to work with a lingering kiss and hug, then she put their room in order and spent the day with Ida at her shop. There was not a wrinkle on her brow nor a flicker of pain in her pretty face. For once in her young life she was glowing with contentment. Ida also beamed with happiness. She was no longer alone, and sharing her home with such a loving couple brought her great peace of mind and joy. Her face was imprinted with a constant, wistful smile.

As for me, my world changed when I became a wife, loved and cherished. Our nights were filled with joyous lovemaking, sharing our blessings and planning our future. Also, Boone Valley opened up when I changed my focus from the inner world of the saloon, to Hattie's house and its occupants and the activities of her store.

Hattie continued to retain that special glow about her that

reflected the love of a good man and the new world she and Barnaby would create for each other.

Hattie shared with me the details of the mercantile business — the ledgers, list of suppliers, and how and when the goods were transported to Boone Valley. Some days I worked with the clerks to familiarize myself with the variety of customers and their needs — men accumulating tools for their search for gold, and women seeking housekeeping items. Shovels, picks, pans, pots, bowls, spoons, ladles, knives, clothing and food products were sold each day.

Streets and walkways continued to be crowded with seekers, finders, losers, winners. The women moved quietly beside their husbands, or shopped on their own. As I caught their eyes, I smiled hello, but they were shy and few returned my greetings. Only when waiting on them did we exchange a few words. Then they would describe their origins and the route they had traveled to reach Boone Valley. I admired them so much. These women had the courage and overwhelming responsibility of providing a home of sorts, as well as feeding and clothing their families. Somehow they fashioned a dwelling out of wood, canvas and calico. If the couple was childless, the woman led a solitary life until the companionship of other women became available.

Bolts of calico were brisk sellers. That common fabric was not only used for clothing and curtains, but also divided one part of a small dwelling into a sleeping area. These women looked longingly at other materials — colorful cottons and laces — that were beyond their few coins. Their worn and mottled hands wistfully touched the merchandise they were unable to buy.

Hattie patiently continued my training, and with a sense of humor. "Come now, Sam," she would say, "you learned to play the piano and what to do with all those notes. Now the notes you play are hardware, clothing, tools. It took me a while to learn everything Martin did when he set up shop. Back in Missouri all I did was wait on customers and take in the money. When he started this store, he taught me everything and he was patient … most of the time. But I learned, and it was a good thing I did. I had to do it all by myself after he died."

"And quite well, from what I see, Hattie. You have your hand on every single item that comes in and goes out, and your clerks respect you."

"Well, they should. I pay them good wages, and they know I'm always fair. I don't mind giving them a day off now and then to do business or be with their families. And, as you know, the store is open on Sundays, but only for half a day. Frank opens at noon, and closes at five, and only two men will work at that time. They decide among themselves who will do the clerking that day, and it seems to work out."

As for life at the saloon, word was passed to us that Orrin was furious when so many of his people attended the weddings. Only Zola and the night bartenders served the customers, and Zola whined and complained until Orrin told her to shut up and get back to work. Marina, feeling some obligation to her new employer, left the reception early and filled the saloon with happy music. The men listened respectfully, moving only to go to the bar to pick up their drinks.

By three o'clock the girls and bartenders returned to their duties without comment, and soon the energy and activity returned to its norm. Orrin's ranting and raving had no effect. The Waiter Girls only smiled and briskly went about their duties, cheerfully sharing the details of the weddings with the customers. That brought smiles to every face, except Orrin's. Even his threats to hold back their pay brought no response from the staff who just nodded pleasantly.

Two weeks after their wedding, Hattie and Barnaby pre-pared for their return to Missouri. There was one great celebration at the house that Saturday night. In attendance were Ambrose, Frank and Jim from the store; Ida; Andrew; Myra and Charlie; Marina; Corby and Maggie; Elmo and his wife; Rev. Norton and wife Della and daughter Marcy; Robert and Flower; and of course Rainbow and Warren. Rev. Norton and his wife and daughter brought large containers of food for the farewell feast, and there was an abundance of punch and wine.

The house was filled with conversation and once more Marina provided beautiful music. Rainbow stood next to Hattie, holding her hand tightly. Warren likewise took a position next to Barnaby and stayed close all evening. The children had come to accept that Hattie and Barnaby were leaving, and were content that they would be seeing them in the future.

Once the food had been served and Della Norton's glorious cake admired and tasted, a quiet came over the group. Grant stood to say, "Come, one and all. Let us stand and raise our glasses as we bid a reluctant, but happy, farewell to our dear friends, Hattie and Barnaby. Every one of us has been blessed in one way or another by their friendship. All we can do now is wish them happiness and a safe journey to Missouri. May God watch over them and keep them safe, and may joy and happiness be theirs forevermore."

All present repeated, "May joy and happiness be theirs forevermore."

Overcome, Hattie and Barnaby stood close together, hands clasped, heads touching. Then Barnaby responded. "Dear friends. It's gonna be hard to leave y'all behind. Hattie was sayin' the other evening how we all came here searching for somethin' — gold, riches, a new life. My dear Hattie and I have been fortunate to find what we were searching for, and more. Now it's time to go back to our families. But we'll be rich in the friendship and love y'all have given us. From our hearts we wish that everybody here finds what they've been searchin' for and that life richly blesses each one of you."

This was followed by tearful hugs. Grant said later that he had never been with a gathering where there was such an exchange of love and speaking from the heart. What these people had endured and brought to each other was openly expressed and acknowledged. The next morning was a difficult one as Grant and I helped Hattie and Barnaby pack the covered wagon. Rainbow and Warren stood to one side looking sad and yet ready to say goodbye.

Hattie approached and took their hands. "Youngsters, we are family, not by blood, but because we decided that's what we really want. We'll always be your Aunt Hattie and Uncle Barnaby, and you'll always be our very own Rainbow and Warren. We're not really saying goodbye, we're saying that we'll meet again. So don't you be sad when you think of us. All right?"

There were nods of agreement, then the three of them shared a hug that lasted a long time. Barnaby came over to join them.

Hattie came to take my hands, and shook her head. "Samantha, wherever would we be now if you hadn't knocked on my door? Even now my heart jumps when I think of it. You and Grant not only changed our lives, but you trusted us with your wonderful secrets, and we'll guard them carefully. You have taken the place of my lost daughter, and it pleasures me that my new family — you, Grant, Rainbow and Warren — will be filling this house with happy times."

Close to tears, I replied, "Hattie, my dear friend. Thank you doesn't seem enough to say. You took me in when I was bewildered and desperate. I prayed for substance and change in my life, and someone or something had the wisdom to bring me here to you. You must admit we had a good old time getting to know each other!"

Laughing and crying, we hugged. "And remember this, dear friend, the affection you and I share will keep us strongly tied to each other in the years to come."

We heard laughter and turned to see Barnaby sitting on the grass next to Warren, with Grant standing nearby, smiling broadly. Hattie and I approached in time to hear Barnaby say to Warren, "Young'un, I been savin' this for last. I've been wantin' to give you somethin' so you'll remember me and Hattie every single day. Somethin' that's been special and important to me." He stopped, then winked at me and Grant.

"From now on, Warren, you'll have my mule, Biscuit, for your very own. Me 'n' Biscuit have been through good times and bad. He's been my partner and was there when I found my gold. So, do you think you 'n' Biscuit could be partners?"

Warren's face went from surprise to radiant. He quickly and emphatically nodded yes!

Barnaby went on. "Now you be sure to be good to him. Give him a carrot now and then, he likes 'em a lot. And above all, talk to him. He likes it when you talk to him, and even acts like he understands what you're sayin'. Who knows, maybe he really does!"

Warren stood and put his arm around Barnaby's neck. "Don't you worry, Uncle Barnaby. I'll take real good care of Biscuit. I'll feed him, and talk to him just like you said. We'll get along just fine."

Barnaby picked up Warren in his strong arms. "When you're ready, you go on down to the livery stable and Jasper there will hand Biscuit over to you. It's all arranged. He's a fine old mule, and I'll be easy in my mind to know he'll have you to care for him."

Rainbow put a small arm around Barnaby and added, "And I'll be there to help. I promise."

There wasn't a dry eye when we waved goodbye to Hattie and Barnaby as their wagon slowly moved out of sight. Grant and I sat on the front steps with Warren between us, elbows on his knees, looking downcast and sad. Rainbow sat in my lap, crying softly.

Grant looked at me, shook his head, then said sternly, "Well, it's all right for some people to sit around looking sad, but right now we've got a problem to solve."

I took my cue and said, "Well, I can't imagine what it is, Grant. Is it something Warren and Rainbow and I can help with?"

Grant said firmly, "You bet it is. It's something the four of us will have to decide, and the problem is this: What are we going to do when Biscuit comes to live with us? Shall we bring him in the house so he can sleep in the bedroom with Warren?"

Rainbow raised her head and giggled. "Don't be silly. Mules don't belong in the house! He can go in back of the house."

I shook my head. "Think about it, youngsters. The vegetable garden's back there, and if we put Biscuit there, he'll eat all the plants as soon as they grow."

Warren was worried. "I don't want him at the livery stable. He'll be lonely, and I want him to be close so I can see him every day."

Grant said in a serious tone, "Why don't we save some money and build him a stall out in back, next to the house but away from the vegetable garden?"

Rainbow said sadly, "But he'll get cold and wet when it rains. I couldn't sleep if I knew he wasn't happy out there."

Grant frowned and went through a visible thinking process. "Well, I guess we could build him a small barn of his own with a roof on it, and special places for his food and water. Then when the weather gets bad, he'll be nice and snug. How does that sound?"

"Could we really do it, Papa Grant, if we all helped? That way me and Rainbow could watch him, see that he gets plenty of hay and water, and I could say good night to him before I go to bed."

Grant stood. "Tell you what, youngsters, let's go in the house right now and draw a picture of Biscuit's new home. If we really work at it, I can get the lumber and maybe have his new home ready in a week, 10 days at the most."

The tears were gone, and two youngsters began planning Biscuit's new home. As we walked into the house arm in arm, I gave Grant a hug. "You're a super special man, I must say. You managed to take the sadness out of this day and give those children something positive to think about. That's just one of the many things I love about you — the way you care for others."

He hugged me in return. "Haven't you noticed that it's easier to give these youngsters the kind of love and attention that we gave to our own children?"

"I know the answer to that," I said. "When we raised our own children, we learned some of the do's and don'ts of child care. Hopefully we can help these two grow up to become fine, responsible adults."

"Amen," he said as we walked with our children into our new home.

The following week we played musical chairs with the living arrangements. The last of our personal things were removed from Grant's small house and settled into the big house.

Next, Andrew moved from his house to the one we had just emptied, which provided more comfortable lodgings for a man of the law who was becoming well known and respected in Boone Valley. Early that week he joined us at the house for a delicious lunch prepared by Myra. Once it was done, Warren and Rainbow hustled Charlie out to the back to show how Biscuit's new home was progressing. Myra was busy filling the coffee cups. Patting a chair beside me, I said, "Myra, take a minute and sit with us."

She protested. "There's lots to do, getting you settled in. I'd better not."

Grant would have none of it. "With all of us moving here and there, something has yet to be resolved. Please sit down."

Myra sat, uneasily, next to me.

"We have a problem, Myra," Grant began. "With all of this

moving going on, Andrew has taken over my old house, and now his house is empty. The four of us have talked it over and agree that the best use for that empty house is for you and Charlie to have it. You'll have much more room and, best of all, you would be closer to us so you won't have so far to walk. It has a small fireplace so it'll be warmer. You'll certainly have more space, and Charlie will have a small yard to play in when the weather is nice."

Myra began to protest, saying she couldn't afford or manage larger living quarters. Andrew took over and reassured her.

"Myra, please. You'll be doing me a favor if you move in the house before some of those crazy miners see that it's empty and take it over. As for payment, you can help me now and then. I'm not much of a housekeeper, and some days it would be a pleasure to come home to a clean and orderly house. And there's another benefit. I'll be nearby and could easily bring you here each day when I go to work. On days when I visit Grant and Samantha, I'll be glad to see you and Charlie safely home."

I added, "It sounds like a wonderful arrangement. Grant left all of his furniture behind because this house is already well furnished. Andrew will also leave his house as it is, so it's ready for you and Charlie to move in right now. Will you do it, Myra?"

Myra lifted up her apron to wipe the tears in her eyes. "I never had people be so kind to me before. Workin' here and knowin' you all has been a real pleasure, and now a nice house for me and Charlie. I don't know what to say!"

Grant slapped his knees. "Then it's settled! Just say when you want Andrew and me to move you and Charlie, and you've got yourself a new home!"

The very next day the last move of our musical chairs was accomplished. Myra and Charlie were happily settled in their snug and secure living quarters, and all was well with our comfortable circle of friends.

The next Sunday morning before the store opened for business, I met with the staff — Ambrose, Frank and Jim. They seemed uneasy, not sure of what I would be asking of them. I brought a jug of apple cider and we settled around the small table in the storeroom as I filled the cups.

I began. "As you know, Hattie has been training me to take over the store. She made it clear how dependable and cooperative you all have been."

The three men visibly relaxed.

"Also, I know you've never been tempted to rush off to the gold fields to try your luck. All of you have families. Well, starting this week your salaries will be raised by $15 a month. And after working with the books, I hope to add a small bonus at the end of each month."

Now the men sat back in their chairs and grinned.

"I'm doing this for two reasons. First, to keep you happy in your work, and second, to encourage ideas and suggestions how to improve the business."

Frank spoke up. "Mrs. Douglas, this is more than we hoped for. You're being very generous and we'll do our best for you."

Smiling I went on. "Now I want us to be able to speak freely and openly about any concerns or problems. We'll meet like this once a month to talk things over and see where we're going."

Every man was in accord.

"You may know that Mr. Douglas and I have bought property in the valley near Sacramento. During the next few years we'll spend more and more time there as the land and buildings are developing. For this reason, I'm making Frank the Assistant Manager and he'll be in charge during my absences."

Each man eyed the others, then nodded in agreement.

At that meeting I did not disclose several other ideas I had. Knowing the gold rush and its demands would decline, I would offer a percentage of the profits with the hope they would put the money aside for the time when Boone Valley was no longer a busy community. I discussed all of this with Grant, and he seemed to think my ideas were sound and my approach, while new and different for this day and age, would be accepted by the three men.

The men had their first taste of big business, 20th Century style. I was not only a married lady and a property owner, but now had my own business. No doubt I could become a first-rate tycoon, scaled down to Boone Valley size!

Chapter Thirty-Eight

Once our lives adjusted and functioned smoothly, time seemed to move swiftly without our noticing. Before we knew it, Rainbow was 8 years old and quite a little lady with definite ideas and opinions. Warren was approaching his teens. He made sure Biscuit's quarters were just right and secure from the weather. He connected with the animal with great affection, so much so that Biscuit followed him anywhere, anytime, without a lead rope. The ripe stalks of our carrot patch were used daily to show Biscuit love and encouragement. Biscuit could now bow his head when asked, walk in a circle, or fetch a carrot from the fence and bring it to Warren. Of course, Grant helped with the training, but it was hard to tell who had the best time — Grant, Warren or Biscuit.

Always anxious to take his four-legged friend into town, Warren begged for errands. He would often sneak into the saloon and, if Orrin was out of sight, spend a quick moment with Wong Kee and his other friends.

My takeover of the store was going well, mostly due to the three dedicated clerks who seemed to enjoy our monthly meetings. We openly aired successes, concerns and ideas for the future. The men became confident and more involved in the business. We jointly decided to hire someone to act as cashier on the busiest days, so I brought in Ellen, a new arrival in town. Left to fend for herself when her husband took off for the gold fields, without children or resources, she found the job a blessing. Once a teacher, she brought a no-nonsense attitude to work that blended well with the staff.

Thanks to Grant's observing eye, Ellen impacted our lives in another way, and he mentioned it one morning at breakfast.

"Sam, you don't have time to tutor Rainbow and Warren anymore. Why not bring Ellen here three days a week to teach the children? Even Charlie, who's bright as a button with more energy than a locomotive, could begin learning."

Yes, little Charlie was now a robust 4-year-old. Always rushing up and down the stairs, in and out of the backyard (tracking in dirt from the garden). Myra was finding it hard to contain him and keep up with the housework. His curiosity kept him busy, looking into things and asking questions. I commented to Grant one day, "Charlie's like a car without brakes going down Telegraph Hill!" It was a truth that made us roar with laughter.

Grant's idea was right on target. Ellen, thank goodness, was able to harness Charlie's raids on the house and garden and soon his voice was singing the ABCs, or acting out stories he had been told. When it was necessary to divert his attention from irritating behavior, we found a workable solution. When asked, he delighted in telling a story, or reciting the ABCs or lesson for the day. Grant was convinced that Charlie's life work would be either acting or performing in a circus!

So now it was early spring, 1855, and work on the main house and other structures in the valley was nearing completion. The Chinese settlement had grown to a population of 24, and new crops were in place and thriving. The production of fruits and vegetables from the first major planting was most satisfactory and sold well in Sacramento and the smaller communities in the valley.

Grant shared this news with enthusiasm. "Our time is coming, Sam. We can move into the main house by early fall and avoid another cold winter here. We'll turn your store and my brewery over to the men we've been training. After that, a trip up here every month or so should be enough to check on things, go through the books, and bring the profits back to the bank in Sacramento."

I was concerned. "Be careful when you travel. So many

people are coming to the area, and some of them try to make it the easy way — highway robbery."

It was hard not to worry, but Grant assured me, "I am careful, and I've been able to travel down the mountain with groups of seven or eight. The men all carry guns, and I carry mine."

I was going to have to accept that such trips and their risks were part of life in 1855, and trust Grant to take care of himself.

"What about Wong Kee? Is he ready to join the Chinese settlement? By the time we move in, he could be familiar with the layout and the farming activities."

"Yes. I'll go to see him and work out the details. I know he's still secretly training his replacement at the saloon."

Then I brought out an envelope and removed the contents. "And now some good news. We received a wonderful letter from Hattie and Barnaby. Let me read it to you."

"My dear Samantha and Grant. Here we are in Hannibal after a long visit with my kinfolk in Washington, which is near St. Louis. How good it's been to see all my dear friends and relatives, or at least those who are still with us. Several cousins have passed on to their reward, as well as my oldest brother who meant so much to me. How I shall miss him.

"My dear Barnaby and I haven't decided whether to settle in Missouri or explore the states north of here as you advised. Since arriving, we've heard many heated arguments about what's happening in this state. Some folks are sympathetic with the South and the use of slaves, and others are firmly against it. We're trying to learn all we can. Now we're visiting with Barnaby's relatives and will pay particular attention to what they say. It's hard listening to the worries these people have when we know the trials that are ahead for them. Barnaby and me talk often about the black days our dear friends and relatives may face, and what would be best for our own future. But it is better for us to know and do something about it, than

sit still and wait for the sky to fall in.

"Give our special love to dear Rainbow and Warren and tell them they are in our thoughts and prayers every day. This goes for you two as well. We'll look forward to your letters during our stay here, which should be at least two more months.

"Kindest regards from Hattie and Barnaby."

Anxious to see our new home, I joined Grant on his next trip to the valley. My heart almost burst when the wagon approached the first group of buildings.

"Oh, Grant, why didn't you tell me how beautiful it is?"

"I didn't want to spoil your first look. Do you approve?"

How could I not approve. The house was right out of a first-class Western. Here was our dream. Rather than a two-story house similar to Hattie's, it was Western style, U-shaped, one story with two bedrooms on each end. The kitchen/dining area was at the center, with a generous living room and a fireplace made of rock slabs. We played with the idea of having a pool, but decided the nearby river would provide all the recreation we could want.

About five 500 yards from the front entrance was the barn and corral for the animals. Beside that, waiting for feathered occupants, was the chicken coop. The windmill to provide the water was off to the east. Coming closer to the house, I could see to one side an outhouse. It had a regular door, two small windows set high on each side, and Grant had mounted a weather vane on top. I teased, "I love the windows, but a weather vane?"

He laughed. "Well, you never know when a storm may be brewing. I believe in being prepared. And you might notice the covered walkway leading to the house, so comfort in sunny or stormy weather is taken care of."

What a funny, thoughtful man. I looked inside the outhouse and found to my delight seating capacity for four, separated by partitions for privacy.

Behind the house the Chinese had planted a small vegetable garden for us. Some areas were already ripening, and I made a note to take back some of our first crop.

Grant showed me through the house with great enthusiasm.

All the drawings we had made by lamplight on wrapping paper from the store, were now transformed to wood, stone, and cozy living space — bedrooms, kitchen, hallways, closets, fireplace. It was our very own home, true to the dreams we had put on paper.

There was a building off to one side, beyond the barn. "That wasn't on our plans. What is it?"

"That's the bunkhouse. We'll need a few men to feed and care for the animals, to scout the territory. It didn't occur to me until just recently."

"Of course," I agreed. "There will be all that plus other heavy work we haven't even thought of. I guess we'll learn in time how to be proper ranchers."

We went on to the Chinese settlement, a 15-minute ride. We passed green fields bursting with the bounty of their efforts. Later we saw rows of young fruit trees not quite ready to bear the luscious bounty to come.

The Chinese community consisted of a row of small wooden houses, side by side, on a dirt road that was lined with young trees. The atmosphere was quiet and men who were not working the fields bowed to us as we rode by.

An older man approached as we reached the center of town. Dressed in gray pants and jacket with the traditional black hat and braided pigtail, his face was serene and without lines, and he stood with dignity and patience.

Grant introduced us. "Sam, this is Chung Wu, the elder and leader of this community. He sees that all goes well here, and I've found him to be a wise and helpful neighbor."

The man bowed deeply, then invited us into his small house for tea. There he and Grant discussed the colony, the farming activities, and plans for future crops. The Chinese were concerned only with producing the fruit and vegetables from the large fields.

As the sun set and darkness approached, we spent our first night in our incomplete but future home. Grant had made sure that we brought warm blankets, candles and wine for a cozy evening. We spent a memorable evening toasting the completion of our first real home together, and the joy we would share when Rainbow and Warren moved in. Holding each other tightly during the night, we agreed that our future could not be any richer nor hold any more promise than at that moment.

On the return trip to Boone Valley the next day, we made use of the uninterrupted time for intense and open dialogue about our past, present and future. We were always aware that small ears or others might overhear. Even when Andrew visited and became involved in our plans, it was necessary to remind him to speak quietly and cautiously.

"Grant, here's something we haven't thought of. What shall we name our property? Should it be something like Shangri-La, or the Ponderosa?"

We passed names back and forth that day, searching for one that would reflect what this land and new life meant to us. Nothing seemed quite right, so we put it aside, hoping some inspired thought would come through.

We rode silently until Grant spoke. "Sam, I don't believe we've been brought here to change the world or disturb the chain of coming events. Could it be that your Universe sent us here for a reason?"

My answer was thoughtful. "I'm sure nothing we do will go down in history or is meant to. But I believe this. Because of what we know, we will raise two exceptional children who will contribute to the world. We want their lives to be of value and rich in potential. We can teach them to treasure the good that is to be found, the pleasure of a perfect day, the richness of a sunset, a garden filled with color, and to appreciate the soul of another human being."

"All that and more, my dear," Grant added. "Looking back, what were we expecting from our lives before we came here? We were each pretty well settled in the pattern of living we had chosen. With my divorce behind me, the demands of my work took most of my time, seeing my girls now and then, and not much beyond that. I really hadn't thought about what I wanted for myself."

He paused, then continued, saying, "Wait … I remember something. Before Boone Valley, I was in these mountains fishing. My mind was touching on the possibilities before me. Someone exciting to love and perhaps marry." He looked at me with a broad smile and a wink. "I pictured a home filled with easy laughter, contentment, warm communication. Yes, I spent several hours visualizing such a life for myself, and then I never thought of it again. I wonder …"

I had to interrupt. "You may not have thought of it again, but I'll bet you anything that your subconscious grabbed it, bundled it up, and held on tightly. That must have been your prayer to the Universe."

Grant went on with his thought. "Something else just popped into my head — something I read years ago. I think it goes like this: Nothing happens by chance, there is a purpose for everything that happens."

I replied. "Yes, I've heard that. But how does that apply to us?"

"My dear, were we brought here to meet and fall in love? Why were we given the gift of future vision? Why were we given these two great children to love and guide to maturity?"

"Do you think the cause was our yearnings for more colorful, soul-pleasing lives?"

"Lady, that sounds right to me. But what follows now? We appreciate and treasure the gift the Universe has given us. It enables us to enrich our lives, but in the process we can also quietly share this gift to benefit others. Is that how it's supposed to work?"

My body was energized by the thought. "If this is true, we must thank and bless the Universe every day for the rest of our lives."

For the remainder of the ride to Boone Valley we seemed to be wrapped in a white cloud of love, protection and grace.

I broke the silence. "Grant, I think I know the perfect name for our new home. How does this sound? 'Celestial Acres'?"

He took my hand, held it against his chest, then slowly nodded. There seemed to be nothing more to say.

Shortly after our return, we invited Andrew for dinner to fulfill a special request. After dinner Warren and Rainbow went into the parlor to play, and the three of us settled down and spoke quietly.

Grant turned to Andrew and said, "We brought you here to ask a favor that is very important to us."

Andrew smiled. "I thought I sensed something in the air. What can I do for you?"

I took over. "Grant and I are determined to send messages to our children in the 20th Century, and we have developed a plan. We each will write letters to our children explaining what happened to us, and saying that we greatly love and miss them. We'll put these letters in envelopes addressed to where the children will be living in 1996."

Grant continued. "On the outside of those envelopes we will instruct: PLEASE HOLD IN TRUST UNTIL CHRISTMAS OF THE YEAR 1996, THEN SEND TO THE ADDRESSES INDICATED."

Andrew raised his eyebrows. "Ingenious, to say the least.

But how can you be sure they will be delivered?"

"That is the problem. Our first thought was, through you, the envelopes could be entrusted to the Wells Fargo office in San Francisco, which we know will continue to be an important banking institution throughout the West."

"Well thought out!" Andrew was impressed. "The letters could be put in a Wells Fargo vault."

"Andrew," Grant cautioned, "it won't work."

"And why not?" Andrew asked.

"Because, my friend, as Sam and I were discussing the idea, one important fact brought us to a dead stop. We hate to tell you this, but in 1906 San Francisco will suffer a major earthquake and fire. Much of the city will burn to the ground. The Wells Fargo offices will be badly damaged. Very little of their historical and business records will survive. The company will recover, but there is no way to know that our letters would survive."

Andrew was wiping his brow. "This is indeed shocking news. My whole career is tied up in Wells Fargo."

Grant hastened to emphasize, "The company will survive and, as is happening now, will have offices throughout the western states. Only the home office in San Francisco will be destroyed, and rebuilt better than ever. Besides, that earthquake is some fifty-odd years from now. You'll be well into retirement by then." Andrew looked relieved.

I inserted, "But, there is still something you can help us with." Andrew leaned forward, eager to learn more.

Grant lowered his voice. "In the letters, we will direct the children to come to the ghost town of Boone Valley and dig up evidence of our story. Sam and I saw that the Wells Fargo brick structure was still standing in 1996. Sam will get a metal box at the store, and in that box we'll put our wallets, credit cards, and wedding rings, proof that the information in our letters is valid. Before we leave town, we would like to bury the box somewhere under the building for our children to uncover. It will prove that we did indeed live here in Boone Valley, and that our stories are absolutely true."

Andrew shook his head. "You two have really thought this through, and I admire the details of your plan. But where can you put your letters with the confidence they will be forwarded in 1996?"

"We haven't worked that out yet. We know there's a solution, but it just hasn't come to us."

Andrew smiled. "Wouldn't you love to see the look on the faces of your children when they read those letters?"

I said sadly, "That's just the trouble, Andrew. We won't be seeing their lovely faces ever again."

After a moment of silence, I leaned over to touch Andrew's arm. "You know so much about us, so please excuse me if I ask you a very personal question on another subject."

He looked uncomfortable, but indicated he would not mind. "It's crystal clear how you feel about Myra and Charlie. Has she allowed herself to show similar feelings for you?"

Andrew moved his coffee cup in a circle on the table, eyes downcast. Then he spoke, words coming slowly, with effort. "Myra, being the lady she is with a husband somewhere out in these mountains, has not said or done anything that I could take as encouragement. Her husband took off three years ago, and still no word. She rarely speaks of him, but it's clear she's a wife without much hope. Bringing her into your home has been her salvation. We all know that."

"And you've said nothing so far?"

"No, but when I was helping her move into my old house, there were times when our hands would touch, or our eyes would meet and we'd be unable to speak. It's there, I know it is, but the shadow of her husband is always between us."

Grant said, "Sam and I were in somewhat the same quandary and you helped us find the answer. There must be men in these mountains who have either seen her husband or heard rumors of a newcomer found dead in his tent. If he's still alive, he couldn't be so unfeeling as to stay with his claim rather than come down to spend time with his wife and child. Let's ask around. In the meantime, let her know that she has someone willing to take her and Charlie into his heart."

Andrew sighed and nodded.

There was so much going on in the lives of our friends, Grant and I often spoke of the difficulty of leaving them behind. Ida Penny came into the store one day and was happy to share news about Flower and Robert.

"Samantha, they are a serenely happy married couple. They show such joy, and when we have dinner together we talk and laugh and tease each other. Flower glows with happiness. Robert's face wears a perpetual smile. As for me, I've never been happier. Oh, I realize they'll have their own home someday, but for now we bring each other the belonging that was never there before."

I saw this myself at church the following Sunday. Flower and Robert joined us outside after services, and we all went to Norton's Café for lunch and had a lovely visit. Robert indicated they had no plans to move because their present situation was so pleasant. Grant and I knew that the declining Gold Rush activity would affect their situation, but by then they would be equal to any adjustment in their lives.

Maggie and Corby were also thriving, and whenever we met she brought news from the other Waiter Girls. Zola was still a dark figure, but her status as Orrin's favorite sustained her.

The Grayson sisters, Genna and Sarah, had become bright and popular additions to the Waiter Girls, always with a witty comeback regardless of the teasing and jibes from the customers. Their songs became part of each evening's highlights. As a result, I heard Orrin had wisely increased their salaries. As their popularity grew, the girls loudly speculated they might find better working conditions in Sonora or Volcano, other busy boomtowns. Orrin had no choice but to ensure their continued presence.

Marina also added to the popularity of the Majestic. Her afternoon programs were well attended, the chairs filled with regulars who would not miss one of her concerts. As before, the program ended on a high note when Willis joined her at the keyboard. The Majestic was now the most popular saloon in Boone Valley. I decided I would sneak over one afternoon and listen from the kitchen.

That opportunity came, and I entered through the side door and into the kitchen, ready to greet Wong Kee and have a great visit. To my dismay Orrin was there. Wong Kee was working away at the stove. Though not invited, I joined Orrin at his table and noted how his wardrobe had been upgraded to a well-cut jacket, bright white pleated shirt, and a multicolored brocaded vest. His hands were on the table before him holding a mug of coffee, and on his fingers were three large, flashy diamond rings.

Indicating the jewelry, I commented, "I'm pleased to see things are going well for you, Orrin. Would you say it was due to the combination of the afternoon concerts, the Grayson sisters, Hurdy-gurdy Girls, and the personable and contented Waiter Girls?" He was so pleased with his obvious success that he didn't bother to take offense and merely nodded in agreement.

"How about the service and deliveries from my store? Has everything come as ordered and on time as promised? Any complaints?"

That brought the shadow of a smile and another nod.

Just then Willis entered and it was good to see that he, too, was showing the results of his increased salary and growing popularity. His suit was new, well cut and put together with shirt and tie.

His hair was not slicked down but nicely combed, and his smile reflected confidence and pleasure with his accomplishments. I stood to give him a hug, then gestured for him to join us. At this Orrin made his version of a tsk-tsk and left the room. Jointly Willis and I shook our heads and chuckled.

"It sure is good to see you, Mis' Samantha. I've been wantin' to tell you how nice everything is for me these days, practicin' and playin' duets with Marina. She is such a fine professional, she's taught me a lot. And the oddest thing, I'm havin' a good time when I'm playin' at night. Before it was just a job, but now I'm finding what good fun it can be."

He took a second to find the right words. "I just wanted to say it's all because of you. I was thinkin' the other day that things weren't too good when you first came along. You talked with the Waiter Girls and helped them change the things they didn't like. And now look how pretty they are in their uniforms." Then he laughed out loud. "And when you challenged me to that darn piano duel, I was real mad at you. But look how it all turned out? I found out what fun playing duets could be. And you and your husband were responsible for bringin' Marina in here, and she's a wonder."

Just then I was aware of Wong Kee standing beside us, listening. Willis glanced up at him and said, "Wong Kee doesn't say much, but he has lots of good things to say about you."

I smiled up at my friend. "You really helped me, Wong Kee, when I had dragons to fight. Can you sit down and visit? I haven't seen you in weeks and I've missed you"

He bowed and I could see a shadow of a smile. "No time, much to do."

Just then we heard music coming from the saloon. Marina had begun her afternoon program. Willis stood and pointed to the door. "I'd better get out there. I always like to listen to her play. Shall I leave the door open so you can hear?"

"Oh, yes. I've been looking forward to it. It's been a while, and I do want to say hello."

Willis left the door open halfway so Marina's wonderful music came through.

"So, my good friend, Wong Kee, how are you these days?"

Wong Kee nodded. "Be better soon."

"Grant will be talking with you about moving to the valley. I understand your replacement is well trained and ready to take over. Our house there is almost finished, so you can go down any-time and get your own house ready. If we move this summer, July or August, you would be a big help when we settle in. And of course your kitchen in our house will need your special touch. I can hardly wait to move into our new house with the children, and you'll be there helping us and cooking all sorts of wonderful dishes."

It wasn't a smile, but his face was beaming. "I cook good for you. Many good things."

"Oh, I'm sure of that. What about friends you have made here? Will you be sorry to leave them behind?"

He raised his eyebrows and answered, "Good friends now busy in your fields. Not many stay here."

"And we're thinking of calling our whole area Celestial Acres. Do you approve?"

There was a for-sure smile on his face now, though it was small and didn't last long as he bowed. "Is good."

Before turning back to the stove, Wong Kee as usual put his wise and well-considered comment on the thought: "When heart is happy, peace, contentment are flowers that bloom."

Amen.

Chapter Thirty-Nine

"Sam, what are we going to do about the letters to our children? I haven't a clue what will work for us."

"Don't give up. The answer will come when we need it. The Universe brought us this far, and somehow we'll know what to do. Do you know yet what you want to say?"

Grant sighed, "Not a word. I'm working on it in my head, what to write and how to say it. These are the most important letters we'll ever write. How do we tell your sons and my daughters that we're off in another dimension?"

This dialogue continued as early spring approached and the move into the valley occupied more of our time. We made arrangements to sell the house for $500 to Josiah Stevenson, the Wells Fargo bank manager. I would write Hattie to let her know the house was in good hands and send her the money.

Rainbow and Warren pestered us for specific details. To them a life that included horses and chickens, and a river to swim in, was exciting to contemplate. Warren had Biscuit, so Rainbow led intense discussions regarding the pony she wanted. Grant began to describe the realities of living on a farm and the responsibilities we would share.

"You realize, youngsters, there will be chickens to feed, eggs to gather, the care and feeding of Biscuit and Rainbow's horse, and other small chores that you'll be expected to do. The good news is, on nice days the four of us can saddle up and ride around our property, look over the fields filled with vegetables, the trees heavy with fruit, and visit the Chinese community. Lots for us to see and do."

Their happy faces told us they were ready to take on any and all assignments.

One lovely morning in May Grant announced, "Y'know, Sam my girl, we could start the process of closing our activities here and make the big move before September.

Just as we finished breakfast, there was a knock on the kitchen door and Wong Kee stood there radiating strength and dignity. Grant brought him in and pulled a chair to the table.

"Dear Wong Kee," I said, "this is the first time we've seen you outside the saloon in a very long time and, wonder of wonders, sitting down and relaxing. What a happy day! Does this mean you said farewell to Orrin? How did he take it?"

"No see him. No go kitchen yesterday. Chen Lee there. Mistah Smithas not happy. Chen Lee work, make coffee, breakfast, say nothing. Friends there happy for me, kind to Chen Lee. Mistah Smithas can do nothing."

"Nicely done, Wong Kee," Grant said as he set a cup of coffee before our guest. "And this will be your first trip to the Chinese settlement. I'll be interested to hear what you think of it."

We went through the details of the move — what to take and when, the delivery of a new stove from Sacramento, and bringing in the pots, pans and provisions for his house and ours. Wong Kee would settle into his small house, and then set up the kitchen in ours.

The plan was to send four wagons down twice — first with the furniture, except the bedroom and kitchen things. Wong Kee could settle in, complete his move, supervise the unloading and set up at our house.

I wondered, "What about the wagons, Grant. Will you have enough?"

"You forget, my dear, the first thing that newcomers want to sell is their wagons. Although if the poor devils are completely out of funds, that's where they'll live for a while. Sam, you've seen those wagons scattered about. If there was a used wagon lot on the edge of town, it would be packed with special deals."

"And what about drivers?"

Wong Kee answered, "Many Chinese drivers ready to help."

Three weeks later Wong Kee returned from his trip to the valley, full of news and accomplishments. The stove had been delivered from Sacramento and placed in our new kitchen. One of the farmers returned to China, so Wong Kee bought his house and was able to move right in.

Grant couldn't wait to ask, "What did you think of the Chinese community? Do you approve?"

"A most happy home."

Then he shared further news, learned through Chung Wu, the elder of the community. They anticipated the arrival of prospective brides from China. Shyly Wong Kee admitted he was looking forward to meeting one young lady from his village in China. In no time the farmers expect the community to be filled with families, children and special occasions. There was no doubt that Wong Kee was now a very happy man. On his face was a wide, happy smile that lasted.

In a burst of joy, I hugged this lovely man. "Wong Kee, I'm so very happy for you!"

Grant was beside me, shaking his hand. "Good for you, fellow. We're delighted and will look forward to welcoming your bride."

Wong Kee's face had a radiance we had never seen before. We saw it more and more as we worked together on the development of Celestial Acres.

Wong Kee became serious again and began to speak at length, far more than we had ever heard from him. We listened closely as he spoke of the young ladies coming from China, and especially the one who would be his wife. He described what it would mean to the men who would be seeing, after many lonely years, babies, children playing in the yards, and women in their homes. He said he hoped to have many children, and in time, generations to extend his family.

Grant and I listened in wonder and appreciation, and with a growing sense that Wong Kee had a particular reason for telling us all this. He continued, saying, "Chinese have strong traditions. Important part of our history."

Then, unexpectedly, he said, "You want send letters to your children?" Indeed, we had told Wong Kee of our desire to leave this legacy for our children. We nodded, but remained silent.

Wong Kee then proposed, "Leave letters with me. I pass on to those who come after me. It will be sacred trust between our families. We be honored to hold letters through generations until year and date they are to be delivered. This would be a vow my descendants will honor and fulfill."

Grant and I sat back in our chairs for a moment, stunned and speechless. The grand scope of this gesture made us choke with emotion. Then Grant said softly, "We are blessed, Wong Kee, that you will be part of our world at Celestial Acres. You have graced our lives in many ways, and we'll be privileged to watch your family as it grows and prospers. We accept your pledge with our hearts full of gratitude."

Wong Kee bowed deeply with honor, and Grant and I bowed in return.

Grant and I held each other closely that night, speaking of the many blessings the Universe had bestowed on us. We vowed to be worthy of them, and to pass them on with blessings to whomever may grace our lives in the coming years.

Soon the actual move was in motion. One early morning in July, four wagons were ready to make the first trip down to the valley. They were heavily loaded with furniture, household goods, the piano, and Wong Kee's possessions. Grant drove one wagon, and Wong Kee and two of his compatriots drove the others. Five days later Grant was back, terribly tired, but he proudly reported the details of the successful journey.

"Everything is going beautifully. It's beginning to feel like Celestial Acres is really our home and the start of a wonderful new way of living. There are chickens in the coop, clucking and squawking like crazy. I hired two men to care for them and watch over the place. It was wonderful waking up mornings and hearing the roosters crowing."

Rainbow, Warren and I were hanging on every word. "What do you say, family, that we get all this packing done and move into our very own ranch as soon as possible."

Clapping my hands, I showed my approval. "I'm all for it! But I don't know if Rainbow and Warren want to pitch in with all the packing and stuff."

"We can do it, we can do it!" Rainbow was jumping up and down, and Warren was repeating, "Let's go! Let's go!"

Even though Grant and I would be returning on business every month or so, it was a wrenching experience to leave Boone Valley and the fine people who had become so much a part of our daily lives. There were dinners, parties and long farewell speeches. Special moments were recalled and cherished.

When we said farewell to Maggie and Corby, she whispered in my ear, "Dear Samantha. It seems we'll have the gift of a new baby next year. We know you'll be happy for us. Corby and I agree that if it's a girl, we want to give her your name. If it's a boy, we would like to call him Grant. Is that all right?"

I was touched by the thought and answered, "Grant and I would be honored."

In time the remaining packing was done, and one early morning in August the caravan was ready to make the final trek to

Celestial Acres. In the first wagon, Grant handled the reins with Rainbow beside him. In the second wagon, Andrew Locke drove the team, which to him was another adventure. Once we arrived and unloaded, he would go on to San Francisco to take care of business with Wells Fargo.

The third wagon was in the care of a new arrival, a boot maker who had just brought his family of seven to Boone Valley. He badly needed the money he would earn by driving one wagon back to Boone Valley, and in the process deliver to our friends there some of the bounty from our farm.

The fourth and final wagon was in the care of a young Chinese boy who would become a new resident at the Chinese settlement. I rode with him, and Warren followed on Biscuit. When Warren or Biscuit tired of the long journey, Warren joined us in the wagon, and relieved Biscuit for a few miles.

The sun was just beginning to show over the mountains as we rattled through town. When we passed the Mercantile Store, Frank, Ambrose and Jim were lined up in front, waving. A few days earlier we had come together to discuss the last details of Frank's role as the manager and the continued assistance of the clerks. They knew Grant and I would be back in four or five weeks to check on our properties.

As we approached the Majestic, the rising sun lit the crowd of people sending us on our way — the Waiter Girls, some of the Hurdy-gurdy Girls, Corby and Maggie, Elmo, Marina and Willis. Even Zola was there, arms crossed tightly, showing in her own way that she disapproved, even to the end. Some late nighters, still enjoying the evening's festivities, were beside her, waving and cheering!

Ida Penny, Flower and Robert were not present, and that was just as well. They knew we would stop by to see them on our occasional trips.

Fifteen minutes later the procession came to a halt, and Grant came back to help me down from the wagon. We walked hand in hand to the Wells Fargo building. This early in the morning neither staff nor clients were there, and Grant and I would be free to perform one last ritual connected to our unexpected arrival in Boone Valley.

Andrew joined us and led the way to the northeast corner of the building. He indicated a square cement block on one corner of the foundation. A shovel leaned against the wall where Andrew had dug a hole at least two feet deep. My metal box would be buried there.

The night before that box was open on our bed, and after a short prayer, I had placed in it my wallet with its IDs, credit cards, and $50 of 1996 currency. Added to that was my watch, and the pure gold ring Harland made me from nuggets he had unearthed. Next I tucked in two red bandannas from the store and two wool scarves knitted by Rainbow. Folded neatly beside all this was a copy of the Boone Valley Register dated February 10, 1855.

Two photos of Rainbow, Warren and me, arms around each other and smiling, came last. On the backs I signed our names and added the date. Two months earlier a traveling photographer had come to Boone Valley and was immediately hired for the portraits. Added to the metal box, they would be evidence of my presence in Boone Valley. Grant had similar photos for his box.

On the other side of the bed, Grant placed carefully selected items into his box, and put his photographs on top. Grant used his own metal box for what he wanted his daughters to see. This was a painful, separate ritual that would conclude our former lives. We had not yet decided if we should try to bring his daughters and my sons together once they had received our letters. Finally we agreed that if the Universe determined that such a meeting was to be, it would happen.

I handed my box to Andrew who placed it into the waiting hole, then covered it with the dirt that was piled to one side. At another corner of the building, Andrew had dug another hole where Grant solemnly placed his metal box. We watched together as Andrew filled that hole and tamped the earth down firmly. Saying a quiet prayer, I sent love and blessings to my sons who would, I hoped, examine the contents and understand why their mother suddenly disappeared from their lives.

Hand in hand Grant and I walked back to the wagons. For a moment he held me tightly, kissing my cheek.

"That was hard, Sam," he said. "The hardest thing I've ever had to do. But now it's done. We've wrapped up the past and put it behind us. From now on we'll live in our new future and make it all it can be. What's ahead of us is rich in possibilities — working together, raising two lovely children. That, my dear, is our gift of love from the Universe."

Looking into his soft brown eyes, I answered, "My dear, we're saying goodbye to what has been. I'm ready for whatever is waiting for us."

Our hands clung tightly together until, little by little, we let go and headed for the wagons waiting to take us down the mountain and into the world of 1855 – our world.

Chapter Forty

August 1856

To my dear sons, Casey and Connor,

You both may be too young to understand or accept the facts that I must present to you at this time, but I ask you to consider the following:

Have you ever looked up into the night sky, observing the thousands of stars, at what is called the Universe?

The Universe in all its mystery is full of wonders, strong and constant. It is all existing things, including Earth and its creatures, and all the heavenly bodies. It is there waiting to serve and become part of your lives. My blessing is that at a most critical moment in my life, the Universe responded to my prayers with a loving embrace. This is what I hope to convey to you, and that once you have read my letter, you will believe.

I am writing to you from a far distance … one that you may find difficult to believe. It is important that you both understand that my sudden absence and separation from you was not a deliberate act, but one beyond my control. My love for you would not have allowed me to suddenly disappear, to miss watching you develop into young men of the 20th Century, knowing your families, and witnessing the quality of your lives. But this was taken from me.

Put aside doubt and skepticism. Read this letter carefully with an open mind and try to accept what I am about to tell you.

Forces that I still do not fully understand removed me from the world we shared. I have agonized over our separation, and will for the remainder of my life. I have loved and missed you every day.

However, by the time you read this, I will have been dead for many, many years. I entrust my story to you and ask that it be restricted for your private information. You may find it beyond belief, but as you both mature and develop a broader understanding of the world and its mysteries, you may accept my truth. In the end, I shall lead you to where you can find undeniable proof that what I tell you is exactly what happened.

When we last saw each other, you had gone off to college. The separation was difficult for me, but you went with my love and blessing. Your father and I were left in an empty house without your voices or presence to comfort us. He suggested that we go to our second home at Rocky Crest. We hoped it would help us to adjust to a life without our two fine boys at home.

The daily routine developed from the start. Harland's free time allowed him to resume his hobby of rock hunting, while I tended to the cabin, fixed the meals, and tried to find ways to pass the hours.

This may or may not explain the decisions I made at that time. One day, out of boredom and frustration, I left Rocky Crest and rode one of your mountain bikes through the hills and mountains — deep in thought, searching for answers when even the questions were not clear in my mind. I traveled farther and farther until I came to an old ghost town. The town was Boone Valley. It was a sorry sight with its deserted streets and broken-down shops and houses. It was late, I was lost, and I ended up spending a lonely, cold and unhappy night saying my prayers and asking for guidance. On looking back, I am convinced the Universe must have heard my prayers and answered them in a most unusual way.

On awaking the next morning, I was astonished to find I was still in Boone Valley, but the town was no longer old or dilapidated. It was a new and bustling town filled with people, just like a scene from the Westerns you enjoyed watching on TV. My first reaction was that I might be on a movie set, or that I had lost my mind and was either insane or hallucinating. To my horror I finally had to accept the fact that the year was 1852, at the height of the California Gold Rush, and in the midst of all of its activities.

Please accept that I had no idea why or how I got here, or whether this was a momentary or permanent transition, but I was here and I had to try to find my way back to you. But it wasn't meant to be.

Think about it.

What would either of you do if you woke up tomorrow in the 18th Century? Who would you talk to? Where would you go for help? You're a product of the 20th Century with all of its education, advantages and customs. How would you live?

Somehow I had to survive and find ways to be part of this time in history. I made friends, found work. But all through this, I missed you both terribly and agonized over when or if I would ever see you again. What would you think of me? There was no way to send word that I was alive and well, and amazingly in another time and place. Alone and confused, I had to accept in time that I could never return to you.

As I write this, my new life here has spanned almost five years and many changes. And I have changed! No longer am I the mother you once knew. Of necessity, I'm more resourceful and confident in my ideas and philosophy. I found work, first playing the piano at a saloon, then managing a general store, and finally running a ranch. Two young children came into my life — a boy of 12 years and a girl just 9. Their mother worked as a Waiter Girl at the saloon. One night she was accidentally shot and killed, and I decided to take over their care. As a result, these youngsters have helped to fill the vacancy in my heart that throbbed whenever I thought of you.

But, my dear boys, I have found that life in these times is simpler, quieter, slower paced, and less complicated. Cooking over a wood stove and eating dinner by lamplight is pleasant. How I wish

I could bring you here for a visit so you could see for yourselves that this new life has brought me satisfaction.

So here I am. It is now 1856, and it's hard for me to fathom what forces or heavenly assistance was given to me. But for my peace of mind, and yours, I felt it was important for you to know the facts of my disappearance.

My dear sons, my love and hope for your future happiness are with you always. When you think of the past, remember me with love and try to visualize what has become of me. When you think of the future, be aware that my love and special blessings will be with you no matter where you may be.

One last thought, dear boys. I will leave it to you whether or not to share this letter with your father. It will be your decision. Either show it to him now, or wait a few years until you mature, then read it over again and again until your understanding is firmly in place.

Daily I think of you, miss you, and love you.

Your loving mother, Samantha

P.S. When you have read and digested the above, then and only then, read the letter enclosed in the second envelope. In that letter is a key. Please do not lose or misplace it because it is most important and a part of the understanding I hope to bring to you.

NOW I ASK YOU TO WAIT AT LEAST FIVE OR MORE DAYS FROM NOW BEFORE YOU READ THE CONTENTS IN THIS SECOND ENVELOPE.

Second Envelope

Dearest Casey and Connor,

I trust you have waited at least five days and the shock of my first letter has lessened somewhat.

Now, my dear boys, in this second letter I'm going to send you on a quest, a treasure hunt. As soon as you can, get up to Rocky Crest. Find your way to what is left of Boone Valley. Be sure to take a shovel and the key that is enclosed in this letter.

When you enter the town, you will see to the left a brick building with iron shutters, all that remains of the Wells Fargo office. You will notice that at each corner of the structure is a cement block. Go to the block in the northeast corner and dig underneath it. There you will find a metal box that I buried many years ago. In it you will find undeniable proof that what I have told you is true. If you have any doubts about my story, this proof should dispel them. See what has been waiting there for these many years and believe.

There are forces in this Universe that are always at work, and may be difficult to accept, but one of them changed my life. May you find peace and understanding in the items I left for you so many years ago. Regretfully I will not be there to help with your transition into adulthood, but I hope you will find comfort in knowing exactly what became of me, that I did not leave you by choice, and that I have built a satisfying life here in this time and place. Continue to think of me with love, and understand without a doubt that my love for you is undying and has lasted through these many years. Please visualize me opening my arms to hold you, and remember that your mother, Samantha, loves you and will continue to love you — *for all time.*

Epilogue

It is still December, actually six days before Christmas. Casey and Connor Malcolm are on a trip into the Sierra Nevadas. Casey is driving carefully through the melting snow scattered on the roads, while Connor sits grimly beside him. They haven't spoken for several miles, each lost in his own thoughts.

Connor, just 18 and into his first year of college, finally speaks.

"No matter what you say, we shouldn't have told Dad we're up here to ski when we're really going all the way up to Rocky Crest."

Shaking his head, Casey replies, "We've been all through this. We're not ready to tell him. The letter delivered by Manny Wong looks pretty old, and we agreed the handwriting looks like Mom's. She's been gone about three months, and this trip may prove whether or not the letter is really from her. I admit it's all hard to believe, but for our sakes, and hers, we've got to check this out."

Connor sits quietly for a few miles, then observes dryly, "Dad will skin us alive if he finds out we came all this way without telling him. But, all right, I agree that it would be hard to show him what we've learned so far."

For the rest of the trip to Rocky Crest they listen to the latest weather reports, then stop at the next town to buy food and a map from the Chamber of Commerce. After some thought, the man at the counter recalls he has heard of the ghost town. He presents a map and circles the general vicinity of Boone Valley.

The boys decide to spend the night at the cabin and start out early in the morning. The next morning is clear and cold, no rain or snow, and they feel ready, able and excited to complete their search. Although the map does not specifically identify the location of Boone Valley, it shows the local roads, large and small.

All in all, it takes them three hours to find the town. Finally, after driving up a faded road indicated on the map, the car groans up and over a hill, and there in the distance are scattered dilapidated buildings. Next to the road and barely readable is a sagging sign announcing, "Welcome to Boone Valley."

The boys trade victorious smiles and continue on. Moments later, Connor points and yells, "There it is! The Wells Fargo building with the iron shutters, just like she said!"

Casey quickly stops the car. Connor grabs the shovel, and his brother follows, carrying the precious letter in the faded envelope.

They take turns digging, and it is not long before the shovel strikes something other than earth. They dig more carefully and soon uncover a metal box. It is worn and rusted, but still holding together. Casey pulls it out gently. The lock is corroded, but with patient jiggling the precious key finally works and the lock clicks open. Sitting side by side on the dirt, they slowly pull out the contents one at a time. First is the tintype of Samantha, kneeling on the ground with her arms around two children.

Connor explodes. "It's her! It's her! Look, she's smiling, and she's wearing those old-fashioned clothes. She looks very happy!"

Casey draws out more of the contents, and Connor, astounded, begins to weep. "My God, Casey, it's her driver's license and wallet. I really wasn't sure what we would find, but this is too weird. Up until now this seemed like a fairy tale, and now … now I guess I believe her letter. She died years ago and we'll never see her again!"

Casey nods and puts his hand on his brother's shoulders. They sit silently for several minutes, holding Samantha's things and struggling to accept the truth of her death and the finality of their loss.

Finally Casey speaks. "At least Mom had a full life even if it wasn't with us. And she never stopped loving us." Tears roll down his cheeks. "She didn't leave us, and she didn't die young. I'm glad for that."

Connor sits up suddenly. "We could talk to Manny Wong? He might know or be able to find out more about his ancestors and how they knew Mom."

Casey nods. "That would be good." But he frowns. "We'll have to be careful. I think for now we should keep all of this to ourselves, share it with no one else, including our father. I don't think he'd believe it, and it would just upset him."

Connor adds, with a faraway look in his eyes. "Maybe so." Drying his eyes, he brings out the box, returns all that was taken from it, and puts it under his arm. Turning, he says, "Brother, maybe we can get home before dark, and on the way there will be lots to talk about."

Looking around the building, he adds, "I have a feeling that Mom will be riding with us all the way home. I feel that we found her instead of losing her. She may be gone, but her strength and determination will always be a part of us."

Nodding, Casey pats his brother's shoulder as they slowly walk away from the Wells Fargo building.

Outside the sun is high and a light breeze whips dust along the street in the empty town. Casey and Connor stop for a moment and look down the main street of what was once Boone Valley. They picture it as it was—a place bustling with miners, shopkeepers and saloon girls, and for a moment they can imagine their mother standing in the dusty road. She has happy tears in her eyes, a smile on her face, and her arms open wide. They smile, too, and then go on their way.

From that day forward they became mature and thoughtful

young men who were warmly convinced that, present or not, their mother loved them dearly, and would for the rest of their lives.